The Agilist's Guidebook

A Reference for Organizational Agile Transformation

The Agilist's Guidebook

A Reference for Organizational Agile Transformation

Chandan Lal Patary

ZORBA BOOKS

ZORBA BOOKS

Published in India by Zorba Books, 2018

Website: www.zorbabooks.com
Email: info@zorbabooks.com

Copyright © Chandan Lal Patary

ISBN Print Book - 978-93-87456-64-8
ISBN eBook - 978-93-87456-65-5

Zorba Books Pvt. Ltd.(opc)
Gurgaon, INDIA

Printed at Repro Knowledgecast Limited, Thane

Scholarly Peer Review by
Dr. Badri N Srinivasan, Ph.D.

About Dr Badri N. Srinivasan

He is working as an enterprise agility coach and has 20+ years' experience with a Ph.D. in Management. He has extensive experience in process implementation and organizational change management processes and process improvement initiatives in the travel, retail, manufacturing, real estate, mortgage and banking, healthcare and financial services domains. He is a Certified LeSS Professional (CLP), SAFe 4.5 Agilist (SA), COBIT 5 professional, Kanban Management Professional (KMP), Certified Scrum Professional (CSP) and Project Management Professional (PMP)®, certified Six Sigma Green Belt (SSGB) and other related certifications.

He is researching the characteristics of agile teams. His focus areas are cognitive psychology, brain research, enterprise organizational transformation and business agility, Innovation, Strategy, People Leadership and the impact of all these factors on organizational growth. He is also a Health Coach focused on yoga, meditation, Tai Chi, Jiu-jitsu and related Indian, Daoist, Chinese and Japanese arts.

His extensive experience includes coaching, managing, mentoring and training Scrum Masters, Product Owners, and project/program managers and implementation of enterprise agile practices in various organizations related to process, technical, scale, leadership and DevOps areas. He is also a blogger/writer, and he has published many articles in various magazines/online forums-Scrum Alliance, InfoQ, PMI– Knowledge Shelf, DZone, Agile Record, Agile Journal, Sticky Minds, techwell.com, LinkedIn and Methods, and Tools. He can be reached by email at thirumangaiazhwar@gmail.com, and through my LinkedIn Profile- https://in.linkedin.com/in/badrisrinivasan.

Contents

Acknowledgments

This book has been shaped by the contributions of many people. I'd like to thank everyone who reviewed chapters, shared stories, or advised. All my friends and colleagues from the current and previous organization pushed me to form this book.

This book is a true collective endeavor of so many brilliant individuals whom I have been fortunate to know and to work with.

I have been able to develop my proficiency because of the hundreds of team members and clients with whom I have had the honor of listening to, coaching, advising, and learning from while conducting my work.

Thanks to all the colleagues with whom I have debated the thoughts and corroborated my understanding.

Special thanks to the many previous managers who have shaped, enabled, and backed my growth and development over the 19+ years of my performing career.

I am lucky to have received valuable leadership instructions from each one of them and I am indebted for the opportunities they have given to me.

Thought leaders who I have never met but admire from afar and who have built my thoughts and actions, including

Kent Beck, Craig Larman, Alistair Cockburn, Mary Poppendieck, Martin Fowler, Roman Pichler, Jim Highsmith, Lyssa Adkins, Robert C. Martin, Henrik Kniberg, Ken Schwaber, Jeff Sutherland, Dave Thomas, Jeff Sutherland, David Anderson, Mike Cohn.

Special gratitude to my wife, my kids, and my parents, all of them have aided, touched and fortified me to achieve this chore.

Preface

Thank you very much for taking up this workbook. I am confident you are already coaching teams or aspiring to coach yourself and others down the line. Either you are a manager or a leader and you want to improve skills and pick up techniques. When you turn each page, you will get possibilities to push yourself to a much higher level to perform. This is all about coaching. It aids people to discover their unknown areas and scale up their potential.

You may be a manager or a leader and coaching is something you already do in various shapes and forms. In the new era of working in an organization where hierarchies are diminishing and more individual contributor roles are becoming prominent, perhaps you have asked to do more of a coaching role in your daily job. I am happy to work with people like you. I know exactly what you are passing through. I know how much more effective you can become by supervising less, stressing less, checking less and coaching more. The idea of this workbook is to retrospect and how you can help yourselves and others by changing some thinking, bring out the best from you and help others do the same.

As a Coach, you can have a profound impact on those with whom you work with and encourage each one of them to do the same to others. I hope each page will help you to think differently to execute differently at your work. I wrote this workbook to help you become the kind of coach who brings extraordinary value to leaders and is remembered with gratitude and respect. This workbook may highlight some things which you are already doing and help you make them more conscious and deliberate. This workbook will also challenge you to reflect and change some of your current ways of working.

My primary intent is to share with you what it means to be a coach rather than simply teaching you coaching techniques. Coaching is a human communication and change process that is as individual as we are. Yes, you can accept best practices and learn from those with greater experience than you, but who you will be as a coach cannot be separated from who you are as a human being. That is what gives coaching such potency; it is also what makes it a demanding path to walk.

The coaching process needs commitment, investment, and action from you and those you coach. I have written this workbook to equip you to help people change the aspects of their lives that have the real impact: their behavior, their work, their relationships, and their attitude. These are the changes people need to turn dreams into reality.

Who is The Agilist's Guidebook for?

This workbook is for all the Agilist who choose to enable organizational agility transformation. The role could be anything, e.g. Product Owner, Scrum Master, Agile Leaders, Chapter Manager Etc. This workbook has emphasized the practical challenges in agile transformation and how we can prepare ourselves to overcome all these challenges.

What's in it for you?

The formation of this workbook, **The Agilist's Guidebook- A Reference for Organizational Agile Transformation**, consists of five parts:

Few challenges which I have across which I would like to highlights in these five chapters

1. How do we get a coach who is being an agile coach?
2. How do we create an agile center of excellence with the help of excellent agile coaches?
3. How do we sustain Communities of Practices initiatives and build learning organization?
4. How do we strengthen the role of agile masters and Product owners?
5. How do we change the command-and-control style to servant leadership styles?
6. How do we bring an agile culture and create more Agile leaders?
7. How to break silos and improve collaboration?
8. How to evaluate and sustain the agile transformation?

9. How to improve team engagement and motivation of the team members?
10. Characteristics of the best Agile team, how to build more such teams?
11. Facilitation and presentation challenges, how to improve?
12. How to coach tough, high attitude and high ego team members?
13. How to engage business in agile transformation?

This workbook will highlight below chapters.

Chapter I, How to develop ourselves as a better coach by focusing on a few of the essential areas.

Chapter II, Coaching on Leadership development

Chapter III, Coaching focus on the High-performance team, how a coach can help?

Chapter IV, Coaching focus on right mindset and how to change this?

Chapter V, Coaching focus on Organizational Transformation

What problem are we solving?

In the realm of software development, Agile is a philosophy. Agility is a mindset.

On February 11-13, 2001, The Lodge at Snowbird ski resort in Utah observed a meeting between seventeen advocates of lightweight methodologies, seeking to discuss and identify any common ground for software development. The meeting in 2001 and the Agile Manifesto had a widespread and significant impact on software engineering, project management, contract management, career paths for many, tooling and corporate strategy.

Manifesto for Agile Software Development says.

We are uncovering better ways of developing software by doing it and helping others do it.
Through this work we have come to value:

Agile disrupts business models, culture, hierarchies, and operations.

According to a report by Tata Consulting Services (TCS), the responsive enterprise can "shift rapidly to where customers want it to go next—the next buying experience they want, the innovations they desire, or the new way they want to do business with your firm altogether."

Everybody desires to adapt so that they stay relevant to the business.

In a swiftly evolving technological and business environment, we are under constant adaptive pressure to evolve.

Agile has secured its place within the software development community where it originated and evolved, and now Agile is expanding into many other areas of the professional workplace.

WHY Agile?

- The embrace of adaptive feedback can help businesses thrive
- The more iterative approach allows them the flexibility to adjust to the changing needs of customers and the continuous churning of market conditions.
- Better customer satisfaction, Customer Delighted
- Value Driven (Define by Customer)
- Shared ownership to build the right solution
- Better team morale and team productivity
- Built-in Transparency
- Build Blame free, fail fast, continuous learning culture

Profit in business comes from repeat customers that boast about your project or service and that bring friends with them.

—W. Edwards Deming

If we glance into the Version one survey report for Agile Transformation failure reasons, we can clearly find what areas we should concentrate more.

1) **Organizational coaching capability has to improve**
2) **Overall mindset of the team members**
3) **Leadership capability**
4) **Building a high-performance team**
5) **Organization development (Structure and Culture)**

How to can we move from Agile Adoption to Agile Transformation?

Agile adoption is "doing" agile. "Adoption" is the action of taking up or to pushing something into the result.

Mindset exists in the next two levels, values and beliefs.

The Agile mindset there are three elements:

1. **Values**: What you consider the most significant to the current situation
2. **Beliefs**: What you hold to be true in that type of situation
3. **Principles**: Which standards guide your choices, decisions, and actions?

For individuals, embracing these values can mean a huge personal transformation.

From Doing-Agile, team members need to understand and become Being Agile in a process.

Example of changes given by **Robert B. Dilts**

The speed of a car is a function of the change in the distance it makes in relation to time (environment).

Pushing the gas pedal or brake of a car with one's foot is behavior which alters its speed.

The capability of keeping the speed limit is a function of mixing a mental map with one's perceptions to control the way in which one uses one's foot.

Respecting the speed limit is a result of valuing laws and trusting that there are penalties if they are not kept. If one does not value the speed limit, one will not keep it, even if one is capable.

Being a "good driver" is a function of aligning all of them.

Organizations often fail in agile transformation due to the wrong assumption that because they are "doing" – they have "become." It could be untimely to "adopt" a practice before understanding "why" the practice was designed.

Agile transformation is "being, becoming or changing character or condition to one of agility." This is much more difficult to achieve. It involves a mindset change in all the people in an organization which can be uncomfortable for most.

Most organizations identify the benefits of agile but aren't sure how to generate or inspire Agile "behavior" or when to present frameworks and practices. Presenting frameworks and practices too early could be counter-productive.

This workbook highlights a few of the challenges that Agilists are facing during agile transformation and how a coach can strengthen their skills and help organizations to transform.

Why Guidebook?

This workbook has listed all the challenges Agilist will encounter when embarking on Organizational agile transformation especially at the large-scale agile transformation.

This workbook is from my experiences while exploring the coaching assignments and agile transformation work; I realized that all the procedure would **equip coaches for better performance. At least this** procedure will guide what can be done. It does not aim to present **a solution** but identifies all these factors which I have come across and helped me to steer through the confusion.

Who is this book for?

If you answer "Yes" to all these questions

a) Do you face challenges related to organizational agility transformation and do not get any specific answer without spending much time?
b) Do you get questions from the leaders related to people issues related to agile transformation and do not know where to get the answer?
c) Are your playing the role of Product owner, scrum master, agile leaders and looking for tips to make yourselves aware regarding transformation challenges?
d) Do you want to learn from others who have traveled the same path in Organization agile transformation journey?

This workbook is for you.

Who should probably back away from this workbook?

If your answer is "yes" for these below points

a) Are you part of the agile transformation journey? Do you think you know enough and no need to know anything new?
b) Do you think there is only one way to implement Agile? Cannot learn from other's mistake?

This workbook is NOT for you.

HOW TO USE THIS WORKBOOK?

This workbook talks about the **Pancha Bhoota model** to reinforce the organizational agility transformation.

What is this Pancha Bhoota?

Pancha Bhoota or Pancha Maha-Bhoota, five major elements, also five physical elements, is a group of five basic elements, which, according to Hinduism, is the basis of all cosmic creation.

According to the ancient theory of life on earth came into existence because of these elements. They say that our body as a whole is a complex constituent of **Pancha Bhoota**. These five elements are believed to be the basis for the creation of all cosmic rays. All the five have unique characteristics and account for different kinds of experiences

These elements are **Prithvi** (Earth), **Jal** (Water), **Agni** (Fire), **Vayu** (Air), **Aakash** (Space). These elements have unique characteristics and these also account for various faculties of human experience.

What is the Pancha Bhoota model?

Five elements in the **Pancha Bhoota Model** are the enabler which will benefit the organization to gain agility.

Each element is liable to strengthen the different structure in the organization. Each of the five elements has a special relationship with the other elements based on their nature. These relationships form the laws of nature. All these elements function in parallel within an organization.

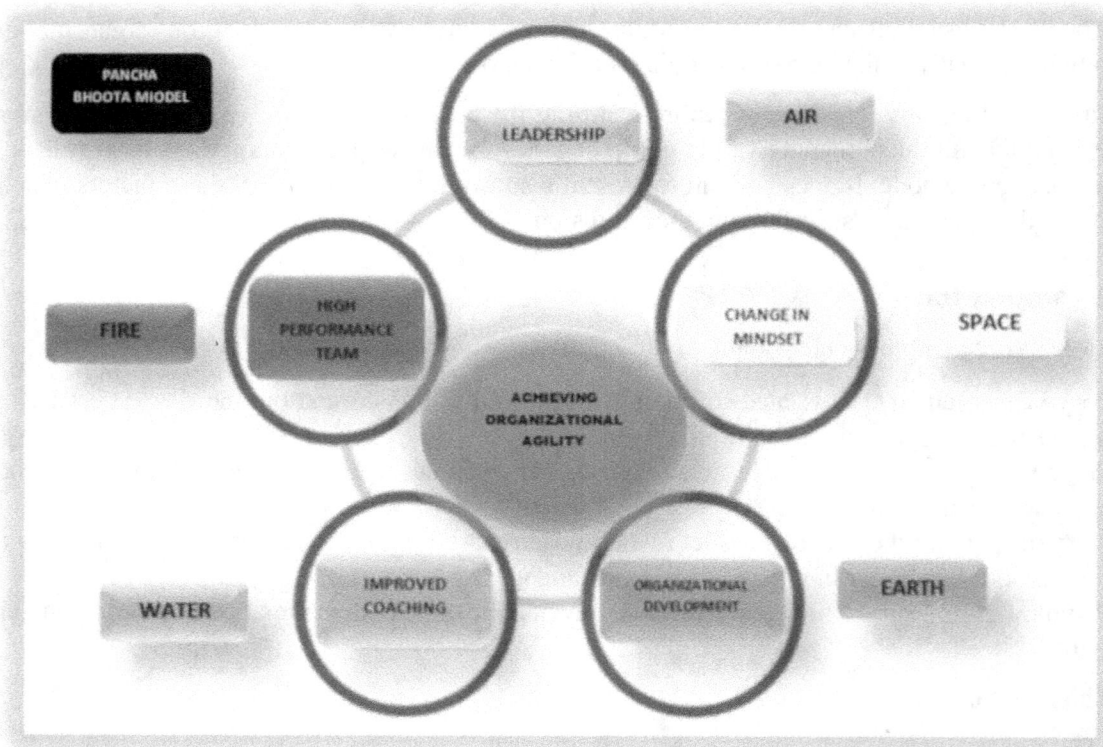

Each chapter or elements in **Pancha Bhoota Model** highlights various challenges a coach will come across around these **elements**. How he/she will prepare to handle such a situation? Though there is no connection between one subchapter with another, from a system point of view, they are interrelated. They distinctly talk about one area where someone has to do more research and develop their strength.

Each chapter will have several **mind maps** which reveal large concepts and break them down into a simpler format. Those mind map aspects have to be thought through and elaborate on further study. These mind maps are Gene in the lamp! The moment you expand those mind maps, the real value will be recognized.

*I have used **XMind** tool to develop all these Mindmaps.*

You as an individual need to set up a development plan for yourself after reading this workbook. Continual development of our skills is essential to survive in today's marketplace. Competitive pressure and fundamental changes will remain the hallmark of the business environment. Thus the need for new and upgraded skills will continue. Lifelong learning is not simply an educational concept; it is a business necessity.

The most significant key to our successful growth is our sense of personal responsibility for our development. For effective development to occur, we need a plan and on the way take feedback whatever actions we are taking. This workbook will guide you to evaluate your present skills and take action wherever improvement needed.

People develop a lot of their sense of security and confidence—what psychologist Albert Bandura calls "**self-efficacy**," from anticipated habits: from doing things the same way again and again. It is not possible for the content of what we do to stay the same, and if we try to artificially maintain it, it causes problems, because we are then adjusting to the reality far too late and in a rough way. Any organization whose members can face unpredictable and uncertain situations (which are the norm) with confidence and effective action, because they have learned a behavioral routine for doing that, can enjoy a competitive advantage.

I have always considered the world as my classroom, soaking up lessons and stories to fuel my path forward. I hope you do the same.

The worst thing you can ever do is think that you know enough.

Never stop learning. Ever.

That is why you accepted this workbook. Now, turn the page and learn something about this **Pancha Bhoota Model.**

Note: This workbook is an extraction from my experience. This book's content is my observation, my experiments and my learnings which I have shared with all to read like a story. You do not have to agree with me, neither have to follow what I have shared. It has to be read like someone else story. If you want, you can experiment with these concepts and understand from your own journey. I am certain you will discover a new world.

"**Companies that** *change may survive, but companies that* **transform thrive. Change brings incremental or small-scale adaptations, while transformation brings great improvements that ripple through the future of an organization.**"

– **Nick Candito**

1 Enablement of Coaching Skills

1.1 Introduction:

"For the past 33 years, I have looked in the mirror every morning and asked myself: If today was the last day of my life would I want to do what I am about to do today"

—Steve Jobs

What am I doing for the coaching community? This is the thought that inspired me to compose this chapter.

Coaching skills are the core of the organizational transformation process. This chapter highlights most of the soft skills required for a coach. The call of each topic is based on the challenges I have undergone during the organizational transformation process. It is vital we as a coach understand the numerous causes which influence the organization transformational challenges and do one's homework around these factors. Once we equip ourselves with various the elements, it is easy to help the organization.

This chapter is devoted to enhancing coaching skills. I was executing all these steps when I was working as a coach. It helped to prepare myself to become a better coach. I get maximum satisfaction as a coach when I get good feedback from the team which I get most of the times. How can we establish that all these wonderful feedbacks get constantly?

In **the Pancha Bhoota model,** coaching is the **Water** element. If we strengthen the coaching area, water element will be purified in the organizational health context.

Why Coaching?

- Raise the standards of team members performance
- Redesigned team members engagement models
- Eliminate some steps which do not add value to the team members
- Challenge the assumptions and belief of the team members
- Set high standard targets for achievement
- Discover their strength and weakness and help the team
- Confront them whenever any negative thoughts are blocking them

We as a coach have to stretch ourselves from the comfort zone to let the magic happen. To achieve that we have to continually rediscover ourselves to support the organization in a stronger way.

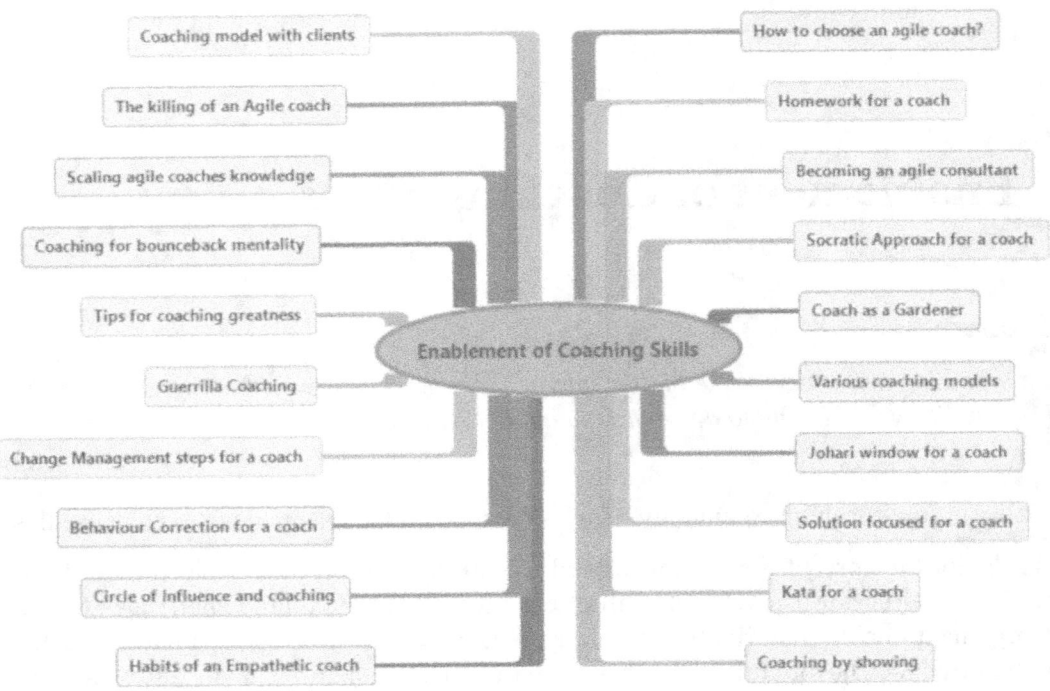

1.2 How to Recruit an Agile Coach?

"Selecting the right person for the right job is the largest part of coaching."

—***Phil Crosby***

Why this topic?

People who have done it once, are handy people for the greater mission. The learning curve will be less. Once we have experimented with the water, we will be well aware of the challenges and the solutions. It is important to validate the coach experience, especially how they have handled the various organizational challenges. I was part of the recruitment panel for a long time. I discovered some mechanisms to validate the coach experience which has worked with me. I have shared all these.

If I have to find an agile coach.....what should I look at in the initial rounds of discussion? That was the thought had come to my mind.

There are so many agility coaches!

Let us ask, ***have you DONE questions a couple of times***?

Have you DONE? **Really**? If not, please do not waste each other's time, if yes, please come up with real-life stories which someone should be able to challenge and understand the context and evaluate. You win-I win, we win.

Let us check through mind maps...

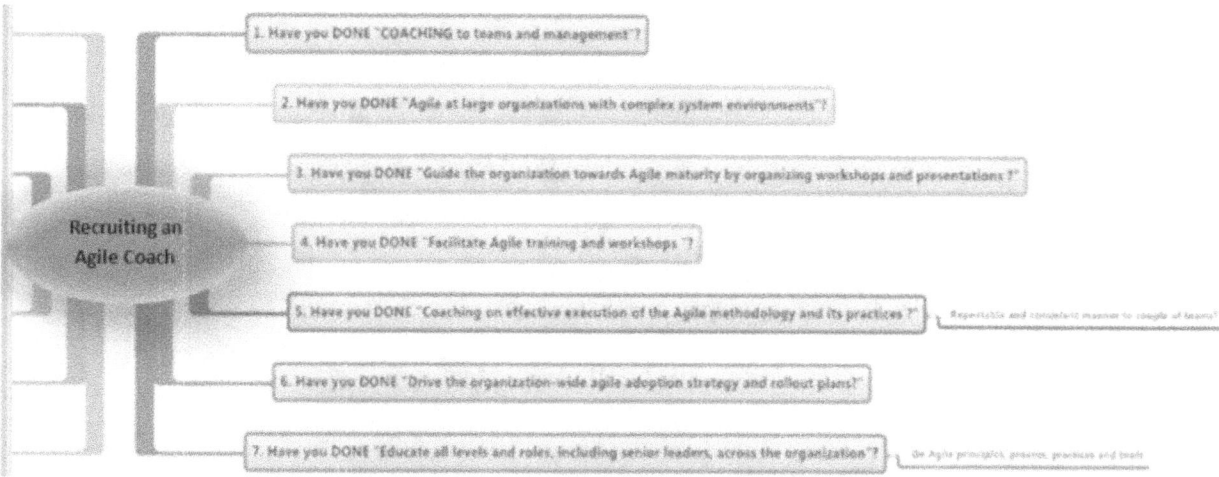

Let us use both sides of the brain...

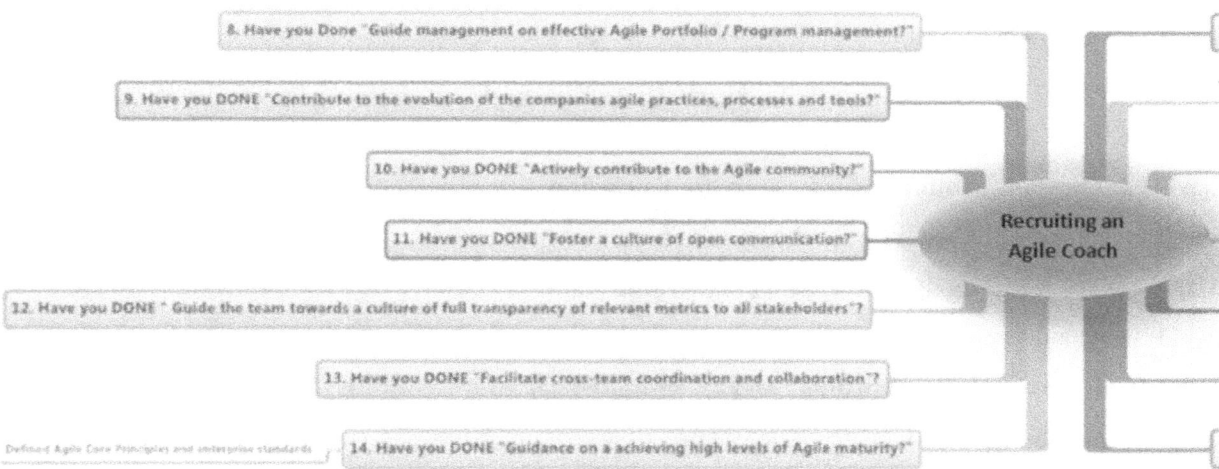

Most of the time these mind maps work. People cannot pretend for a long time; once we go deep and look at their experience, their legitimacy will come out.

I have taken hundreds of interview till now with the same approach. I look for the real experiences, real stories and challenges they had faced. "Have you done?" please tell the truth.

What actions they had taken in that context and what the outcome has been.

Using Gherkin Language for Coach Interview?

Gherkin is a Business Readable,Domain Specific Language created especially for **behavior** descriptions.

How about applying the same in Coach Recruitment?

We need to start by giving different scenarios and expectation from the candidate is how he/she behaves in those scenarios.

For example,

Feature: To check the Facilitation Skills of a Coach

As a Recruiter, I want to evaluate the Facilitation skill of a coach so that I am convinced that the workshop will be conducted effectively and efficiently

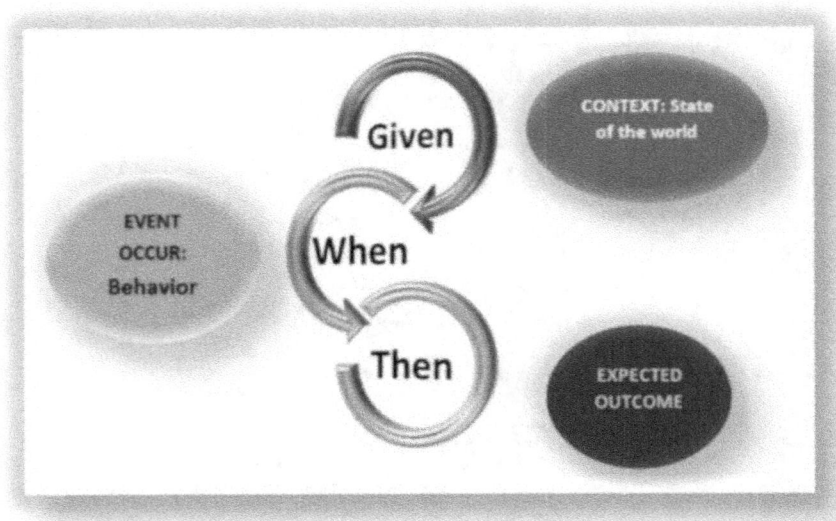

Scenarios 1: Coach is conducting a Leadership workshop

Given: There are 50 participants

When: Audience gets disengaged

Then: as a Coach "What will you DO?"

Scenarios 2: Coach is conducting a Leadership workshop

Given: You are asked to explain agile values with a game

When: Audience is the young, interested in playing the game

Then: "What should you do as a Coach?"

Feature: Design a two-wheeler which can run without Fuel

Given: Passenger on the two-wheeler

When: It Rains

Then: It should protect the passengers from the rain

And Transport also from point A to Point B

Feature: Effective Daily stand up

Scenario 1: Team members are cross-talking

Given: Daily stand-up are hijacked by one person

When: He/She is dominating and taking more time with irrelevant information

Then: as a coach "What you should be doing?"

Scenario 2: Team Members are late in the stand-up

Given: Daily stand up start at 11 AM

When: 2 team members join after 11.15 AM and started their status update

Then: As a coach "What you should do?"

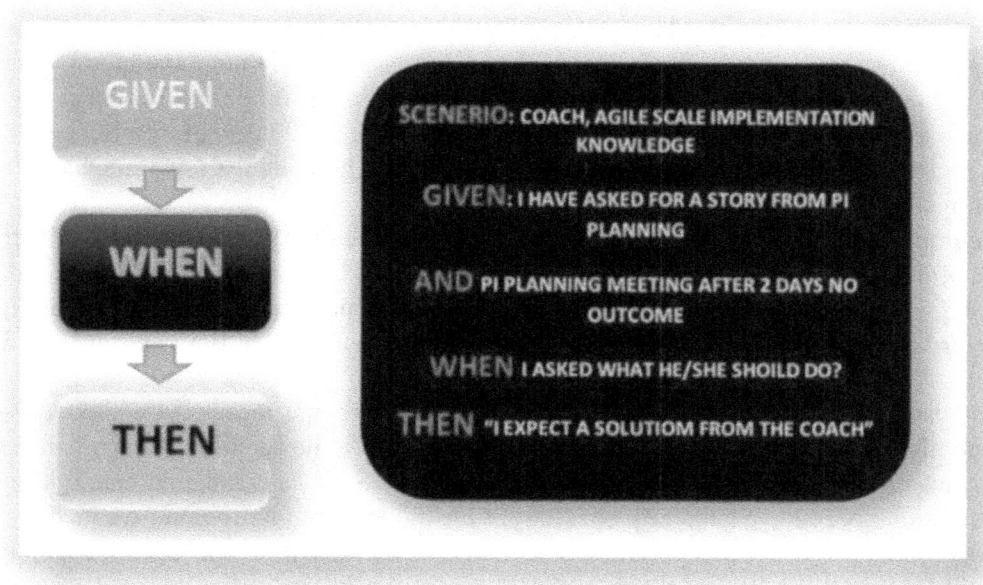

One more area to deep dive into, provide all these anti-patterns and ask candidates to come up with a few points to address these.

- Product manager does not have long-term product vision? He/she has requirement visibility for one month!
- Confidence exist within the team that "we know what to build, nobody should tell us " Feedback is not taking
- Micromanagement is high as higher management has too much concern about investment and not getting rapid ROI. Transparency is missing.
- Team members blame each other's, team members hesitate to take responsibility, they are not self-organized.
- Team members are scared of failure, no encouragement of failing fast. They know higher management will criticize failure.
- Senior managers are expert in command-and-control belief, pretend to be an agile expert.
- Product managers are headstrong, high attitude domain experts. Always scaring team members as they are investing money.
- Managers are concerned about how many hours have been logged. Someone from the top asking for ROI
- No fun for the team, only concern about the budget and team members are treated as robots/resources.
- Tasks have been pushed to the team at standup meeting; standup is like interrogating meeting.
- Team members are not cross-functional, so cannot complete the end-to-end delivery of requirements/features
- Scrum master was a project manager, completed all the certifications of Agile, spent his/her significant career as a taskmaster and MPP (Microsoft project plan)
- Team members openly say Agile will not fit into their context, it has been pushed, and nothing can be done.
- Mechanical agile process. Doing Agile.
- Retrospective meeting team members feel, "Why Again!! O not again!"
- Attrition rate is very high; good people are leaving from the organization, new recruitment are not considering fitment of the agile mindset
- The flexible, agile process, sometimes demo meeting skipped, sometimes sprint date extended, sometime standup skipped (very flexible)

Provide all these use cases to resolve.

- Agile Initiative in Local Pockets: Management team says let us start local agile but the Global team will come later. We have seen many such initiatives for agile transformation fails because Management says let us start with a local team, if it is successful we will spread to other sides as well. The natures of the projects are distributed agile development. Management says let us not rock the boat!

- The manager knows everything about agile: Mid Manager says, we do not have to know agile, we know anyway! They are power point masters; it will take 30 min class on Agile for the team at any moment! Let us first train the team and transform them! My Product manager is 40 years of experience; do you think he needs agile training? Let us start with developers and testers! These are the few sentences we keep getting into agile transformation projects.

- We have completed agile training and have several team members certified, why still things are not changing? Mid manager says I know everything about Agile, Team is trained and certified, Sr. manager is wondering why things are not changing?, what's to be done next? I cannot hire a coach, it is expensive may be affordable for a couple of days. But I want to get faster cycle time and quality delivery from the project.

- There is no plan for agile adoption in the team. No team can become successful without a systematic plan for agile adoption. There should be a clear roadmap and plan for agile adoption. In an organization, the team owns the plan. Project management approach should apply- Start date and End date with milestones for the agile adoption program. We identify backlog for the agile adoption program, we identify one Program manager as Product owner for this program. If it is missing an agile program will not become successful.

- What should I do with my Project managers? HR manager asks, my organizational structure, instead of Pyramid, it has a bulge in the mid-area of the pyramid! There are many mid-level managers, most of them are designated Project Manager, Sr. Project Manager, Very Sr. Project Manager, etc. what should I do with them in the new structure(if at all we have to create), please help us to restructure this organization to accommodate Agile adoption process.

- In Agile, all the principle and practices are not required! The team thinks so, we are customizing agile practices based on our need, we are doing scrum but whatever we feel like we are following. We are doing the demo, but whenever it is ready! We are doing standup, but when all the team members are available, most of the time it got cancel, we are doing retrospect, but whenever we feel there some significant delivery is ready then, etc., we are following Agile BUT we are changing wherever we feel so.

- We have PMO and QA departments wherein a weekly Deep Dive session gray hair Boss is asking for much metrics which team has to provide! Teams are forced to show the agile adoption progress through various metrics. Metric is a must and sometimes too much behind for the metrics to assess the agile adoption progress. Where is the Data? Once data is present, Next data and NEXT data and it never end.

- Organization belongs to the Organizations category which is using traditional management methods rely on detailed planning, command-and-control, and a hierarchical structure. Have several Line managers who used to do MPP (Microsoft Project Plan) and handle timesheet approval and used to do appraisal management several times in a year and very busy person, what they will do in agile adoption? OK, some of them have become Agile Guru!!, now what to do with the rest, their contribution to the entire agile transformation process?

- We are not best paymaster, we cannot afford Generalist, we have many specialists in our legacy business, what to do now? We are in compliance domain, many things to take care, especially detailed documentation, etc.

- The product manager is very busy, does not write requirement elaborately, he needs some junior product manager to write down user story and the detail acceptance criteria and review with him! He cannot explain the market need to the team (Busy). Team struggles to know what needs to be built. His/her feedback is good, team members are taking more time to catch up with the requirement. They do not have the market orientation etc. blame game.

- Developers believe it is the test engineer's job to do testing! I am a Developer, Architect feels; I am here to sketch UML diagrams, not getting a salary to do coding! We need more team members to do blah blah jobs. No recognition, no appreciation. "On Failure" Looks for the person to blame. On top of that Attrition rate is >15%, One more point we have a Bell curve policy where anyway some team members will not get good hike whatever performance level he/she might do. Good performers are not a good bootlicker! They do not have the Godfather to get a good hike.

- Interconnected departments are still in the legacy process, they are in the waterfall way of executing the work not supporting Agility.
- Command and Control type boss, asking for Detail plan, asking for detail estimation! Team members are still controlled by Line managers. Trust is missing.

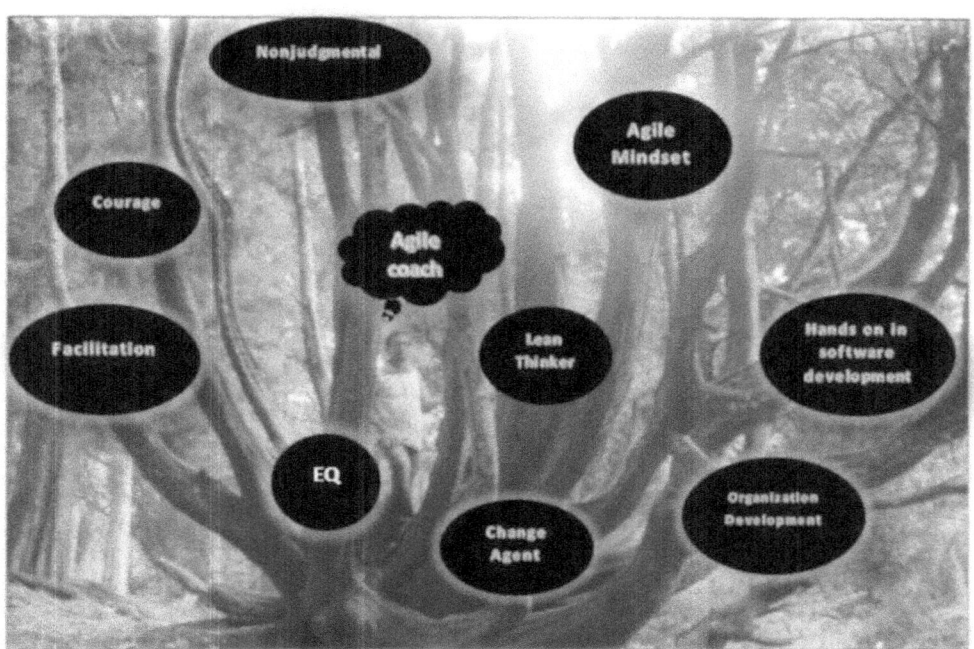

How can coach help to improve the situation?

What actions are you going to take from this lesson?

1. _____

2. _____

3. _____

Thinking Question:

Are you doing sufficient to recruit your fellow coaches in innovative ways through which we can learn from each other and we solve a bigger organizational topic?

1.3 How an agile coach prepare for the new assignment?

" So while the complexities change, the work of coaching stays the same, keep your clients at the center of the work, push them to use their strengths more and to temper their weaknesses, and illuminate blind spots because these are what really gets in the way"

—Stacy Feiner

Why this topic?

As a coach when we engage with the team, we have to do the homework, so that we can start contributing to the moment we start the engagement. Without doing proper homework, it will be a waste of everyone's time. All the assumptions need to be validated during the initial discussion. Some of my homework patterns. I have shared here.

The shoe that fits one person pinches another; there is no recipe for living that suits all cases.

- Carl Jung

When we start a new assignment, let us look into these aspects and see where a team stands and then help teams to increase the maturity against all these areas.

The motto should be to produce great software by applying agile.

A coach can transform a team by changing their way of thinking, doing, and unlearn the old way of operating. How can a coach help? Good observation skill, structured feedback, mentor and support to the team members. Coach has to be optimistic and should have the characteristics of a good leader (walk the talk).

Let us have a look at how an agile coach should start...

- What is the **business or context** team is operating? How many team members? At what experience level? Let us understand the business complexity. It will help us to proceed considering many factors which influence the business. E.g., are we working for the banking application development, developing any mission-critical software which will be used in the healthcare domain, or some gaming application product, etc.?
- What are the current practices followed by the team and what are the ways we can optimize the working practices? **Optimizing** the work will help you to know the value flow and identify the waste in the value stream process flow. All these exercises will help us to take any initiative that is valid for the team .Adaptability and fitment to the team will be higher if we consider all these factors.
- When we have understood the flow, analyzing the current operating model we can **simplify** the workflow and explain to the team members about the benefit of the new way of working. Couple of iterations the team will experiment with the new way of working and improve wherever required which will become a standard process for the team for their need.
- In this discovery path, the team will solve this new initiative together, which will help the team to increase **bonding** among themselves and they will become **self-organized** over a period.
- As a part of coaching, the coach needs to identify how this new process brings **technical Excellency** as a part of the deliverable. There are several software practices that can be initiated which can enable technical excellence in product development. All good design practices is an incremental way can enable teams to grow and develop a **superb product**.
- As a part of coaching, the coach needs to see how we can sustain any initiative team has taken to improve the current situation. As people's involvement is very high, the coach needs to always help the team members to grow and build process around people. Need to empower team members to decide and see how any initiative if it fails should also result in learning.
- **People development** is an ongoing agenda which coach should always keep in his/her work list. Deploy best practices available in the industry and improve the people and their competency. Check with the line organization what can be done to improve the team members complains if there are any.
- Agile coach needs to **demonstrate** to all the stakeholders how we are becoming better and better. There should be some mechanism to collect the data which shows this evidence. It could be a demo or a deliverable which the end user appreciates. There should not be too much overhead metrics which demotivates the team members.

- The agile coach need to support the team members they way meeting has been conducted, the workshop has been conducted, **communication** is happening with the stakeholders. How can we maximize the output if there is any gap?
- The agile coach needs to help to create an environment where team members are willing to contribute, share, care with others. A place everyone would like to be a part of. This will take some time to build such a cultural transformation. The goal is to create an environment where everybody cares for each other, respects each other, willing to experiment and fail and learn from the same. No blame whenever an incident happens. Encourage positive ways of looking at the event.
- Avoid any type of **command-and-control** symptom. Except for the team no one decides. The team decides and we trust the team members. No manager should tell the team what to do and how to do. No manager should micromanage any situation.
- The coach should focus on **collaboration**, how efficiently team members are collaborating with others. Help them to do this exercise more efficiently. This will result in an efficient execution process.
- Create a culture for collaboration. Encourages team members to be more extroverted and to communicate proactively in a non-judgmental environment.
- Coach needs to ensure **frequent deliverable** from the team which can be consumed by the end user. In this process learning will be fast, the discovery of the **unknown** will be fast. Tools and infrastructure have to enable execution speed and faster frequent delivery.
- Ensuring that the team keeps their focus on producing a potentially **consumable** solution each iteration to the end user. Every certain interval the team captures the end user satisfaction by discussing with them.
- The team assesses the **value delivery process**, if there are gaps, the team works on to efficient this delivery process. Let team build a culture of asking 5 WHY questions so that they validate every assumption.
- Encourage the **storytelling** culture where each team shares the best practices. A coach builds the community of best practitioners. Involve other related departments like HR, supply chain, training, etc. to be part of the agile story so that they also start changing.
- There will always be some **resistance** from the team members regarding the new initiatives, the coach has to experiment with a different approach to get the buy-in from the team members. A coach can propose like we have a common problem and ask help from team members. The new idea will come and the coach can agree with the team and implement to solve the problem.
- A coach has to create a space for himself/herself in the industry by sharing best practices and contributing to the community by writing blogs/books etc.
- Build a designation less world where everyone contributes. No hierarchy and **flat structure**.

"People don't only use a coach when there is a problem with their technique; they understand that no matter how good their technique is, there is always room for improvement."

—John Perry, Sport Psychology

Transformation is a journey for the team, it cannot happen in a month. The coach should have the belief, trust, and patience to see the changes happening. Senior management involvement and encouragement catalyze the transformation process. These are some thoughts which can help an agile coach to start the journey.

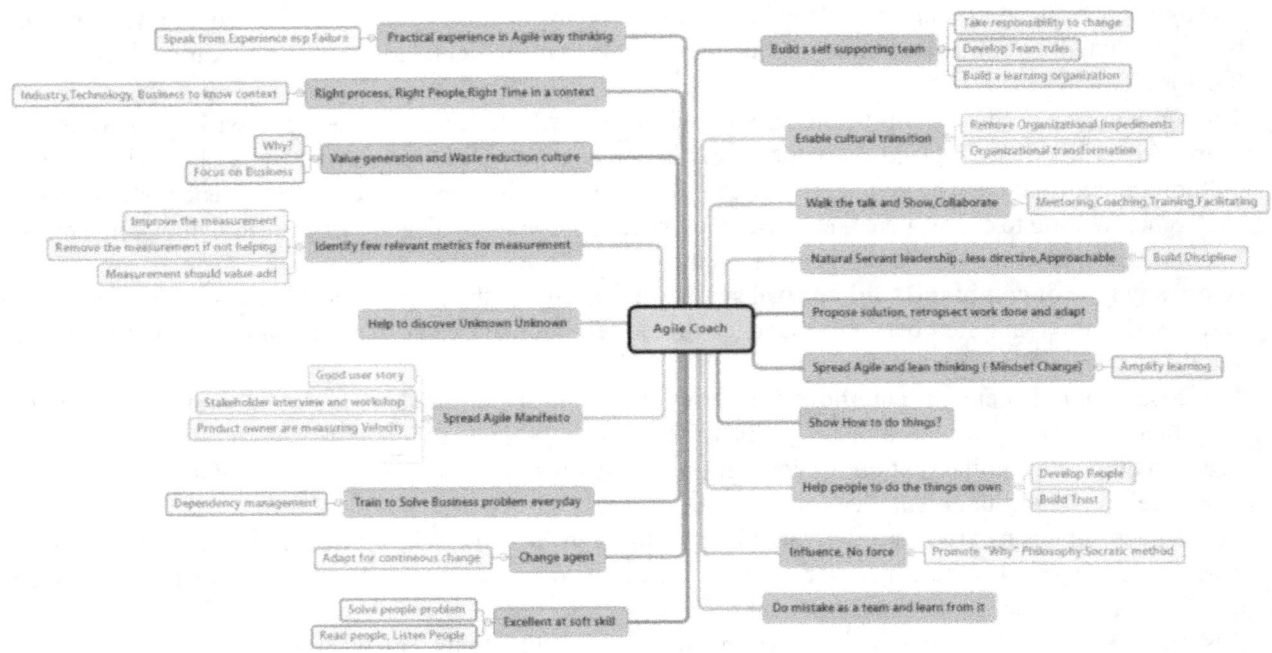

At the end, Let us look for the occasion to increase the execution speed, let us increase incremental delivery, let us reduce the feedback loop, let us adapt fast, let us collaborate, and let us look for an opportunity to involve end user as much as possible, Let us improve value generation, let us build people. Let us build a superb product which customer loves.

Agile Coach Checklist
What is the context ? What problem are we solving ?
Why Change is required? What are the Value and driving forces?
What are the metrics fit in the current context and those generate value and helps decision making
Look for the impediments and help to improve those.
Agile discipline and demonstrate why team members should follow the rules?
What is the big picture? Communicate same to all the team members.
We are always allowed to experiment to solve the unknown problems (Mindset) ?
We are always learning from our mistake
A Good psychological knowledge (socio-psychological knowledge) to understand dysfunctional behaviour and correction?
Propose better framework to use in current contxt, model and tools etc.
Demonstrate throughput improvement, is it Improving iteration on iterartion?
Look for command and control culture and its influences, build servant leadership culture
Look for over planning, insufficient communication , poor collaboration,waste, smell , employee and stakeholder engagement and improve all these factor iteration on iteration
ROI in each iteration, Organize milestone review with stakeholders, is it Improving iteration on iterartion?
Employee happiness index? NPS Rating, is it Improving iteration on iterartion?
Team members are setting their goals, competency and skill development plan, accountable and responsible for the output?

"Coaches are aware of how to ignite passion and motivate people. They have an energy that is contagious and knows exactly how to get their team excited"

- Brian Cagney

What actions are you going to take from this lesson?

1. _____

2. _____

3. _____

Thinking Question:

➤ Are you doing enough to create a study plan based on the various contexts where clients might be navigating through?

1.4 How to Become an Agile Consultant?

"A consultant: someone brought in to build a one-handled wheelbarrow."

—Fennel Hudson

Why this topic?

A Consultant, a person who provides expert advice professionally. How can we position ourselves in the consultant model? I have worked with many consultants most of them are based in Europe. During my work with them, I have learned some of their best practices and noted all these down for myself. I am sharing a few of these points to improve our consultancy abilities.

Want to start an agile consulting business, thinking what type of skills we should have.

All these points are very crucial when we aspire to become a consultant.

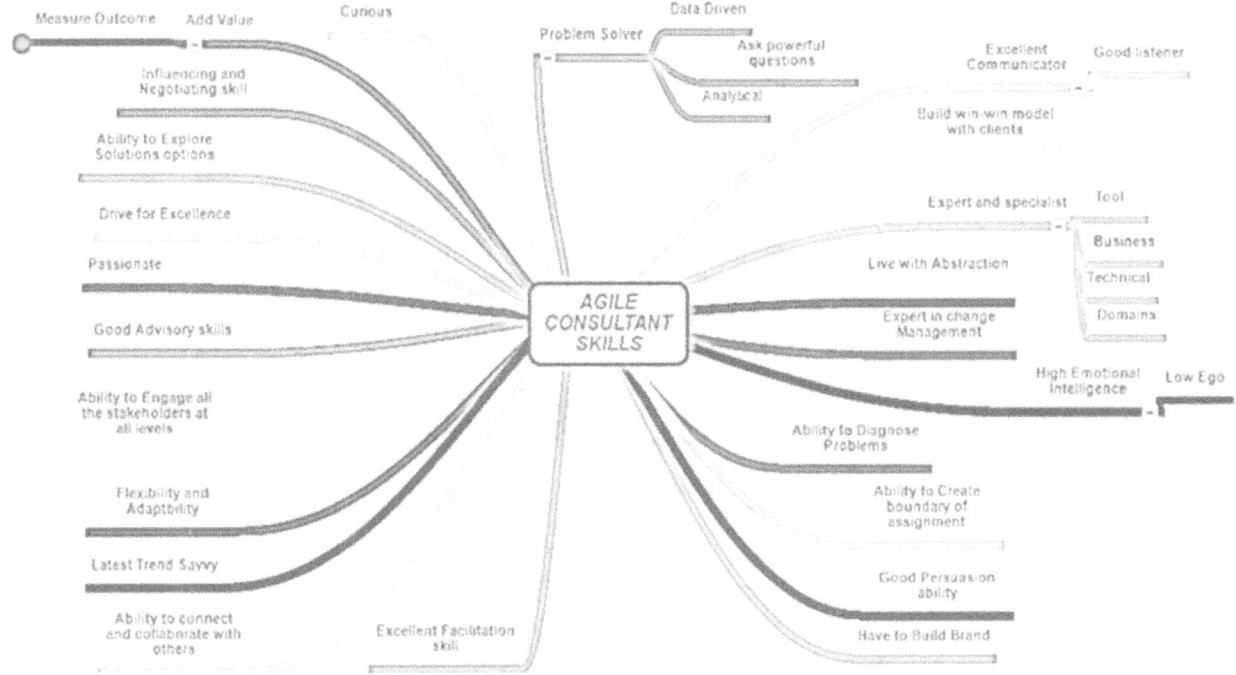

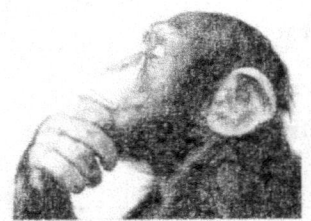

: Why? Why? Why? Why? And Why? Develop better questioning skill.

Improve Likeability factor

: Conveying the moral through stories

Demonstrates that some of the message has to be expressed in a different way

Power of Observation

Can we find family members from this picture?

Assessment points for any agile projects. To become awesome agile consultants, we have to be aware of the below mind map factors.

"As a business consultant, I am a voracious reader of self-help books, case studies of thriving companies, and the biographies and autobiographies of the world's most successful people. I relentlessly implement the best ideas into my businesses"

–Clay Clark

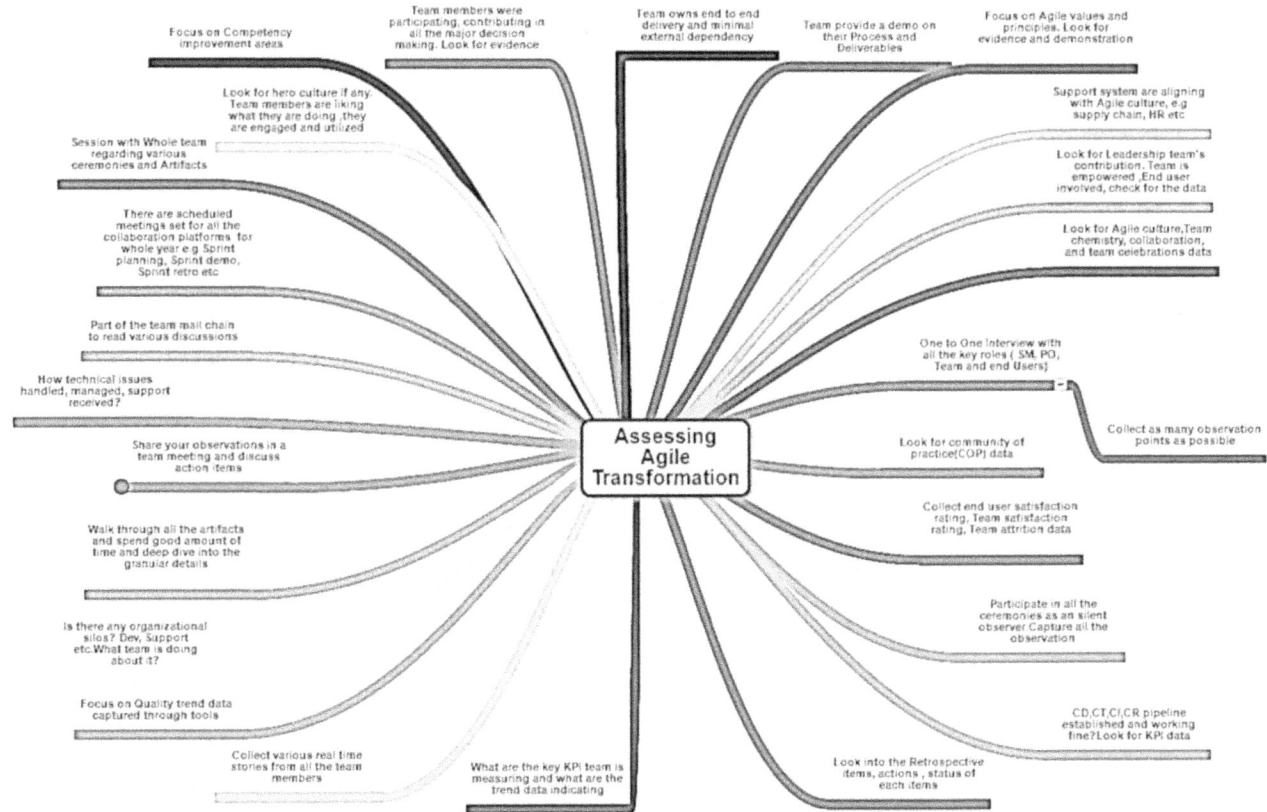

What actions are you going to take from this lesson?

1. _____

2. _____

3. _____

Thinking Question:

➤ Are you doing enough to build the capability to become a consultant or build consultant like competences which can aid in your work?

1.5 What are the various coaching models to use?

"Coaches have to watch for what they don't want to see and listen to what they don't want to hear."

—*John Madden, American Football*

Why this topic?

During my various coaching engagements, I realized that various contexts demand various kinds of model, it is good to know about these models. But not mandatory. It guides the coach to think structurally. We can experiment with these models with our coaching assignment and learn from it

Coaching is a way of enabling others to act and build on their strengths.

To coach is to care enough about people to invest time in building personal relationships with them.

There are a number of coaching models agile coaches can refer.

We as an agile coach should know all the available coaching models. We need to know which one to use when.

There are a few

- o **GROW**
- o **TGROW**
- o **OSKAR**
- o **OUTCOMES**
- o **SPACE**
- o **ACHIEVE**
- o **POSITIVE**

a) **GROW** model: The GROW model was developed by Graham Alexander and John Whitmore. The name is an acronym with each letter standing for a different phase of the model. GROW stands for below picture

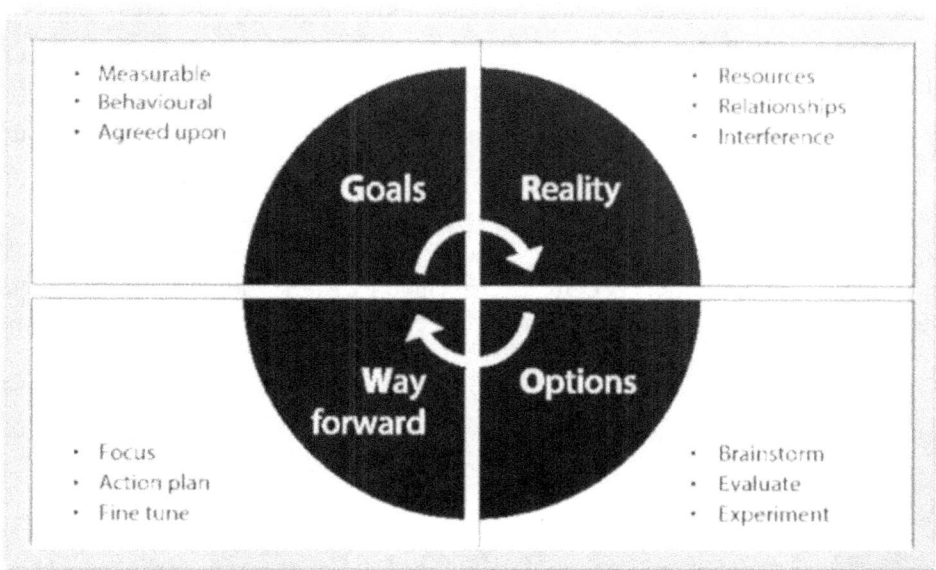

The GROW model is easy to apply and check for the result. These are not sequential steps. The goal must be SMART to measure output. GROW model, devised by Sir John Whitmore in the classic book 'Coaching for Performance,' which first appeared in 1990.

b) **TGROW** model: Eminent coaching Guru Myles Downey felt that additional element would make GROW model more pertinent in the environment of the organization. Downey felt that the first element of a coaching model should be "TOPIC," creating the acronym TGROW.

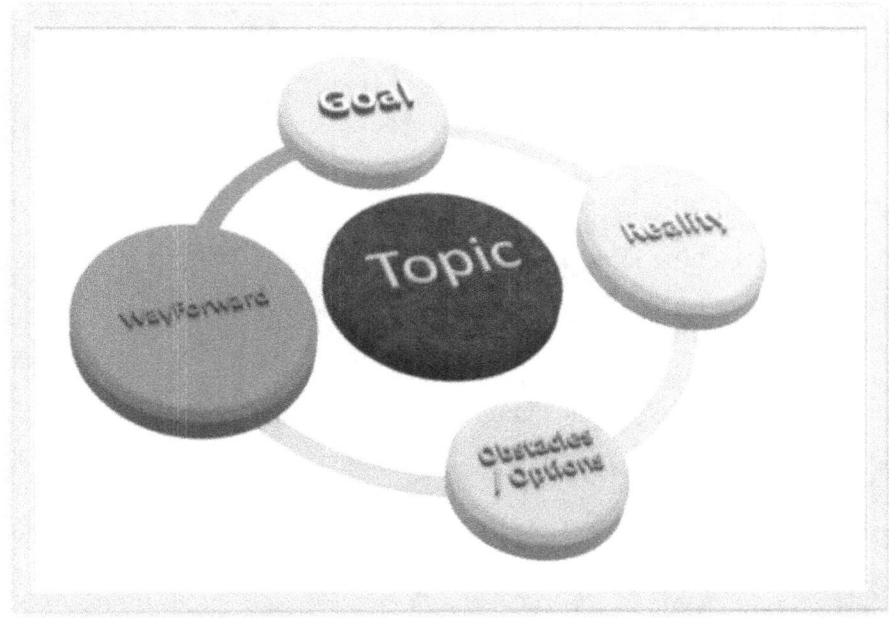

Topic–this covers the wider environment that impacts on the specific issue to be addressed through coaching. It will reflect the level of importance the issue has within that wider area and the impact it may have on the coaches' long-term aspirations.

Goal – a specific, measurable endpoint that the coaches want to attain.

Reality–the current situation the coaches are in now and all the issues he or she is facing.

Obstacles/Options – what is stopping the coaches from attaining this goal – obstacles – and what 'options' are available to the coaches to resolve this issue.

The way forward – the required steps needed to execute the chosen option and attain their goal.

Downey's reasoning for making 'Topic' the first element of his coaching model was the need to have an appreciation of the environment the organization is in.

c) OSKAR model:

One of the most popular coaching models is OSKAR. Invented by Mark with his co-author Paul Z Jackson for a project in the year 2000, OSKAR is becoming widely accepted as an easy-to-use way to harness the positive power of.

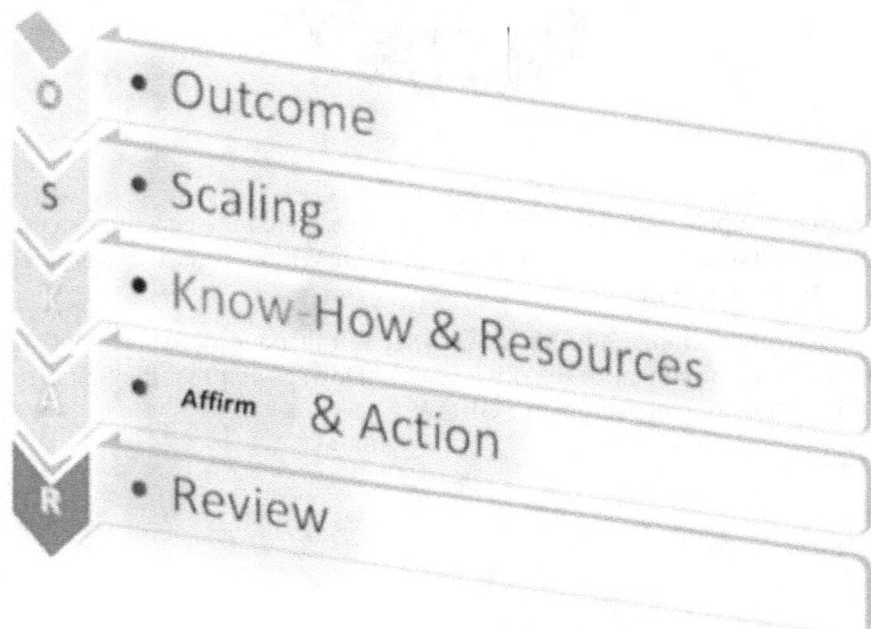

The benefits of this kind of coaching in practice are:

- Positive and progress focus leads to the good motivation for the coaches
- Positive questions lead to the excellent relationship between coach and coaches
- Incisive focus on what works leads to rapid and sustainable results
- Focus on the know-how of what works encourages shared wisdom throughout the organization.

d) OUTCOMES model:

There are some similarities between GROW and OUTCOMES model, but OUTCOMES model is more detail oriented.

OUTCOMES stand for

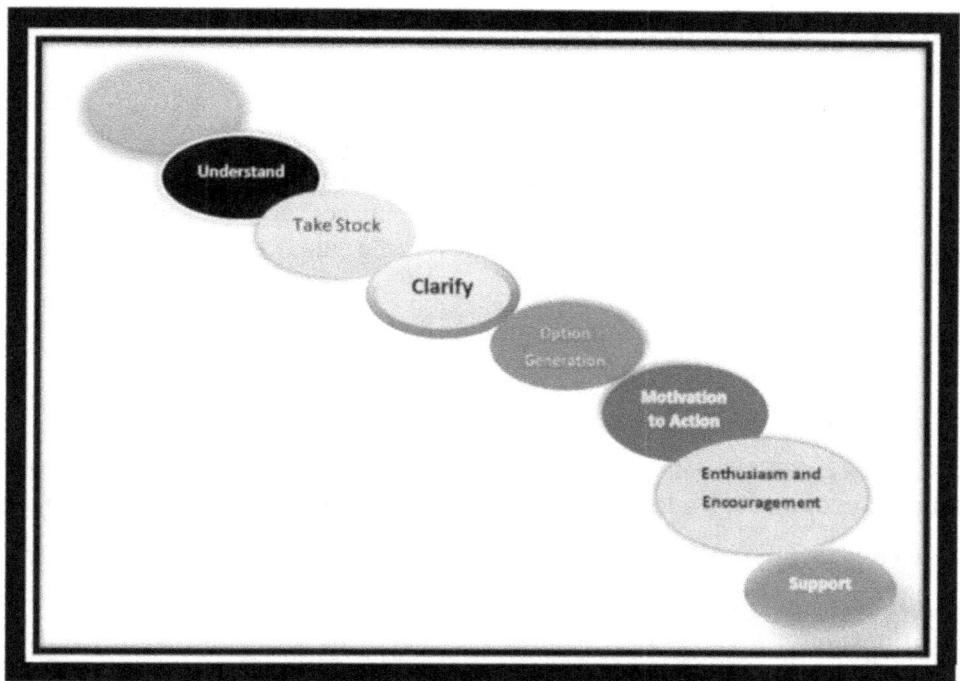

O for Objectives, U for understand, T for Taking stock about the current situation, C for clarifying, O for option Generation, M for Motivation to action, E for Enthusiasm and encouragement, S for Support.

e) SPACE model (Edgerton and Palmer, 2005) is used in the cognitive behavioral approaches to coaching and is the acronym for the following elements:

Social context, **P**hysiology, **A**ction, **C**ognition, and **E**motion. SPACE can be used in parallel with GROW and POSITIVE to help coaches overcome psychological blocks associated with particular problems or issues (including performance-related issues).

f) ACHIEVE Coaching Model: This is a seven-step model developed by Dembkowski and Eldridge (2003).

It includes the following steps:

(a) Assess the current situation,

(b) Creative brainstorming of alternatives to the current situation,

(c) Hone goals (i.e., helping the client to formulate goals),

(d) Initiate options (i.e., helping the client to initiate a wide range of behavioral options to achieve the desired goal),

(e) Evaluate options,

(f) Valid action program design (i.e., a collaboration between the coach and the coachee to develop an action plan),

(g) Encourage momentum (i.e., an ongoing process of providing encouragement and helping the client to keep on track with the plans).

g) **POSITIVE**: POSITIVE model by Libri (2004), is a model developed from the GROW and ACHIEVE models. It aims at producing an 'optimum coaching relationship' and includes asking key questions around:

- The Purpose of the coachee,
- Observations (e.g., of efforts up-to-date),
- Strategy,
- Insight (e.g., on a commitment to a goal),
- Team (e.g., with whom the coachee will share his/her goal),
- Initiate (e.g., when the coachee will start to act towards achieving a goal),
- Value (e.g., question how the coachee would celebrate his/her success), and
- Encourage (e.g., asking about the coachee's progress in the pursuit of his/her goals) (as cited in Edgerton and Palmer, 2005).

An important role of the coach is to ask pertinent questions and listen. Questioning and listening can help the other person set realistic learning goals.

Coach Marshall Goldsmith says,

"My success rate as a coach has improved dramatically as I've realized that people's getting better is not a function of me; it's a function of the person and the people around the person."

Whatever model we follow, Improving coaching is as follows:

- **Communicate clear expectations,**
- **Build relationships,**
- **Give feedback on areas that require specific improvement,**
- **Listen actively,**
- **Help to remove obstacles,**
- **Give emotional support, including empathy,**
- **Reflect content or meaning,**
- **Give gentle advice and guidance,**
- **Allow for modeling of desired performance and behavior,**
- **Gain a commitment to change, and**
- **Applaud good results**

"The [best] coaches… know that the job is to win… know that they must be decisive, that they must phase people through their organizations, and at the same time they are sensitive to the feelings, loyalties, and emotions that people have toward one another. If you don't have these feelings, I do not know how you can lead anyone. I have spent many sleepless nights trying to figure out how I was going to phase out certain players for whom I had strong feelings, but that was my job. I wasn't hired to do anything but win." - Bill Walsh, American Football

What actions are you going to take from this lesson?

1. _____

2. _____

3. _____

Thinking Question:

- Are you doing enough to absorb various coaching models which can help you to perform as a coach in the finest way?

1.6 Agile Coach as a Gardner?

"To be as good as it can be, a team has to buy into what you as the coach are doing. They have to feel you're a part of them and they're a part of you." - Bobby Knight

Why this topic?

The organization is a garden and team members are like plants. With that analogy, how we are fulfilling the coach role.

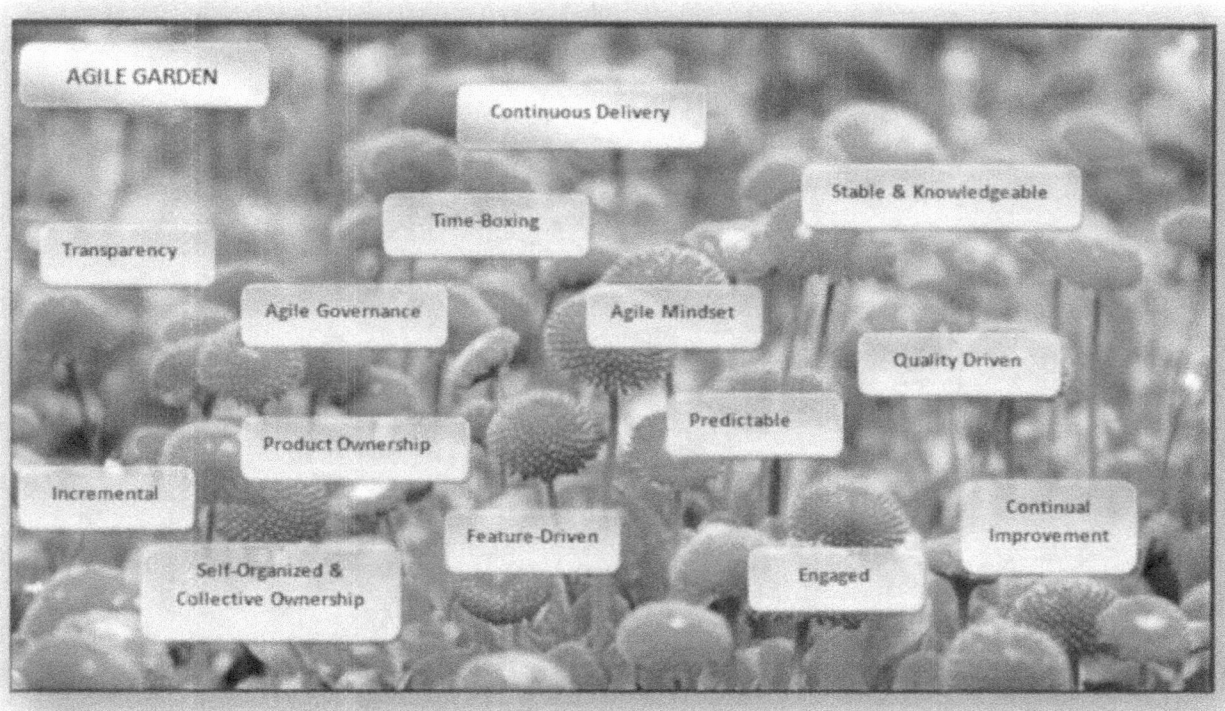

As an agile coach are you taking care of your garden?

Gardeners are in charge of growing and maintaining all kinds of plants in a variety of settings. These could be public parks, gardens, sports grounds, and schools.

Agile gardener, you need to do the same for the team or organization at the enterprise level

> Pruning shrubs => at enterprise level remove all the unwanted parts
> Checking the health of the plants by identifying any pests or diseases and controlling them = > Look at the team level and find the smells within the team.
> Raising plants from seeds or cuttings = > at the enterprise level, a coach needs to identify at team level if there are such things that need to be done.
> Cleaning and maintaining tools and equipment => at the enterprise level, are we aware of the all the centralized and standardized tools? Is everybody aware of all these tools?
> Applying nutrients to plants and maintaining moisture levels => Talk to the leaders and managers, share your thoughts with them about the people concerned which you observe during your coaching session.
> Using machinery such as lawnmowers, rotators, and hedge trimmers => Automate the improve process. Collect the anonymous feedback and take actions on them
> Digging, planting and weeding flower beds and borders => Coach, Mentor and have one to one to sessions with all the team members and leaders
> Do basic landscaping and designs for the beautification of the gardens=> Work with the team and team setup. Inject fun into the work and create an ambient which is fun filled.
> Must have passion in plants = > at organizational transformation what do we need to be a passionate agile gardener? Passionate about team development. Understand pain points from the team members.

These are some thought-provoking questions which agile coach can ask and look for, the evidence to improve the organization as a garden.

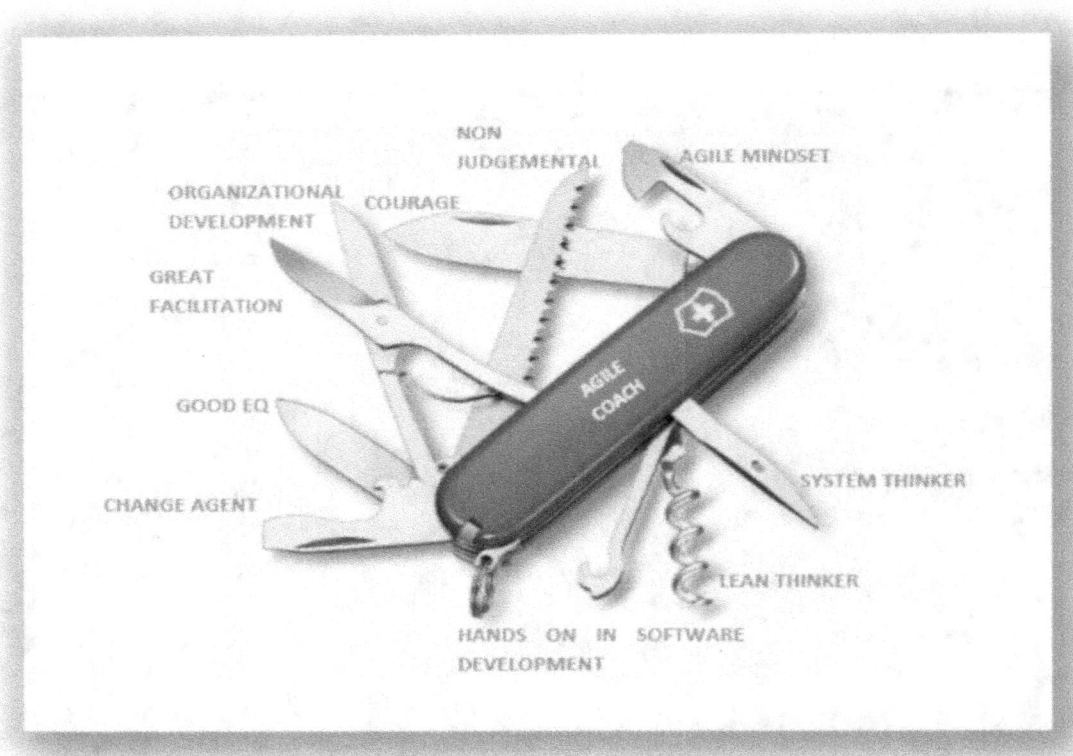

"Good coaching may be defined as the development of character, personality and habits of players, plus the teaching of fundamentals and team play"

—Clair Bee

What actions are you going to take from this lesson?

1. _____

2. _____

3. _____

Thinking Question:

➤ Are you doing enough to aid your organization's Garden? What else can you do?

1.7 How to apply the Socratic Approach to Coaching?

"I cannot teach anybody anything. I can only make them think."

—Socrates

Why this topic?

Socrates was a great coach. In one of the stories, I came across these facts and shared the same in the coaching clinic. Colleagues started using this concept and got benefited. It is important to question all the assumptions and validate.

The ancient Greek philosopher Socrates describes this as the **"Allegory of the Cave."** You find it in Plato›s Dialogues. The Dialogues are a series of conversations between Plato and his old teacher, Socrates.

Socrates says a philosopher is like a prisoner who is freed from the cave and can now see reality as it truly is.

Socrates lived in ancient Greece. He was a master at **asking powerful questions**. Instead of lecturing, he taught by posing his students **a series of thought-provoking questions**. Through these, he **engaged** his students' **minds** in the learning process. He **uncovered** their **assumptions**. He slowly but surely got to the **heart of the issue**.

Socrates would start a class by asking **"What is the virtue?"** or **"What is good?"** We use these words all the time. But do we really know what they mean? Today, many universities around the world use the "Socratic Method" in their teaching—one of the most famous of these is Harvard Business School. Socrates summed up this method very clearly. He said,

"The highest form of Human Excellence is to question oneself and others."

Socrates was a vocal critic of Athenian society and government. He was finally sentenced to death for his apparent attacks on the ruling classes. Without a struggle, he drank a cup of poison hemlock. It gradually reached his heart and he died, leaving his enduring reputation as one of the greatest philosophers in history.

Implement the Socratic mindset and find the answer, <u>**Enquiry on all the assumptions.**</u>

- Question all the points which other mostly ignore or do not give much importance.
- Use questions to stimulate others on an inspiring ride of knowledge and finding.

When we adopt the Socrates mindset, we approach almost every conversation differently.

DO NOT	DO
TELL	ASK THOUHGT PROVOKING QUESTIONS
BEING THE EXPERT	INVITE OTHERS TO CONTRIBUTE EXPERTISE
CONTROLLING KNOWLEDGE	HELO DRAW OUT OTHERS EXPERIENCES
ASSUMING MEANING	ASK ABOUT THE MEANING OF THE WORDS
MANDATING SOLUTIONS	SOLICIT SOLUTIONS FROM OTHERS
SHOWING HOW SMART YOU ARE	SHOW OTHERS HOW SMART THEY ARE
ANALYZING	SYNTHESIZE AND LOOK AT THE BIG PICTURE

"Remember that there is nothing stable in human affairs; therefore avoid undue elation in prosperity or undue depression in adversity."

—Socrates, 469–399 B.C.

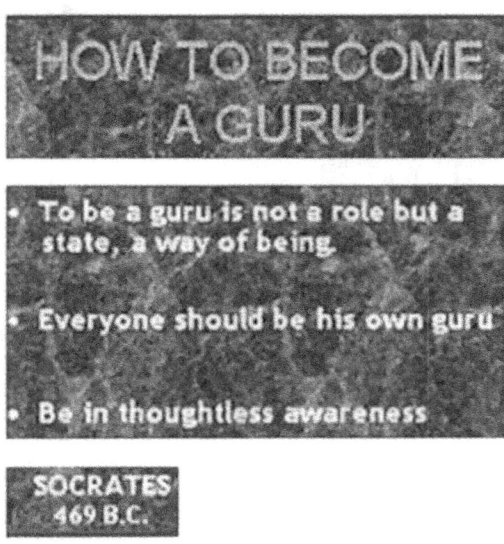

What actions are you going to take from this lesson?

1. _____

2. _____

3. _____

Thinking Question:

> ➤ Are you doing enough to practice what Socrates said and reap the benefits?

1.8 How to Use Johari Window to Improve Coaching effectiveness?

"Coaching is people management–getting people to do what you want them to do and like doing it"

—*Anonymous*

Why this topic?

This model helped me know the person's personality and why should we spend the time to discover the hidden part of a person's personality. I was not able to influence many team members, when I started looking into myself, why, then this model helped me to connect with the people and take them along on my journey.

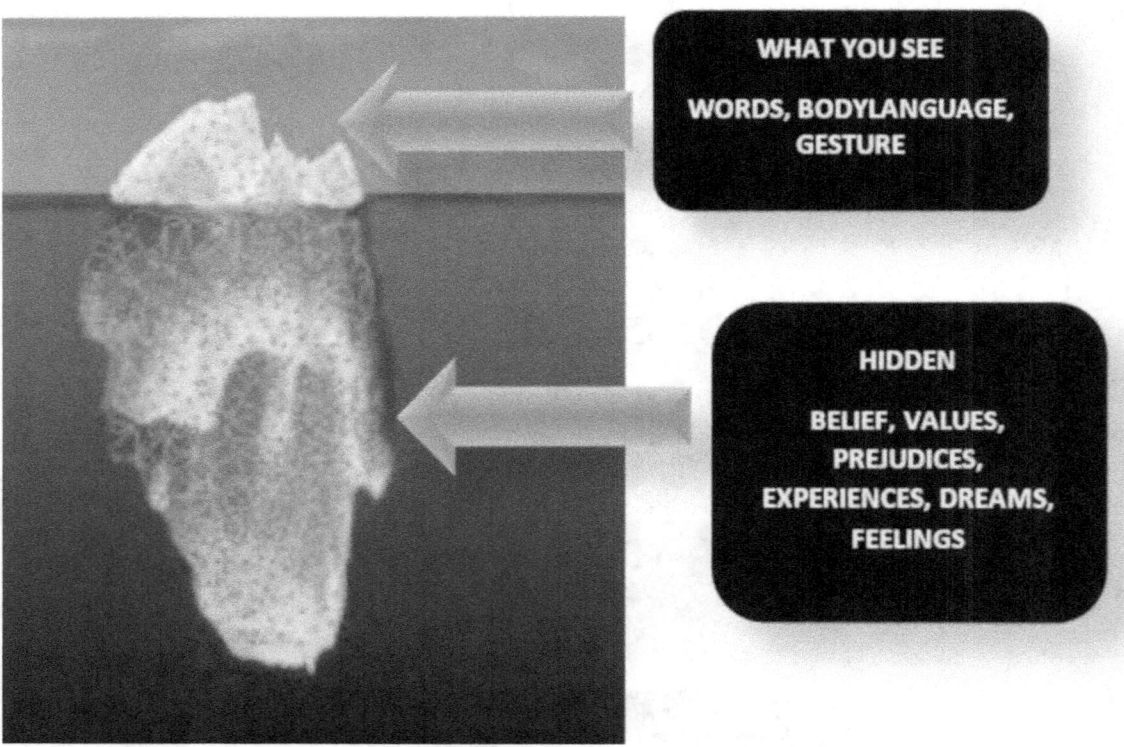

WHAT ABOVE PICTURE TELLS US?

Only a very small percentage of who we are is visible (tip of the iceberg), whereas the very core of our values, emotions, behaviors, and natural reflexes, stem from something much deeper, hence the mass iceberg formation that remains invisible under water.

How can we coach effectively with the above state where visibility is very less?

So what should be our major skill require to start coaching?

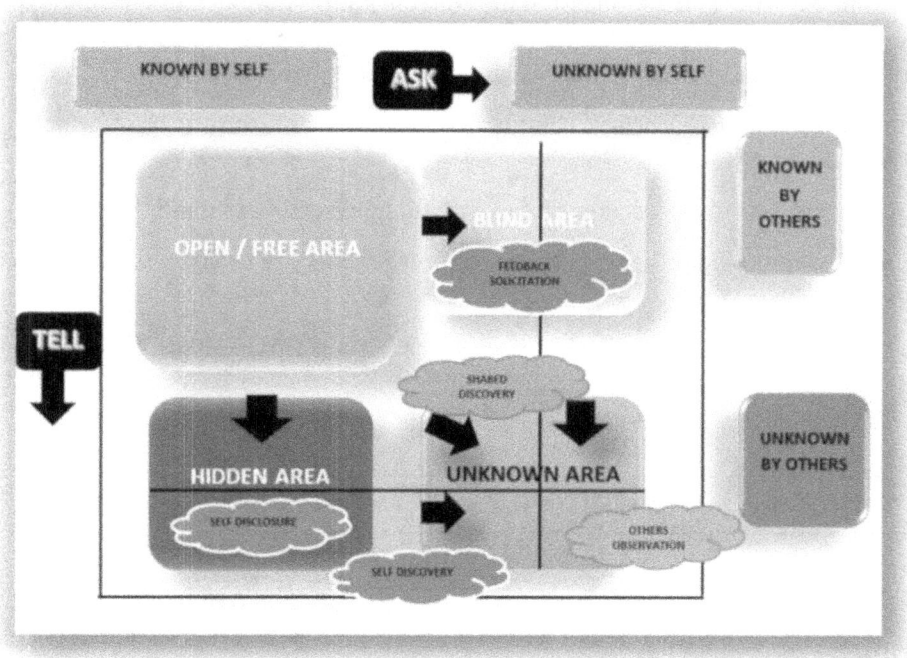

In a coaching conversation, both coach and coachee are focused on what is going on in the coachee's mind?

HOW CAN WE REDUCE THE BLIND AREA?

HOW CAN WE REDUCE UNKNOWN AREA?

The **Johari window** is a tool created in 1955 by two American psychologists, Joseph Luft (1916–2014) and Harrington Ingham (1914–1995). Today the tool is used extensively to help people better understand their relationship with self and others.

A coach can help team members become aware of their "blind" quadrant opportunities for growth, through feedback, discussion, and the goal-setting process. Listen and learn.

Asking *for and listening to feedback* from others is the only way to move out of the blind area

Disclosure (transparency–*telling* the others) is the way to bring the "Open Area" down to the hidden area

SELF DISCLOSURE OR GIVE FEEDBACK

As a COACH we can build trust with others by disclosing information about ourselves, with the help of feedback from others, we can learn about ourselves and come to terms with personal issues. The ultimate goal of the Johari Window is to enlarge the Open/free Area.

An example

A coachee who says 'I had delivery pressure and could not get any time for a coaching session' is reporting all the following simultaneously:

1. A fact
2. A topic for conversation
3. An implicit relationship
4. An appeal to the coach
5. An expression of himself or herself as a coachee

All of these things come together at the moment of the conversation. The coach has the choice of doing nothing, following up on any of these messages, or indeed continuing with or proposing a completely different type of conversation or conversational content. An overwhelming variety of choices.

In the coaching conversation, the coachee continually produces new information which can find a place somewhere in the Johari window.

At the same time, the coach has great freedom in the way (s) he responds to that information.

> *"Coaching is unlocking a person's potential to maximize their own performance. It's helping them to learn rather than teaching them."*

> —*Tim Gallwey*

What actions are you going to take from this lesson?

1. _____

2. _____

3. _____

Thinking Question:

➢ Are you doing enough to use Johari concept to know more about people and connect with them in a bigger way?

1.9 How to use Solution-Focused Approach to Coaching?

Why this topic?

This topic was born from, the discussion that some of the projects are very critical and challenging in nature, a coach has to help the team by sitting with them, understand the end to end issues and solve the problem with them by doing hand holding.

Solution-Focused Brief Coaching has emerged from **Solution-Focused Brief Therapy (SFBT).**

Solution Focused Brief Coaching uses questions that emphasis and redeploy the coaching sessions on results, clients' fortes and on the prospect.

The investigations aid to emphasize the parts of life that are 'problem free', such as interests, fortes and times of relaxation.

The elementary standard of the Solution Focused work is to converse around resolutions instead of difficulties.

Once a solution has been identified, the path to reach it can be identified as well. The coach implies - with the usage of the present tense for the solution and the past tense for everything that relates to the problem - the client has already reached the solution and needs "only" to document the steps needed to reach there.

The original idea came from the Milwaukee's Brief Family Therapy Center, with Steve De Shazer, Insoo Kim Berg, and Yvonne Dolan being the most well-known contributors. Its development started in 1978 and continues to date. It has been used successfully in psychotherapy and coaching, proving to be a very effective alternative to problem-oriented techniques.

OSKAR is a framework for solution-focused coaching.

The model focuses on the solution rather than the problem and by finding out what works and doing more of it, and stop doing what doesn't work and doing something else.

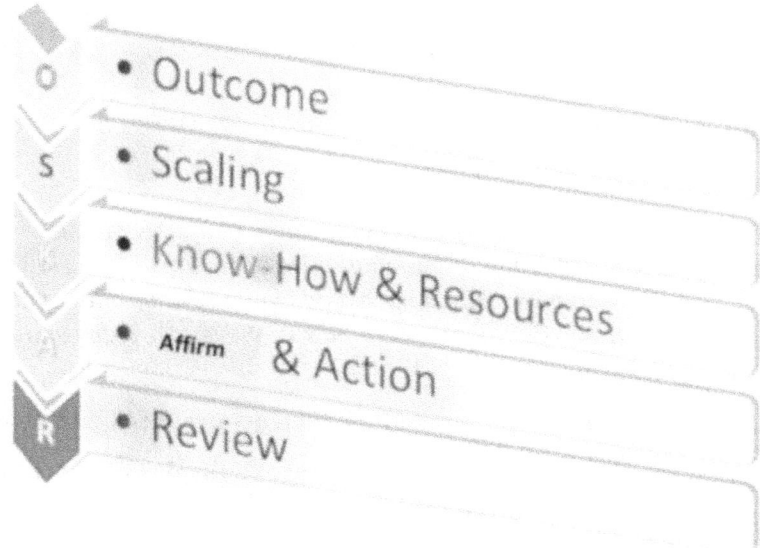

Albert Einstein is supposed to have said, 'No problem can be solved by the same consciousness that created it'.

Solution-focused coaching thus avoids drawing attention to the problem. It prefers to draw clients' conscious attention to solutions.

Solution-focused coaching, moving away from the problem: the coach tries to find situations when the problem does not arise, looks for reasons for those positive experiences, and attempts to build on them. Conversations are structured as follows:

- **Objective**: What do you want to achieve?
- **Solutions now**: What is going better already? How exactly? What positive exceptions do you experience?
- **Characteristics of solutions**: What tells you that things are going better ('miracle question')?
- **Feedback for solutions**: Positive evaluation and compliments.
- **Reinforcement of solutions:** Reinforcing what is already going well with the aid of homework.

1. OUTCOME: What is the objective of this coaching? What do you want to achieve today? What do you want to achieve in the long term? How will you know this coaching has been of use to you?

2. SCALING: On a scale of 0 to 10, with 10 representing the Future Perfect, and 0 the worst it has ever been, where are you on that scale today? You are at n now; what did you do to get this far?

3. KNOW-HOW & RESOURCES: What helps you perform at n on the scale, rather than 0? When does the outcome already happen for you - even a little bit? What did you do to make that happen? How did you do that? What did you do differently?

4. AFFIRM AND ACTION: What's already going well? What is the next small step? What would you like to do personally, straight away? You are at n now, what would it take to get you to n+1?

5. REVIEW: What's better? What did you do that made the change happen?

What actions are you going to take from this lesson?

1. _____

2. _____

3. _____

Thinking Question:

Are you doing enough to help others to propose solutions when they ask for?

1.10 How to use Coaching Kata?

Why this topic?

During our coaching engagement, we had many challenges. Many unique challenges. It is not written in any book. The challenges are very specific to the geographically distributed projects. How do we help each other as a coach? The concept was born so that we should have a coaching kata backlog and we should have a kata session to help each other, to grow professionally. More topics we have, more discussion, we have and we are growing as a coach in terms of knowledge

Kata is a Japanese word describing **detailed patterns of movements practiced either solo or in pairs.**

The kata is not intended as a literal depiction of a mock fight, but as a **display of transition and flow from one posture and movement to another, teaching the student proper form and position, and encouraging them to visualize different scenarios for the use of each motion and technique.**

When we are driving a car for the first time and when we are driving a formula one race on the highway! Imagine the transition state of growth in between.

How many kata sessions they have to complete to reach a state where Roger Federer and Rafael Nadal are today?

How did you build the habit? Through routine practice

> "WE ARE WHAT WE REPEATEDLY DO. EXCELLENCE THEN, IS NOT AN ACT, BUT A HABIT."
> - ARISTOTLE

What is coaching Kata?

Coaching Kata is to teach and coach the improvement kata by using real-world problems as practice.

In the coaching kata session, one experience coach (mentor coach) who is already familiar with a similar type of experience guides mentee coach.

Mentor coach will not provide the solution.

A mentor should teach the basis of improvement kata.

A mentee should always identify the next step with the guidance of a mentor.

The challenge is how to find such mentors?

We have many such mentors, we need to be humble enough to look for those people and learn from them.

Coaching Kata questions for improvement...

The five questions:

1. What is the target condition?
2. What is the actual condition now?
3. What obstacles are now preventing you from reaching the target condition? Which one are you addressing now?
4. What is your next step (PDCA experiment)
5. When can we go and see what we have learned form taking that step?

From Toyota Kata by Mike Rother

How about Coaching Dojo?

A coaching Dojo is a workout in programming which aids a programmer to improve their skills through rehearsal and reiteration.

The Dojo was intended as a safe place to practice and learn coaching skills.

Coaching Dojo needs three members.

One being a person who proposed a "kata" (essentially a person with an issue to discuss), one person who coached them through the kata, and another who observed the coach and provided feedback.

Let us swapped until everyone had a chance of trying out each role.

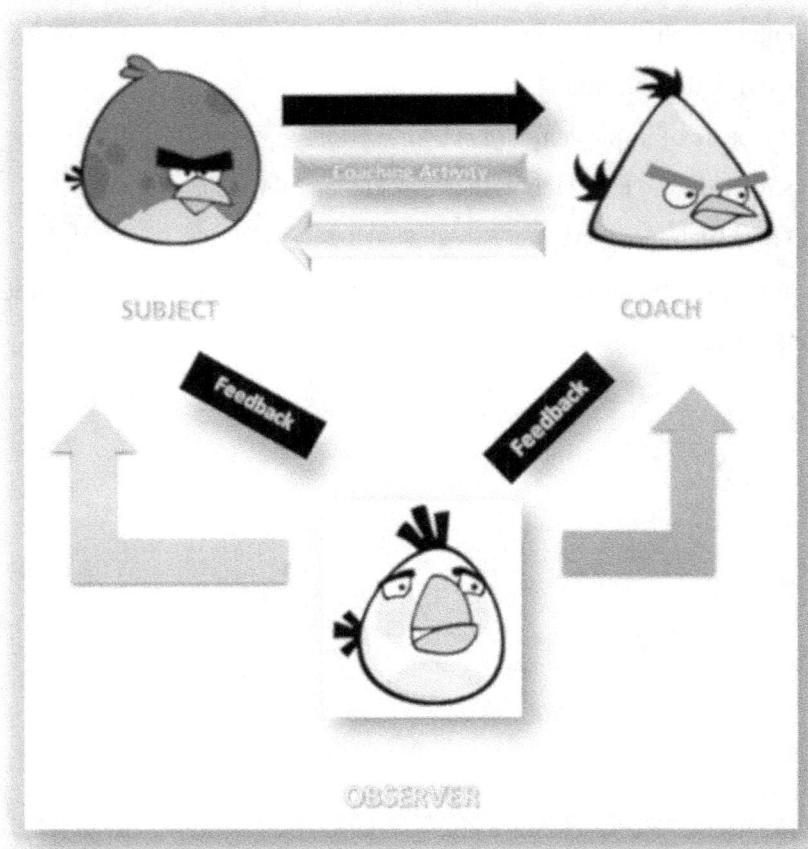

Few coaching dojo assignments which we can start for practice:

1. Team members do not need a coach! Team members are not open for coaching. **As a coach how should I proceed?**

2. Team members are not willing to change. They are efficient and productive in the current way of executing the project. Do not want to hear anything about Agile. Agile process is overhead for them. **How should I coach such a team?**

3. Line Manager/Sr. Manager, wants the coach to solve all the team issues. The team is demotivated with the work and pressure from the other side of the organization. **How should I coach such a team**?

4. Product management team members are headstrong, high attitude individuals. Not willing to participate in any coaching session. **How do I coach?**

5. How do I do Planning Kata? What should be the example that can be given to continue with the planning kata?

6. Not willing to change the team structure, the current structure is the inefficient way of operating. Old role still exists, not willing to leave those positions, **How do I coach such a team?**

7. Old governance model. Metrics are driven, too much data-driven, which is significantly influencing people's behavior and culture. **How do I coach such a cultural transformation?**

8. Most of the team members are doing agile. The mechanical process, they are not agile. Team members are expected to be told what to do, how to do it, and when to do it. They don't want to problem solve, they don't want to take risks, and they don't want to be accountable. **How do I coach such a team?**

9. Team members focusing on Project assignment (Start to Finish!), Start date, and end date. No long-term commitment. **How do I coach?**

"Practice doesn't make perfect. Perfect practice makes perfect."

—Vince Lombardi, American Football

What actions are you going to take from this lesson?

1. _____

2. _____

3. _____

Thinking Question:

Are you doing enough to create a space where we as a coach can run the kata session to strengthen our skills?

1.11 How to do "Coaching by Showing"?

"Coaching is a profession of love. You can't coach people unless you love them."

—Eddy Robinson

Why this topic?

This topic came from the seagull coaching side effects, as a result of such coaching, sustenance of the agile transformation is at risk. We agreed that we have to support the team, whoever asks for it. Every coach has to do the homework and dry run the kata session if required and support the team.

In our coaching Dojo session, we discussed the importance of this concept, where we walk the talk. By seeing us doing, people start changing themselves. We become the role model for the team and that change is sustainable.

Coaching by **"showing how to,"** this is what I have learned from my in-laws.

When my daughter was born, my in-laws were with us and they took care of all the childcare requirements at an early stage of my daughter. She has completely demonstrated us how to take care kid's end to end necessities for initial 4-5 months. But it was for a very small duration as she owns one school for kids, she has to go back for her commitment. After she left, we started owning the complete childcare requirement with confident as she has demonstrated hands on to us.

She is a very good cook, every year whenever she visited us, we have a few new dishes, the same continues after she left. She demonstrated to us how to cook all the new dishes. Later it is much easier for us to continue to prepare the same dishes

She coaches my wife about all the aspects of parenting and child care. When my son was born, we did not have much trouble with the childcare as already we have been coached by my in-laws.

My father didn't tell me how to live;
he lived, and let me watch him do it

- Clarence Budington Kelland -

Learning by doing, coaching by showing.....that is what the key message I have learned

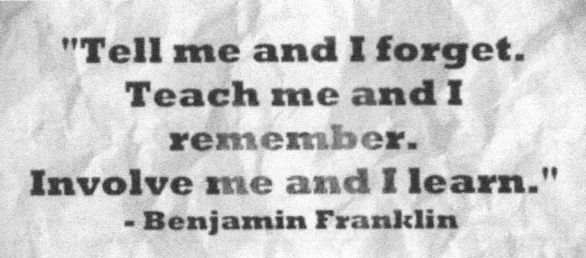

Same concepts I have been applying with the scrum team. During my coaching, I play a scrum master role for one sprint, product owner role for one sprint and demonstrate how to run the sprint. They observe how I am doing and take over from there.

Teams regularly have a lot of enhancement chance in how they do their Sprint Planning, Daily Scrum, Review & Retrospective, and their Backlog Refinement. I facilitate these workshops to show how they could be done effectively and then tries to increase team ownership of these events.

In this process, there were lots of questions and clarification which I would have missed which are very specific to that context. It helps teams to get inspired to know why we are doing certain steps.

I am not telling theory to my team and finishing, I live with them with their problem and show them how to address the challenges as a team. I am an active participator—reviewing the dashboards, asking thoughtful and appropriately placed questions, and surfacing opportunities for acknowledgment and recognition. It is important for a coach, who is trained to listen deeply and to come from a place of inquiry, to be aware of who, how and when their questions are offered.

I discover that consultancy service to the team where I provide information does not work, promote self-discovery works for the long term.

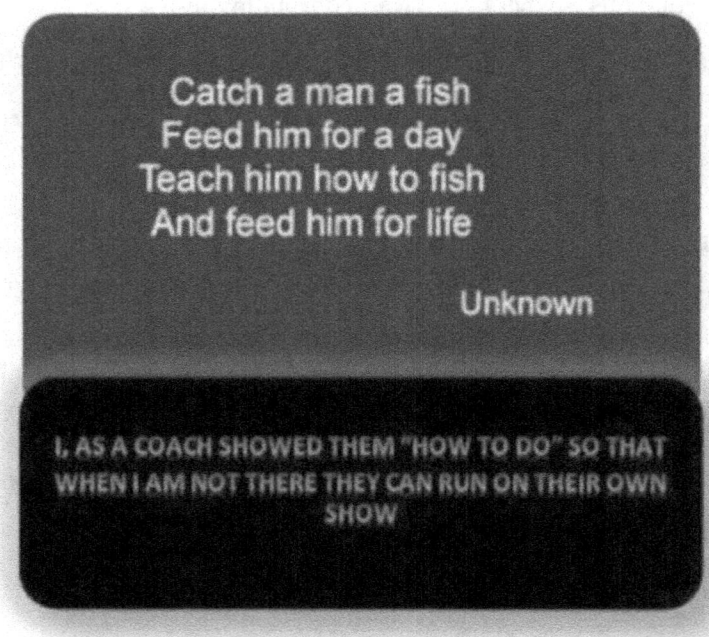

It is well accepted by the team and it is a game-changing moment.

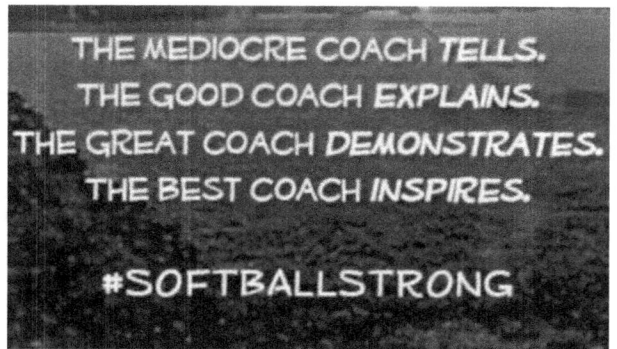

What actions are you going to take from this lesson?

1. _____

2. _____

3. _____

Thinking Question:

Are you doing enough to help others by showing them how to do? What is the feedback on this approach to improve?

1.12 What are the Seven Habits of a Highly Empathetic Coach?

> *"We think we listen, but very rarely do we listen with real understanding, true empathy. Yet listening, of this very special kind, is one of the most potent forces for change that I know."*
>
> —*Carl Rogers*

Why this topic?

This thought came to my mind when we are doing the design thinking workshop, we were emphasizing the empathy aspect with the people who will build the product and consume the solutions. Why not we as a coach also start exercising the same with coaching team? That's how I started digging more into this.

Few of my fellow coaches are sharing stories from their team, where scrum masters will not allow others to talk.

He/She will keep talking about what the scrum guides say and what we should do, etc.

He/She as a scrum master will not listen to the team members.

Later they come to the coaches for help, complaint is "team members had stopped co-operating with me, what I can do?"

When my fellow coaches looked into this problem they realized, as a coach we have to explain what empathy is all about and how empathy can help others.

As a scrum master or a product owner, we all should develop this skill.

Why is Empathy important as a coach?

1. It helps us to understand the unspoken parts of our communication with others.

2. It helps us to **understand** and motivates others.

3. It helps us to understand the pain points about others so that we **connect** with them in a better way.
4. It helps us to understand what they need from us, and how we can treat them according to how they want to be treated.
5. It helps us to **evaluate** more clearly how our words and actions **affect or influence** the surrounding people
6. It helps us to **resolve** any potential **conflict** that may arise from misunderstandings.

What is Empathy?

Empathy is the capacity to **understand or feel** what another person is experiencing from within their frame of reference, i.e., the capacity to place oneself in another's position.

It means being as good at listening to the thoughts of others as saying your own;

We all have our viewpoints, standards, experiences, and cultural understandings that make us distinctively us. When we amalgamate these kinds of stuff together, particularly in an original situational or cultural setting, we are broadening our skill to understand and empathize with others.

When we are empathetic toward someone else, we consider before we speak or act, and instead, find a way to make them feel supported, loved, cared for, or even just simply understood.

Three Types of Empathy: Psychologists have identified three types of empathy:

Cognitive empathy, emotional empathy, and compassionate empathy.

Cognitive empathy: Understanding someone's thoughts and emotions, in a very rational, rather than emotional sense.

Emotional empathy: is also known as emotional contagion, and is 'catching' someone else's feelings, so that you literally feel them too.

Compassionate empathy: Understanding someone's feelings and taking appropriate action to help.

What are the 7 habits?

1. **Getting Curious About Strangers**
2. **Listening and Being Vulnerable**
3. **Offer Your Support**
4. **Practice Emotional Detachment**
5. **Be fully present when you are with people**
6. **Try another person's life**
7. **Ask better questions.**

Practice these seven habits for six months to build empathy into your personality, things will start changing for you

"If you judge people, you have no time to love them."

—*Mother Teresa*

What actions are you going to take from this lesson?

1. _____

2. _____

3. _____

Thinking Question:

Are you doing enough to build your empathetic abilities which can be applied to coaching?

1.13 How to use Circle of Influence for Coaching?

"Simply put, Coaching is where you work with someone to connect with yourself, redesign your environment and your life, and then take action to implement it!"

—*Emma-Louise Elsey*

Why this topic?

As an enterprise coach, we have many organizational commitment to meet. We have to influence many executives, some of them are super powerful people. To understand how much we can stretch ourselves to help them, we need to know this concept.

When I was working with a few powerful executives, I was curious to know, how can I get the work done for them? Then I started my homework to understand the entire game plan.

Stephen Covey, in The Seven Habits of Highly Effective People, introduces the concept of the **Circle of Concern and Circle of Influence**.

A Circle of Concern includes the wide range of concerns we have, such as our fitness, our families, complications at work, troubling neighbor, or interstate conflict.

A Circle of Influence encompasses those concerns that we can do something about. They are concerned that we have some administrator over.

Stephen Covey defines proactive as "being responsible for our own lives.....our behavior is a function of our choices, not our circumstances.

Proactive people emphasis on matters within their circle of influence. They toil on stuff they can do something about.

The nature of their energy in doing this is a positive, expanding and amplifying. They increase their Circle of Influence."

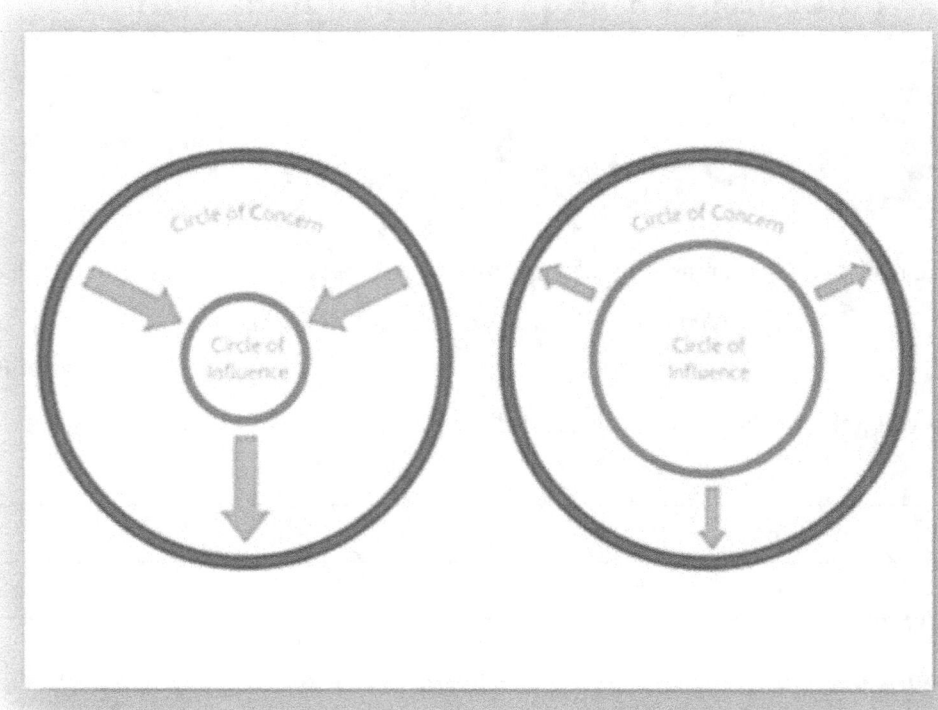

Reactive people incline to neglect those themes that are under their control and influence. Their attention is elsewhere and their Circle of Influence shrinks.

Steven Covey tells us that in life our Circle of Influence is most often smaller than the Circle of Concern.

We can't control the economy or a company merger. As we react, we tend to focus on the Circle of Concern, which depletes our energy, because we have no control over it.

The energy focused on the Circle of Concern is negative.

If you focus on the Circle of Concern and neglect the Circle of Influence, eventually the Circle of Influence will get smaller. This will add to feelings of pressure, weakness, and powerlessness because you cannot change anything in the Circle of Concern.

Where do we spend most of our time and energy?

As an agile coach, most of us are working as Individual contributors.

Most of the thing in the transformation which creates turbulence goes beyond our influence area.

How can we increase the circle of influence on a daily basis by listing down the things which we can control?

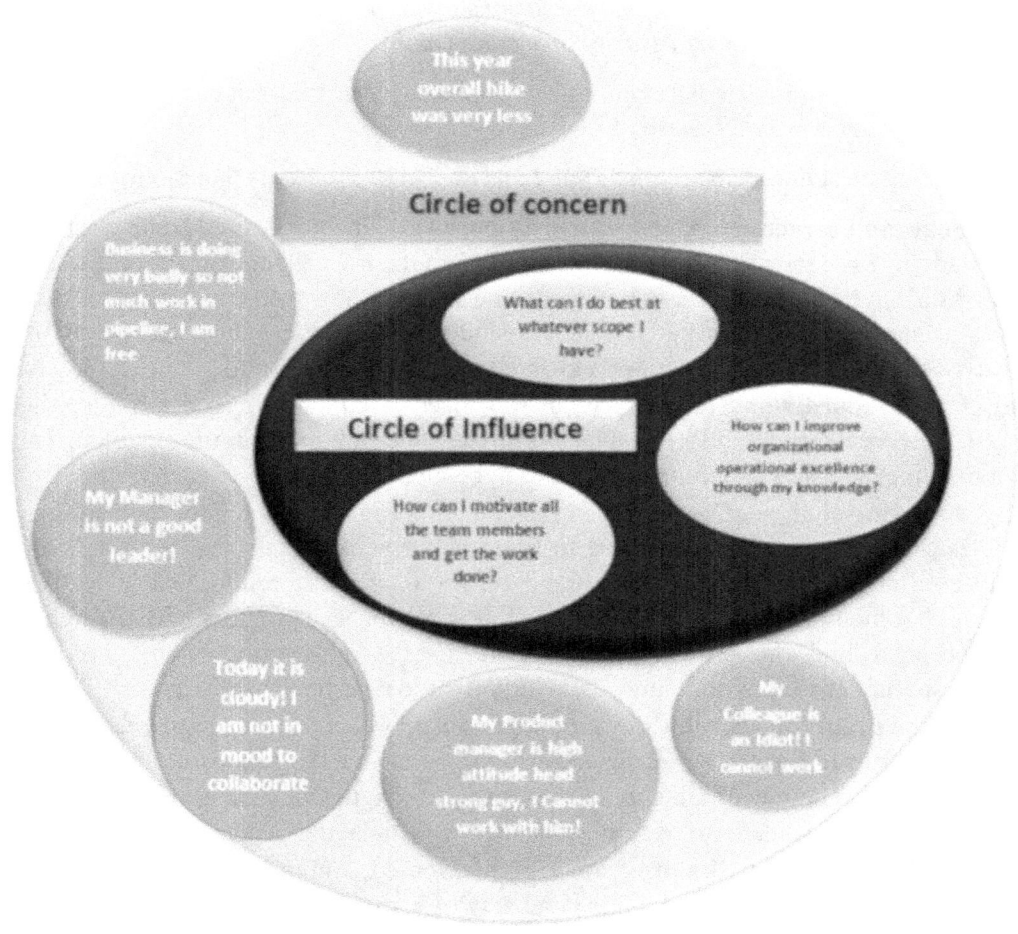

What actions are you going to take from this lesson?

1. _____

2. _____

3. _____

Thinking Question:

Are you doing enough to build your influencing abilities through which we can control our situation and ignore the parts which are beyond our control?

1.14 How to use Behavior Analysis and Modification for coaching?

"Between stimulus and response, there is a space. In that space is our power to choose our response. In our response lies our growth and our freedom."

—Viktor E. Frankl

Why this topic?

When I worked with a few team members who are working with the same systems for 20+ years and they are not willing to accept any other thoughts, how can we influence them? The change for them is tough. As a coach is there any way we can help them for a new way of operating easily?

Behavior modification, *a formalized technique for promoting the frequency of desirable behaviors and decreasing the incidence of unwanted ones.*

The techniques used by behavior analysts are as varied as the list of processes that modify **behavior**.

- **Identifying goals and target behaviors**. The first step is to define the desired behavior. Is it an increase in time spent studying? A decrease in weight? An increase in the use of language? A reduction in the amount of aggression displayed by a child? The goals must be stated in observable terms and must lead to specific targets. For instance, a goal might be "to increase study time," whereas the target behavior would be "to study at least 2 hours per day on weekdays and an hour on Saturdays."

- **Designing a data-recording system and recording preliminary data**. To determine whether behavior has changed, it is necessary to collect data before any changes are made in the situation. This information provides a baseline against which future changes can be measured.

- **Selecting a behavior-change strategy**. The crucial step is to select an appropriate strategy. Because all the principles of learning can be employed to bring about behavior change, a "package" of treatments is normally used. This might include the systematic use of positive reinforcement for desired behavior (verbal praise or something more tangible, such as food), as well as a program of extinction for undesirable behavior (ignoring a child who throws a tantrum). Selecting the right reinforcement is critical, and it may be necessary to experiment a bit to find out what is important to a particular individual.

- **Implementing the program.** Probably the most important aspect of program implementation is consistency. It is also important to reinforce the intended behavior. For example, suppose a mother wants her son to spend more time on his homework, but as soon as he sits down to study, he asks for a snack. If the mother gets a snack for him, she is likely to be reinforcing her son's delaying tactic, not his studying.

- **Keeping careful records after the program is implemented**. Another crucial task is record keeping. If the target behaviors are not monitored, there is no way of knowing whether the program has actually been successful.

- **Evaluating and altering the ongoing program**. Finally, the results of the program should be compared with baseline, pre-implementation data to determine its effectiveness. If the program has been successful, the procedures employed can be phased out gradually. For instance, if the program called for reinforcing every instance of picking up one's clothes from the bedroom floor, the reinforcement schedule could be modified to a fixed-ratio schedule in which every third instance was reinforced. However, if the program has not been successful in bringing about the desired behavior change, consideration of other approaches might be advisable.

Where can we apply these concepts? e.g., scrum master is not doing the ceremonies, product owners are not attending the demo meeting, team members are not writing user stories, this is not interest, that is not working, those managers will always blame, etc.

How do we change the world?

"The fastest way for a person to change or more precisely to change their behavioral pattern is to remove the environmental triggers that support the unwanted behavior."

— Sasha Tenodi

What actions are you going to take from this lesson?

1. _____

2. _____

3. _____

Thinking Question:

Are you doing enough to help your team members to change their routine behaviors which are not enabling them to perform better?

1.15 What are the Change Management approaches for effective Coaching

"I cannot say whether things will get better if we change; what I can say is they must change if they are to get better"

—Georg C. Lichtenburg

Why this topic?

How can we sustain the transformation, in search of this question we had to dig deeper and realize these artifacts? Without such thought, investment will be a waste.

Why People are not changing, the way they were working? This is the persistent question we have in our mind when we coach the team and go back to the team and see they have gone back to their original habits.

I was wondering what else we need to do to ensure that changes are retained with the team members and those new changed practices, sustains.

I put my heart and mind into the coaching but when I have found **old habits were returning**, I tried to find the gaps and improve.

"Habit is the intersection of knowledge (what to do), skill (how to do), and desire (want to do)."

— Stephen R. Covey, the 7 Habits of Highly Effective People: Powerful Lessons in Personal Change

What I have found and learned is

Learning experiences are like climbing mountains. Once we climb the peak we acquire the required knowledge and skills. It is not knowing more, but doing more with the knowledge.

As a good coach, I would love to create more **mountaineers**, who will be able to climb any mountain.

If I keep telling my team members how to climb the mountain, it does not help them until they practice the same to climb small hills.

Few **passionate** team members practically apply the information and demonstrate the same by doing. All the secrets are in **DOING** more with the information.

Motivation is also the key driver for applying this knowledge.

We need to know when to use which information. Which tool will be useful for what time?

Having a skill is different from having knowledge

To teach **skills**, the **practice** must be part of the learning journey. Skill will develop when they practice with the new knowledge which they acquired for some time.

When I find old habits of these mountaineers are blocking their new leanings, we need to help them to **unlearn** some of these old habits and superimpose these new leanings.

We need to reprogram through their conscious mind so that the automatic process do not hijack them.

Now, after addressing all these issues, **Knowledge, Skill and Motivation**, still old habits are coming back, what do we do?

Let us look into the **context** or the setup where those mountaineers are performing. Can we do some change in that environment to get the support from it? I see it works.

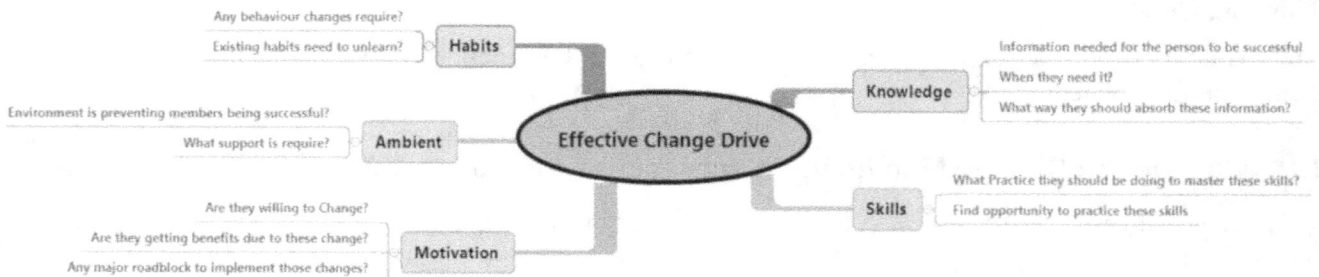

When I was staying alone in my earlier career, I had to cook food for myself to save money. I purchased a few books of cooking to learn, how to prepare fish curry. I did not know how to cook various chicken and fish curries. 3 years we had practiced preparing chicken and fish curries. Initially, it was horrible to eat, but over a period, it was consumable curry! We used to put a lot of spices to make it awesome.

Now when I prepare the same curry at a family gathering, I carry the same old habit, put a lot of spices which nobody likes. I consciously tried to come out of that old habit, but it is taking time. Trying to unlearn some of those old habits which do not work anymore in a family set up. The family does not like spicy food!

I get many appreciations for my cooking! Which encourages me to experiment more and try new ways to satisfy my end users!

I do not like to cook weekdays as I am too tired to do that, if some family members appear, I do not get that passion for cooking. But at the weekend I like to cook, I get the **motivation** to cook. Until I get a bigger **inspiration** on weekdays, I do not cook!

I look for the perfect ambiance to cook. If the materials are ready, equipment, utensils are there, I love cooking. If I go to my friend's house when they ask me to prepare dishes, if there are not enough utensils I feel annoyed to cook, and it reflects in my delivery (curry will not be tasty!!)

> Your earning ability today is largely dependent upon your knowledge, skill and your ability to combine that knowledge and skill in such a way that you contribute value for which customers are going to pay.
>
> — Brian Tracy —

I realized it needs **knowledge, Skill (practice), Motivation, ambiance** to do a better job. When I teach cooking with my kids, I make sure all these factors are there, so that they can produce wow output.

"Change cannot be forced on people. The best way to instill change is to do it with them. Create it with them"

—*Lisa Bodell*

What actions are you going to take from this lesson?

1. _____

2. _____

3. _____

Thinking Question:

Are you doing enough to build various way to sustain change management?

1.16 How to apply Guerrilla Coaching for Agile Transformation?

"Coaching works because it's all about you. When you connect with what you really want and why - and take action - magical things can happen."

—*Emma-Louise Elsey*

Why this Topic?

To change the organizational culture for agile transformation what else can we do. In one of the brainstorming sessions, this idea was coined and we start elaborating on it.

This thought came in a conversion with a couple of leaders where they are asking how we can rapidly do something which can change the organizational culture, the DNA of the people.

Have you heard of **Guerrilla warfare**?

The Spanish word **"guerrilla"** is the diminutive form of "guerra" (**"war"**).

It is a form of irregular warfare in which a <u>small group of combatants</u>, such as paramilitary personnel, armed civilians, or irregulars, use military tactics, including **ambushes**, **sabotage**, **raids**, **petty warfare, hit-and-run tactics, and mobility** to fight a larger and less-mobile traditional military.

In ancient times these actions were often associated with **smaller** tribal policies fighting a **larger empire.**

The term "Guerrilla coaching "is traced to guerrilla warfare, which focuses on <u>unusual strategies to attain an objective</u>. The term itself was from the inspiration of guerrilla warfare which is an unconventional warfare was using different techniques from usual and small tactical strategies used by armed civilians.

But how does that translate into the work we do every day? In coaching, guerrilla techniques, mostly play on the element of **surprise**. It sets out to make highly **unusual** coaching that catch people **surprisingly** in the sequence of their day-to-day routines with little budget to spend. This contains high vigor and resourcefulness, concentrating on grasping the attention of the team members at a more individual and unforgettable level.

Guerrilla coaching is unexpected. That makes it memorable.

Guerrilla coaching will bring innovation.

How can we start this Guerrilla Coaching?

1. Walk into the team daily stand-up without informing the team members. Stop attending for the next couple of days. Share your observation about the improvements (Surprise visits)
2. Review the team product backlog with the peer coaches and share the observations by the peer coach itself to the team for improvement
3. Call for the meeting with the Product owner to share the mid-sprint review comments.
4. Facilitate one of the sprint demo meetings (Other than the first sprint) and explain various factors to be taken care, Repeat such events
5. Invite the other scrum team to visit the team you are coaching, Let the team explore each other and learn from each other
6. Witness, pay attention and ask queries to know the client's condition
7. Ensure that clients develop personal competencies and do not develop unhealthy dependencies on the coaching or mentoring relationship.
8. Invite for a one whole day coaching and training workshop where we will discuss many topics, Pain points, and solutions
9. Invite leaders to demo meeting of the other team, which they are not managing or accountable. Share observation points
10. Team members from other departments, coach your team. Cross coaching and learning from each other.
11. Invite executives for floor walk or a Gemba walk without informing the team members, share improvement feedback.
12. Coach build coaching competency through demonstration and sessions (Coach Get award based on the maximum best follower they produced)
13. Share experiences, and examples from another team to inspire other team members
14. Use Directive and non-directive coaching style, e.g., tell, ask, provide answers, ask for solutions, and share the source of knowledge

15. Invite team members for community contribution or Meetup, Development them for Meetup presentation
16. Reward the team members for their extra miler contribution in a large gathering one in four months.
17. Play Agile manifesto game with the team, which principles are working and which are not and what can team take action.
18. Take everyone out for a walk. Discuss the best things happening around transformation.
19. Call for open space agility discussion at the team level, department level.
20. Call for a shop floor quiz competition on Transformation, recognized top 5 winners and ask them to speak about their transformation journey.
21. Invite leadership team members for the town hall presentation and share with all what they have done and opened for Q&A
22. Call for competition, Best Collaborative team and Best Collaborative person of the quarter. Recognized them and ask them to present their case studies to all the public.

How fast can we move to **participate** or delegate state of coaching?

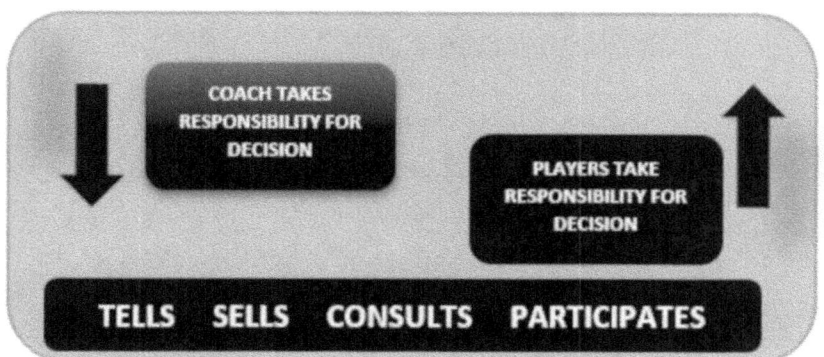

"Don't tell people how to do things, tell them what to do and let them surprise you with their results."

—*George S. Patton*

What actions are you going to take from this lesson?

1. _____

2. _____

3. _____

Thinking Question:

Are you doing enough to use guerrilla coaching at your work? What is the impact?

1.17 What are the Tips to coach for Greatness?

"I absolutely believe that people, unless coached, never reach their maximum capabilities."

—*Bob Nardelli*

Why this topic?

To answer the question, what are the best coach's characteristics? What do we look for from a coach?

These are the some of the factors need to be taken into account when we coach one to one.

Be it a scrum master or manager or Product owner, we have to coach them to improve their current performance level.

All these actions start with us, first, we demonstrate as a coach, we are the role model for others.

It will be much easier to influence others when we have scaled ourselves at a higher level, Walk the talk!

We as a coach need to ensure that we ask for all these factors. We ask them questions to find these points and make them realize to change some of their thoughts if needed.

These mind map highlights the aspects of coaching greatness to focus into. In our coaching engagement, we ensure we bring into all these points for discussion.

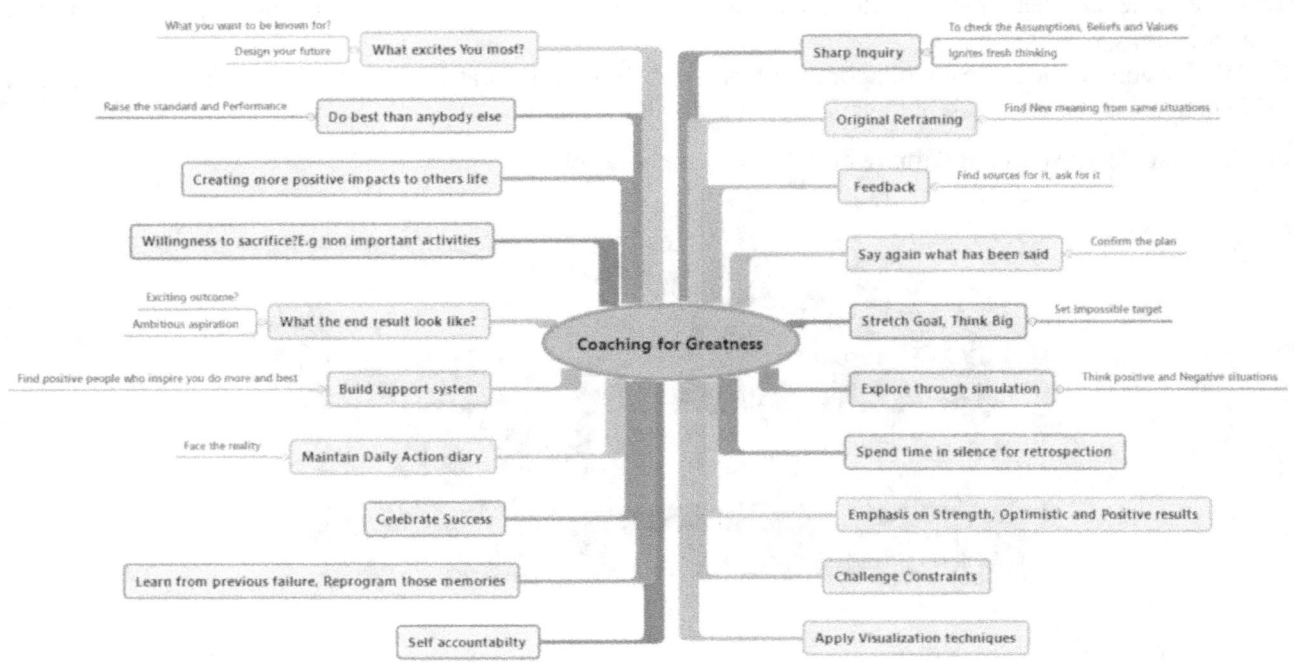

"What a man can be, He must be. This need we call self-actualization "

—Abraham Maslow

What actions are you going to take from this lesson?

1. _____

2. _____

3. _____

Thinking Question:

Are you doing enough to use coaching greatness aspects and benefits out of it?

1.18 How to Scale Agile Coach's Knowledge?

"My biggest motivation? Just to keep challenging myself. I see life almost like one long university education that I never had -- every day I'm learning something new."

—Richard Branson

Why this topic?

This thought arises as a part of the organizational scaling engagement. We were preparing ourselves and gearing ourselves to satisfy the need of the scale coach. We have interacted with many colleagues in Europe and realize it is a completely different area. I have listed down a few which can help us to become a better scale coach.

As a part of my job, I do a lot of recruiting, Most of the time I find, we have many coaches who project themselves with few scaled agile certifications. Their thoughts are revolving around those frameworks and justifying those frameworks steps. When I look at my own organizational transformation, I realized it would be good if the scale coach knows the big picture about the Organizational aspects.

Let us think about, how an agile coach can scale their knowledge?

I am getting resumes about scale coaches! Which are full of Certified Bullet Train Engineers! Certified Large Scale FIFA coach! Etc. are claiming themselves as an expert Scaled Agile coach.

When I hire them, they are failing in basic Scaled Agile implementation.

What was missing was Organization Culture (OC), Organization Behavior (OB) and Organization Structure (OS) related knowledge?

I am sure coaches who have launched these 20 or 30 Bullet trains in an organization, they have studied several months about the OB, OC, and OS.

I felt Scale Coach could educate themselves about scaling their knowledge in OC, OB, and OS.

We can create Certified OcbsS (Organizational Culture, Behaviors and Structure specialist)! We can name anything BUT importance is knowledge of all these areas.

It would be great if people equipped themselves with this knowledge so that I can get a Scaled Agile coach who can help Organizational scaling Agile and Transformation.

Why OC, OB, and OS?

We look for all these capabilities when we hire coaches who are an integral part of enterprise agile transformation.

Organizational culture (OC): It is a structure of common Values, standards, and principles, which manages how people perform in organizations. These shared values have a strong effect on the people in the organization and prescribe how they dress, act, and complete their jobs. Every organization matures and keeps a unique culture, which delivers rules and borders for the behavior of the members of the organization. Let's explore what elements make up an organization's culture.

Organizational behavior (OB) is the study of the way people interact within groups. Understanding, forecasting and managing human behavior, both individually and in a group that occurs within an organization.

Organizational structure (OS) is an arrangement that contains obvious and unspoken institutional rules and policies designed to outline how numerous work roles and responsibilities are delegated, controlled and coordinated. Organizational structure also regulates how information flows from level to level within the company. For example, in a centralized organization, decisions flow from the top down, while in a decentralized organization, the verdicts are made at various diverse levels.

DO YOU see CONNECTIONS AMONG ALL THESE OC-OB-OS for Scaling Agile?

As an Enterprise Agile coach when you master all these points, how easy it will be for you to start the scaling engagement?

Instead of just thinking about Launching bullet train from point A to point B, let us understand what problem we are solving in the context of the organization.

Not just Certified Hammer Engineers, looking for nails everywhere!

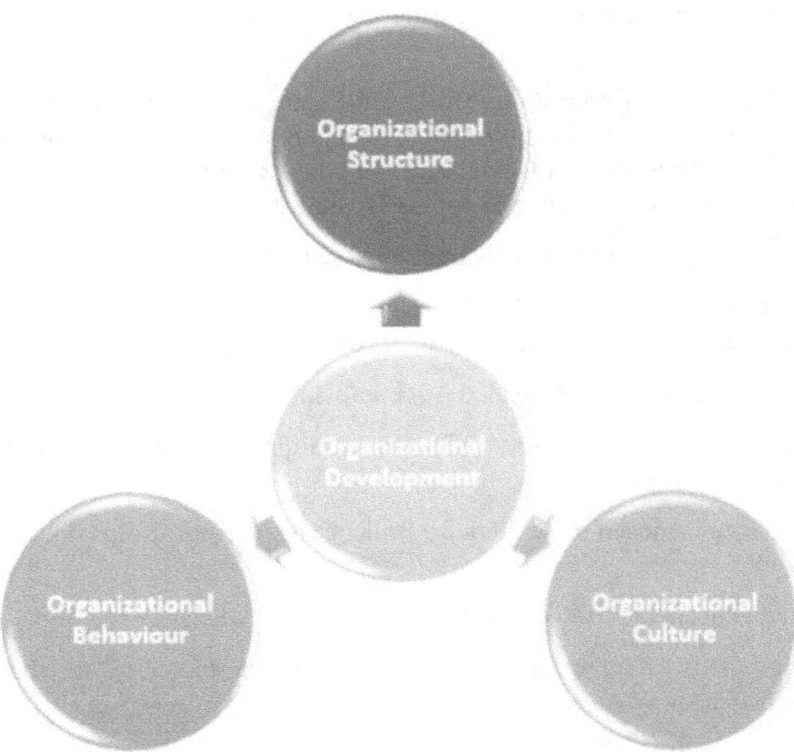

If a coach builds expertise in these points, it will be easier for him/her to start scaling an agile engagement.

- OC chooses the way employees to interrelate in their workplace.
- OC represents certain predefined policies which guide the employees and give them a sense of direction in the workplace.
- OB aids in clarifying the interpersonal relationships employees share with each other as well as with their upper and junior team members.
- Knowing OB helps to make any change within the organization easily.
- OB balances the cordial relationship in an enterprise by maintaining effective communication.
- OB has three units of analysis: the individual, the group, and the organization.
- OS helps us to provide the foundation on which standard operating procedures and routines rest.
- OS helps us to determine which individuals get to participate in which decision-making processes, and thus to what extent their views shape the organization's actions

We as a coach need to know various frameworks and models related to OS, OB, and OC.

E.g. do we know more about these OB models and benefits?

	Autocratic	Custodial	Supportive	Collegial
Basis of Model	Power	Economic sources	Leadership	Partnership
Managerial Orientation	Authority	Money	Support	Teamwork
Employee Orientation	Obedience	Security and Benefits	Job Performance	Responsible Behaviour
Employee Psychological Result	Dependence on Boss	Dependence on Organization	Participation	Self Discipline
Employee Needs met	Subsistence	Security	Status and recognition	Self Actualization
Performance result	Minimum	Passive co-operation	Awakened Drives	Moderate Enthusiasm

Can we explain more about Schneider Cultural Model and how can we benefit out of this model?

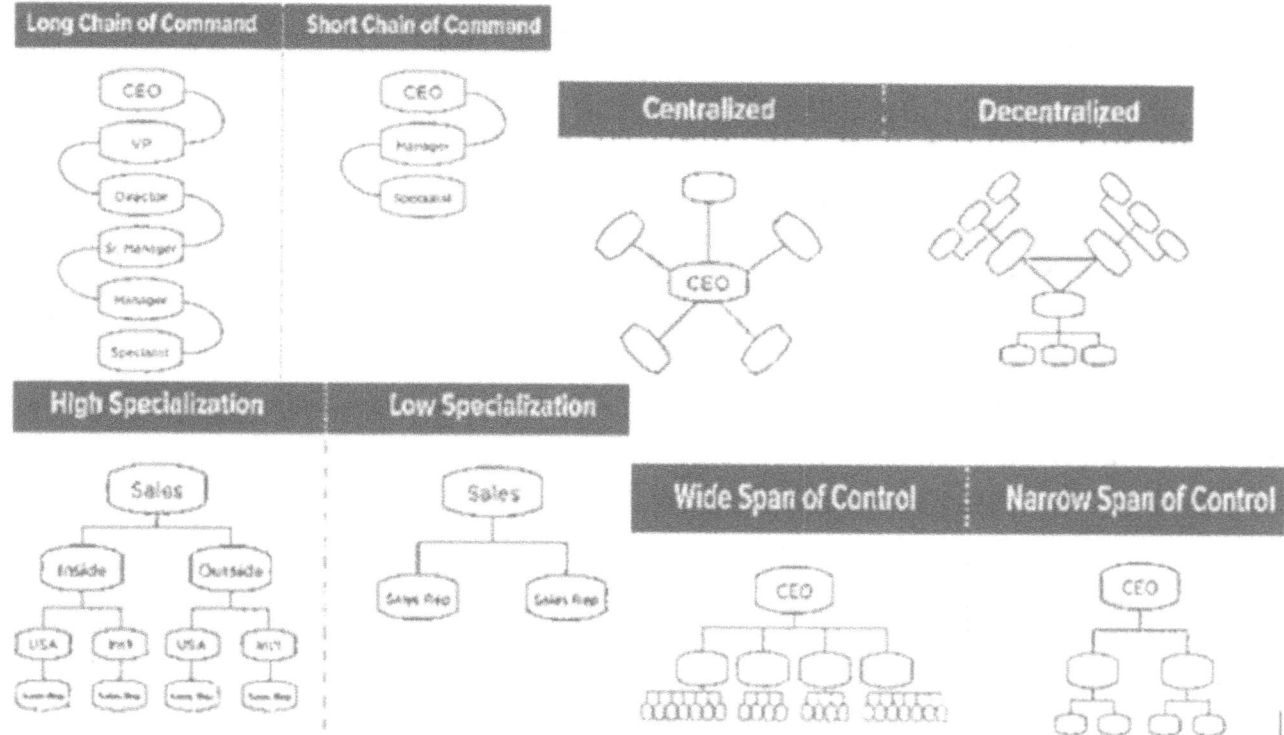

OS, OC and OB world are very wide and vast, once we know these deeply, it helps the coach to structure the dialogue with Executives to help them for Organizational development and transformation.

By the way, how do you prove that you are OS, OC and OB experts? Your questioning skill will demonstrate that!

What actions are you going to take from this lesson?

1. _____

2. _____

3. _____

Thinking Question:

Are you doing enough study to scale your knowledge in the area of organizational change management aspects and their impacts?

1.19 What is coaching for Resilience Mindset? How to do it?

> *"Our greatest glory is not in never failing, but in getting up every time we do"*
>
> —*Confucius*

Why this Topic?

Most of the time I had found that team members are getting demotivated by small failures, I started searching what story I can share with my coaching partners? That's how I discovered these thoughts and started sharing in my sessions.

One widely used cliché in sport **is** *"The game is 90% mental"*. It seems to have originated from a quote that is usually attributed to baseball legend Yogi Bera: *"90% of baseball is mental…the other half is physical."*

Martin Seligman (1990), a pioneer in the positive psychology movement, coined the term explanatory style to describe personality attributes related to how people perceive troubling events and how this contributes to their pessimism or optimism.

I have personally applied this style several times in my career. And now in coaching, it is important to explain the same to other team members.

In Authentic Happiness (2002), Dr. Seligman describes an optimist as one who believes the cause of a positive event is **personal** (as a result of one's own skill or ability), **permanent** (almost always present), and **pervasive** (across all domains).

A person's explanatory style has three key components: **Permanence, Pervasiveness, and Personalization.**

We need to re-look at our explanatory style. If required, we have to change.

Permanence: Relates to the perception of time. Events are perceived as permanent or temporary.

Pervasiveness: Relates to the perception of space. Events are perceived as global or specific.

Personalization: Relates to the perception of causality. Events are internally or externally caused.

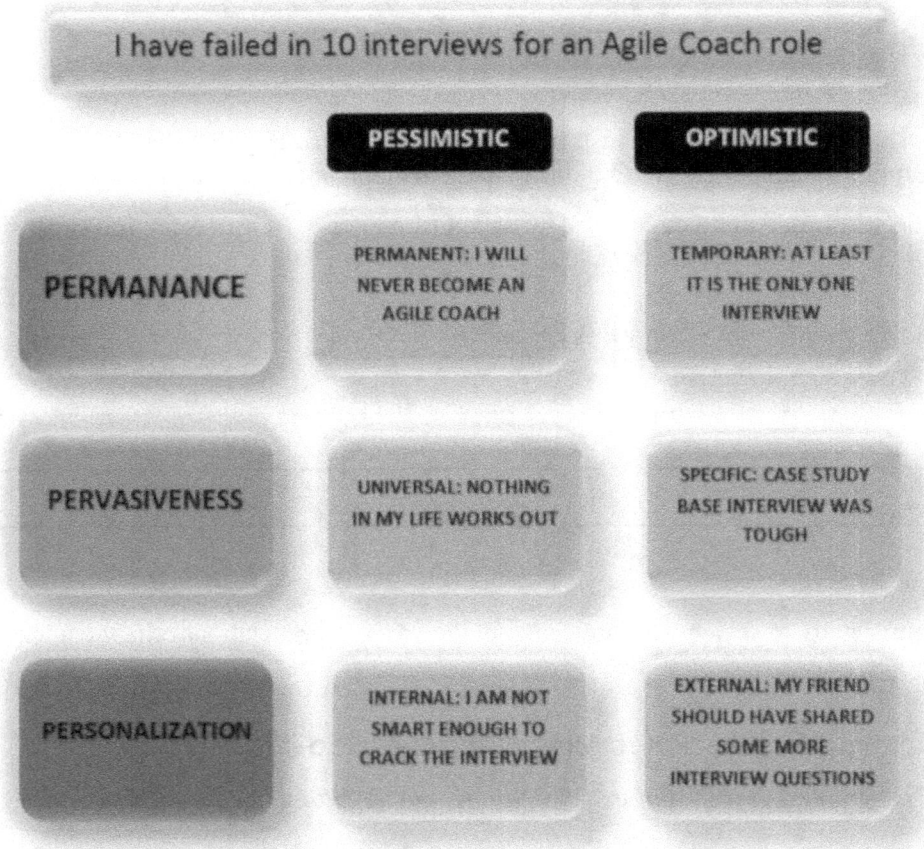

One of my friends was always having an impression that he will never be able to get an on-site opportunity. He will never be able to take his family abroad. I shared with him about Permanence which refers to how long a person believes a troubling situation will last. Most troubling situations do not last forever and are linked to time frames that eventually expire. He was almost in a depression situation. After several attempts now he and his family are in Italy.

I have learned to look at all these troubling events as a temporary phenomenon. Negative emotions increase with troubling events. This time does not last for long. If we do not change our mindset, we will fall into this permanence trap. If we start believing that temporary events last long, we start losing faith and experience deteriorating confidence level.

One of my friends was jobless for six months and was not able to crack any interview after having so many years of experience in the software development. He had started thinking, I will never be available to get a job, and there is no market for senior C++ developers in today's market, etc. I shared the same topics about pervasiveness which refer to how extensive my friend perceives specific problems to be. He often overestimates the extent of his problems and negative personal characteristics. And it was affecting his personal life. His wife started criticizing his capability. The financial problem is also causing more issues at home. This situation was affecting every aspect of their lives, including his married life and health. Now by putting a good effort and networking, he got a job in Chennai, India.

He was falling into the pervasiveness trap as he allowed his thoughts about context-specific troubles and personal attributes to become pervasive and influence other facets of his lives that are not affected.

With both of my friends, the on-site aspiring friend, and the jobless friend, were thinking that the problem they were facing was because of their problem or because of others. My on-site aspiring friend was blaming all the managers not to give him an opportunity as he is not buttering them or not in the same community, etc. My jobless friend was blaming himself for not being able to get a job related to C++.

My friends fell into the personalization trap when they assign responsibility for their problems exclusively to themselves or others.

In the world of athletics, athletes are constantly facing events deemed positive and negative by not only themselves, but also by friends, family, and in some cases, by thousands or even millions of people.

At face value, one might estimate that having an optimistic explanatory style would lead to greater and steadier performance.

Deepa Malik ecstatic after winning Silver at Rio Paralympics 2016. Deepa Malik's name is synonymous with grit and courage. From Paralysis to a Paralympian. What can we learn from her story?

As a coach, I have to change the people's explanatory style through coaching.

We have to shift a person's explanatory style towards an optimistic way of thinking, which in turn alleviate depressive symptoms. **Fear of failure from the working environment has to change through mindset change.** We do not want to be over-optimistic, but balanced.

As Seligman points out," Learned Optimism works not through an unjustifiable positivity about the world, but through the power of 'non-negative' thinking."

What actions are you going to take from this lesson?

1. _____

2. _____

3. _____

Thinking Question:

➢ Are you doing enough to learn from failure and build a mindset which is more optimistic?

1.20 Which Coaching approach to use with Clients?

A good coach can change a game. A great coach can change a life
                    —*John Wooden, former UCLA basketball coach*

Why this Topic?

Over a period of time, I have realized that it is important that we draw up an agreement by capturing all the points to avoid any conflict with the clients. I realized it later and started hunting for the model, how to do this homework? This is how this chapter is born. I have applied this concept several times.

I was looking for some structural model to start the coaching journey with the clients, that was the trigger for me to search for the below post.

When we are dealing with the client for coaching measuring model, we are wondering how we demonstrate the output and how we will measure the success of the coaching program.

I have used several steps what has been mentioned in the book **"The Behavioral coaching model"** - **Suzanne Skiffington & Perry Zeus** which had worked for me nicely.

Let us walk through each aspect.

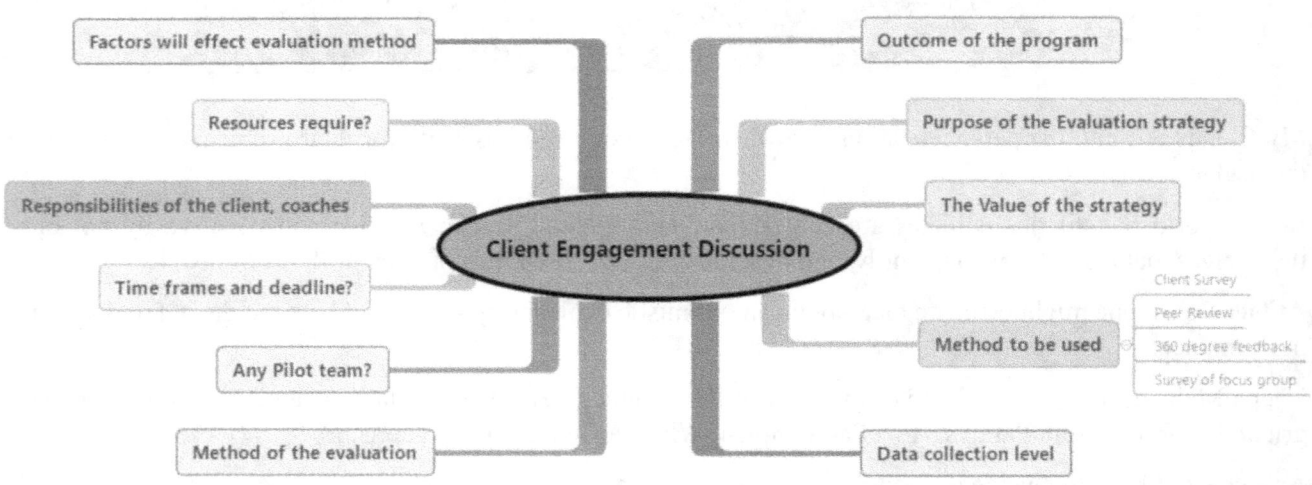

It is better to decide the measurement part, should this drive through ROI (Return on investment) or ROE (Return on expectation) or a combination of both?

One of the critical points is checked if the coaching **contract is short term or long term**?

E.g., if we are getting into 3-6 months coaching contract, then we should calculate the ROI at the end of this period.

If the coaching focus is more on soft aspects, the real benefit will be realized at the end of the program, or it may take more time.

If the focus of coaching is intangible, it is not appropriate to use ROI, ROE is a superior method in this case.

Some of the intangibles coaches' measures include changes in job satisfaction, change in leadership and management style and the changes in teamwork.

ROE measurement?

An ROE involves setting out the plans for the coaching program, gaining consensus on the objectives and then tracking the program to ensure that the objectives and goals have been met.

The underlying assumption of conducting an ROE is that as long as the coaching program focuses on the organization's business objectives and results in positive changes, then it will be valued by the organization.

Coaches have to establish the goals of the organization and those of the individual coaches, the changes that have to be made to meet these goals, the degree of learning that has to occur to effect these changes and how they will be measured.

In the end, we have to see how these learnings have to be applied on the job, as well as the overall business impact, may not be the monetary advantage.

ROE can encompass and measure productivity, organization strength, customer service, reduced customer complaints, level of conflict and job satisfaction.

ROI measurement?

An ROI can present, measure and evaluate the financial returns of the coaching program. It can also quantify reaction to and satisfaction with the project, the amount of learning, application, and implementation.

ROI = Net coaching benefit/ Coaching cost * 100

It can be calculated at three months to six month period

Coaching benefit can include in ROI

- Bottom line profitability
- Sales figure
- Retaining team members who have undergone coaching
- Cost savings
- Quality of production case and services
- Overall productivity

Some of the soft skill data

- Leadership skill
- Management skill
- Conflict resolution
- Workplace optimism
- Job satisfaction
- Better time management
- Team commitment
- Client satisfaction

Coaching cost

- The direct cost of coaching (Research and development cost, fees, travel expenses, accommodation, assessment cost)
- Time including any follow-up contact via telephone, email and video conference
- Cost of the team members involvement while in a coaching session
- Cost of the time to the organization in overseeing and administrating the program

Reporting mechanism to the client:

Coach has to frequently report to the client regarding the coaching progress and client expectation as outlined in the contract. Maybe monthly, maybe once in 3 months for a six-month program report has to send.

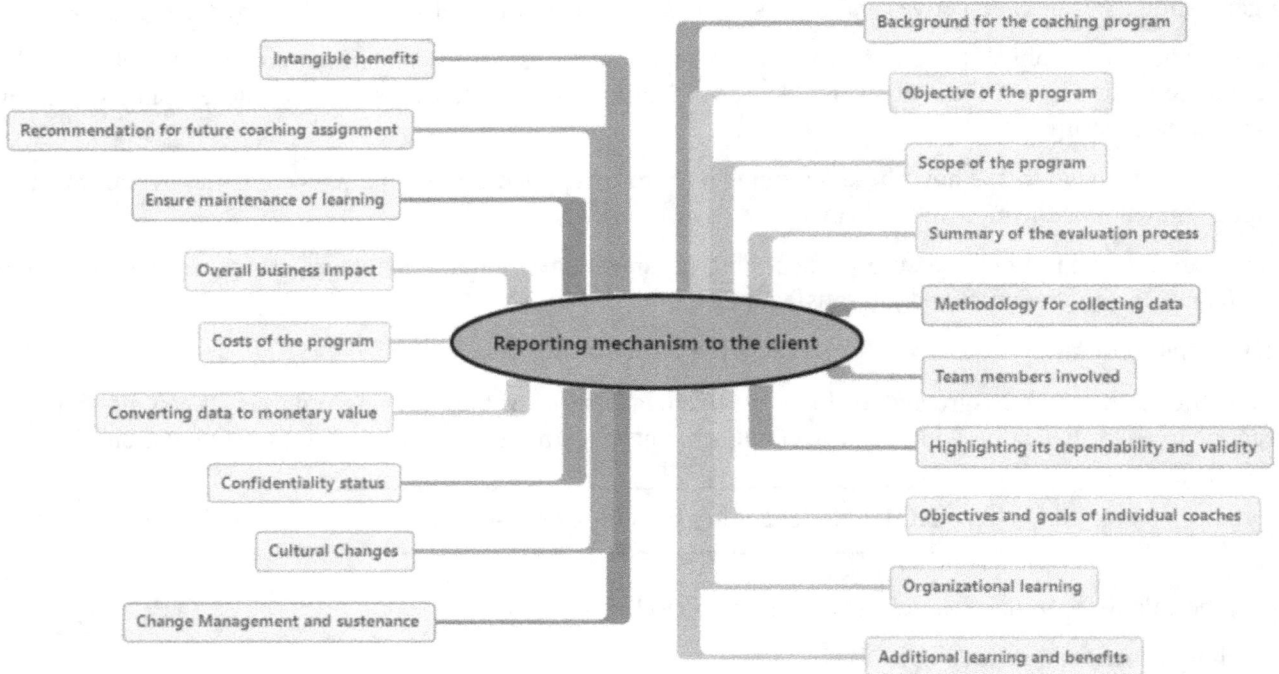

With this structure, it is easy to imagine the coaching model or an engagement model with a client. There will be a promising effect before and after.

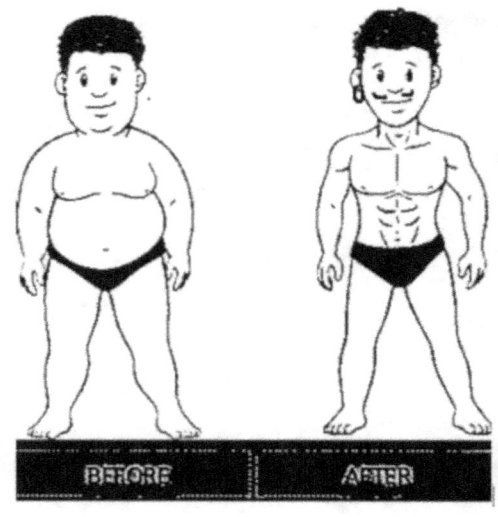

What actions are you going to take from this lesson?

1. _____

2. _____

3. _____

Thinking Question:

➤ Are you doing enough to understand how to create a contract based on the client's context?

1.21 How Will Agile Coach get neutralized?

"Victory or defeat is not determined at the moment of crisis, but rather in the long and unspectacular period of preparation."

—Anonymous

Why this topic?

This topic was bothering me for a long time when I was not able to engage with various coaching engagements. I was getting an escalation from various teams regarding my engagement. I was listing down what are the various factors which neutralize coach to perform at the expected level. It is good to know all these factors so that we can watch as a professional coach and gear up for it

WHO KILLED MY AGILE COACH?

An investigation started after the "killing" of an agile coach who came into the organization to transform the team.

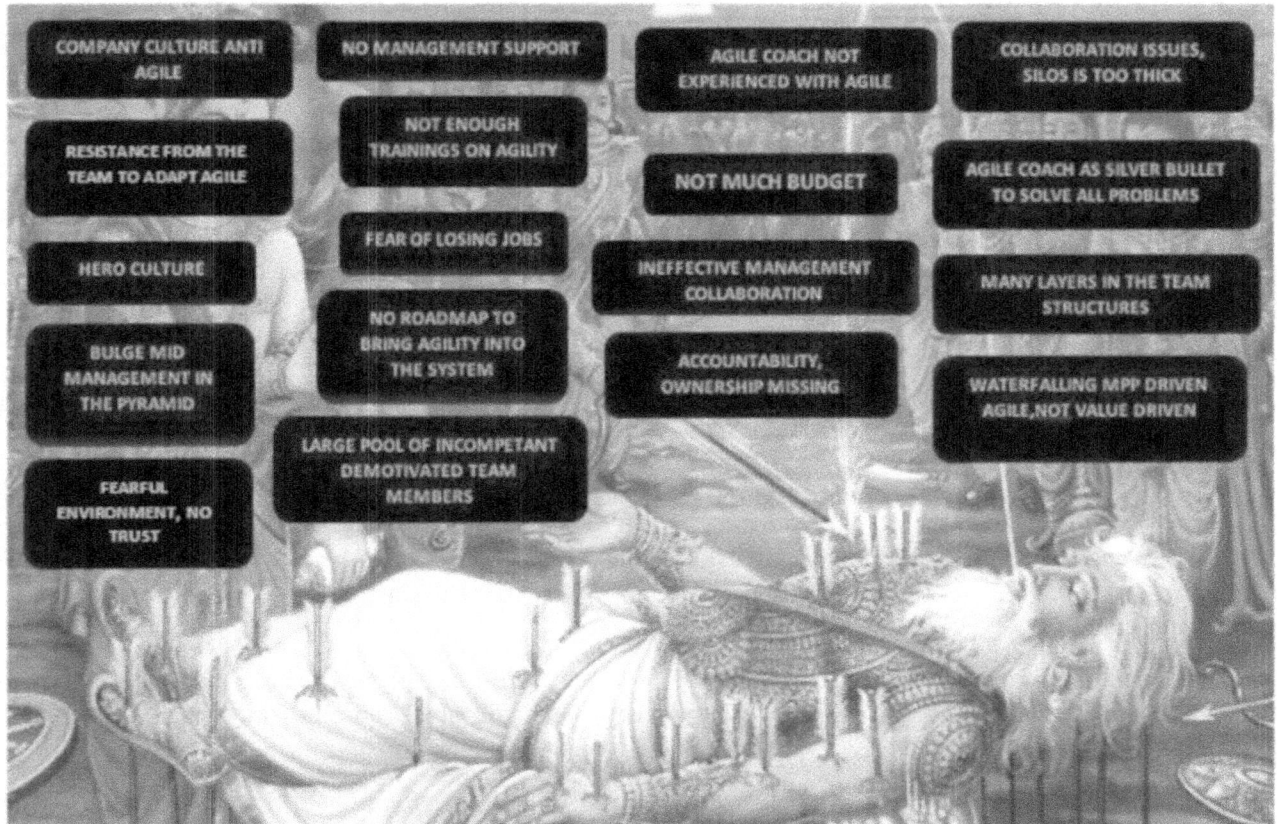

Killing - He lost his job, sacked from his job, criticized badly etc.

The organization was a large legacy enterprise which exists for multiple decades.

Agile coach came across all the below issues and under the load of all these issues he collapsed and was killed by all these issues.

Moral of the story is

COACH WILL GET KILLED IN THE BATTLEFIELD IF WE DO NOT HAVE ENOUGH STRATEGY, SUPPORT, TO BRING THE AGILITY INTO THE ORGANIZATION IN A SYSTEMATIC WAY

- DO WE HAVE AGILE BASE CAMP WHICH HAS AUTHORITY AND POWER TO HANDLE ANY NEGATIVE FORCES?
- DO WE HAVE DIRECT REPORT TO THE CEO OF THIS BASE CAMP WHERE ALL THE COACHES WILL EXIST?
- DO WE HAVE SUFFICIENT MONEY TO RUN THE TRANSFORMATION?
- DO WE HAVE COMPETENT AND CAPABLE COACHES TO RUN THE TRANSFORMATION? WHO ARE THE RADICAL CHANGE AGENTS?
- DO THIS BASE CAMP EMPOWERED TO TAKE ANY ORGANIZATIONAL CHANGE INITIATIVES?
- DO WE HAVE AUTHORITY AND EMPOWERMENT TO ESCALATE ANY TOPICS?
- DO WE HAVE KATA SESSIONS HAPPENING AMONG COACHES?

"It is not the strongest of the species that survives, nor the most intelligent, but the one most responsive to change."

—*Charles Darwin*

I want to share one more story which worth to mention here,

Learning from Corporate Abhimanyu

This is a famous story from the **Epic Mahabharata**. All of us know about this story.

What I am finding is, **Abhimanyu** like character are everywhere in the organization.

What can we learn from this story?

In the organization transformation Journey, we come across many leaders who are the change agent acting like Abhimanyu. They live a very short life with the system. They got killed on the battleground. Abhimanyu is often quoted as an example of his partial knowledge about **Chakaravyuha**.

Abhimanyu was the son the Arjun. He was a great warrior prince, who acquired the most secretive knowledge of strategic warfare from his father Arjun and his maternal uncle Sri Krishna. Abhimanyu inherited both courage and fighting ability from his father, Arjun, and his grandfather Lord Indra. He was considered to be equal to his father owing to his prodigious feats.

Abhimanyu learned the art of breaking into the chakravyuha when he was in Subhadra's womb. It was then Arjuna was narrating the art of breaking into chakravyuh to Subhadra. But he did not know how to destroy the formation once he was inside, as Subhadra fell asleep while listening to the story and (Abhimanyu in her womb) could learn only half of the technique. This is the reason why he was only able to enter/ break and not come out of the chakravyu.

The whole organization is filled with trap, especially when we are doing organization change management implementation or organizational restructuring. Everywhere you may find chakravyuha. How will you survive if you have half knowledge?

Only two people knew how to break this chakravyuha, Krishna and Arjun. At that time they were away. All other Pandava generals turned to Abhimanyu for help.

Abhimanyu replied that though he knew how to enter the formation, he had no idea how to get out, and only his father, Arjun and Krishna knew the full secret. Bhima recommended that all the Pandava warriors will follow Abhimanyu into the array and fight the Kauravas.

Abhimanyu agreed and led the charge. Despite Dronacharya's efforts, Abhimanyu sliced the creation and started to massacre the Kauravas. But before the remaining Pandavas could enter the formation, the entrance was jammed by Jayadratha, King of the Sindhus and Abhimanyu's fate was closed literally.

A strategy was formed and a joint attack on Abhimanyu followed. Karna cut off Abhimanyu's bow and stopped his attack, Kripa killed his two chariot-drivers, and Kritavarma slew his horses; Abhimanyu took up a sword and a shield but these weapons were cut off by Drona and Ashwathama (though in other versions of the story, the perpetrators change while the acts remain the same). Abhimanyu then took up chariot-wheel and hurled it at Drona, but Kripa and Aswatthama protected Drona by cutting the wheel. With variations depending on the version of the story, Abhimanyu continues to fight, picking up discarded weapons as he requires. In one prominent ending, Abhimanyu wages war with a chariot-wheel killing hundreds of warriors; he is killed when many warriors concurrently attack him from all sides after which Abhimanyu and Laxman Kumara involve into a mace fight and get unconscious at the same time. Laxman Kumara wakes early and hits Abhimanyu on his head, thus killing him.

"Fools rush in where angels fear to tread"

How can you not become corporate Abhimanyu?

1. Understand the organization culture by discussing with as many people as possible
2. On critical assignment, be aware of the consequence of the assignment not done
3. Courage is good, but there is a limit, how much we can take up
4. Sacrifice, if it is for a good reason, take a call
5. Are you equipped with enough knowledge to face the situation? Acquire the experience needed to run the show
6. Ask the difficult questions to discover the unknown
7. Take a measure of your daily performance
8. Build a safe, failure immune, the checklist for yourself. Most of the large setbacks happen due to ignoring small setbacks
9. If you are not in the fail-free learning culture, do not dare to experiment
10. Raise Objection, whenever you find something is suspicious. Same like attorneys, in court, are constantly trying to say "objection? It is an attempt to control the documents and testimony that gets into "the record."
11. Do not fall prey to loss aversion.
12. Learn about corporate scapegoating and how to not become victims

John C. Maxwell said, "A man must be big enough to admit his mistakes, smart enough to profit from them, and strong enough to correct them."

What actions are you going to take from this lesson?

1. _____

2. _____

3. _____

Thinking Question:

➢ Are you doing enough to learn the ploys which coach will pass through and how can a coach make themselves rough?

1.22 Key Takeaways:

The real benefits will be realized when we do research in our area and implement all these thoughts and find out what benefit we are getting and what value we are generating for the team and the organization. In the **Pancha Bhoota Model, Water** elements once strengthen it will be easy to achieve Organizational agility.

What we have discussed in this chapter is

1. Effective use of the coaching contract model. Choose the best one suitable under the specific context.
2. Coaching to improve tenacity among team members. Parts of optimism and explain these to the team members.
3. Importance of knowledge around the Organizational structure, Organizational Behavior and, Organization culture
4. Tips for coaching greatness
5. Steps for Guerrilla coaching benefits.
6. Effective change management drive and internal factors to be taken care.
7. Behavior Analysis and Behavior Modification benefits
8. Benefits of the circle of influence
9. Empathic coach and improve empathy
10. Benefits of coaching by showing
11. Usages of kata can help coaches to improve their expertise
12. Parts of solution the focused approach
13. Application of Johari window in coaching
14. Usage of the Socratic approach
15. As an organization is like a garden, an agile coach as a gardener needs to take care of the plants for its growth.
16. When coach will get exterminated in an organization
17. Coaching model which can guide coaches
18. Preparing to become a better consultant.
19. Preparation to become a better coach
20. Finding a better coach, Looking into the various aspects before we select a coach

In the next chapter, we will discuss about the Leadership development or strengthen the **Air** element in the **Pancha Bhoota Model**.

2 Enablement of Leadership Skills

2.1 Introduction:

This chapter features some of the attributes which we as a leader have to be mastered. How an agile coach can coach the leaders to become agile leaders. It is one of the toughest tasks to persuade senior executives for coaching engagements. In the **Pancha Bhoota Model,** this is the **Air** element. If we strengthen this area **Air** element of the organization will become strong. It will serve to accomplish organizational agility.

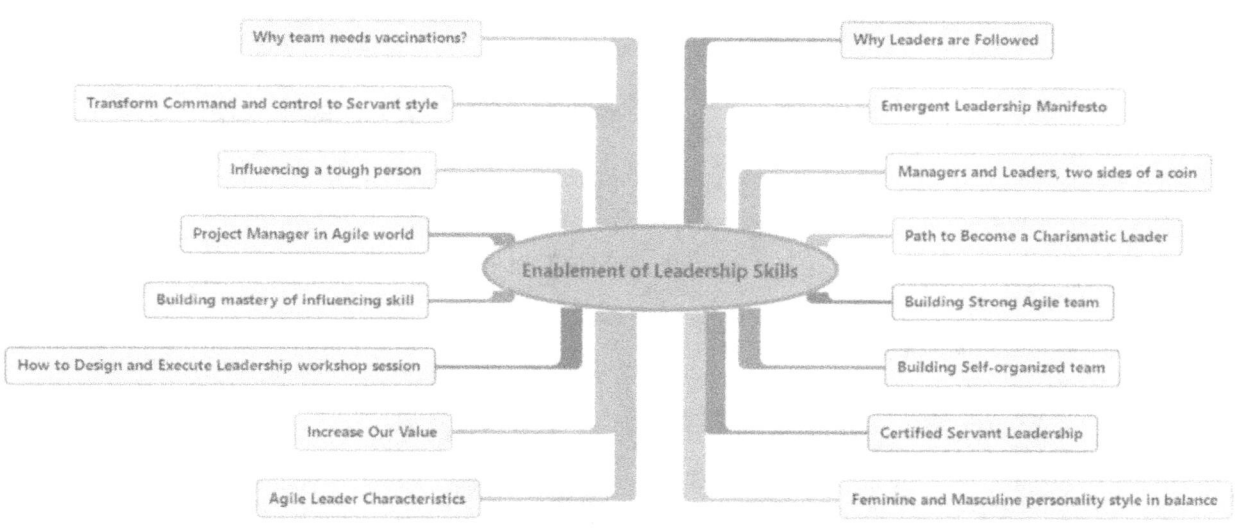

"Leaders are made, they are not born. They are made by hard effort, which is the price which all of us must pay to achieve any goal that is worthwhile."

- Vince Lombardi

2.2 Why Leaders have disciples?

"If you believe lack of authority prevents you from leading effectively, it is time to rethink your understanding of leadership."

—Mike Bonem and Roger Patterson,

Why this topic?

I have this query from many managers with whom I am taking a coaching engagement. Million Dollar Question? Is not it? How can I demonstrate to them efficiently in a simple language?

Below mind map highlights some key factors about the conventional leadership styles.

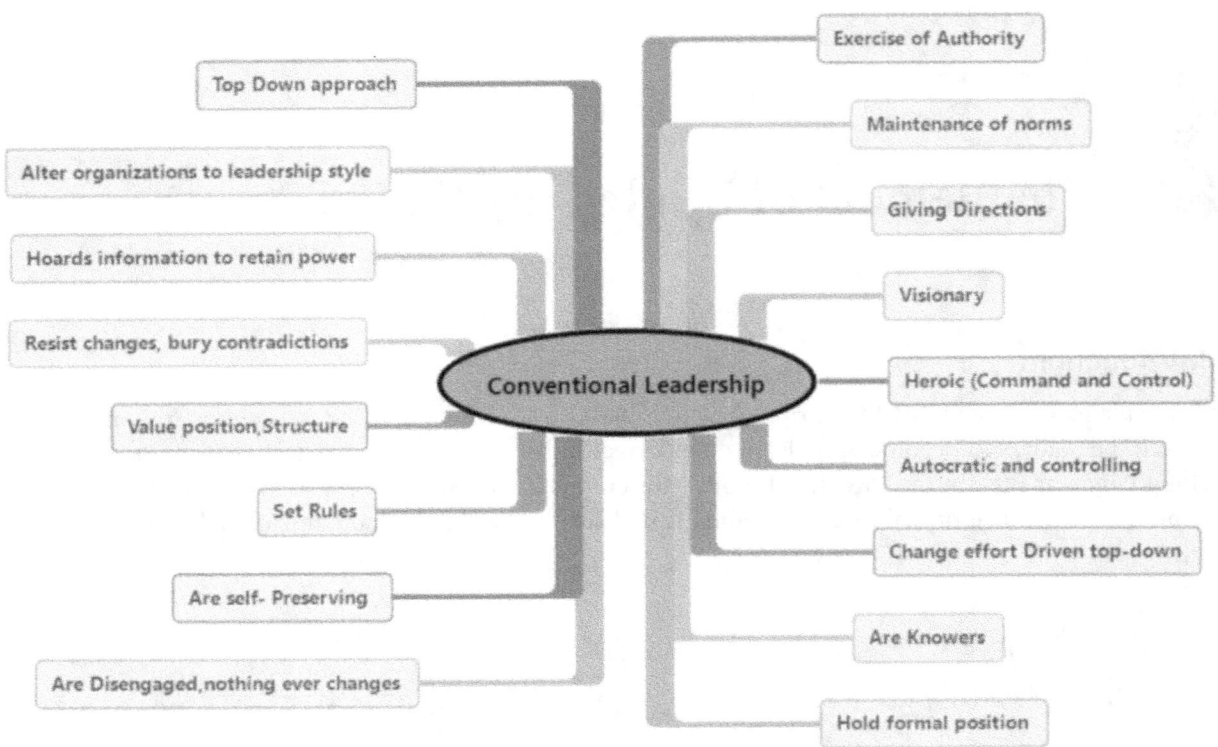

I am in search of finding the answers to these questions.

These thoughts are not the ultimate list, but it evolved based on the observation of many good leaders with whom I have been working.

Look at the picture, **why** people follow them?

They inspired us for some reason.

They know why they exist? And **inspire** others by sharing the **purpose**. Real **alignment** with all the below factors.

It is not the **positional power** because of which people are following leaders, you have **something** as a leader because of which people are following you.

Oh! Yes, people follow the **commander**, why?

They follow for survival!

These leaders say something which **touches our emotions**. They **engage** us through their **dialogues**, which is unique and we **someway** like it, do not know why BUT we like them, and we want to be with them

We follow because they connect with us emotionally

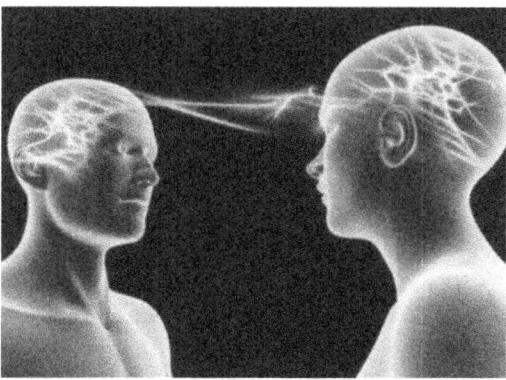

Emotion matters more than logic and reason.

The Right type of people attracts the right materials. The way the magnet attracts iron.

Why are there so many followers for the world's second richest Hindu temple?

Annually 2.5-3 crore pilgrims have Darshan of the Lord Venkateswara, Every day in the Hundi box(Donation), Temple get count 3+ crore of Indian rupees? **Belief?**

Common people believed that something good will happen in their life if they visit Tirupati Balaji temples.

Can we create a similar impression in people's mind? The **Belief** that something good will happen if they follow someone...

Why so many followers?

Capture the Heart and Mind of the people. Not by Hate!

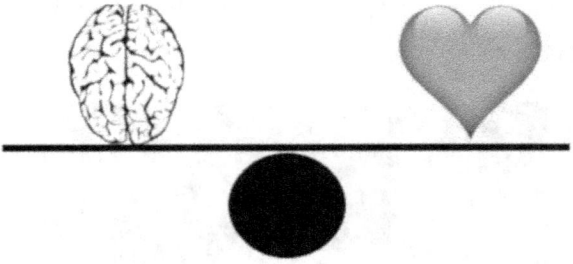

Heart and Mind have to be in balance.

What can Leaders do to influence **emotions** and the **logic** of followers?

Why do so many visitors going to the Taj Mahal? **Beauty? Pride**? **Feel-good factor**? It is one of the wonders of the world.

As a Leader, can we provide assurance and hope to our followers?

Servant leadership: living for others and helping others.

Building **Trust** among followers. Can Leaders and followers trust each other?

Very few powerful steps, but with many years of conscious practice, we can master all these. Look around yourself, you will find many such leaders.

What actions we can take as a leader to strengthen each area and achieve mastery

A follower shares an influential relationship between leaders and other followers with the intent to support the leaders who reflect their mutual purpose."

—Rodger Adair

What actions are you going to take from this lesson?

1. _____

2. _____

3. _____

Thinking Question:

Are you doing enough to build leadership capabilities to influence your followers?

2.3 Emergent Leadership Manifesto (Scaling Leaders)?

"There are two ways of spreading light: to be the candle or the mirror that reflects it."
— Edith Wharton Vesalius In Zante (1564)

Why this topic?

Leadership is in a complex world is experimental, It is more collaborative and democratic. During our leadership coaching, we have to enlighten the leaders with numerous concepts to alter their mindset.

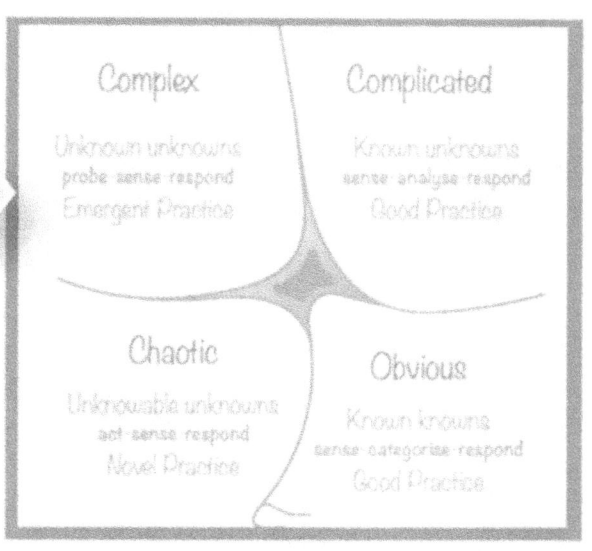

We cannot determine what will cause a particular outcome but we can run some experiments to see if they move us in the right direction so we probe, sense and respond (P-S-R). This is also the domain of multi-hypothesis as there is no right or wrong answer so we may want to run a series of experiments or in fact run a number in parallel. This is the domain of emergent practice.

Collaborative Team Power	Over	Positional Power
Share information with the Team	Over	Keep the information with self for Power
Allow team to come up with Decision	Over	Exclusive Decision maker
Ask powerful Questions and allow team to come up with solutions	Over	Provide Solutions
Creative and Innovative	Over	Predefined, Prescriptive
Holarchy	Over	Hierarchies
Lead by servant leadership style	Over	Lead by Command and Control
Consider People have Mind, Body and Spirit	Over	People as Resources
Learn from Failures and Encourage Team	Over	Punish for Failure
Encourage creativity	Over	Discourage Deviation
Inspire Trust with Engagement	Over	Trust build with Transaction

Provide space to have more than one leader at the same time	Over	Emphasize characteristics or behaviors of only one leader
One instance can be a follower, in another instance can be a Leader.	Over	Leader always have the control over followers
Rely on team capability, experiment and innovation with Flexible Process	Over	Rely on standard practices and heavy weight process
Collaborative Discussion	Over	One way Communication
Empowered team; Locus of control is shifted to team	Over	Hold Power to Self
Value driven approach	Over	Plan Driven approach
People Interest first	Over	Self Interest
Win-Win conflict resolution style	Over	Win-Lose conflict resolution style
Team Leadership	Over	Individual leadership
leadership emerges over a period of time through communication	Over	leadership is not assigned by position

LEAN LEADERS

❖ EAGERLY EMBRACE THE ROLE OF A PROBLEM SOLVER.

❖ REALIZE THAT NO MANAGER AT A HIGHER LEVEL CAN SOLVE A PROBLEM AT A LOWER LEVEL—PROBLEMS CAN ONLY BE SOLVED WHERE THEY LIVE, BY THOSE LIVING WITH THEM

❖ BELIEVE THAT ALL PROBLEM SOLVING REQUIRES EXPERIMENTATION

❖ UNDERSTAND THAT NO PROBLEM IS SOLVED FOREVER. THE CRITICAL, PROBING MIND OF THE LEAN MANAGER STAYS ACTIVE IN THE PURSUIT OF PERFECTION.

- JAMES WOMACK

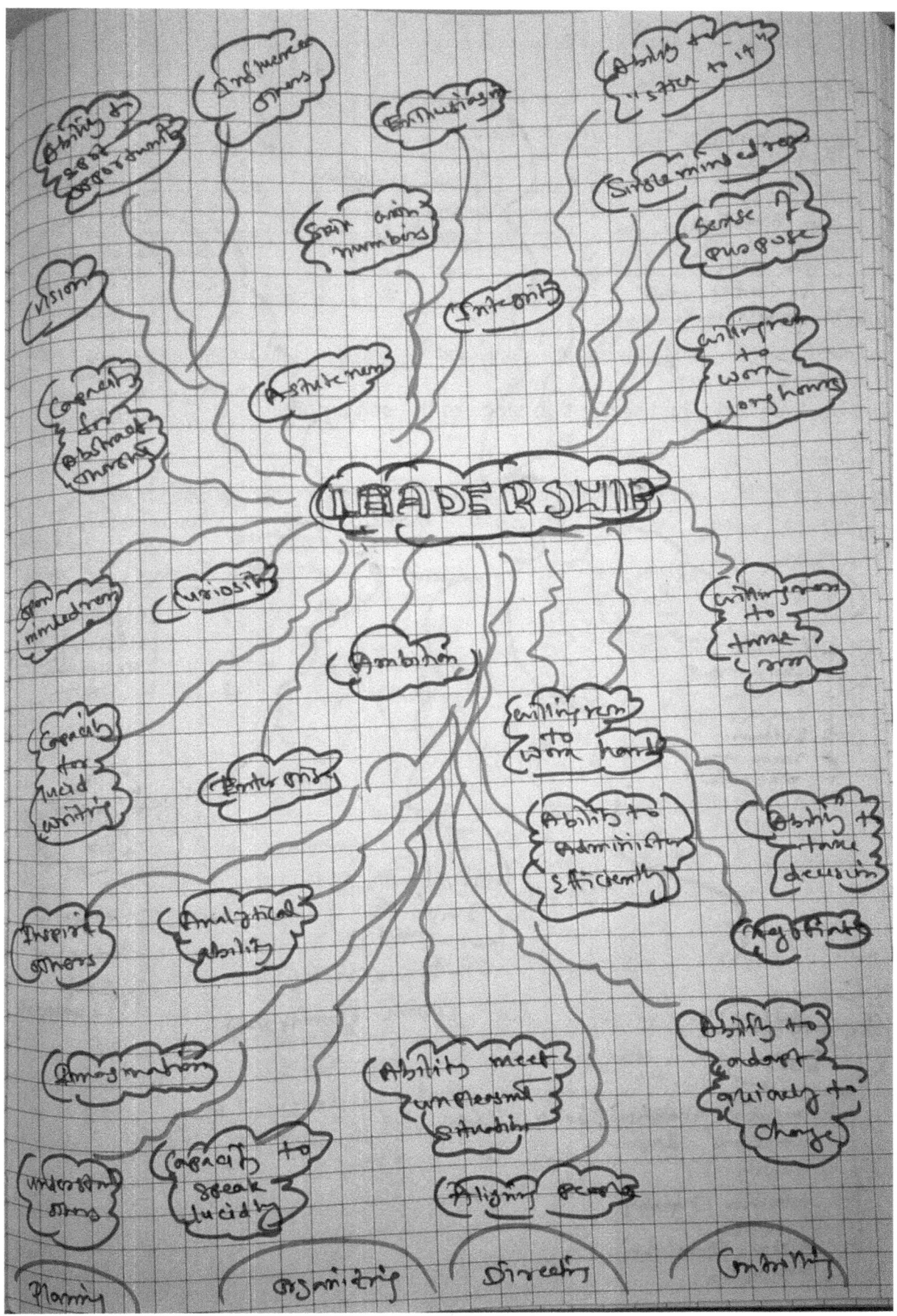

"True leadership must have follower-ship. Management styles can vary, but even an autocrat needs people who believe and simply don't follow from fear"

— *James Robinson III, RRE Ventures*

What actions are you going to take from this lesson?

1. _____

2. _____

3. _____

Thinking Question:

Are you doing enough to build your leadership skills and help others to build their skills?

2.4 The Manager and the Leader, two sides of the same coin!

Why this topic?

Elucidation this to my fellow leaders whom I was coaching, how can I easily explain this thought?

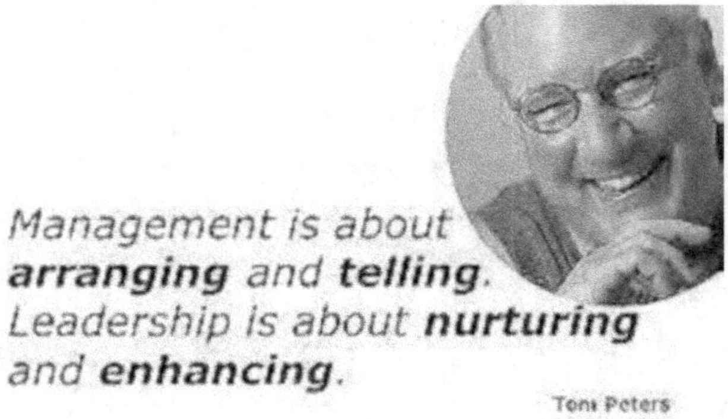

Management is about **arranging** and **telling**.
Leadership is about **nurturing** and **enhancing**.

Tom Peters

It needs the balance of both the worlds.

We cannot say, he/she is a good leader, but a poor manager, and vice versa.

MANAGER	LEADER
FOCUSES ON NOW	FOCUSES ON FUTURE
PREFER STABILITY	PREFER CHANGE
CONTROLLING	INSPIRING
MINIMIZE RISKS	TAKE RISKS
WORK FOCUS	PEOPLE FOCUS
MAKE DECISION	FACILITATE DECISION
REACTIVE	PROACTIVE
PLAN DETAIL	SET DIRECTION
ADMINISTRATOR	INNOVATOR
ASK HOW	ASK WHY
DO THINGS RIGHT	DO THE RIGHT THINGS
MAINTAINS	DEVELOPS
EYE ON BOTTOM LINE	EYE ON HORIZON
RULE ORIENTED	OUTCOME ORIENTED
TRANSACTIONAL	TRANSFORMATIONAL
SHORT RANGE	LONG RANGE
RESULT	ACHIEVEMENT
THE HEAD	THE HEART

A leader must not only give followers a structure, organization, and control but also show courage, purpose, commitment, accountability and a sense of value.

Management focus produces an essential order, consistency, and predictability, and then leadership produces change and adaptability—to new competitors, new products, new markets, new regulations, and new customers. Both sets of skills are necessary, and both must be in balance.

Every High-Performance Leader should have both strong management and strong leadership skills.

> "*Management is efficiency in climbing the ladder of success; leadership determines whether the ladder is leaning against the right wall*"
>
> —*Stephen Covey*

It is very easy to acquire the scientific part which is Management, but it is tough to acquire the art part which is leadership.

I have worked with many good managers and good leaders. Few of them are successful in the corporate ladder because of their management skills, a few of them have to leave because of the poor management skill and some of them started their own company due to their excellent leadership skill.

WHEN I TALK TO MANAGERS I GET THE FEELING THAT THEY ARE IMPORTANT.

WHEN I TALK TO LEADERS I GET THE FEELING THAT I AM IMPORTANT.

What actions are you going to take from this lesson?

1. _____

2. _____

3. _____

Thinking Question:

Are you working out enough to find out the manager and leaders roles so that you can make an impact while coaching?

2.5 Building self-Organized team?

"Self-organization has a curious feature in that the degrees of freedom for the separate parts are greater than the degrees of freedom for the collection. The reduction in the degrees of freedom is in the form of relationships and these relationships are essentially information and so it appears that information is generated by a loss of freedom."

—R.A.Delmonico

Why this topic?

"The best architectures, requirements, and designs emerge from self-organizing teams", as indicated in the Agile Manifesto

What are the characteristics of a self-organized team? When we glance at these pictures what comes to our mind? Awesome teamwork, world-class performance? How to reach this height of maturity?

Self-organization is a process by which a system—several components together with interaction rules—becomes ordered in space and/or time. Often, self-organization leads to emergent properties, meaning that the whole system has characteristics that differ qualitatively from those of the component parts without the interactions. Self-organization is usually distinguished from self-assembly because self-organized structures rely on a continuous input of energy to be maintained. - Jonathon Howard

A broad definition of self-organization is given by Haken (2006).

"A system is self-organizing if it acquires a spatial, temporal, or functional structure without specific interference from outside. By 'specific' we mean that the structure or functioning is not impressed on the system but that the system is acted upon from the outside in a non-specific fashion. For instance, the fluid which forms hexagons is heated from below in an entirely uniform fashion and it acquires its specific structure by self-organization."

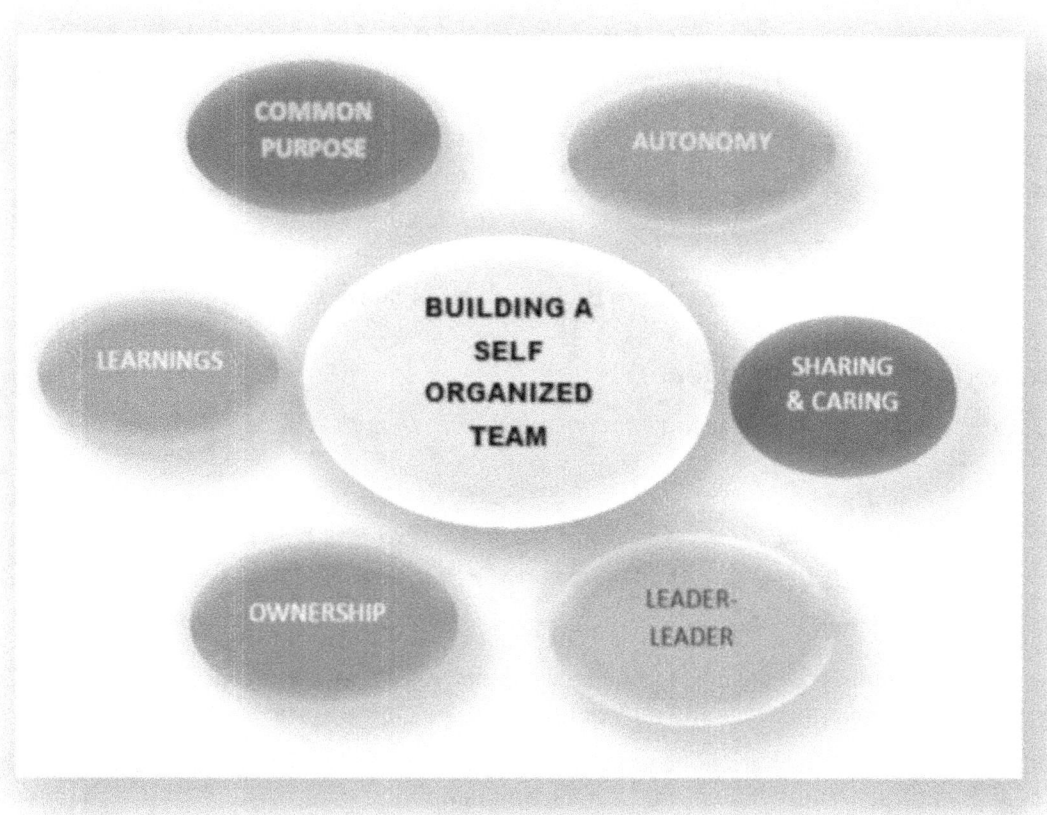

A self-organized team should have the below characteristics:

1. **They are Autonomous**
2. **They have a common purpose**
3. **They learn from each other continuously**
4. **They take ownership**
5. **They share and care for each other's**
6. **They are a leader - leader on their own(Shared leadership)**

To achieve all these aspects whatever is required team needs to do to achieve world-class output.

Hackman provides us with an authority matrix to distinguish four levels of team self-organization

*   **Manager-led teams that leave team members only the authority for task execution while managers monitor and manage work processes, design the context and set the direction.**
*   **Self-managing teams put members not just in charge** of task execution but also for managing their progress.
*   **Self-designing teams give members the authority to modify the design of their team and/or aspects of the organizational context in which they operate.**
*   **Self-governing teams have** the responsibility for all the four core functions as shown by the corporate boards of directors, worker cooperatives or start-ups.

"Organisms live in a stream of energy. In a stream of energy, you get increasingly complex levels of self-organization."

                                                                    —***R.A.Delmonico***

What actions are you going to take from this lesson?

1. _____

2. _____

3. _____

Thinking Question:

Are you doing sufficient to support the team to become a self-organized?

2.6 Characteristics of an Agile team?

"The strength of the team is each individual member. The strength of each member is the team."

—Phil Jackson

Why this topic?

Every manager asks me to help them to form an outstanding agile team, How to accompany them?

Coaching is more an Art than a science.

There is no magic formula; the coach has to understand every team as each team is unique. The Coach's main job is to build an excellent agile team and move on.

I could find a few barriers which are indicators and those need to be handle carefully. The team should realize these issues and fix these issues with coaching and mentorship.

At the initial stage, the coach will be the communicator, leader, role model and a collaborator. Initially, there will be resistance as the change is tough to digest and the team needs a shoulder to cry on. The agile coach plays a critical role as a transformer and change agent. The team should be able to see the change after some time.

Below are a few influencing factors.

- **Definition of Done:** The team member needs to know what done means in all the assignments they are working on. If I am playing a game, I need to clearly know what done means for that game. Same applies when I am writing a user story or executing a test case, what that done means for that specific work. It has to be very clear without much ambiguity. Do all the team members know their DONE criteria all the time?
- **Ego checking: It** is the big killer in the team-building process. As analytical people, we engineers often associate our ego with our work. But this brings some potential negative side effects. We should have improved our emotional capacity to control our ego to effectively work with the team members in various circumstances.
  The agile team members should have more generalists not many specialists. All the team members have to contribute and do all types of jobs from architecture to documentation. "I am an architect, I cannot do testing assignment" will not help the team to deliver solution fast.
- **Follow the sprint, and the demo and learn from the execution mistake:** As soon as something is vaguely usable; it is better to get it released in a raw form to the public. It becomes apparent very quickly where the successes and failures are, and so the programming team is expected to learn, iterate, and push a new version out as quickly as possible.

Are we learning from others and doing the same for improvement?

Most of the time team members feel that others are pointing at their mistake and all they do is start defending their solution instead of looking at the bigger picture. If this pattern continues, the team feels sprint demo meeting are to find fault. The Product owner, architect and all the stakeholders have to help each other to build an environment where all own to build a better product and solution. The only way the team maturity grows and also increases learning by making mistakes. Make more mistakes, fast and learn from the mistakes. This positive attitude has to be adapted by all the team members for the improvement.

- **Keep Time for Learning**

To become an effective team, we need to share the knowledge and learn new stuff continuously. This is the only way the team learns and the agility grows. If the team members focus too much on velocity and that becomes the measure of productivity, it will impact their learning. Continuous value generation requires a good amount of time for knowledge building. Otherwise, the technical debts will also increase.

- **Assumption checking:**

We have to check all the project assumptions by asking questions. The acceptance of wrong assumptions is the killer of many initiatives. We assume that "If We Build It, They Will Come.", are we sure they will come?

We have a habit of accepting everything at face value without challenging, and most of the time this habit causes some issues. Let us change this habit.

- **Communication Patterns of Successful Cultures:**

Communication is the major contributor to team handling. Communication, especially with geographically dispersed teams, is very crucial. All the techniques have to be applied, e.g., internet, video conference, chat, telephone to effectively pass the messages to the team members, and collaborate with the team. Essential to run the meeting effectively with a proper agenda and to follow all the meeting rules. A noble universal rule around communication is to include as little people as needed in synchronous communication (like meetings) and to go for a wider audience in asynchronous communication (like email).

- **The Servant Leader:**

In today's world, the old style of management has disappeared where command and get the resulting style is not effective at least with the knowledge workers. The cure for the "management" disease is a liberal application of what we call "servant leadership," which is a nice way of saying that the most important thing a manager can do is to *serve her team*; much like a butler or majordomo tends to the health and well-being of a household. The manager has to trust the team members and be honest in all the aspects. He spread humor and joy in the team so that the place is lively and nice to work.

- **Take ownership**

Team members have to own the failures and success, and they have to own the outcome and responsibility. Build it is a practice to own. If we are passing the blame, it creates a negative atmosphere and soon the place will be difficult to stay.

- **Low performer**

How does one coach a low performer effectively? The best analogy is to imagine you're helping a limping person learn to walk again, then jog, and then run alongside the rest of the team. Meet with the engineer every week to check on the progress, and be sure you set explicit expectations around each upcoming milestone so that it's easy to measure success or failure. If the low performer can't keep up, it will become quite obvious to both of you early in the process. At this point, the person will often acknowledge that things aren't going well and we need to decide to quit. In other scenarios, the determination will kick in and he'll "up his game" to meet the expectations. Either way, by working directly with the low performer, you're catalyzing important and necessary changes.

- **Build a culture of trust**:

Whatever is required, we have to create and build a trust culture. We have to keep our promise whatever it may be, and it will create a trust culture among the team members, Let us be honest and follow this practice. People tend to enjoy interacting with people who they believe like them. No blame culture.

- **Attitude**:

Attitude is contagious, and we have to build a learning attitude from all the context, Let us experiment and learn from each other that could be an excellent attitude. Building a negative, pessimistic, blame game, fault finding attitude should be avoided.

- **Walk the talk and energize**

Demonstrate every concept wherever possible. Help the team to remove all the roadblocks. Make them comfortable. Team members should also demonstrate the same over a period of time. Are they doing?

- **People Are Like Plants**

The way, a gardener takes care of his/her plants, the same way, a coach has to mentor and coach all the team members. The result will be tremendous. Are they listening? Team members have to play like a world cup winning team, where all are contributing for one common vision "To win"!

Value Driven Delivery Culture
The Team is committed to deliver what is needed.
The Team knows the actions that need to be taken.
The Team can understand the importance of this project.
The Team can be trusted.
Leader Helps the Team to take ownership and doesn't take it back.
Leader Conveys the vision, the value, and the urgency.
Leader Helps the Team focus.
Connects the customer with the Team directly.
Enables the Team.
Has time for strategic thinking.
Team Takes ownership
Team is accountable
Team Can optimize what it does.
Team Stands or falls together.

There are many soft skills which influence the agile team but the above few I have understood to start with and found all these factors are common and universal and most of the agile coaches have all these challenges.

Traditional Team:

1. Driven by Managers
2. Direction given by Managers
3. Functional expertise
4. The Project manager is ultimately responsible
5. Command and Control Leadership
6. Large Teams
7. Single skilled team members
8. Many Specialist
9. Decisions making by the leaders
10. Focus on individual success

Agile Team:

1. Driven by self-organized team
2. Directed by the team
3. Cross functional team members
4. All team members are accountable
5. Servant leadership style
6. Small teams
7. Multiskilled team members
8. Many generalists
9. The team takes the decisions
10. Focus on team success

"Individual commitment to a group effort - that is what makes a team work, a company work, a society work, a civilization work."

- Vince Lombardi

What actions are you going to take from this lesson?

1. _____

2. _____

3. _____

Thinking Question:

Are you doing enough to supplement your knowledge to establish the best team and aid others in building the same?

2.7 How to Become a Charismatic Leader?

"We are all seduced by charismatic people, whether it's in your office or on the bus or on the train. There are people who just, like, come through the door, and everybody turns around and looks at them and feel drawn to them."

—Edgar Ramirez

Why this topic?

As the organization is becoming flat, and the hierarchies are vanishing, it is significant to recognize further the charismatic leadership style, what is this style of leadership?

Charisma is a Greek word meaning a **"Divinely inspired gift."** In the study of leadership, charisma is a special quality of leaders whose purpose, powers, and the extraordinary determination differentiate them from others.

A case in point is Steve Jobs of Apple Inc. and Pixar, whose name frequently surfaces in discussions related to charisma. Several years ago, he was nominated, the Time magazine person of the year by an entertainment executive, and given this accolade: **"He is a true visionary who continues to lead the technological revolution. Year after year, Apple creates must-have products that shape how we live our lives. Jobs and Apple continue to lead us to a wonderful new technological future."**

Charismatic leaders use impression management to deliberately cultivate a certain relationship with the group members. In other words, they take steps to create a favorable, successful impression, recognizing that the perception of constituents determine whether they function as charismatic leaders.

AM I DOING THE SAME?

Jane A. Halpert performed a statistical analysis of the effects charismatic leaders have on followers and found that the three dimensions are the most important. One key dimension is the **Referent power**, the ability to influence others because of one's desirable traits and characteristics. If we like a leader, he or she might be able to exercise referent power.

Another dimension is **Expert power**, the ability to influence others because of one's specialized knowledge, skills or abilities. An important part of Steve Jobs' charisma stems from his expert powers reflected in imagining and designing electronic devices such as the iMac and iPod.

The third dimension of charismatic leadership is the ability to get group members excited about their work or to experience **Job involvement**.

Job involvement is a key component of job satisfaction, and one empirical study has provided evidence of the relationship between charismatic leadership and job satisfaction.

The outstanding characteristic of charismatic leaders is that they are charismatic, and therefore they can attract, motivates, or lead others! They also have other distinguishing characteristics.

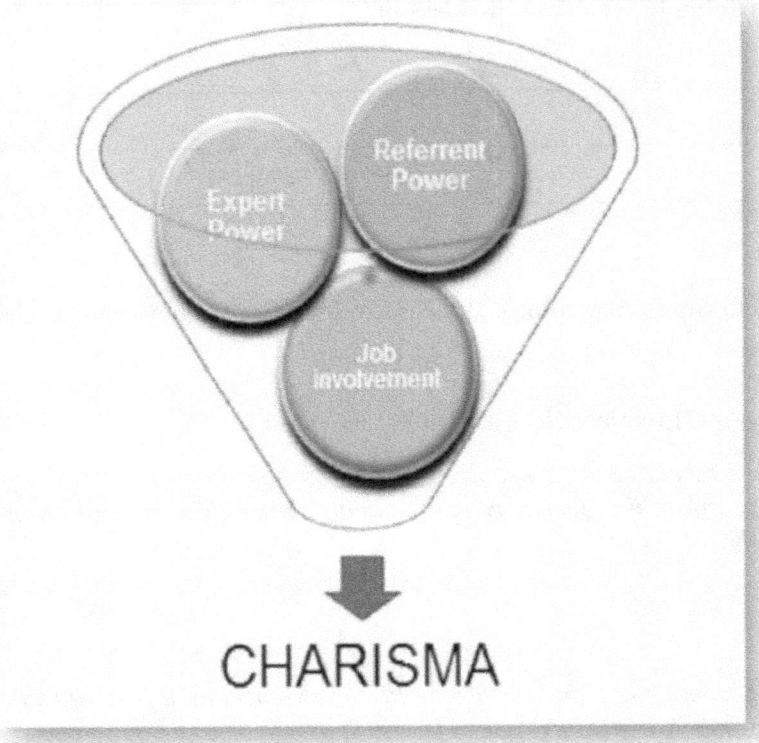

1. Charismatic leaders are visionary because they offer an exciting image of where the organization is headed and how to get there.
2. Charismatic leaders have masterful communication skills. To inspire people, the charismatic leader uses colorful language and exciting metaphors and analogies.
3. Another key characteristic is the ability to inspire trust.
4. Charismatic leaders have an energy and action orientation. Like entrepreneurs, most charismatic leaders are energetic and serve as role models for getting things done on time. Emotional articulateness and cordiality are also distinguished.
5. A key characteristic of charismatic leaders is the ability to express feelings openly.
6. Another trait of charismatic leaders is that they romanticize Risk. They enjoy risk so much that they feel empty in its absence.
7. In addition to valuing risk, charismatic leaders use unconventional strategies to achieve success. The charismatic leader inspires others by framing unusual strategies to achieve important goals.
8. A final strategy for becoming a more charismatic leader is a combination of the ideas already introduced: **being dramatic and unique in significant, positive ways and that is a major contributor to charisma.**

I am walking through this path......coming across many mentors who are having all the above characteristics, I am admiring them and practicing all the skills to become a charismatic leader......are you?

"Truly charismatic people, in my experience, don't come along very often."

—*Francesca Annis*

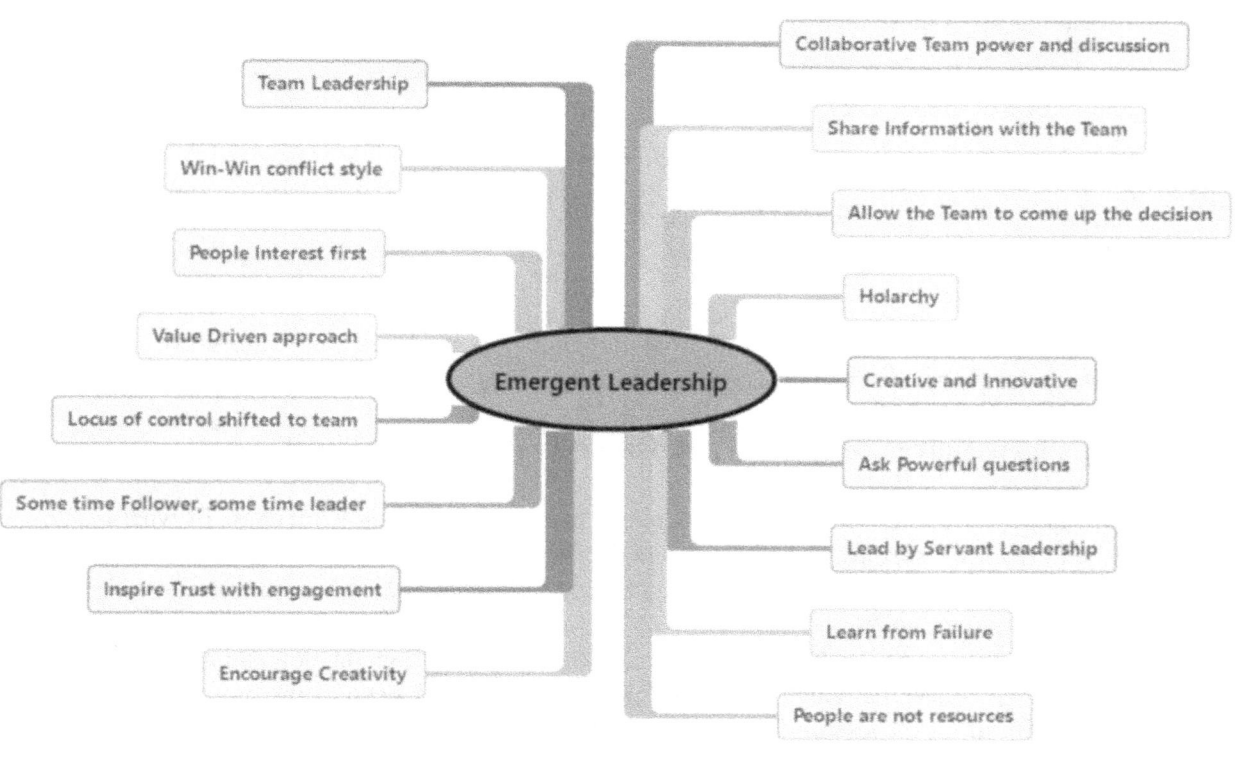

What actions are you going to take from this lesson?

1. _____

2. _____

3. _____

Thinking Question:

Are you doing enough to build knowledge about this leadership style? What else can you work out?

2.8 Certified Servant Leader! Looking for Certified Servant Leader (CSL)?

"Serving others prepares you to lead others."

—Jim George

Why this topic?

What are the few key characteristics of servant leaders, which I can share in the leadership workshop?

I have been asked to look for a better servant leader and how to measure if at all possible, best servant leaders!

I was wondering what are the **characteristics of** someone who is demonstrating servant leadership consistently and which we can **measure** and leads to some kinds of recognition, which I call as a **Certified Servant leader (CSL).**

Mastering servant-leadership is a lifelong learning process.

These attributes are often the result of having developed a highly moral and spiritual character.

Can we observe the team members through the lens of the below characteristics?

At least I have started using these factors to assess the best servant leaders, who can be a role model for others.

The following **12 characteristics** of Servant-Leadership have been identified by Larry Spears, CEO of the Greenleaf Center for Servant Leadership.

He calls them as being thoughtful to the improvement of servant leaders.

I was looking at individuals who are demonstrating most of these characteristics, I am confirming in my mind if he/she is the best CSL (Certified Servant Leader)

Let us have a look at each element

1. Does he/she **seek to listen** receptively to what is being done and said (not just said)? Listening also encompasses getting in touch with one's inner voice, and seeking to understand what is being communicated? Does he/she **seeks to identify and clarify** the will of the group?
2. Does he/she **understands and empathize** with others? Does he/she **accepts and recognize** people's special talents?
3. Does he/she **heal self and others**? Do others believe he/she has a **strong awareness** of what is going on? Does he/she look for cues from their opinions and decisions?
4. Does he/she **seek to convince others**, rather than coerce compliance? Does he /she **successfully construct an agreement** within groups?
5. He/she is a **great dreamer**? Do they have the ability to look at the organization and any issues within the organization from a conceptualizing perspective? He/she is **thinking beyond the day-to-day realities**?
6. Does he/she **understand the lessons from the past, the realities of the present** and the **likely consequence of a decision in the future**?
7. Does he/she responsible for **preparing it for its destiny**, usually for the betterment of society? Does he/she desire to prepare the organization to contribute to the greater good of society—not unlike preparing the prince to serve the greater good of the kingdom?
8. Do employees believe that he/she is **committed to helping them develop and grow**? Does he/she believe that **all employees have something to offer beyond their tangible contributions**?
9. Does he/she has a **strong sense of community spirit and work hard to foster it** in an organization?
10. Do employees believe that he/she is **willing to sacrifice their self-interest** for the good of the organization? Does he/she have a **natural desire to serve others**? Does he/she **desires to make a difference for others** within the organization and will pursue opportunities to **make a difference and to impact the lives of employees**, the organization, and the community—never for their own gain?
11. Does he/she **understand the deep human need** to contribute to personally meaningful enterprises? Does he/she **nurture the individual's spirit** through honest praise and supportive recognition? Does he/she remind employees to reflect on the importance of both the struggles and successes in the organization and learn from both?
12. Do those **served to grow as persons**; do they, while being served, **become healthier, wiser, freer, more autonomous,** more likely themselves to be servants?

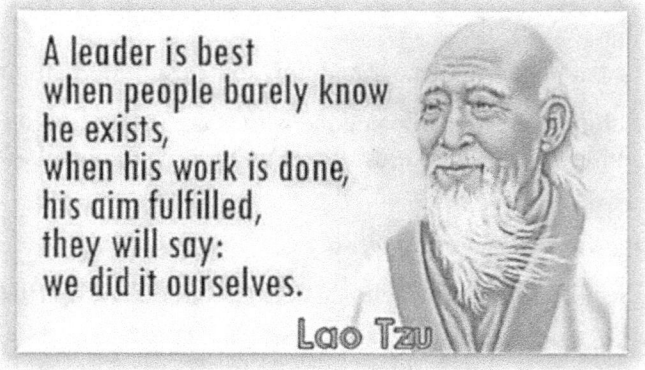

Maybe we can start observing all these above aspects and recognize individuals who are demonstrating such characteristics?

"In a servant leadership culture we learn by choice or example that if we want to be great, we have to serve others respectfully."

—Vern Dosch,

What actions are you going to take from this lesson?

1. _____

2. _____

3. _____

Thinking Question:

Are you doing adequate to bring out the servant leadership attributes in yourself and later coach others to obtain the same?

2.9 Do you have a Feminine and Masculine personality style in harmony?

"What is the most beautiful in virile men is something feminine; what is the most beautiful in feminine women is something masculine."

—Susan Sontag

Why this topic?

Every individual is unique, and their leadership styles are varied, and it is useful to know both of these styles.

Coaching has to be a balance of both the **masculine** and **feminine** qualities. Though these qualities are different, one isn't necessarily better than the other.

Do not believe?

Experiment and see the benefits.

In Taoist philosophy, 'yin' is the feminine principle, representing the forces of earth, while 'yang' is the masculine principle, representing the spirit.

Marianne Williamson

It is the balance between the **HARD** and **SOFT** part of the characteristics.

It should be a healthy balance. An **Unhealthy** hard and soft part will cause a problem.

Please have a look, are you applying a balanced approach?

What action can we take to increase the balance based on your dominant personality style?

Masculinity and Femininity—Complements

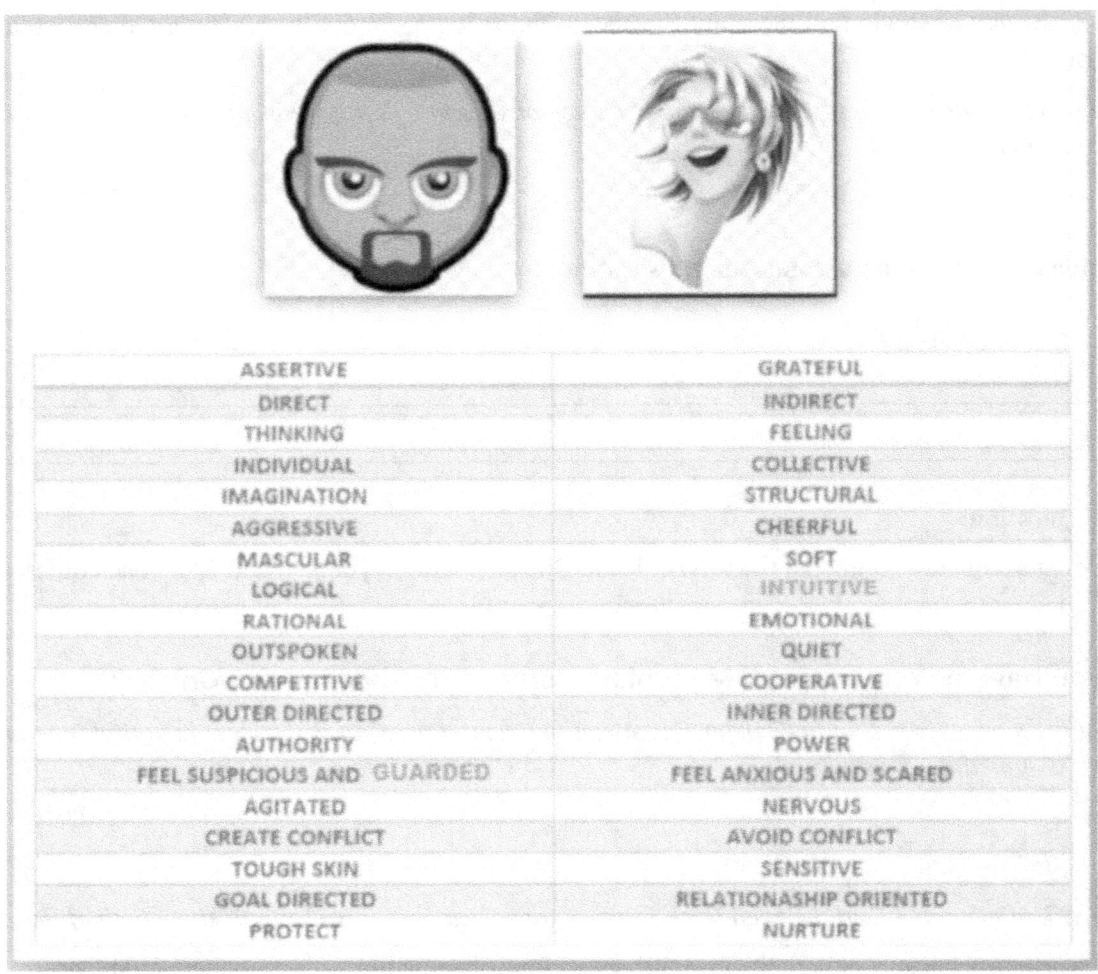

ASSERTIVE	GRATEFUL
DIRECT	INDIRECT
THINKING	FEELING
INDIVIDUAL	COLLECTIVE
IMAGINATION	STRUCTURAL
AGGRESSIVE	CHEERFUL
MASCULAR	SOFT
LOGICAL	INTUITIVE
RATIONAL	EMOTIONAL
OUTSPOKEN	QUIET
COMPETITIVE	COOPERATIVE
OUTER DIRECTED	INNER DIRECTED
AUTHORITY	POWER
FEEL SUSPICIOUS AND GUARDED	FEEL ANXIOUS AND SCARED
AGITATED	NERVOUS
CREATE CONFLICT	AVOID CONFLICT
TOUGH SKIN	SENSITIVE
GOAL DIRECTED	RELATIONASHIP ORIENTED
PROTECT	NURTURE

As a coach, if we demonstrate only the Masculine styles or only the Feminine styles, the end result will not be as expected. It has to be a balance of both.

According to yoga philosophy, the male energy is known as **Shiva,** and the female energy is known as **Shakti**. The male energy is represented by the **sun** and the feminine by the **moon**.

The important aspect is that we as a person have to be in constant **balance** to be able to achieve the best of our worlds, mental, physical and emotional.

Both sides, male and female have to attain a harmonious whole.

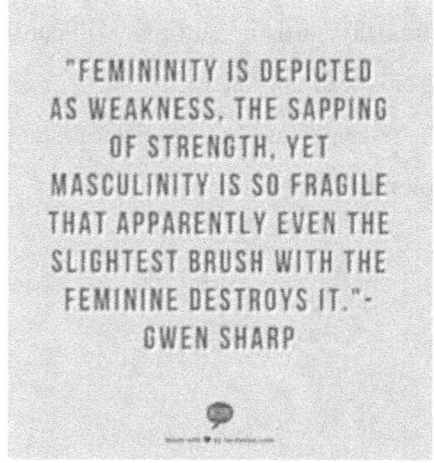

"FEMININITY IS DEPICTED AS WEAKNESS, THE SAPPING OF STRENGTH, YET MASCULINITY IS SO FRAGILE THAT APPARENTLY EVEN THE SLIGHTEST BRUSH WITH THE FEMININE DESTROYS IT." - GWEN SHARP

While doing coaching, we have to apply the Masculine style or the feminine style based on the circumstances. For that, we need to know both these styles.

Some of the **Feminine Qualities** which helps us in coaching - Be Affectionate, Be Empathetic, Be Patient, Be Soft and so on.

A Coach shouldn't be all masculine or all feminine -- they need to change their style depending on who they're working with and the needs of the situation.

"I definitely believe that we really need to stop putting things in masculine and feminine boxes and realize that men and women both contain masculine and feminine energy."

—Nelly Furtado

What actions are you going to take from this lesson?

1. _____

2. _____

3. _____

Thinking Question:

Are you doing sufficient to figure out the personality of the individuals so that you can support your coaching team members?

2.10 When I find my Agile Leader, How do I recognize him/her?

"I am not afraid of an army of lions led by a sheep; I am afraid of an army of sheep led by a lion."

—Alexander the Great

Why this topic?

Many of my team members were seeking that to share with them, how an excellent agile leader should perform? I have started netting all the information and subsequently shared with them.

I was searching for my role model **Agile Leader** for a long time. I was preparing myself for that time.

How do I identify that person, what are the characteristics I should be looking forward to recognizing that person as my **role model Agile Leader**?

After a long search, I have found the person and now many more such people I have come across. The method which helped me to identify that person is, shared with all of you.

1) What I have observed according to the Agile Leader, **Customer is the center of everything**. The customer is the king. The customer defines the expectations, wants, and needs. Leaders ensure that the customer gets full satisfaction through product and service.

2) The environment is dynamic and unstable, the agile Leaders confirm that the team members are **aligned and adjust to the varying demands of the customer**. They take actions to ensure that the changing needs are addressed and the customer agrees to the changed offering. The changes could be different offerings in services, new features, anything which brings customer satisfaction. Agile leaders are flexible and take extreme steps to address these changing needs.

3) **Customer Satisfaction and Team satisfaction**: Agile leaders balance these both aspects. They take actions on a daily basis to address these two areas of satisfaction. They develop themselves to exhibit leadership characteristics to achieve both. They take several initiatives to change the culture and measure the improvements for both of these areas.

4) **Feedback** from customers and team members: They take continuous feedback from all and take visible actions to change the ecosystem. Team members and customers accept and agree that there are developments in the shortest timeline based on their feedback.

5) **Co-creation**: Agile Leaders encourage all the team members to participate in co-creating the solutions. They inspire and encourage through their charismatic leadership to all the participants in the solution building process. They never stop until they see effective collaborations are happening. They do all these steps without using much positional power to improve the co-creation in the organization. They use their network to bring experts from various areas to help each other.

6) They **cultivate great people**: Agile leaders are constantly building people capabilities. They ensure competency is at the expected level. They take care of the team member's emotional health. They create an environment where team members feel the best place to work. They create a leadership production factory through continuous coaching and mentoring.

7) They **invest in infrastructure**: To align with the Digital world, they invest in the latest cutting-edge technology. They fight for the best tools and technology. They are tech savvy and adapted the latest technology. They train the team members to educate themselves and create an ecosystem which is full of the latest technology.

8) **Experimental mindset**: Agile leaders are learning from the mistakes. They encourage team members to fail and learn from their mistakes. They create a community where they encourage team members to share what mistake they did and how as a team we should avoid the mistake in the future. They give full freedom to the team members to fail fast. They build a culture of learning from failure. They have understood that survival in today's world is only through learning by experiments.

9) They bring **standardization,** wherever applicable. They ensure we are not reinventing the wheel. Uncertainty is costly. Common processes, tools, and techniques enable greater understanding and communication among all the participants when implementing change. Lack of standardization often results in redundancy and conflicting approaches that can lead to waste and an inability to adapt to the needs of the customer, especially in a reasonable period.

10) **Transparency**: They are the believers of the effect of visual information radiator. They always communicate to bring transparency. They share the goals, vision and inspire team members through effective communication. They develop master communication skills.

11) **Walk the talk**: They demonstrate what they preach. They do not talk in the air. They fight from the front. They inspire their team members through this process. If they do not know anything they take the help from the team members, but they ensure that they accept that they do not know everything.

12) They **re-skill themselves**: They are continuously learning. They ensure all the team members are learning and growing. They keep track of all the team members' knowledge, including self for the improvement. They **create a learning organization**. They encourage team members to look into their profile in each quarter and check if they are constantly learning.

13) **Continuous improvement** culture: They build an organizational culture of continuous improvement. They ensure the elimination of waste on a daily basis. They maintain the waste removal backlog where they retrospect with the team members at certain intervals and celebrate the waste removed.

14) **Break silos** culture and increase alignment: They look for the continuous value flow of the business. They look for collaboration and alignment opportunity. They remove all the silos with the help of all stakeholders. They work with all the team members to minimize dependency.

15) They are always on the ground, and they are **connected**. They do not believe in the Red/Amber/Green traffic signal based power point presentation. They get the **information** from the real world. They fly to various countries at certain intervals to get the real information from the team members. They prefer face-to-face interaction with most of the team members. They are not sticking to the few important team members.

16) They implement **small incremental** delivery and get **feedback** from the stakeholders. They manage the **queue** properly and implement **work in progress limits**. They **decentralize** the operational decisions and own the strategic decisions. They link strategy with operations.

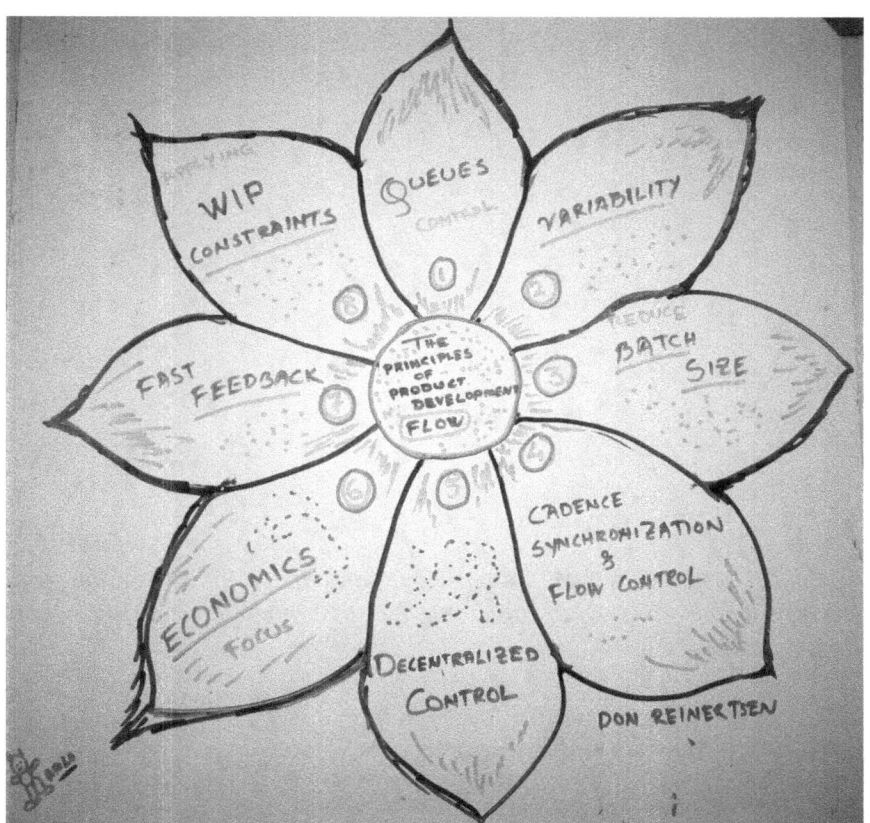

17) They **think systems**: They look at the big picture and help team members to achieve the same. By adhering to such a perspective, team members begin to appreciate the importance of their roles and those of others in contributing to customer satisfaction.

18) They **build trust** as a culture. Allow people to take ownership and come up with ideas to improve the organizational setup. They believe in TDD (Trust-Driven Development).

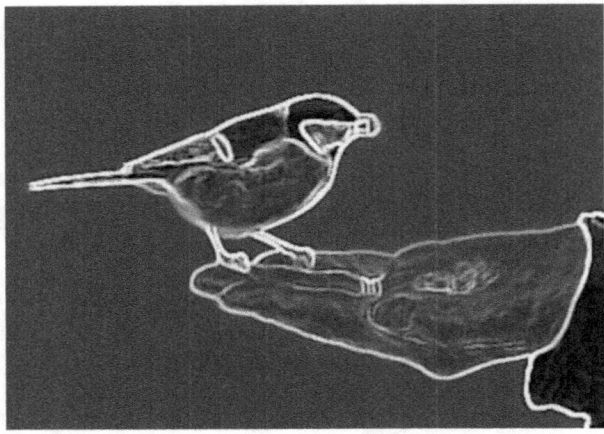

19) They believe in a **flat structure:** They are not behind designations or higher positions. They understand that layers slow down the decision making. Communication becomes more difficult; management gets out of touch with what is occurring in the lower-level ranks; negative conflict often erupts as members of executive management compete for greater growth in power and control; and procedures become so intertwined that making change is next to impossible because it defeats the power and control of certain people or organizations.

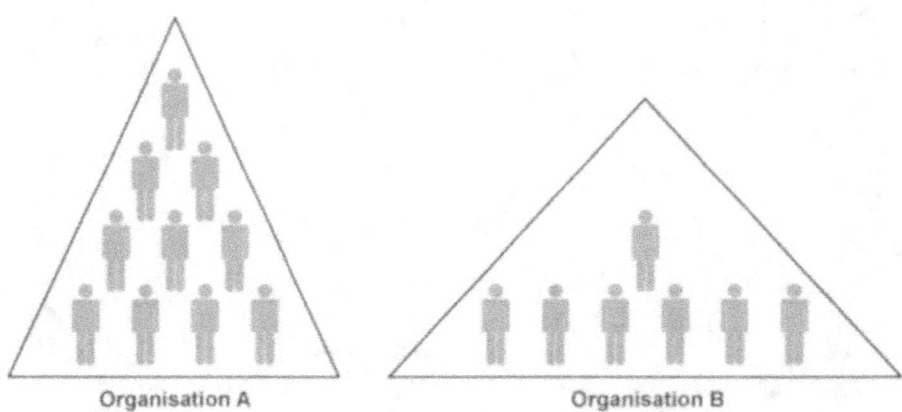

"Leadership is not about a title or a designation. It's about impact, influence, and inspiration. Impact involves getting results, influence is about spreading the passion you have for your work and you have to inspire teammates and customers."

—*Robin S Sharma*

What actions are you going to take from this lesson?

1. _____

2. _____

3. _____

Thinking Question:

Are you doing enough to reinforce your learning on agile leadership? What else can you look at?

2.11 How to Increase your personal worth?

"To get them hooked and booked for life, you must consistently feed them – value!"

—*Bernard Kelvin Clive*

Why this topic?

This theme was developed based on the examination with a few team members who were getting very low salary and a few who were getting a remarkably high salary, and most of them were enquiring, how to improve and sustain the high salary?

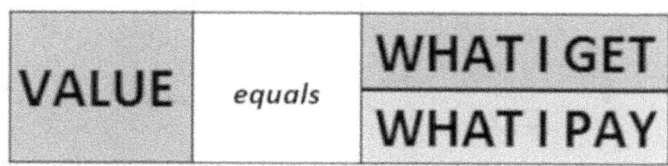

The theory of supply and demand lies at the heart of market economics.

Profitability requires scarcity and this is increasingly provided by the uniqueness of knowledge.

The more abundant the supply of a good or service, the lower its price will be, even to the extent that it may not be profitable to produce and sell.

The more scarce the supply, when the competition is held back by barriers such as patents, expertise or other forms of knowledge, the more likely the good or service will generate a profit.

Where there are such barriers, the price of a good or service no longer relates directly to its cost of production, but rather to its customer value, which in turn relates to its uniqueness or the costs that the buyers would incur, if the product were not available.

In the pharmaceutical industry, if there is a high demand for a product for which you have a patent and no alternative exists, the future is a lucrative one, even if the R&D costs have been substantial.

Thus scarce and valuable knowledge can help deliver exceptional profits.

Where does scarcity lie and where is it likely to develop?

In our finite world, there will always be bottlenecks, blockages or things for which there is a need but which are unavailable. But as someone somewhere will come up with innovative solutions, the scarcity will not remain the same for long.

Having the insight and knowledge to understand such changes is as important as the ability to deliver customer value. And if you can anticipate the changes, you will be ahead of the competition.

It is essential first to develop an understanding of how, why and where scarcity will occur…and increase our value by going there first!

When will the customer pay for us? When the customer gets value from our service.

$$Value = \frac{Results\ produced\ for\ the\ customer + Process\ quality}{Price\ to\ the\ customer + Costs\ of\ acquiring\ the\ service}$$

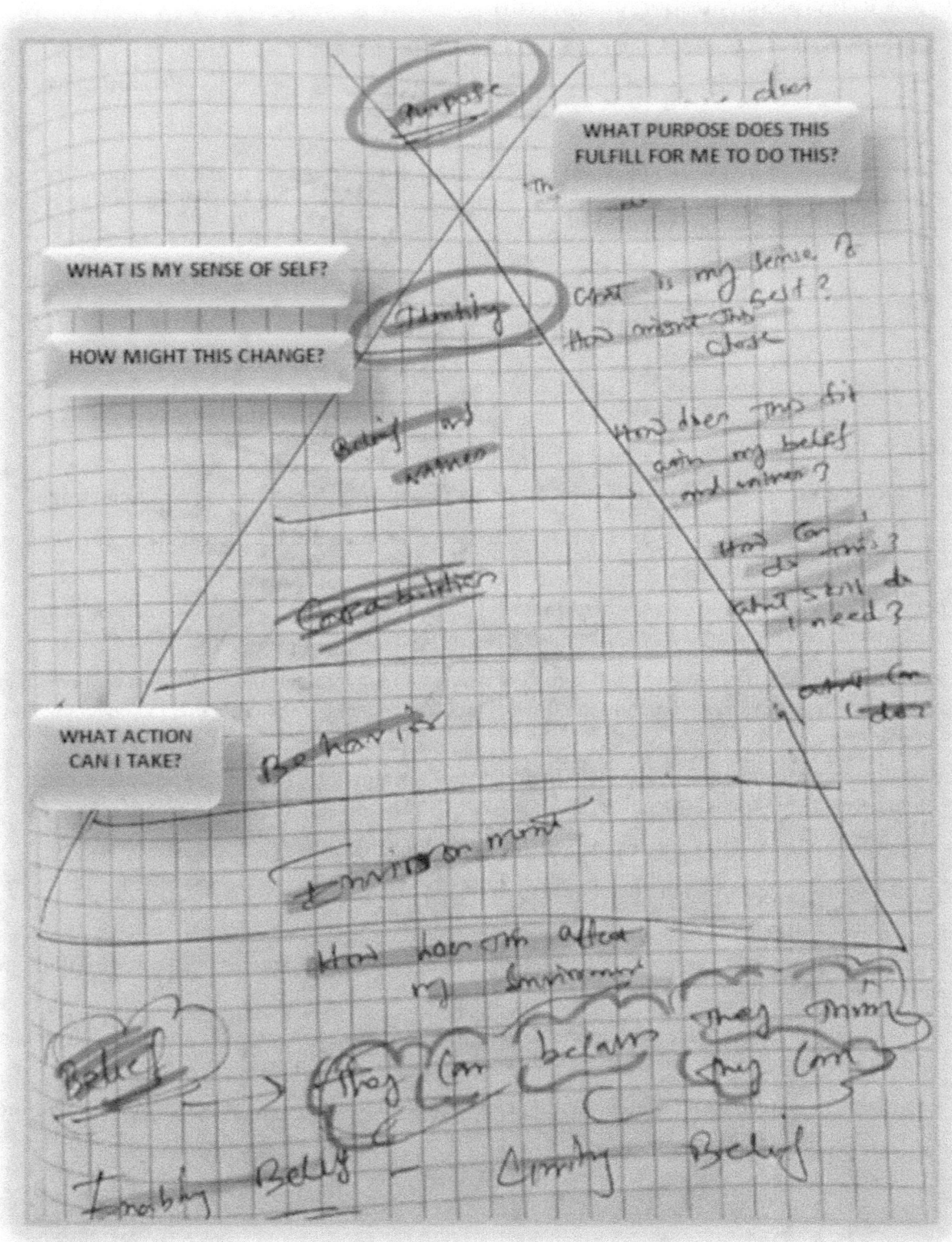

"Try not to become a man of success, but a man of value. Look around at how people want to get more out of life than they put in. A man of value will give more than he receives. Be creative, but make sure that what you create is not a curse for mankind."

—Albert Einstein

What actions are you going to take from this lesson?

1. _____

2. _____

3. _____

Thinking Question:

Are you doing enough to raise your value to the organization?

2.12 How to Influence a rigid Person

> *"One of the best ways to influence people is to make them feel important."*
>
> —*Roy T. Bennett*

Why this topic?

During our coaching engagement, we come across this query. Most of the scrum masters will love to know if there are any procedures which will help them to run the show effectively by influencing rough fellows.

a) How do we handle tough Product owners? Who will not listen to anything?

b) How do we handle tough managers? Who is arrogant, dominating and commanding?

c) How do we work with the team members who are very good at their work but will not listen?

d) How do we handle tough customers who are very demanding? And having less patience?

I have got some checklist items which can be followed and shared with all the team members who can practice these patterns and obtain results.

This is working fine with a few team members and personally with me.

Webster's dictionary defines influence as **"the act or power of producing an effect without apparent exertion of force or direct exercise of command," or "the power or capacity of causing an effect in indirect or intangible ways."**

First, Let us apply Logical persuasion to our target person. Here we will use Logic to explain what we believe or what we want.

So how should we structure this?

a) **Know your audience well**. Understand who they are and how they operate. Know what's important to them and what they would expect from you.

b) **Ask, Why would they say yes and why would they say no**? What would they find convincing and compelling? How might they argue against what you are proposing (and what will you say if they do)? What issues might they raise (and how will you respond to those issues)?

c) **Be clear in your mind** about why they should agree with what you are proposing. Be able to state, as precisely as possible, your premise as well as the principal facts and arguments supporting your premise.

d) Build your case by **finding supporting facts and evidence**. If appropriate, find ways to present or display that information in a compelling way.

e) Make your **influence attempt at the right time**—when other urgent businesses do not press people and when they have time for thoughtful reflection and to fully hear your arguments.

f) **Listen carefully to their responses**. Listening, responding thoughtfully, asking questions that engage people in the discussion and summarizing periodically are techniques that help make logical persuading more effective.

g) **Influence is often a process rather than an event**. We may need to present our case, understand where the resistance lies if people say no, and then return later with a revised case that addresses their resistance.

Sometimes above approach will not work, when things have to be done, in less time, where we do not have time to logically influence them.

We have to apply **Appealing to authority (Legitimizing)**. This should be the last option to use. Use this technique only when you need to.

a) Only quote authorities, they will find credible, and they respect.

b) Refer to policies, procedures, standard practices, rules, regulations, or traditions as the basis for your decision

c) Cite the higher authority in making your request or statement.

d) In writing or speaking, use quotations from respected authorities to substantiate or reinforce the points you are making.

At the end use these steps

1. When you can, do more for people than they expect. Treat them well, and they will remember it—and reciprocate.
2. Act with confidence
3. Avoid being aggressive
4. Try to use a compelling tone of voice
5. Use assertive nonverbal approach to emphasize your points.
6. You are just trying to express your opinion in a clear and self-confident way.

"I always dream of a pen that would be a syringe."

—*Jacques Derrida*

What actions are you going to take from this lesson?

1. _____

2. _____

3. _____

Thinking Question:

Are you doing enough to learn numerous approaches to persuade an individual? What further wisdom do you desire to gain?

2.13 How to Design and Execute Leadership workshop sessions?

[In my home workshop,] generally, I'm mending things, which is interesting because you learn a lot about why they broke.

—Sir James Dyson

Why This Topic?

Most of the time organizations asked to set up in-house training, execute by the in-house coaches. I was part of establishing Agile Training institutes and courses for several years. This is the central need when you start offering training for a wider crowd in an organization.

I have been designing and executing leadership workshops for the last several years focusing on greater customer satisfaction.

Creating a transformational program requires a **deep understanding of the way the mental life, conflict, and relationship triangles function**.

Someone working in this kind of programs will invest a **huge amount of emotional energy engaging with participants, challenging them while simultaneously showing empathy and care.**

In order to create a truly productive, safe environment where executives can experiment with **cognitions, emotions, and behavior**, participants need to be able and willing to engage in self-exploration and self-experimentation.

One of the key challenges is how do we motivate leaders to participate in the workshop? How do we engage them by designing the module effectively?

I am doing several inspect and adapt approaches by researching various pilot approaches.

I have tried this below approach and had got positive responses in the leadership workshop by including all these aspects told by Kolb.

The "**Experiential Learning Theory**" (ELT) of Kolb was constructed on the foundation of a four-stage learning cycle expressed by immediate or concrete experiences provide a basis for 'observations and reflections.'

Sensing and grasping of the experience are transformed through reflection and this allows the emergence of ideas which can then be tried out through actions.

Kolb's model, therefore, works at two levels - a four-stage cycle:

- **Concrete Experience - (CE)**
- **Reflective Observation - (RO)**
- **Abstract Conceptualization - (AC)**
- **Active Experimentation - (AE)**

Activists: Learning is the greatest from relatively short here-and-now tasks. These may be managerial actions on the job or in courses: such an approach as business games and competitive teamwork exercises.

They absorb fewer concept from the circumstances relating to an inactive approach such as listening to talks or reading.

Reflectors: Learn greatest from actions where they can stand back, attend and witness. They like gathering information and being given the chance to reflect on it. They absorb fewer aspects when they are quickly doing things without the chance to plan.

Theorists: Learn the greatest when they can review things in terms of a system, a concept, a model or a theory. They are interested in and absorb ideas even where they may be distant from the current reality. They learn fewer concept from the actions presented without this kind of explicit or implied design.

Pragmatists: Learning is the finest when there is a clear connection between the subject matter and the problem or opportunity on the job. They like being visible to the methods or procedures which can be practical in their instant condition. They learn fewer concept from the learning events which seem far from their truth.

With all these techniques we have successfully executed many leadership workshops with excellent feedback.

We also used the social learning theory proposed by Albert Bandura

There are three core concepts at the heart of the **social learning theory**.

First is the idea that people can learn through **observation**.

Next is the notion that internal mental states are an essential part of this process.

Finally, this theory identifies that just because something has been learned, **it does not mean that it will result in a change in behavior.**

The Modeling Process developed by Bandura helps us recognize that not all perceived behaviors could be learned effectively, nor learning can necessarily result in behavioral changes.

The modeling process includes the following steps for us to determine whether social learning is successful or not

Step 1: Attention

Step 2: Retention

Step 3: Reproduction

Step 4: Motivation

If you are designing a leadership workshop, you also can try these approaches. It is important to take care of all the different types of participants and how we can increase the learning of the participants.

We got an excellent result by incorporating all these concepts into the design modules.

What actions are you going to take from this lesson?

1. _____

2. _____

3. _____

Thinking Question:

Are you doing enough work to design an executive workshop? What are the comments? And what actions have been picked up for these comments?

2.14 Influence, How to master this skill?

Why this topic?

The world is becoming flat and Hierarchical organizations are becoming flat. We cannot push individuals to do the work that we want them to do. We can merely influence them. This is the only way in the coming days. How can we improve this skill? In the servant leadership style, one of the key techniques is influencing the team member. Every leader seek to grasp this skill without exception.

"the only way on earth to influence the other fellow is to talk about what he wants and show him how to get it."

-Dale Carnegie
How to Win Friends and
Influence People (1936)

Influence, influence, the influence of our boss, influence of our peers, the influence of our spouse, the influence of our girlfriends/boyfriends, what not!

Most of the time, we influence others all the time, knowing or unknowingly.

But how to do it effectively….? Which can help us to build a relationship with all the connected team members?

Influence is not some magic power that only a few people have.

Every person on the planet exercises influences all the time.

> *Most of our energy is spent to influence. Influence is a part of nearly every communication. It occurs in virtually every human interaction, every moment, and everywhere. It is so fundamental to leadership that there could be no leadership without it. If we have the power we are influencing if we don't have, we are influencing max. Before anything else, getting ready is the secret to success.*
>
> **—HENRY FORD**

We need to do the good amount of homework. Preparation Is the Key to Influence.

We need to read other's mind and help them with what they want to get the buy-in from others.

"Some people may be uncooperative because they are too busy elsewhere, and some because they are not capable of helping.

Others may well have goals, values, and beliefs that are fairly different and in conflict with the manager's and may, therefore, have no desire whatsoever to help or cooperate."

So we need to know exactly what it is and act on it to help each other.

Interests, which play a critical role, enquire whether your request is aligned with the person's interests and values.

If not, then the person's interests would not be well served by going along with you and, in this situation, most people most of the time will not willingly consent to be influenced. You may not be able to influence people the first time and in the initial moment, you approach them.

- **Influence is often a process rather than an event.**

Sometimes, the influence technique we are using is not one they respond well to. If we keep trying the same approach, we may create greater and greater resistance. If the influence technique we are using is not working, don't keep doing the same thing. Try something else.

- **Culture plays a significant role when we are influencing people.**

What works in South Africa may not work as well in India, just as the openness and informality typical in Australia, even in business settings, may not be as acceptable in Germany or the Netherlands (in fact, it could cause suspicion). The effectiveness of influence depends in part on the conventions, values, and beliefs prevalent in every culture.

People tend to **assume** that what they like, everyone else will like; that what works well for them will also work for others. This is the case because, by and large, most people believe that they are normal and that most other people share their view of reality.

If we are observant, and if we listen to other people and observe their behavior and the environments they create for themselves, we can discover how best to influence most of the people. It will build our capability over a period of time and soon it will become second nature. So we need to consciously make it a habit to build those observation skills.

- **Our business has to have mutual benefits to get the effective influence of others.**
- **Prepare our mind, know who our audience is, know their code, and structure a winning persuasive argument accordingly.**
- **Let us know who, what, when, where, and why about our message and our audience.**
- **Master Persuaders know that information and structure are the seeds for perfect persuasion.**

What actions are you going to take from this lesson?

1. _____

2. _____

3. _____

Thinking Question:

Are you doing enough to enhance your influencing skills and support your coworkers to develop theirs?

2.15 How can Project managers position themselves in an agile world?

"A mind that is stretched by new experiences can never go back to its old dimensions."

—Oliver Wendell Holmes, Jr.

Why this topic?

As an agile coach, I am supposed to coach all the project managers to reconsider themselves in the corporate agile world. I desire to discover a way for them and what are the choices that we have?

As a Project manager, I want to create my position in the agile world

.... So that I can Value-add to the organization and the team.

There is no designation for the project manager in an Agile based project, No role defined!

How can I survive as a project manager in this new world?

I have done a good amount of work as a "Project Manager" and executed many successful projects.

I used to do Project management, which requires careful planning, estimation, coordination, tracking, and control.

What to do now? These activities are no more value added to a project managers to an agile project.

Agile disrupts the task-based management approach!

Edwards Deming suggests that there are two mistakes a manager can make:

- They can react to an outcome as if it came from a common cause (i.e., something that is inherent in the definition process) when, in fact, it came from a special cause (i.e., something that is unexpected or unusual).
- Or, they can react to an outcome as if it came from a special cause when, in fact, it came from a common cause.

How can we avoid a reactive approach?

I have decided to rediscover myself!!

How can I generate value in this new world...?

I have listed down how my expertise can value-add to team members and the organization in agile projects.

I have to resign mentally from my project manager position in an agile project to start with. Classic PM taught me to focus on the project plan as my primary tool to execute and complete the project. I had to manage the golden triangle where "scope, time, cost, quality" factors are part. Need to control all these parameters so that they should not change. Do whatever is required to control all these factors.

So Plan is everything to control.

But in an agile world, the agile project manager focuses on generating business value by whatever is vital to do.

In the agile environment, the PM emphasis is moved from planning to execution

So the change is - Plan driven to Value driven management.

So the Project manager focuses more on facilitating then the tightly controlled plan. No more WBS focused, but help to get the output. Not micromanaging those WBS elements.

Upper management encourages the project manager by not asking to show "% Schedule Variance" metrics and "% cost variance" metrics. There is no punishment for percentage schedule variance. Help the team to create a high-level business needs than control through the static project plan.

Allow changes to happen for better customer satisfaction and plan accordingly. Take the help from the team to solve technical problems to address the business benefits.

The agile project manager makes the plan, changes the plan, and watches out for the factors which will change the plan for the betterment of all the stakeholders. Become more proactive to execute the project.

An important aspect of an agile approach is the phenomenal importance it gives to an individual. Therefore, people, their skills, motivation, and communication are crucial ingredients of a successful agile project. From command and control to servant leadership. Develop people and empower people.

Let us look into our new roles and responsibilities of an **"Agile project manager"**

1. The project manager is a facilitator and a better leader than a Manager.
2. Project manager becomes a coach and mentor for the project team.
3. The project manager is an individual contributor role and we value-add in every possible way.
4. Demonstrate more leadership abilities and walk the talk.
5. Be a Change agent and chaos controller.
6. Influence the team members and lead

7. A data analyst for the team or the data scientist who understands various changing scenarios and shares the information with the right people in meaningful decision making.
8. Analyzing various "what if" scenarios and helps the team with the output
9. Effective stakeholder management. Update information to all the executive team members, external customers or dependent project team members
10. Build trust and relationship with all others so that he/she can help in a crisis.
11. Effective collaboration among the stakeholders. Mentor and coach the team to improve the same.
12. Resolve execution challenges in all possible ways, and remove organizational impediments.
13. Help the team to see the big picture.
14. Facilitate workshops, discussions, conflict resolution, various meetings, retrospective meetings, etc. to help the team.
15. Empower the team, to build a culture of trust. Look for an opportunity to improve the team performance by removing organizational impediments (Infrastructure, policies, tools etc.).
16. Help the team to come out from a heavyweight process to a lightweight process and achieve the results.
17. Project Risk management and minimize any disruptions.
18. Help the team by playing the role of Scrum of Scrum masters to update the executive team members.
19. Help the team by playing the role of a Program Manager for multiple Scrum teams
20. Become a servant leader with excellent service.
21. Taking care of the organizational process compliance and audit (Timesheet, metrics and measurement, financial status, procurement, recruitment, training, PMO updates, other activities)
22. Taking care of the commercial and legal obligation, licensing, certifications etc.
23. Coach the team for the organizational transformation.

As a project manager, we need to learn how to lead in an environment with the empowered teams.

As a project manager, we need to learn by knowing when to lead, when to help, and when letting the team run on its own.

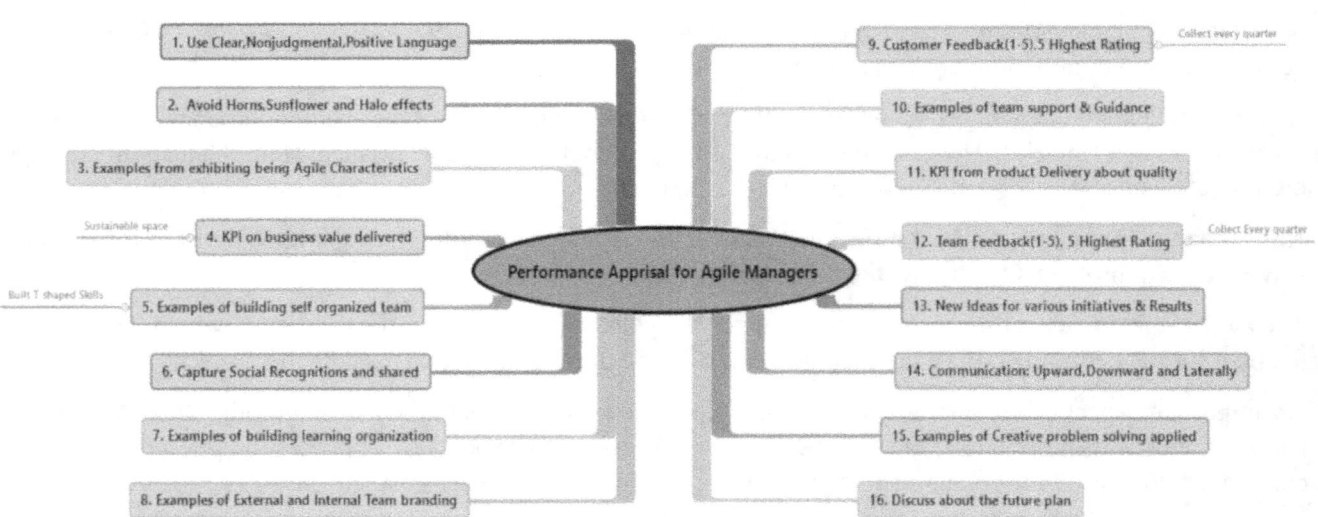

In the classic paradigm, control is very important for the project manager and in order to have control, we need a solid plan—thus the need to maintain an up-to-date plan. In the agile project, we spend more energy on information absorption and analysis.

An agile project manager does more shepherding and less directing.

By doing so I (Project Manager) becomes a valuable team member in the agile world.

What actions are you going to take from this lesson?

1. _____

2. _____

3. _____

Thinking Question:

Are you doing enough to train the project managers?

2.16 How to transform command and control to a servant leadership style?

"You don't need a title to be a leader. "

—Mark Sanborn

Why this topic?

How do we renovate ourselves from a tyranny type traditional leader to servant leaders?

Command and Control is a management style based on a strict hierarchy of authority. Managers have a specific authority to issue commands. Commands must be followed, or discipline is applied.

Mostly used in military work, in a knowledge-driven organization command-and-control techniques are considered counterproductive (e.g., a barrier to creativity).

Many people will not agree that today's leaders are slowly becoming servant leaders compared to positional leaders.

There are some core personality and thinking style that needs to be changed to successfully execute this role.

Robert Greenleaf, the man who coined the phrase servant leadership, defines it this way.

The servant-leader is a servant first. . . . It begins with the natural feeling that one wants to serve, to serve first. Then conscious choice brings one to aspire to lead. He or she is sharply different from the person who is a leader first, perhaps because of the need to assuage an unusual power drive or to acquire material possessions. For such it will be a later choice to serve after leadership is established. The leader-first and the servant-first are two extreme types. Between them, there are shadings and blends that are part of the infinite variety of human nature.

The difference manifests itself in the care taken by the servant-first to make sure that other people's highest priority needs are being served.

The best test, and the most difficult to administer is:

Do those served to grow as persons?

Do they, while being served, become healthier, wiser, freer, more autonomous, more likely themselves to become servants?

And, what is the effect on the least privileged in the society; will they benefit, or, at least, will they not be further deprived?

When we focus on others, we tend to change our thought process. We want to influence our customers, teams, even though they may not directly reporting to us, but leaders provide services to them.

We become servant leaders, how do we think now?

- **Think about all the team members**
- **Think about a win-win situation for all**

- **Think about other benefits**
- **Build trust**
- **Reduce selfishness gradually**

Greenleaf (1977) says others will only follow leaders who are proven and trusted servants.

Greenleaf goes further to see the leader as essentially not involving the overt use of power at all. Servant leadership, as he calls it, involves putting the needs of those who are being led first. He focuses on higher needs, resulting in mature and holistic development, involving autonomy, freedom, wisdom and increased focus on service. The core characteristics of the leader, then, include listening, empathy, healing, awareness, conceptualization, foresight and the building of a community. In turn, such a leadership looks to make a difference within the institution or project and beyond the group in terms of affecting those in society with the least resources.

Key characteristics

- **Place service before self-interest**
- **Listen first to express confidence in others**
- **Inspire trust by being trustworthy**
- **Focus on what is feasible to accomplish**
- **Lend a hand.**
- **Provide emotional healing**

Servant leaders are committed to serving others rather than achieving their own goals. Aspects of servant leadership include placing service before self-interest, listening to others, inspiring trust by being trustworthy, focusing on what is feasible to accomplish, lending a hand and emotional healing.

In all the sessions while discussing with the leaders, I have highlighted all these points. I personally implement all these in my personal life.

What actions are you going to take from this lesson?

1. _____

2. _____

3. _____

Thinking Question:

Are you doing enough to help the leaders to conform the Servant leadership style and let pass of the heritage leadership style?

2.17 Why do we need to give vaccinations to the team?

The right raw materials can...double or triple the protective power of the immune system,

—*Joel Fuhrman*

Why this topic?

During our agile assessment, we realize that many teams require treatment for their growth!! That is how this topic came to my notice, as an organization is a living organism, it demands all the organism to live healthily.

The **immune system** is a host defense system comprising many biological structures and processes within an organism that protects against disease.

To function properly, an **immune system** must **detect** a wide variety of **agents**, known as **pathogens**, from viruses to parasitic worms, and distinguish them from the organism's healthy tissue.

The immune system is a system, <u>not a single entity</u>. To function well, it requires **balance** and **harmony**.

The amazing thing about the immune system is that it's **constantly adapting and learning** so that the body can fight against bacteria or viruses that change over time.

Same applies to any Performing team. They are at the performing stage because they balance and harmony within the team. Team members can defend themselves from external negative influence and disturbance.

The best team has built a very good defensive system over a period of any external changes.

The team will not take any changes and they will resist until they find a bigger benefit for the team.

Change agents have to influence the team members on the bigger benefit team will get with the new changes. With many workshops, dialogue, open space discussions this defending mechanism can be penetrated and get the buy-in from the team. Else we are wasting lots of energy fighting with the Team Immune system.

As a coach, we need to understand the team immune system.

How can we help this immune system to be the same with new changes?

There are many organizational changes are happening, which team has to adopt and adapt. The team can't be rigid with old process and practices. It always needs changes with changes environment where an organization is operating, same as a human body.

The purpose of vaccinations is to introduce a pathogen (i.e. virus, bacteria, etc.) to the immune system so that a person can develop immunity to the pathogen without having to experience the disease.

For the team also we need to give vaccinations to improve the team immune system.

As a Coach, we need to inspect the team immune system and provide require vaccination based on the situation.

Sometimes performing team also declines in their performance due to internal conflict.

When your immune system doesn't work the way it should, it is called an immune system disorder.

In **Team immune system**, such disorder, also visible.

Immune Deficiency Diseases:

An immune deficiency disease is when the immune system is missing one or more of its parts, and it reacts too slowly to a threat.

Autoimmune disease:

When an intruder invades your body—like a cold virus or bacteria on a thorn that pricks your skin—your immune system protects you. It tries to identify, kill and eliminate the invaders that might hurt you.

But sometimes problems with your immune system cause it to mistake your body's own healthy cells as invaders and then repeatedly attacks them. This is called an autoimmune disease. In autoimmune diseases, the immune system turns against parts of the body it is designed to protect

Do you see more often within a team? Same performing team got affected by the team members itself or because of competency mismatch, new conflicts arise.

How can Leader ensure to boost Team Immune System?

- **Good Alignment among team members**
- **Team members can give all types of feedback to each other**
- **Trust each other**
- **Committed and fulfill the promise**
- **Learning mindset**
- **Collaborate, Communicate and Care**

If we have all these automatically implemented, The Team Immune system will improve.

What actions are you going to take from this lesson?

1. _____

2. _____

3. _____

Thinking Question:

Are you doing enough to improve the immune system of the team?

2.18 Key Takeaways

All these steps will strengthen the organizational leadership capability which means in the **Pancha Bhoota Model**, the **Air** element will become more robust.

Here are the key points to remember from this chapter:

- Features for which the people follow the leaders, and the Characteristics of outstanding leaders
- It is significant to change the command-and-control leadership style to a Servant leadership style based on the situation
- Project managers need to revive themselves in the agile world through their functional skills and soft skills
- Every team member needs to master the influencing skills in today's world without any excuse
- Manifesto of leadership in a new era
- Manager and leadership characteristics to recognize for all of us.
- Self-organized team characteristics
- Strong agile team behaviors, and How to improve
- Characteristics of the Charismatic leader's, and what can we pick up from them?
- Servant leadership style, and how to build up?
- Understanding masculine and feminine characteristics
- The agile leader styles, and how to establish them?
- Aspects to study while designing a leadership workshop
- Increasing our value at work, Think about and come up with an action plan

In the next chapter, we will consider into the challenges of setting up a high-performance team. By knowing this we will strengthen the **Fire** element of the **Pancha Bhoota Model**.

3 Enablement of High Performance Teams

3.1 Introduction:

This chapter will highlight the virtues of high-performance teams and how coaches can take care of the numerous elements to keep the high level of performance in a team. All these are my views, and there are many alternative factors, I feel these issues once we fix, will allow building a high-performance teams. In the **Panch Bhoota Model,** this element is **Fire.** How to reinforce the **Fire** element?

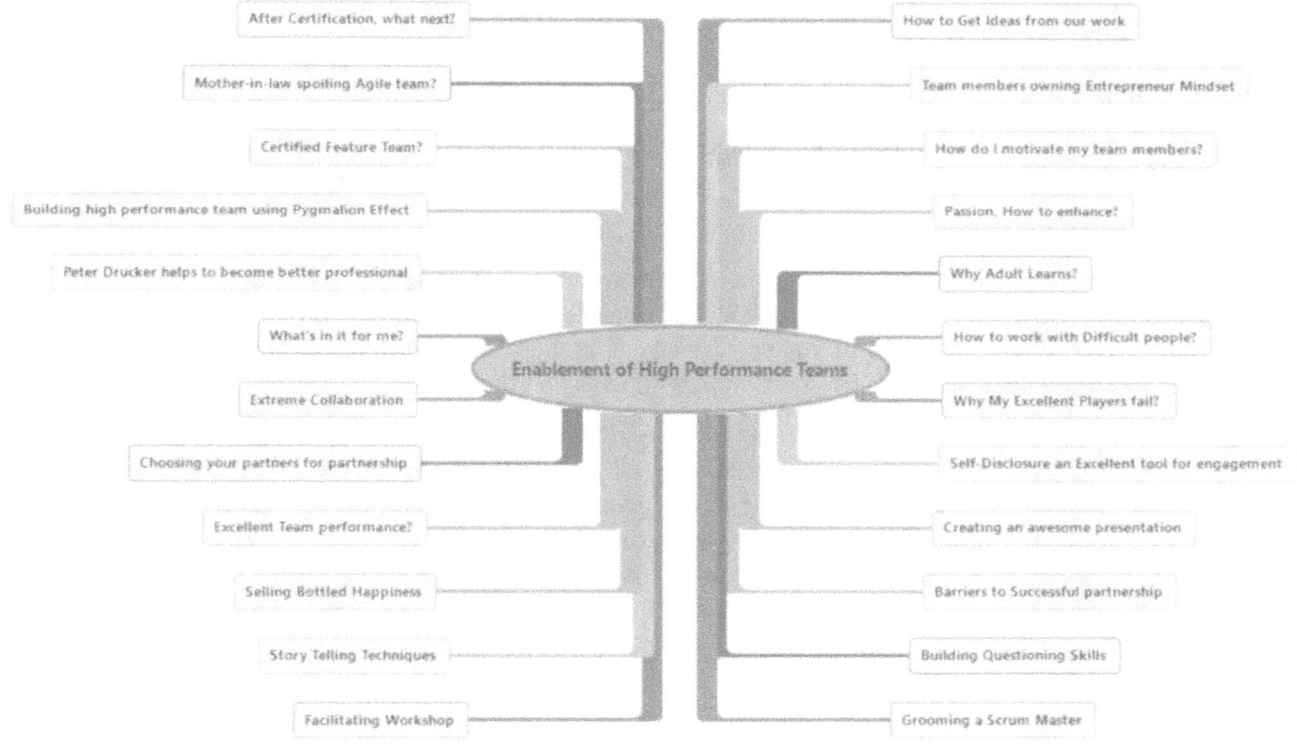

3.2 How to Get Ideas from our work?

> *"Innovation comes from saying NO to 1,000 things."*
>
> —*Steve Jobs*

Why this topic?

We are functioning in a VUCA (Volatile, Uncertain, Complex and Ambiguous) world, where our survival is because of new ideas we are driving and generating value. We desire to produce many such talented individuals as a team member where they are generating ideas for the team.

Aristotle's dictum (and in harmony with his thinking) is that **people also learn by *reflecting* on what they're doing.**

In other words, part of the task is to take stock of your progress as an Idea Hunter regularly.

This could be as simple as asking yourself questions at the end of the week

1. What's my daily "educational process"?
2. Did I read a newspaper in the past few days?
3. Did I take part in any stimulating conversations?
4. What have I learned this week?
5. Did I make connections between my personal experiences and my projects?
6. Did I run any ideas by other people?

Aristotle said, **"What we have to learn to do, we learn by doing."**

We practice idea work in the same general sense that a physician practices medicine—by doing it.

We pick up the habits of the Hunt by digging for ideas consciously and systematically.

Training yourself to notice things is another part of the observational platform. In line with Aristotle's dictum related earlier ("What we have to learn to do, we learn by doing"), **the best advice is to be a more deliberate observer, wherever you find yourself.**

Paying attention to your own experiences as a customer or client is a good place to start.

When you walk into a coffee shop, do the baristas look happy or harried?

What can you learn about an establishment from the people who patronize it—how they are dressed or who they are with?

Do you have any trouble getting the information you need as a customer?

The U.S. Army uses an observational method with its Center for Army. The center's observation teams—typically deployed with the first troops in an operation—look for problems and threats as well as opportunities. Just as important, they record what they see on the spot. Analysts at the center's headquarters in Fort Leavenworth, Kansas, then interpret the data in close conversation with teams on the ground.

They issue warnings and offer guidance to field units through the center's website, often within hours, and post new lessons a few days later. Such was the flow of observation during the wars in the former Yugoslavia during 1990 when one of the first teams discovered that snow-covered roads were likely to have hidden mines. **Speedy recording and sharing of the information were essential**. As one military official told Harvard University's David Garvin, "It would be a shame if a soldier in one battalion made the same mistake tomorrow that was made in a different battalion today."

> *"The heart and soul of the company is creativity and innovation."*
>
> —*Bob Iger*

The most of the great companies where employees produce great ideas, one habit which distinguishing them is

- **Writing down the views and comments**
- **Maintaining them in an easily available place**

That's partly because most of us do not have photographic memories, but also because ideas tend to arrive in bits and pieces that need to be put together over time. And it's easy to forget a fragment that standing alone seems unimportant.

Edison and his team knew there were two products of work: **what you make and what you learn in the process. And your learning is more diverse if you're working on different products for different sectors and industries.**

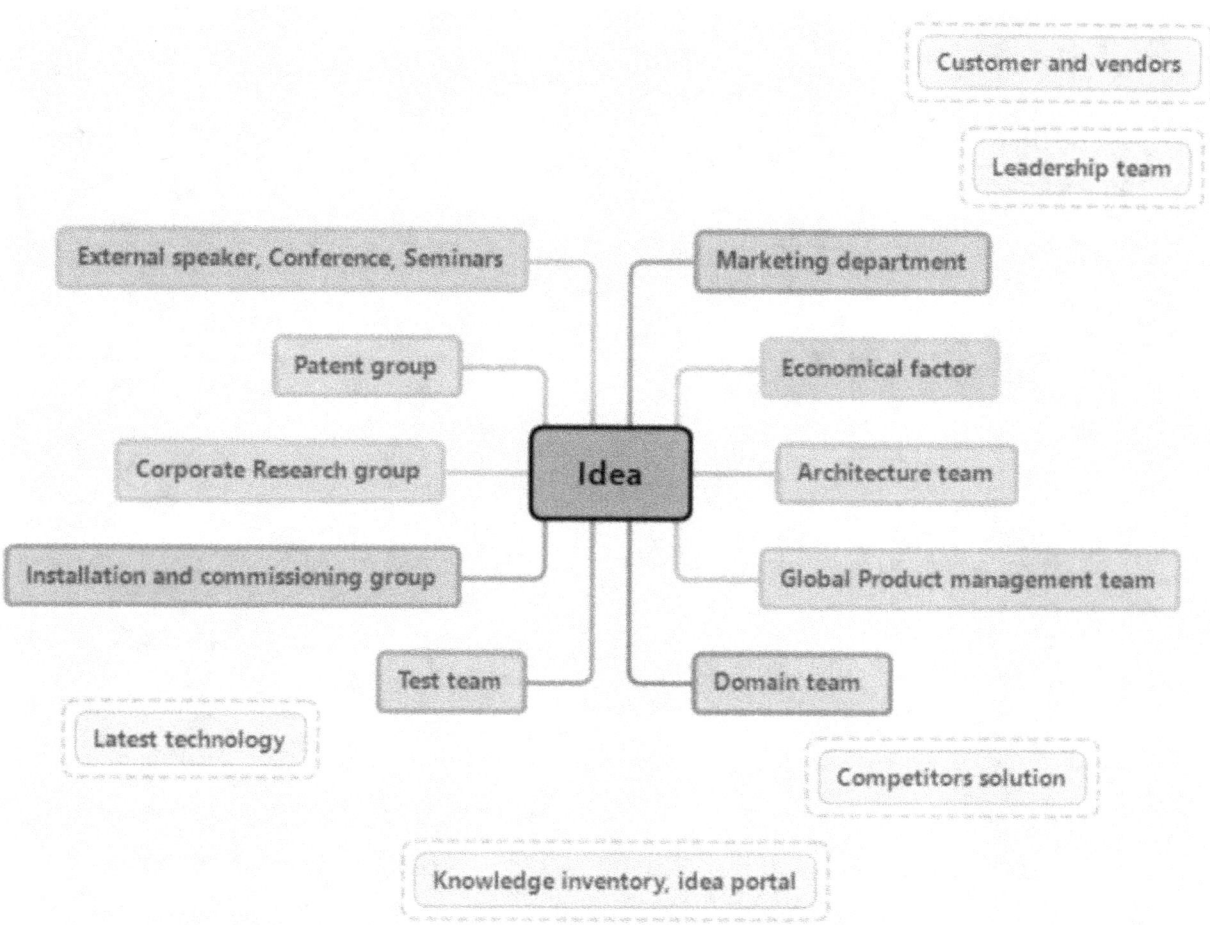

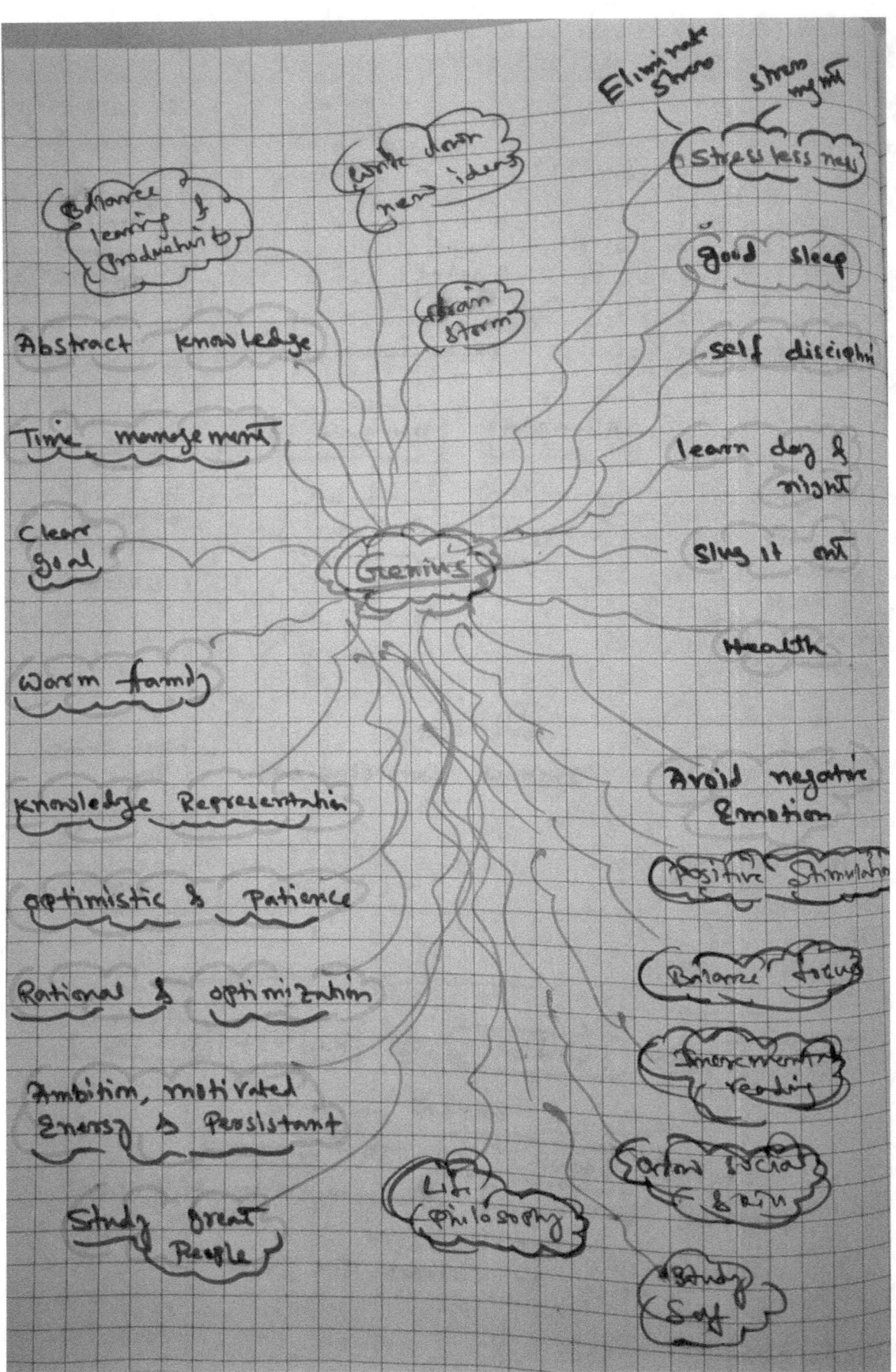

Learning from Edison

Edison's solution was simple

1. He would first work very hard on the problem he was trying to tackle.
2. He would spend many hours looking at it from all different angles, mulling over a wide variety of bizarre and wonderful solutions to his problem.
3. He would read broadly on the topic and talk to anyone who might have some useful input. When he began to feel sleepy, still with all his reading and thoughts on the matter fresh in his mind, it was then that he used to settle down, ball bearings in hand for his pre-planned nap.
4. From the brain's perspective, the reason this strategy was so effective was that he was awakened just after he had dipped into the hypnogogic state, which happens to occur simultaneously with the brain losing control of the hand muscles, sending the metal balls crashing to the floor with a bang.

The problem that Edison quickly observed during his sorties into the creative phase of early sleep was as follows: if he nodded off just for a few minutes, he would often wake up with an innovative idea.

Let us apply all these thoughts and see if we can become an Idea generating machine. It worked for most of the teams with whom I have been working. They had produced world-class products with many awesome features.

"If at first, the idea is not absurd, then there is no hope for it."

—Albert Einstein

What actions are you going to take from this lesson?

1. _____
2. _____
3. _____

Thinking Question:

Are you doing enough to generate ideas at your work and encouraging others to achieve the same?

3.3 How to create an Entrepreneurial Mindset among team members?

"I'm convinced that about half of what separates the successful entrepreneurs from the non-successful ones is pure perseverance."

— Steve Jobs

Why this topic?

How can we build such a team having team members where every individual is like an Entrepreneur? Where they are committed, they own everything, they are motivated to contribute something bigger, better, and they explore to learn more about themselves, and about the organization.

Below factors are the key mindset of most of the entrepreneurs which all the team members should acquire over a period

The Organization will be able to face any challenge when we have below mindset with most of the employees. There is an urgent need about the below mindset if the organization in today's world all the employees have to think like an entrepreneur and leaders have to run his/her own business.

Below are a few characters which are very important in today's world to survive and run the organization. Below mindset changes are very crucial for an organization or team.

1. **Desire and willingness to take the initiative**: All employees should always be ready to jump at the opportunity. They should be willing to step forward and build businesses based on their creative ideas.

2. **Preference for moderate risk**. The path is full of risk, willingness to take the calculated risk is effective. The goal may appear to be high—even impossible—from others' perspective, but team members should typically have to think through the situation and believe that their goals are reasonable and attainable.

3. **Confidence** in their ability to succeed. Team members should have typically had an <u>abundance of confidence</u> in their ability to succeed, and they tend to be <u>optimistic about their chances for business success</u>. Team members might face many barriers when starting and running their assignments, and a healthy dose of optimism can be an important component in their ultimate success.

4. **Self-reliance.** Team members *should not shy away* from the responsibility of making their businesses succeed.

5. **Perseverance**. Even when things don't work out as they planned, team members should not give up. They simply <u>keep trying</u>. Real entrepreneurs follow the advice contained in the Japanese proverb, "Fall seven times; stand up eight."

6. **The desire for immediate feedback**. Team members should know how they are doing and are constantly looking for reinforcement. Tricia Fox, the founder of Fox Day Schools, Inc., claims, <u>"I like being independent and successful. Nothing gives you feedback like your own business."</u>

7. **High level of energy.** Entrepreneurs are highly enthusiastic than the normal person. That energy may be a critical factor given an incredible effort required to launch a start-up company. Long hours—often 60 to 80 hours a week—and hard work are the rule rather than the exception. Building a successful business requires a great deal of stamina.

8. **Competitiveness**. Team members should tend to exhibit competitive behavior, often early in life. They enjoy competitive games and sports and always want to keep the score!

9. **Future orientation**. Team members tend to dream big and then formulate plans to transform those dreams into reality. They have a well-defined sense of searching for opportunities. They look ahead and are less concerned with what they accomplished yesterday than what they can do tomorrow. Ever vigilant for new business opportunities, entrepreneurs observe the same events other people do, but they see something different.

10. **Skill at organizing**. Managers and leaders should know how to put the right people and resources together to accomplish a task. Effectively combining people and jobs enables entrepreneurs to bring their visions to reality.

11. **Value of achievement over money**. The achievement should be the primary motivating force behind team members; money is simply a way of "keeping score" of accomplishments—a symbol of achievement. "Money is not the driving motive of most entrepreneurs," says Nick Grouf, founder of a high-tech company. "It's just a very nice by-product of the process."

12. **A high degree of commitment.** Team members should often immerse themselves completely in their businesses. <u>"The commitment of the team has to do is tremendous; team members usually should put everything on the line,"</u> That commitment helps overcome business-threatening mistakes, obstacles, and pessimism from naysayers.

13. **Tolerance for ambiguity.** Team members should have a high tolerance for ambiguity, ever-changing situations—the environment in which they most often operate. <u>This ability to handle uncertainty is critical</u> because managers and leaders constantly make decisions using new, sometimes conflicting, information gleaned from a variety of unfamiliar sources.

14. **Flexibility**. Team members should have the ability to adapt to the changing demands of their customers and their businesses. In this rapidly changing world economy, rigidity often leads to failure. As a society, its people and their tastes change, team members also must be willing to adapt their businesses to meet those changes. Successful teams are willing to allow their business models to evolve as market conditions warrant.

15. **Tenacity**. Obstacles, obstructions, and defeat typically do not dissuade team members from doggedly pursuing their visions. Successful team members have the willpower to conquer the barriers that stand in the way of their success.

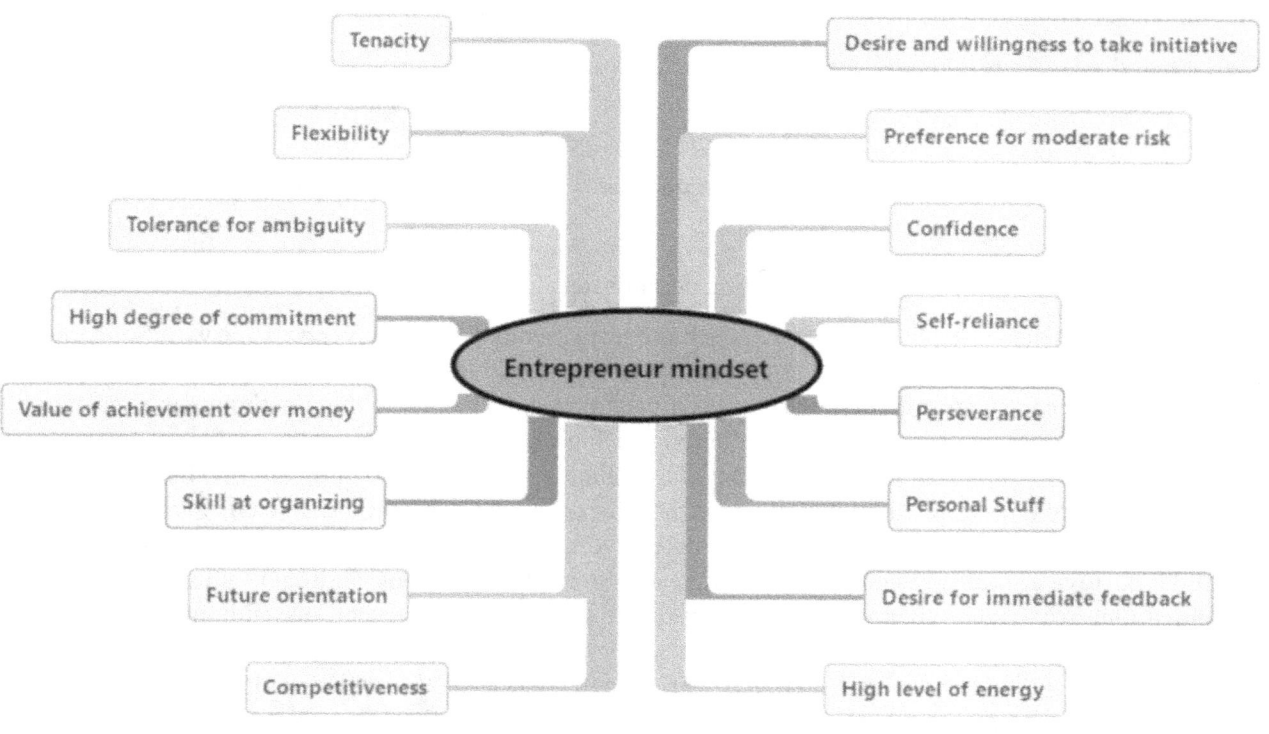

"Entrepreneurship is living a few years of your life like most people won't, so you can spend the rest of your life like most people can't."

—*Student of Warren G. Tracy*

What actions are you going to take from this lesson?

1. _____

2. _____

3. _____

Thinking Question:

Are you doing enough to provoke people to become entrepreneurs or Intrapreneurs?

3.4 Knowing the people: How to work with difficult people?

"When dealing with people, remember you are not dealing with creatures of logic, but with creatures of emotion, creatures bristling with prejudice, and motivated by pride and vanity."

—*Dale Carnegie*

Why this topic?

How to effectively connect with people? We need to follow certain practices. What is the specialty of difficult people? Why are they tough to deal with? Once someone spends a good amount of time within a certain domain, why they become headstrong, high attitude, high ego, and less tolerance level? How to get along with them?

Different people have differing personalities. A character largely determines the way individuals act. A character is a product of genetics and upbringing.

How can we get along with the people by following certain practices?

I have worked in various domains with heavyweight domain experts I have learned a couple of observations which helped me to work with these heavyweight people. They are really good in their area of inspiration or domain.

"Seek the best in everyone that you meet. Seek the worst when dealing with yourself."

—**Sasha Azevedo**

How to work with this difficult person? By doing certain tricks!

1. **Help them:** whenever the time comes, to help these team members in whatever possible way. Soon they will become your buddy. Look for all the opportunity to help them, service mindset. Think of all the probable ways how you can support them to make their life simpler. Sincerely help them without any expectation.

2. **No-Fault Finding**: let us not focus on the individual fault rather, "let us solve the problem," "improve the situation together" mindset. It will help to build the relationship. When we find fault in others, they become defensive and the more we do this it changes their behavior. They become suspicious and generalize that all people are here to find fault. They repeat defensive behaviors when someone approaches them. Let us build a positive culture and energy by helping each other. Not by finding fault, but by experimenting with and learning from each other's mistake. Appreciate the person who is doing the fault, and because of the initiative, they are taking we have come to know about the fault. So no fault finding. Let us forgive more and understand intending to help others. Give constructive feedback to others which help them in their growth.

3. **Unproductive But smart people:** They pretend a lot, fight a lot, fake a lot, we need to have the patience to deal with them. Help them to produce what is expected from them, they will soon come to the original human behavior. Spend more time with them and understand their genuine concern and support wherever possible. They will become cooperative and productive.

4. **Unproductive But Busy Person:** They would love to take more challenges, willingness to contribute more, but as they are over-committed, the output is less. As a result of that, they will be panic, irritated and will not cooperate properly. We need to analyze such a person and assess their capacity vs. commitment. Help them to plan and organize. They will become your pal. It is not their fault to become unproductive, but they want to do so much, there is not so much to do with the current bandwidth so that mostly clutter.

5. **Working with subject matter experts:** We have to give them their due recognition wherever it is due, we have to acknowledge and appreciate their talent, and praise them for their dedication to that subject. They will get along with you. Whenever they need improvement, carefully bring it to their notice so that it becomes a win-win point to discuss. Ask for their help whenever and wherever applicable. Let us not try to show smartness to them by pretending as subject matter experts where we already have experts. Take their help and recognize them.

6. **Arguing and losing temper with team members:** Most of the time in situations where we are working with the high attitude, team members, there is a possibility of an emotional outburst may vent. Avoid involving in such discussions. Do not fight back, as the output will be zero. Be friendly with them, but do not run away. Discuss and resolve the issue at that place only. Share your distressed emotion skillfully and express and discuss for common understanding. Face the conflict and constructively resolve it.

7. **Pygmalion effect:** let us help people by expecting more from them, encouraging them, they are great and they can do more, contribute more. Genuinely expect more from them. Do not underestimate them or tell them.

8. **Modulate your tune:** Neither increase nor decrease your volume too much. Do not allow others also to do the same. The sound has an effect on the ambiance! Manage it professionally. Listen from your heart, do not pretend you are listening, it irritates opponents if they realize it. Connect with the person from the heart. Find out what is the best way we can connect with that person. There is some cohesion between you and the person, use those common factors to influence that person.

9. Understand the underlying **prerequisite** of these team members, based on that need, fulfill that need, be it recognition, appreciation, and support whatever it is. Then we will be able to connect with the team members, whatever may be their ego is. The connection will be at a much deeper level.

10. Let us maximize the **commonality** between the team members, then the **connections** will be much deeper. Let us discover what is the common connection between us (Team member A vs. me or Team member B vs. me) let us all swing in the same direction. Let us all be like a SINE wave. How can we do that? We have to undertake a good amount of homework about each team member.

11. Let us analyze and understand every team member, understand their behavior, intention and truly connect with them to get their support. Let us understand what situation all these team members get annoyed, frustrated and shout, etc. Let us observe all the negative emotional disbursement situation, with the proper analysis, help them and become the best buddy to them.

12. Change is always tough, team members always want to be in their comfort zone, including me. Until and unless I see a bigger benefit and a sure path, I will not change. Same with most of us, we become annoyed and frustrated whenever the change is big, and the output is not immediate. When we expect others to change fast without part of the game, they feel treated badly and they resist the changes. Let us change first before I expect some changes in other, then it will be much easier to influence others.

13. Let us create an ambiance, where people **open up**, more and more and in such a situation, we can be closer to that person. It is our art how can we can reach that open up the situation for a long time to effectively connect with that person so that connection is becoming real and bonding will be permanent.

14. Influence team members for a common set of **purposes**. Agreement with a purpose. There is a reason to be together. It will energize both the party for a **bigger vision** and they will be part of our journey easily. Emphasize the **bigger picture**.

Buddha said, "You will not be punished for your anger, you will be punished by your anger. "

Take a deep breath and learn to control your emotion. It helps in the relationship. Observe your emotional pattern and control when it is going beyond your influence. Always smile, it creates positive energy within the work environment. Practice courtesy, it is contagious and helps to build the good relationship. Let us build a climate of trust where everyone feels like contributing and safe. People will be free to open up and collaborate for a bigger mission.

"Be careful in dealing with a man who cares nothing for comfort or promotion, but is simply determined to do what he believes to be right. He is a dangerous uncomfortable enemy, because his body, which you can always conquer, gives you little purchase upon his soul"

—Gilbert Murray

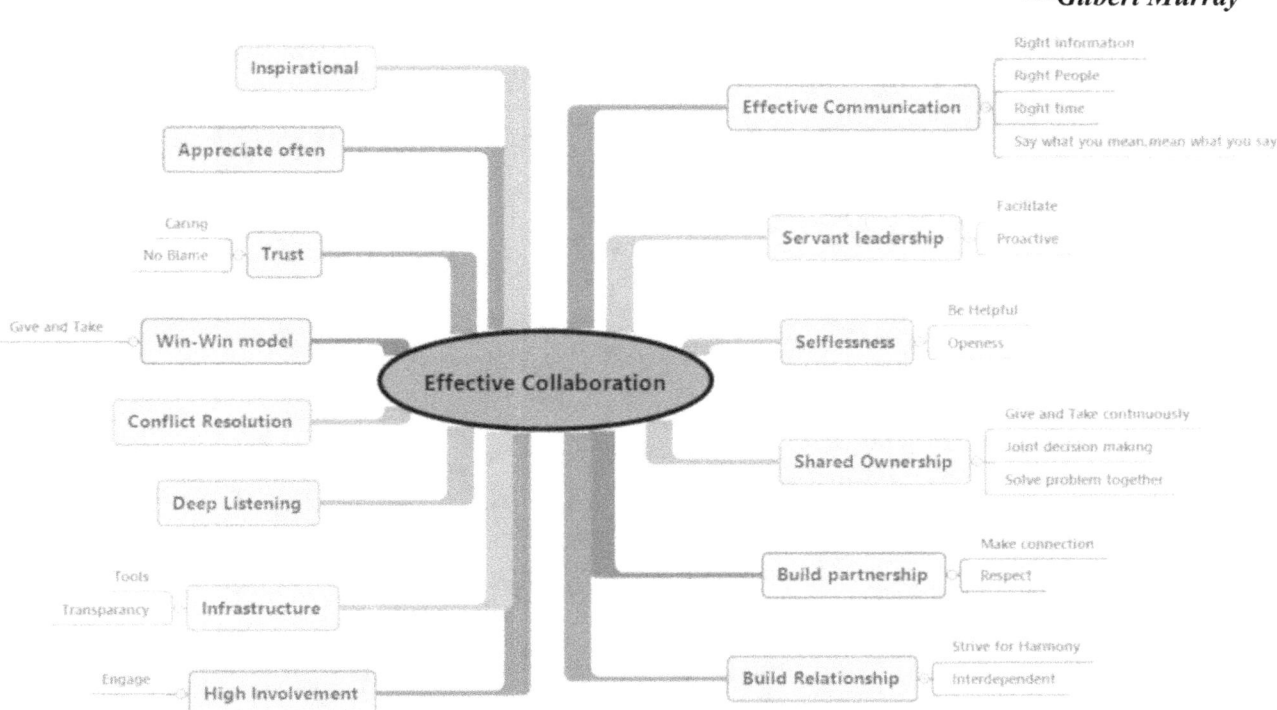

"Everybody has a hot button. Who is pushing yours? While you probably cannot control that person, you CAN control the way you react to them."

—Unknown

What actions are you going to take from this lesson?

1. _____

2. _____

3. _____

Thinking Question:

Are you doing enough to build knowledge to work with diverse types of people so that you can support the team members to establish their collaboration skills?

3.5 How do adults learn? How to coach them?

"The wisest mind has something yet to learn "

—George Santayana

Why this topic?

There are always fresh roles, different skills, and the new ways of working. Everything is constantly changing. As a result of that, we have many older and elder team members are part of the re-skilling program. I had to think about them before we start the curriculum. Why will they learn and how can we establish their journey smooth?

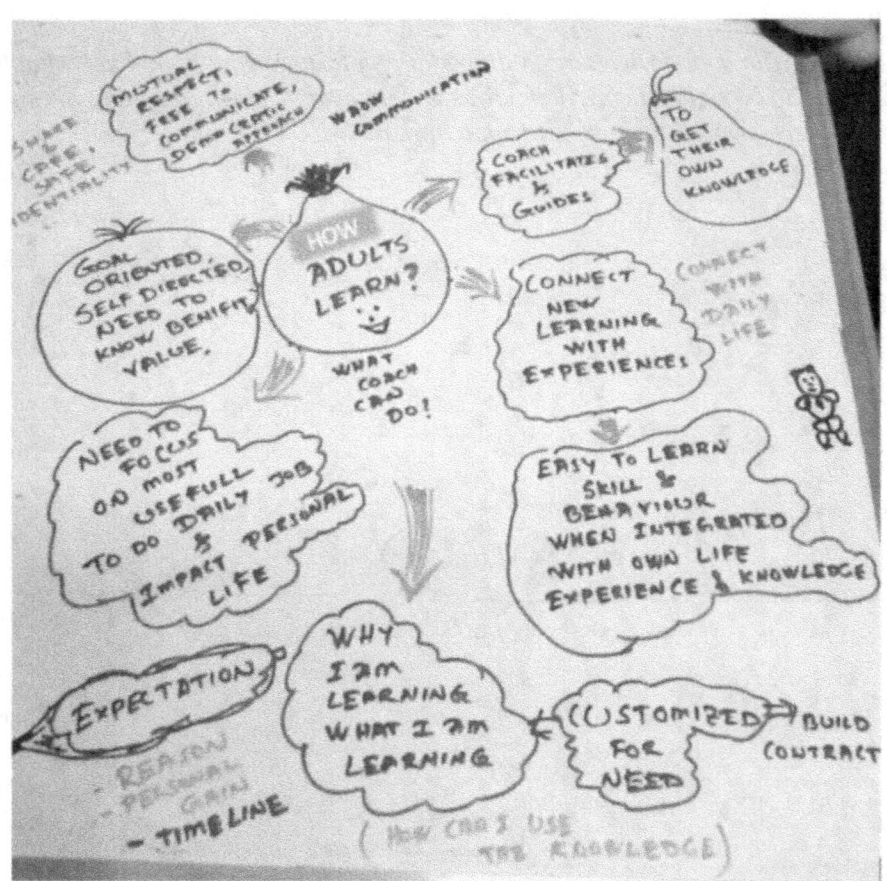

What do you want to take away from this mind map in your current assignment?

"Anyone who keeps learning stays young."

—*Henry Ford*

What actions are you going to take from this lesson?

1. _____

2. _____

3. _____

Thinking Question:

Are you doing enough to inspire people who need to up skill themselves?

3.6 Developing Passion for our work?

Passion is one great force that unleashes creativity, because if you're passionate about something, then you're more willing to take risks. Yo-Yo Ma

Why this topic?

Agile Transformation is all about excellent people developing an awesome solution for the end users, how to the produce fires-in-the-belly for the team members to find such a level of delivery commitment?

Amy Wrzesniewski, a professor of organizational behavior at Yale University, has made a career studying **how people think about their work.**

Her breakthrough paper, published in the Journal of Research in Personality while she was still a graduate student, explores the distinction between **a job, a career, and a calling.**

A job, in Wrzesniewski's formulation, **is a way to pay the bills**, a career is a path toward increasingly better work, and **a calling is a work that's an important part of your life and a vital part of your identity.**

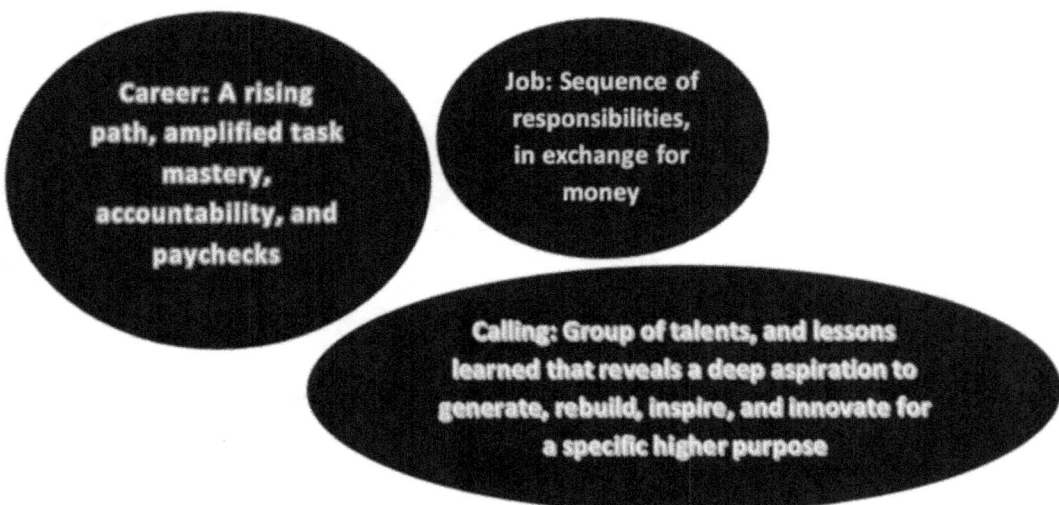

On reflection, that makes sense. **If you have many years' of experience, then you've had time to get better at what you do and develop a feeling of efficacy.** It also gives you time to develop **strong relationships with your coworkers and to see many examples of your work benefiting others**. What's important here, however, is that this explanation, though reasonable, contradicts the passion hypothesis, which instead emphasizes the immediate **happiness that comes from matching your job to a true passion**.

ERICSSON'S 10,000-HOUR RULE

It's tempting to look at truly exceptional achievers–such as Olympic athletes and celebrated musicians–and conclude that they must have been born with a unique gift for what they do.

According to influential research by psychologist Anders Ericsson, however, the path to expertise is available to anyone who's prepared to put the necessary levels of practice.

How much? Studies of elite musicians, athletes, and chess players suggest at least 10,000 hours of practice spread over a period of more than ten years. What's more, not just any kind of practice will do.

Ericsson says it needs to be what he calls **'deliberate practice',** in which you don't just repeat what you know but instead *constantly seek to stretch yourself.*

This inevitably involves forensic self-criticism, repeated failure and a dogged ability to keep dusting yourself down and trying again – a process that's not particularly enjoyable and quite distinct from leisurely practice.

Although Ericsson's perspective argues against the idea of innate gifts, his concept of deliberate practice does, of course, require **a rare mix of motivation, good health, and opportunity.**

Biographies of musical geniuses like Mozart and Michael Jackson nearly always reveal that they started relentless practice from an early age.

Two of the four manifesto items and five of the 12 principles are people oriented!

This emphasizes that applying agile methods is more than simply having a different way of developing software;

The human element is just as important, as is delivering value to the customer rather than merely following a prescriptive development or management process.

Agile transformation is all about **culture** and **people**.

Work closely with your people and invest in them.

> *"Follow your passion, be prepared to work hard and sacrifice, and, above all, don't let anyone limit your dreams."*
>
> —*Donovan Bailey*

What actions are you going to take from this lesson?

1. _____

2. _____

3. _____

Thinking Question:

Are you doing enough to inspire people to create a life with purpose and work for their passion?

3.7 How do I motivate my team members?

> *You can motivate by fear, and you can motivate by reward. But both those methods are only temporary. The only lasting thing is self-motivation.*
>
> —**Homer Rice**

Why this Topic?

The agile manifesto says,

"Build projects around motivated individuals"

How to get the motivated individuals?

"You have power over your mind - not outside events. Realize this, and you will find strength."- Marcus Aurelius

Motivation is one of the most important elements in coaching. Every coach needs to develop mastery skill in Motivation.

	Maslow	Daniel Pink	Alderfer	Herzberg	Berne's Six Hungers	McClelland
Higher Order Needs	Self Actualization	Purpose			Recognition hunger	Achievement
		Autonomy	Growth	Satisfier Factors	Time structure hunger	
	Esteem	Mastery			Incident hunger	Power
Lower Order Needs	Social		Relatedness		Stimulus hunger	
				Hygiene Factor		
	Safety		Existence		Contact hunger	Affiliation
	Physiological				Sexual hunger	

This table is a snapshot of most of the famous motivational theories.

Chip Conley, the founder of the Joie de Vivre hotel chain and Head of Hospitality at Airbnb, used the Hierarchy of Needs pyramid to transform his business.

Similar stuff we have observed with one of the best team managers where she has helped her employees understand the meaning of their roles during a staff retreat…they were able to realize the significance of their job to the company and to the people they were facilitating. By showing them the importance of their roles, the team was able to feel they are appreciated and inspired to work harder.

We all have all these drivers, and if we first satisfy lower order needs and focus to strengthen the higher order needs, the employees will become self-driven. As a leader how can we implement the below fourteen points?

1. How can we provide **sensory, intellectual and emotional** stimulation?
2. How can we provide team member **status to be acknowledged** and also **belonging** to something?
3. How can we create a strong, motivating **work environment** where high performance is the standard?
4. How can we create **a sense of connection and comfort**?
5. How can we create an **enjoyment of passion** about anything, from sports to supporting international causes?
6. How can we encourage people to perform better at work by having and communicating **high expectations** of them?
7. How can we **encourage Happiness**?
8. How can we **stop punishing** for failure?
9. How can we make a major effort to ensure that we offer **competitive wages** and other forms of compensation?
10. How can we grow team members by providing challenging new tasks which are attainable and according to their interest?
11. How can we give team members the freedom to find their own unique solution which is out of the box? Through which they can achieve personal and professional achievement?
12. How can we create a good support system and guidance for the team members so that they get inspired to do the assignment?

13. How can we rotate a team member's job so that they do not do the routine work, and let them **discover new interesting work**?
14. How can I set a stretch goal for the team members and recognize them on the achievement of the same in public?

Maslow arrived at **self-actualization** by observing two of his mentors who, he believed, were exceptional people. According to Maslow, they stood out from the run-of-the-mill crowd in that they were so wholly given over to a sense of mission and performed at such a high level that they appeared at a different stage of personal development than most people.

They were, in essence, the human development equivalent of Olympic athletes. Maslow set about the business of identifying more such people until he had amassed a dozen examples of self-actualizers. From these, he attempted to identify behaviors that were commonly or consistently associated with self-actualization.

He arrived at the following nine criterion behaviors

1. Experiences of flow states that represent total absorption and selflessness.
2. Make daily choices that move one toward growth and away from defensiveness.
3. Have knowledge of and the ability to listen to one's true self.
4. Honesty.
5. A deep sense of understanding of one's mission, destiny, and primary relationships.
6. An ongoing dedication to personal growth even if this means difficult practices and choices.
7. Setting up peak experiences, in part by understanding what to avoid in one's weaknesses and the lack of potential.
8. Engaging in self-reflection to better understand one's preferences, identity, behavioral leanings, bad habits, and other aspects of the self.
9. "Resacralization." That is, breathing a sense of wonder, sacredness, and true understanding of one's perception of the world, into one's relationships, and into one's actions.

People don't believe what you tell them. They rarely believe what you show them. They often believe what their friends tell them. They always believe what they tell themselves.

—**Seth Godin**

Some points from Southwest Airlines

Wikipedia mentions these three facts:

- Southwest Airlines (SWA) is one of the world's most profitable airlines, posting a profit for the 36th consecutive year in January 2009.

- SWA is the largest airline in the United States by the number of passengers carried domestically per year (as of December 31, 2007)
- SWA has carried more customers than any other U.S. airline since August 2006 for combined domestic and international passengers, according to the U.S. Department of Transportation's Bureau of Transportation Statistics.

SWA mission statement – on the SWA website – it reads

"To our employees: We are committed to providing our Employees a stable work environment with equal opportunity for learning and personal growth. Creativity and innovation are encouraged for improving the effectiveness of Southwest Airlines. Above all, Employees will be provided the same concern, respect, and caring attitude within the organization that they are expected to share externally with every Southwest Customer."

Zig Ziglar said that **"people often say motivation does not last. Well, neither does bathing. That's why we recommend it on a daily basis."**

What actions are you going to take from this lesson?

1. _____

2. _____

3. _____

Thinking Question:

Are you doing enough to build knowledge to motivate team members regardless of any condition, where they invariable contribute?

3.8 Why excellent individual Players find it difficult to perform as a team player?

> *"We must all hang together or most assuredly we shall all hang separately."*
>
> —*Ben Franklin*

Why this topic?

Looking for the answer when team members are not able to handle with the other team members, where they were performing very well as an individual contributor. What are those cases when they fail to work as a team member?

A **system** is a set of interacting or interdependent module **parts** forming a complex/intricate **whole**.

Every **system** is defined by its spatial and temporal **limits**, bounded and influenced by its **environment**, described by its structure and purpose and expressed by its functioning.

The term system may also refer to a set of rules that governs a structure or behavior.

Difficult to assess why one player behaves in a certain scenario where he was an excellent person most of the time.

Alternatively and usually in the context of complex social systems, the term is used to describe the set of rules that govern structure or behavior.

It is impossible to predict the **behavior of the whole system** with only knowledge about the **individual units**, because we also need to understand the **interactions or the relationships between the units**.

In other words, **the system is something altogether different from the sum of its parts.**

With any system, the whole is different from the sum of the individual parts.

By shifting the focus from the parts to the whole, we can better grasp the connections between the different elements.

For example: One cannot predict the quality of a couple based on knowledge about the individual partners from before they were married. Eccentric individuals can together form a well-functioning couple.

One of my roommates **who is considered** as an **excellent personality** as a friend when we were in college, is currently a totally dysfunctional couple. The behavior of couples at family environment **and individuals** when we were in collages time is governed by different rules.

Different Levels need different rules.

Though we may hire the best individual team members, but not necessarily as a whole team they will be able to operate in an excellent manner.

The other side of "the whole is different from the sum of the parts" is that "The part derives properties from the whole that it does not have by itself in any other context"

The only way to discover the qualities of the whole system as well as some of the most important extrinsic properties of the parts is by studying it as a whole, taking into account the relationships between the interacting units.

Because in healthy, flexible teams, the relationships and the roles of team members change according to the subject being discussed and one needs to observe the executive team while it is doing its job as an executive team, not while involved in an outward-bound or leisure activities.

When people come together for any purpose for a period of time, a relationship boundary develops around them which has a unifying force and makes those within it act to some degree as a unit, a whole.

As people are drawn to form relationships or join a group, they find they have to communicate, collaborate and share the goals and the must move, interact and change together because their outcomes become connected and they become dependent on each other.

One way to see this is to pay attention to how group behavior is often quite different from individual behavior.

Groups of good children can become harsh to a weaker child or to an animal.

A collection of physically weak students can exercise a sport, empower one another and become a winning team.

Alcoholics and addicts can discover the strength to change in a support group when alone, they are unable to give up their habits.

Individually one may be outshined as a player, but we need to find out how they can perform with others as a group player, and then we can label them as successful.

One may be a very good striker but if he is not able to get the pass from the other player of the team, the team will not be able to win. Good striker alone cannot win the match except a few exceptional penalty kicks!

It is **not a simple cause-and-effect relationship** when an individual behaves differently when they are with team vs when they perform alone, we have to think of them as a system.

Go beyond the **Frame**, enlarge the Frame, and we will discover to a different viewpoint.

Frame 1

Frame 2

There should not be any blame game when we find the good player is not up to the expectation, there could be multiple changes with many emergent feedbacks which influences an individual to perform differently.

Think big, Think systemic to understand the Whole-Part relationship.

"It is literally true that you can succeed best and quickest by helping others to succeed."

—Napoleon Hill

What actions are you going to take from this lesson?

1. _____

2. _____

3. _____

Thinking Question:

Am I doing enough exercise to work with the varieties of team members and describe the trade secret of the game to work as a team?

3.9 Self-Disclosure an Excellent tool for increased engagement in a Workshop

"Employee engagement is the art and science of engaging people in an authentic and recognized connections to strategy, roles, performance, organization, community, relationship, customers, development, energy, and happiness to leverage, sustain, and transform work into results."

—David Zinger,

Why this topic?

I have been taking workshops for a long time and would like to share one common trouble I have been suffering.

How to increase engagement from participants?

Sometimes I feel, Most of the participants are attending as an observer, it was a mostly one-way traffic!

I was wondering how I can engage and encourage more participation and make it a two-way traffic.

One of the techniques worked for me out of several is **"Constructive Self-Disclosure"**.

It has improved the effectiveness of the workshop output.

Self-Disclosure: As a general rule, **relationships grow stronger when people are willing to reveal more about themselves and their work experiences**.

It is a surprising but true fact of life that two people can work together for many years and never really get to know each other.

If we encourage employees to hide their true feelings result is often a weakening of the communication process.

Self-disclosure leads to a more open and supportive environment in the workplace.

Self-disclosure is the process of letting another person know what you think, feel, or want. It is one of the important ways you let yourself be known by others. Self-disclosure can improve interpersonal communication, resolve conflict, and strengthen interpersonal relationships.

Psychologists have long known that self-disclosure is one of the hallmarks of intimate relationships. Revealing our intentions, purposes, objectives, values, and feelings, can increase fondness and moods of closeness.

Social penetration theory states that as we get to know someone, we engage in a reciprocal process of self-disclosure that changes in breadth and depth and affects how a relationship develops. Depth denotes to how personal or delicate the information is, and breadth mentions in the array of themes conversed.

Self-disclosure helps:

Increased accuracy in communication. Self-disclosure often takes the guesswork out of the communication process. No one is a mind reader; if people conceal how they really feel, it is difficult for others to know how to respond to them appropriately.

People who are frustrated by the heavy workload and loss of balance in their life, but mask their true feelings, may never see the problem resolved.

The person who is in a position to solve this problem may be oblivious to what's important to you—unless you spell it out.

Stronger, deeper relationships. Another reward from self-disclosure is the strengthening of interpersonal relationships. When two people engage in an open, authentic dialogue, they often develop a high regard for each other's views.

Often they discover they share common interests and concerns and these serve as a foundation for a deeper relationship.

Increased authenticity. "People trust us when we are honest and reliable, Not an imitation of somebody different."

Jack Welch, a highly successful CEO of General Electric for many years, says the most powerful thing you can do to get ahead is to be real: **"Think of authenticity as your foundation, your center and don't let any organization try to wring it out of you, subtly or otherwise."**

Those who self-disclose are generally more liked by others than those who do not reveal anything at all about themselves.

Research has shown in laboratory experiments with undergraduate students, that strangers who engaged in reciprocal self-disclosure reported more positive evaluations of their partner than two people who did not divulge as much.

Please go ahead and try this exercise.

Next time you are at work, at happy hour, or in a class try engaging in discussions with someone for at least an hour and gradually progress from more superficial small talk to revealing personal and meaningful information.

What actions are you going to take from this lesson?

1. _____

2. _____

3. _____

Thinking Question:

Are you doing enough study/experimentation/research to build a capability to enhance workshop engagement?

3.10 Barriers To Successful Partnership

> *"There are big problems that change the world. If we are working together, that will make us understand each other, appreciate each other, help each other."*
>
> *—Jack Ma*

Why this topic?

As a part of coaching, we demonstrate how to promote the collaboration with others. Now, what are the various tips I can give to my team members to develop partnership?

Agile Manifesto says that we are uncovering better ways of developing software by doing it and helping others do it. Through this work, we have come to value

> *"Individuals and **interactions** over processes and tools*
> *Working software over comprehensive documentation*
> *Customer **collaboration** over contract negotiation*
> *Responding to change over following a plan"*
>
> *More stress on the **partnership** with all the team members.*

In his book "**How the Best Get Better**" management consultant Dan Sullivan describes a pattern of behavior that he has coined as "the Rugged Individualist." Rugged individualists believe he can do everything by himself. He doesn't need anyone else to help him.

It can be a solitary and lonely life. A software developer behaving as a rugged individualist may struggle with coding issues for days because he is too afraid to let others know that he needs help from others. He may isolate himself from his team because he doesn't want anyone to learn the real truth about his lack of skills or abilities.

We need to embrace what Dan calls the unique-ability teamwork. It is based on creative ways to get things done by determining each of our strengths and weaknesses. Rather than trying to improve your weaknesses, focus on your **strengths by surrounding yourself with teammates who have strengths in your weak areas.**

A working definition of a **partnership** is "a cooperative association between units to work toward common objectives through a jointly decided division of labor."

"If you have an apple and I have an apple and we exchange these apples, then you and I will still each have one apple. But if you have an idea and I have an idea and we exchange these ideas, then each of us will have two ideas." — George Bernard Shaw

BARRIERS TO SUCCESSFUL PARTNERSHIPS:

1. Limited vision/fail to inspire
2. One partner manipulates or dictates, or partners race for the lead
3. The absence of a strong purpose and an unpredictable level of understanding of the purpose
4. Lack of understanding roles/responsibilities
5. Lack of backing from the partner organizations with ultimate decision-making powers

6. Differences between philosophies and type of working
7. Lack of obligation; unwilling to contribute
8. Uneven and/or improper equilibrium of power and control
9. Key interests and/or people missing from the partnership
10. Hidden agendas
11. Failure to connect
12. Lack of evaluation or monitoring systems
13. Failure to acquire knowledge
14. Financial and time commitments outweigh potential benefits
15. Less time for effective consultation

The partnership is the key for collaboration and servant style leadership.

> *"Coming together is a beginning; keeping together is progress; working together is a success."*
>
> **—Edward Everett Hale**

What actions are you going to take from this lesson?

1. _____

2. _____

3. _____

Thinking Question:

Are you building enough knowledge power to build the partnership with someone at any moment?

3.11 Building Questioning Skills?

> *"Questions are the root of everything great I have done in life. The most creative ideas ever experienced are often conceptualized by asking simple questions."*
>
> **—Jeff Shinabarger,**

Why this topic?

Many of my teams whom I am coaching, I tell them, "You have to build up better questioning skills". They are sitting in a remote corner and the users are in another part of the world, how they could improve better questioning skills so that they can get the output within a shorter timescale with the required output.

I was imagining I should be giving them something so that they can start applying to develop this skill.

> *"Asking the Right questions takes as much skill as giving the right answers"*
>
> **—Robert Half**

I have learned from the book, **The Art of Powerful Questions, Eric Vogt, Juanita Brown, and David Isaacs** where they have outlined the steps of a game plan that organizations might follow to apply queries to catalyze insights, innovations, and plan for action.

What they have recommended

- **Judging the present condition**
- **Finding out the giant enquiries**
- **Crafting pictures of opportunities, Chances**
- **Growing practical strategies**

To build the ability to ask a powerful question, we need to understand **WHY** we are doing it.

So

1. Start with **Relationship building questions**
2. **START WITH WHY**? Why am I asking these questions? **What is the Purpose**?
3. **Listen** and understand the perspective of the other person.
4. Ask with **Positive Intent**
5. Ask with **Curiosity**, To **discover**, to unearth the hidden assumptions
6. Ask to **promote thinking**
7. Ask to **clarify**, Assumptions, to avoid misunderstanding, to get more information
8. More **OPEN** ended questions, Less **Close**-ended questions
9. Ask for More **Elaboration**
10. Ask for specific **examples, Learning**
11. Ask for specific **challenges**
12. Ask questions related to **Roadblocks** and **constraints**
13. Ask questions to **inspire**, generate **positive energy**
14. Ask Questions to **create** more question
15. Ask more **Chaining** questions
16. Ask more **Funnel** Questions, starting with closed questions

"Millions saw the apple fall, but Newton was the one who asked why."

—Bernard M. Baruch

Use also AI **(Appreciative Inquiry)**

From the *Handbook of Appreciative Inquiry*,

"Appreciative Inquiry is the co-evolutionary, co-operative **search for the best in people, their organizations, and the relevant world around them** ...

AI includes the **art and practice of enquiring demands that reinforce a system's ability to catch, anticipate and improve an optimistic perspective** ...

AI practice stresses on the swiftness of the imagination and innovation. **Instead of adverse, perilous, and strengthening analyses commonly used in our organizations** ... there is discovery, dream, design, and destiny."

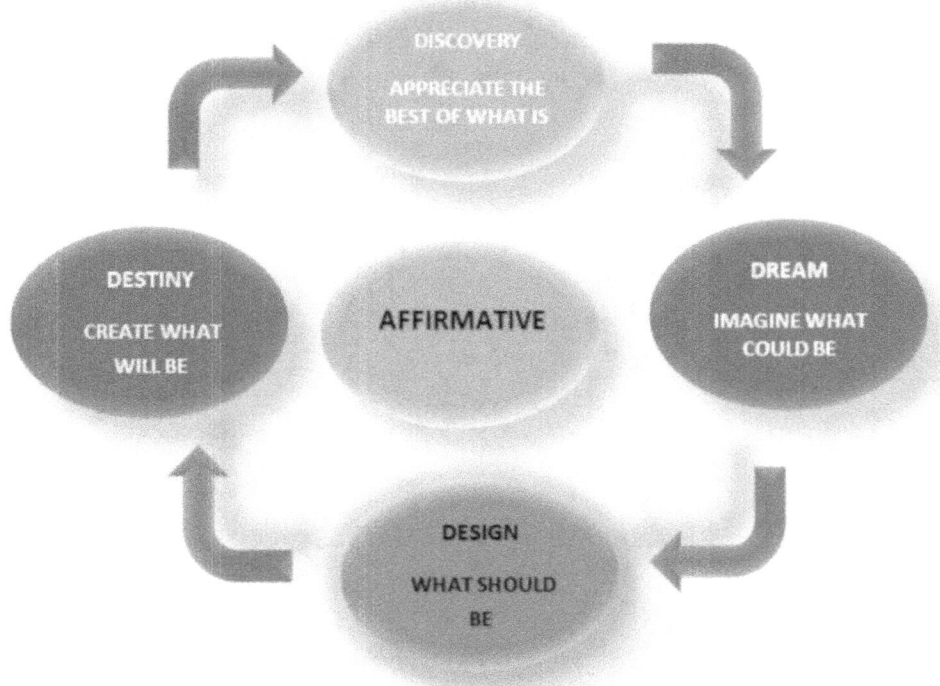

How do I apply this? Start applying with the team whom you are coaching with, whom you are interacting?

How am I getting the benefit? Five points to note

1. While Interacting with the Product Owner to validate their Maturity
2. While Interacting with the Scrum Master to Validate their Maturity
3. While Interacting with the Scrum Team to Validate their Maturity
4. While coaching to understand the gap
5. While providing training, all these Questioning skills help

> *"The wise man doesn't give the right answers, he poses the right questions."*
>
> —*Claude Levi-Strauss*

What actions are you going to take from this lesson?

1. _____

2. _____

3. _____

Thinking Question:

Am I doing enough investigation to strengthen my questioning technique?

3.12 How to Tutor a Scrum Master?

> *"All the best performers bring to their role something more, something different from what the author put on paper. That's what makes theatre live. That's why it persists."*
>
> —*Stephen Sondheim*

Why this topic?

Sustenance of the agile transformation is in a few key roles. If these roles are executed well, sustenance is assured. The scrum master is one of the roles. How can we ensure, SM is well prepared on his/her role?

Planning to conduct a workshop for a scrum master...asking myself what should I share? A couple of my Project Manager friends asked, how can I be a better scrum master?

The comment was made that they need the abilities of all good leaders.

Tao Te Ching Written by Lao-tzu Ch 17

When the Master governs, the people
are hardly aware that he exists.
Next, best is a leader who is loved.
Next, one who is feared.
The worst is one who is despised.

If you don't trust the people, you
make them untrustworthy.

The Master doesn't talk, he acts. When
his work is done, the people say,
"Amazing: we did it, all by ourselves

A great Scrum Master recognizes himself in the acronym made up by Geoff Watts, RE-TRAINED:

1. Resourceful, he/she is creative in removing the impediments
2. Enabling, he/she is passionate about helping others
3. Tactful, he/she is diplomacy personified
4. Respected, he/she has a reputation for integrity
5. An alternative, he/she is prepared to promote a counterculture
6. Inspiring, he/she generates interest and vigor in others
7. Nurturing, he/she enjoys helping teams and individuals to develop and grow
8. Empathic, he/she is sensitive to those around the team
9. Disruptive, he/she breaks the status quo and help create a new way of working

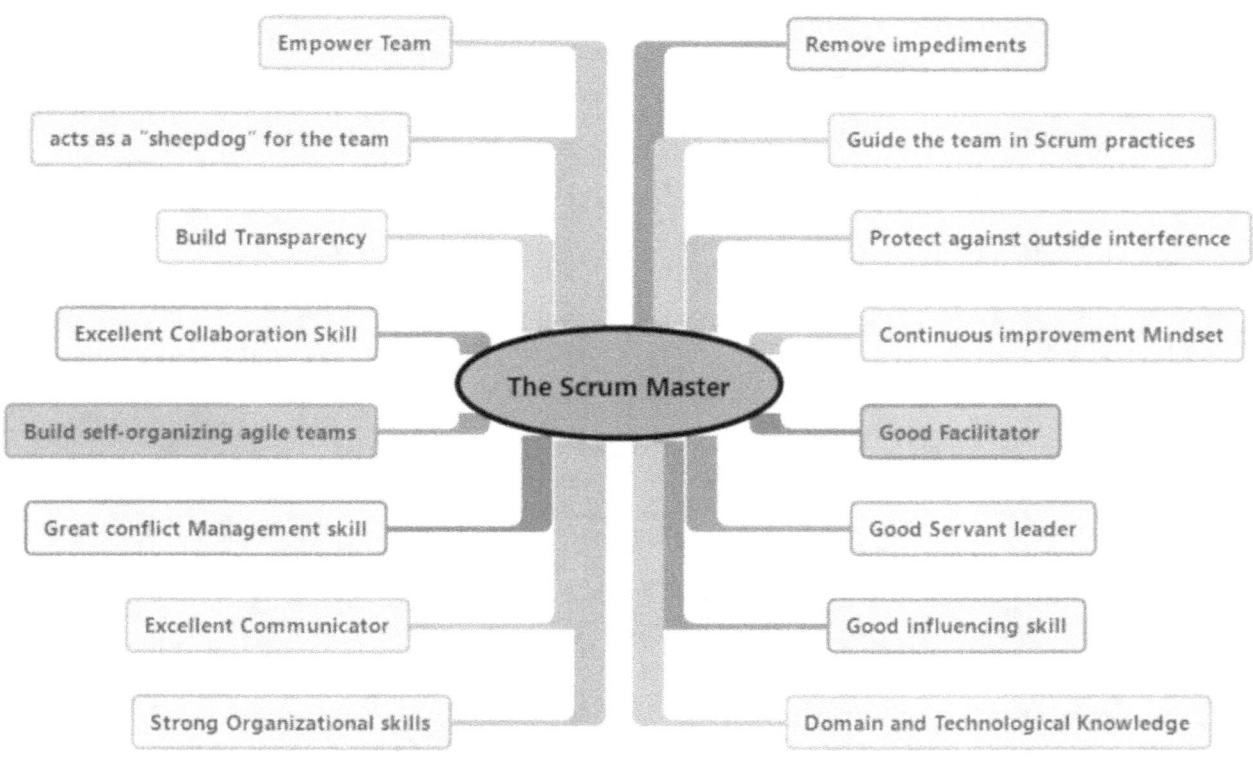

What actions are you going to take from this lesson?

1. _____

2. _____

3. _____

Thinking Question:

Are you doing enough to help your scrum masters to operate at their greatest level?

3.13 Characteristics of Workshop Facilitation? How to master it?

"Tell me, and I will forget. Show me, and I may remember. Involve me, and I will understand."

—Confucius in 450 BC

Why this topic?

As a coach, one of the key intentions is of a master workshop facilitator. How to build up that skill?

Workshop facilitation is about helping a group to gain skills and knowledge.

Unlike the stereotypical role of a schoolteacher, it's not about being in charge.

You don't even need to be an expert in the workshop topic (although it can often help).

The key to good facilitation is that **you and the participants are equals** –

You all share the equal responsibility to create a good learning experience.

A good facilitator will design workshops that combine learning and information sharing with interactive tools for group work.

Facilitators know when they are successful when they look at a group of **happy**, and **smiling** faces.

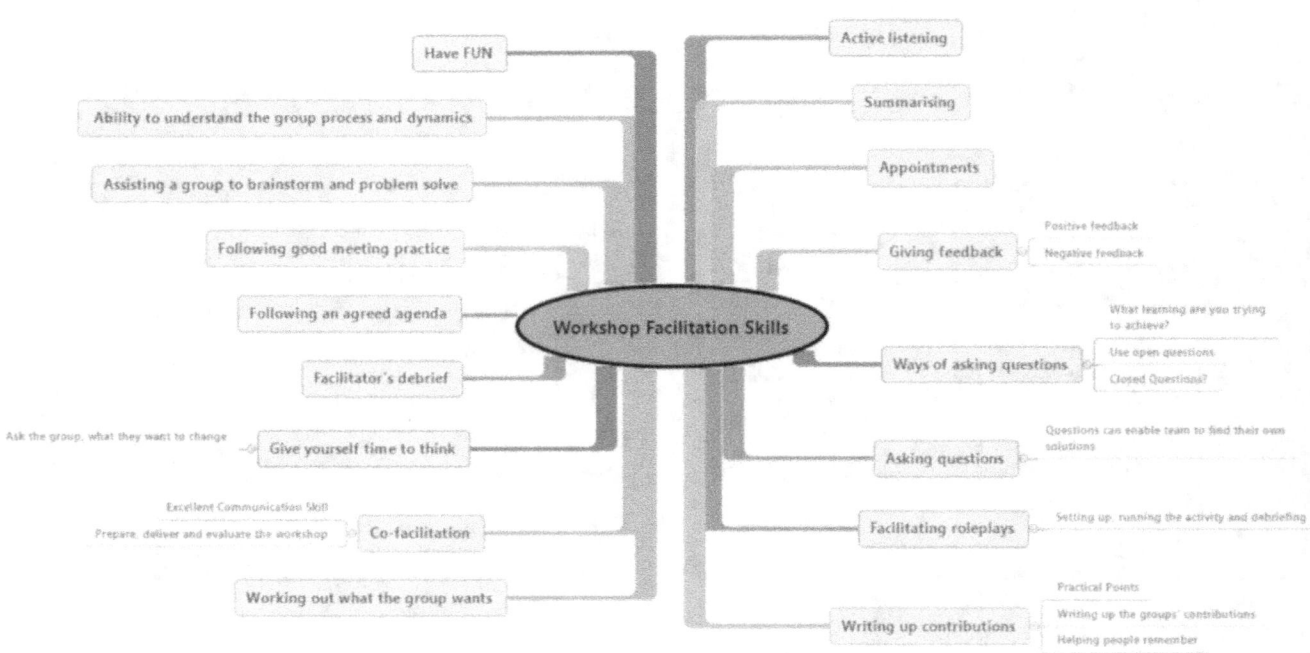

The general concept of learning through experience is ancient.

Around 350 BCE, Aristotle wrote in the Nicomachean Ethics **"for the things we have to learn before we can do them, we learn by doing them"**

To be an effective facilitator, we must know when to take a leadership role and when to be neutral and take a back seat.

This is a difficult balance to maintain!

The importance of being skillful in the role is to design and help the proceedings effectively and remain attentive to the group processes and outcomes, rather than focusing on specific content and opinions involved.

What should we do?

> *"When people who attend experience that their presence is truly wanted and valuable and that their unique gifts are necessary for the best outcome of the gathering, the possibility for authentic engagement, leading to success, is greatly enhanced."*
>
> —*The Art of Convening*, **by Craig and Patricia Neal with Cynthia Wold**

In my workshop what I have observed working with me is

1. I tell lots of stories from my life which nobody can get from Google searches
2. I have worked with GE Medical system, Honeywell Aerospace, Honeywell Building Automation, ABB Power Automation, ABB Industrial automation, and always built large systems, and I have so many stories to share.
3. I am 100% curious to learn from other stories, so I encourage others to tell stories
4. I ensure 100% of the participants are engaged with me
5. I apply fun-filled, light discussions and motivate others
6. I spend a good amount of time on each concept, not always in a hurry to finish, so it allows participants to absorb and feel the Aha moment
7. I collect feedback every hour and I give feedback at every moment. I take action based on the feedback

> *"I never teach my pupils. I only attempt to provide the conditions in which they can learn."*
>
> —*Albert Einstein*

What actions are you going to take from this lesson?

1. _____
2. _____
3. _____

Thinking Question:

Are you doing enough to boost your facilitation skills? What else can you look at?

3.14 Story Telling Technique: How can we become a better Storyteller?

Why this topic?

How do we engage our audience during any presentation? By storytelling!

> *The art of storytelling can be used to drive change.*
>
> —*Richard Branson*

Academics and marketers alike have found that our brains are hard-wired to process and store information in the form of stories.

So, when we hear that **"once upon a time…."** there was a certain character in such and such place, our minds are immediately transported to this imaginary scene.

In fact, according to a professional speaker Akash Karia, **stories are irresistible to the human mind because they activate our imaginations and so we have no choice but to follow the mental movies created in our heads.**

"Inside each of us is a natural born storyteller just waiting to be released?"

—Robin Moore

As a result, they are used by many TED presenters who are some of the most inspirational speakers in the world.

Storytelling accomplishes the essential for human beings cast their knowledge in description method.

Our ancestors probably gathered around the evening fires and expressed their fears, their beliefs, and their heroism through oral narratives.

This long tradition of storytelling is evident in ancient cultures.

Part of the powerful presentation is telling several stories in a session.

How to build that skill ....through practices...

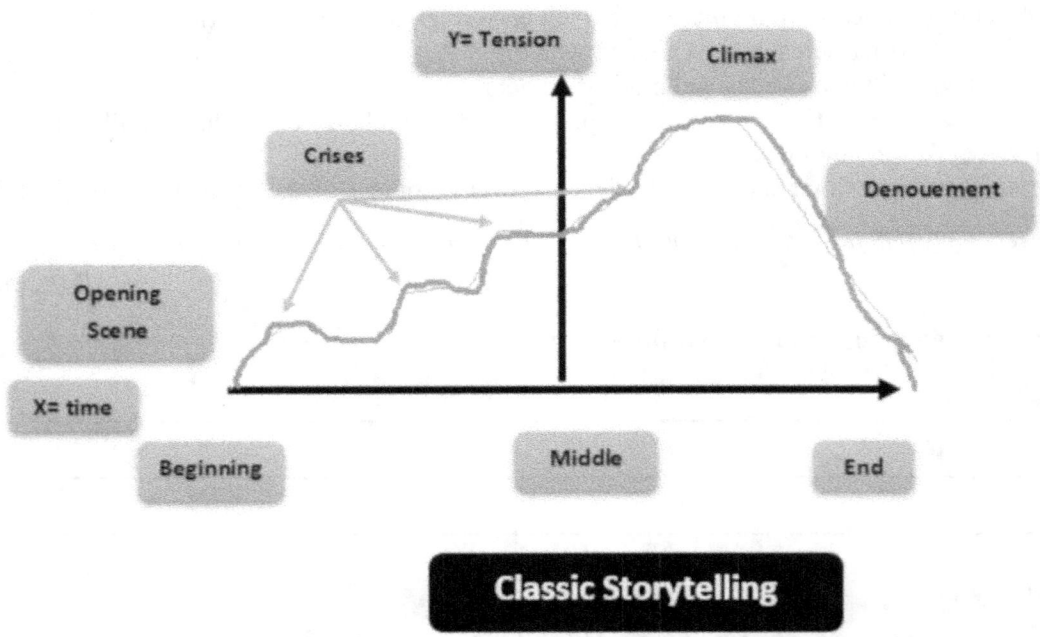

What are the factors to be considered while telling the story?

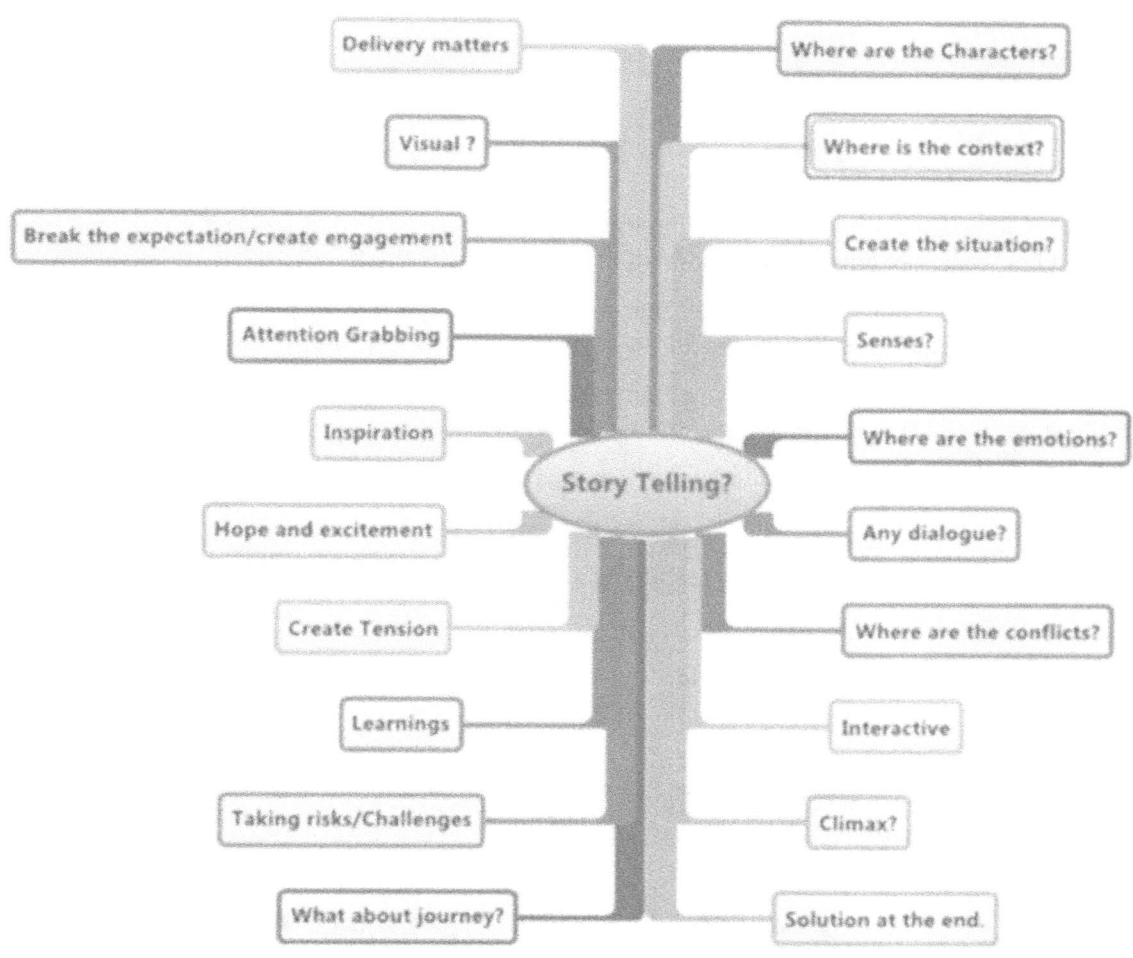

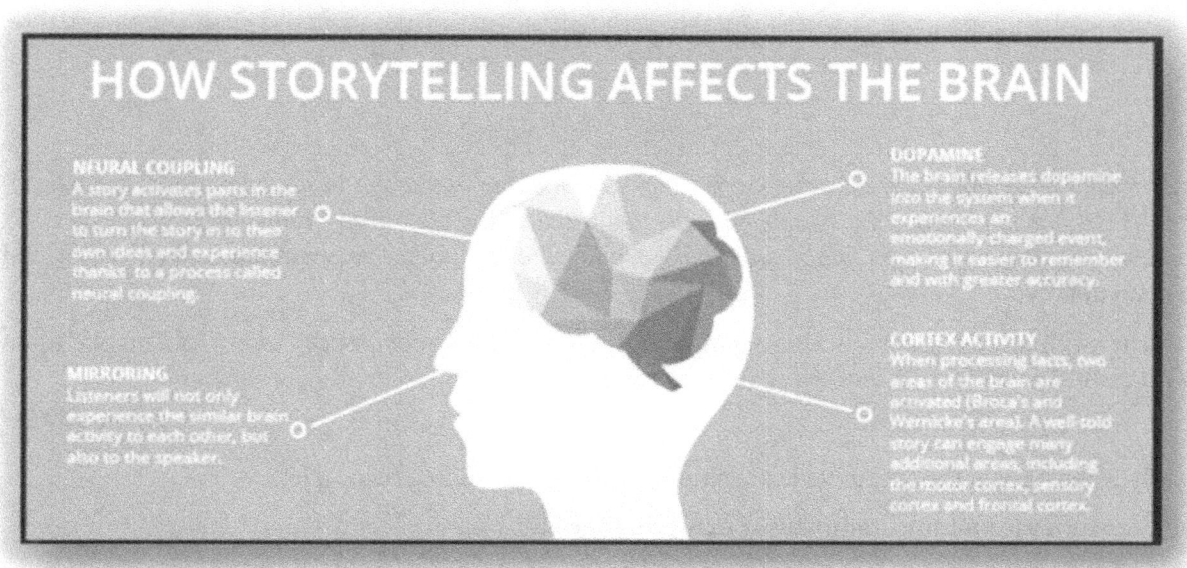

"A successful talk is a little micacle—people see the world differently afterward"

—TED curatour Chris Anderson

What I have learned about storytelling techniques from JK Rowling storytelling structure is

The three parts of any story are

a) **Trigger event and followed by**
b) **Transformation**
c) **Lesson learned from all these.**

All the great storyteller always had retrospect into their life and describe their struggling life. They inspire us by their stories saying what they have learned from all their experiences.

The same story is about Oprah's life. She also connects with the audience by inspiring the people by sharing the struggling life she had and she had overcome through learnings.

An inspiring storyteller identifies their life core purpose. Their message flows from the meaning they attach to their own life story, their fight, and recovery, strain, and achievement

Stories have a unique power to move people's hearts.

—*Peter Guber*

Storytelling is a game-changer

Build your story with

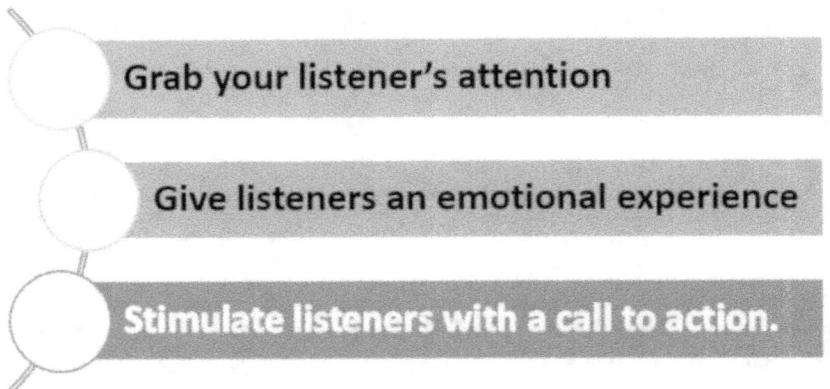

"Listeners are rarely hooked if they don't sense some compelling challenge in the beginning. They won't stay engaged if they're not excited by the struggle in the middle. And they won't remember or act on the story unless they feel galvanized by its final resolution," explains Peter Guber, The chairman, and CEO of Mandalay Entertainment group.

"Everybody likes to tell a story. Little children do it effortlessly. Great artists do it with talent and years of practice. Somewhere in between stand you and me."

—*Sylvia Ziskind*

Especially when we run the executive leadership workshop, storytelling helps a lot.

Telling life stories is an important way of exploring the self.

Executives should be given an opportunity to deal with such questions as: **Who am I? Where am I going? How will I get there?**

Through storytelling, executives gain a way of working through internal crises and developmental challenges. Stories also help to arrive at a meaningful personal life integration. Other people's stories lead to learning empathy, psychological astuteness, and further self-reflection.

Program designers should think about how to maximize the benefits of **storytelling** by creating opportunities for people to tell their stories and for the other participants to identify the issues together and talk about them.

Every story will reveal specific present-day dilemmas that have grown out of underlying problems—dilemmas that can be remedied by addressing those deeper issues.

These dilemmas will be the basis for "contracts" between the presenter and the rest of the participants.

Storytelling can be done by giving a hot seat to each participant at a certain moment in the program, or by running parallel small group coaching sessions in which the participants take turns to present their stories, supported by self-discovery tools described in this book.

When we talk about building a great product through a design thinking approach, it is all about stories. How we tell better stories to our end users and team members. We have to create a design culture by creating better stories.

What actions are you going to take from this lesson?

1. _____

2. _____

3. _____

Thinking Question:

Are you doing enough to build our storytelling technique by studying various books and working ourt storytelling techniques in the seminars?

3.15 Nurturing happiness in teams?

"Remember that the happiest people are not those getting more, but those giving more."

—*H. Jackson Brown. Jr*

Why this topic?

How can I make my team members happy, this is the thought that triggered me to look into this thought?

"Happy chemicals" - Dopamine, Endorphin, Oxytocin, and Serotonin.

These chemicals spurt our brain when we see something good for our survival.

As a coach, I would like to take away the anxiety from the team.

How can we increase these chemicals? If I can sell these chemicals in a bottle in the tea stall, team members will surely buy from me!

Let me put Dopamine in the bottle first.

Let us focus more on these activities to get more Dopamine.

Dopamine has been called our "motivation molecule."

Increased Dopamine = Extra Productivity

1. "When we receive a **reward** of any kind, **dopamine** is released in our brains. As we get rewarded over and over again for something, we learn that we should keep doing whatever that is very deep, and it's hard to unlearn those kinds of behaviors."
2. "**Dopamine** surges when we are structured and finish jobs – regardless of the job being minor or big.
3. As with creating a checklist, getting a streak going is a great way to increase dopamine levels. A streak is a visual reminder of how many days in a row you've **achieved something**. Let us create a stretch goal and achieve it, that we will have a purpose, and once we achieve the purpose Dopamine will increase. It will drive us.
4. When we are feeling hopeless, throw on some of our preferred songs and jam out! **Music aids to a rise of Dopamine level**.
5. Let us have a **celebration** time where the team demonstrates their **hobbies**. **Creative hobbies** of all kinds increase Dopamine levels.

Dopamine produces the joy of finding what you seek–the "Eureka! I got it!" feeling.

Let us put **Endorphin** in the bottle.

1. Find more reasons to laugh. It's an everyday, immediate way to give yourself an endorphin rush. The act of laughing stimulates the production of endorphins and helps you feel better instantly. Laughter helps to relieve stress and has many other physical and emotional benefits. Build a laughing club.
2. **Smile**, but make sure it's a real one. True smiles, called Duchenne smiles, result in the production of endorphins, giving our mood a boost
3. Give in to gossip, gossiping stimulates pleasure centers in the brain and releases endorphins. Scientists believe that since we're social animals, and gossip developed as a way to stay connected, Let us be positive in gossiping
4. Celebrate with **chocolates**, eating dark chocolates increases Endorphin. Research suggests that chocolate's not the only food that can produce pleasure. All pleasant foods make your brain release endorphins to elevate your mood. Celebrate a team lunch or dinner frequently.

124

5. Take a **group fitness class**. Athletes who run together could tolerate twice as much pain (a sign that endorphins are present) as athletes who run alone. Workout with others to improve your endorphin flow.

Let us put **Oxytocin** in the bottle.

Feelings of alienation and dealing with loneliness, as well as a lack of intimate relationships, are the outward manifestations of reduced oxytocin levels.

1. Give a gift. Our first human oxytocin studies showed that **receiving gifts** raised oxytocin. So why not make this a regular practice? The key is not to expect a gift in return but to **surprise** someone for no reason.
2. Oxytocin is great when **you're out with friends** or **solving a problem with coworkers**. It might not be so great when you need to pick a leader or make any other big decision that requires independence, not conformity.

Let us put **Serotonin** in the bottle.

1. **Light** boosts Serotonin. Heading into the sunshine, even on a cool day, is the quickest way to boost your mood. Let us go out and spend some time. Research has found a positive correlation between serotonin synthesis and the total hours of sunlight during the day. In the postmortems of humans, serotonin levels are higher during the summer months than in the winter months
2. Prolonged periods of **stress** can deplete **serotonin** levels. We should stay away from stressful situations as much as possible and find healthy ways to deal with stress once it comes your way.
3. Relive **happy memories**. Though it may sound corny, reliving happy times may be enough to give your brain a serotonin boost. Let us talk to our team about some happy memories and share.

WHEN YOUR BRAIN RELEASES ONE OF THESE CHEMICALS, YOU FEEL GOOD

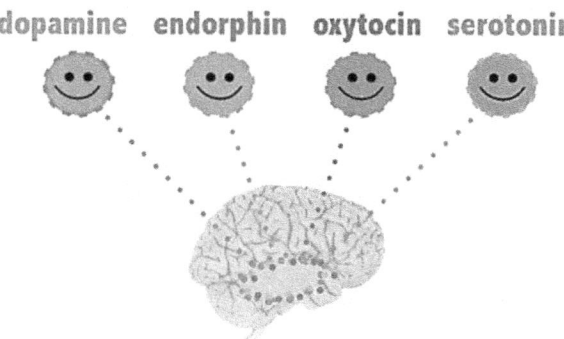

Each of the happy chemicals motivates a different type of survival behavior.

Dopamine motivates us to get what we need, even when it takes lots of effort. **Endorphin** motivates us to ignore pain, so we can escape from harm when we are injured.

Oxytocin motivates us to trust others and to find safety in companionship.

And **serotonin** motivates us to get respect.

Let us give this Bottled happiness to the team to improve their happiness.

One of our favorite business books is Tony Hsieh's Delivering Happiness (BusinessPlusUS, 2010).

The author founded a company called Zappos in 1999. Zappos grew from zero sales in 1999 to $1 billion worth of sales in 2009.

Hsieh says this success was the result of making customers happy — and he achieved that by making his employees happy.

Zappos has a set of 10 core values that the staff created together. They provide the foundation for the company's culture and are a guide on how to treat customers, suppliers, employees and sales reps in a mindful way.

These values include

1. Creating fun and a little weirdness
2. Being adventurous, creative and open-minded
3. Pursuing growth and learning
4. Building a positive team and family spirit
5. Being passionate and determined

Happy people show greater activation in the left pre-frontal cortex.

Happier staff are more productive, creative, take fewer sick days and are more likely to be promoted.

So good work doesn't make you happy but being happy creates good work.

Today's generation requires more happiness at the workplace because Generation Z is wired differently.

MOOD lifting Exercise at Office, Try it!

Before I start interacting with the team for coaching engagement, I check the mood of each team member. When our mood is good, the absorption rate of information is very high.

First, we all have to feel relaxed before we get into any serious discussion.

What coaching effectiveness will come on change management when our team members are down due to some reason?

Most of the time first I have looked into the mood of the team and uplift the mood of the team members. It worked for me and helped me in my coaching.

We need to lift our team member's mood of happiness and then we can get down to business. That should be the starting point for any coaching, mentoring session.

HOW? To lift the mood

Good mood reflects an energized, engaged state of mind and involves feelings such as interest, alertness, joy, excitement, and enthusiasm.

As a servant leader, we all need to push the team members to reach this state. For knowledge workers, it is essential for us to be in a good mood state to contribute at the higher the level most of the time. And the sad mood is contagious.

When we are in a good mood, the world is a beautiful place, nice things happen, people smile at us, we get the results we want and feel at peace inside.

We don't even think about our frame of mind because we are **alive, positive and happy**.

Feeling low, in mood is described in a number of ways, such as **being fed-up, down, sad, worried, worn-out or frustrated.**

We have days when the vibration is low, we are in a negative head-space and nothing seems to work out for us. People growl at us, the lunch is tasteless and the traffic terrible.

This is the time to grab hold of the reins and take control of our mood instead of letting it control us.

What actions can we take in our workspace?

WALK, WALK AND WALK:

Whenever we feel lethargic, bored, sad, or low – simply start walking. This is especially beneficial for those who are working for long hours at a desk. Sitting in one place for too long can cause a hindrance in blood and oxygen circulation, which, in turn, disturbs hormonal chemistry in the brain leading to bad moods and irritability.

GOOD COMPANY:

Review the surrounding people on a day-to-day basis and check whether they are bringing our mood up or down. We will notice that among friends, family, and colleagues, some energies us and others drain us. When we begin working on our own positivity levels, we will naturally start magnetizing towards upbeat, happy people, and repelling negative ones.

LAUGHTER:

One greater mood lifter is laughing.

Laughter is an antidote to all kinds of mental and physical ailments.

"Laughter instantly lessens the flow of stress hormones, lowers blood pressure, relaxes muscles and triggers a flood of endorphins,."

"We often think that we smile in response to being happy, but the reverse is also true," "We can influence mood by manipulating our facial expressions. The facial muscles provide feedback to the brain, and we experience less negative emotions if we smile."

Create a Pleasure desk-space:

Create your workspace with many vibrant colors, posters or objects which inspire you. Some people are keeping cute teddy bears, Spiderman, some past great moments, memories etc. to energize them at their desk.

COLOR:

One greater mood lifter is color.

If you wake up in the morning with little energy, or you need to prepare for a business meeting, this is where the power of colors can help.

Color stimulates our eyes and our brain when used properly, it can make us feel happy, energized and focused.

Warm colors (like a red, orange and yellow) tend to be energizers, increasing heart rate and circulation; cool colors (such as blue and lavender) act like sedatives—decreasing your heart rate and adrenaline production.

The important thing here is that if we find a certain color relaxing or motivating, wearing that color can give us a mental boost.

Breathe Easy:

One greater mood lifter is right breathing or concentrated breathing.

Close your eyes and refocus your breathing pattern. Shifting to deep breathing will soothe your nerves, send oxygen to your brain and refresh your mind. Inhale slowly through your nose to the count of eight. Fill your belly—not your chest—with air. Exhale through your mouth to the count of 10 to 16. Repeat five to ten times, until you feel calmer.

Great photos and posters:

Looking at the great artwork which is a form of visualization.

Looking at calming, peaceful scenes can help people relax and de-stress.

Most of the offices are now days put a lot of large sizes, high-resolution photos, paintings etc. to energize team members with many positive statements.

I have asked my team members to weekly put some good posters, quotes at the desk and change it often.

Clean up your workplace:

Our emotions and mental wellbeing can be intrinsically linked to how disorganized our workspace is. **A cluttered desk or office can negatively affect our mood, resilience, and ability to work productively. Look at your office work, if it is messed up like below image than most of the time you will be sad.**

Clutter is mentally draining – and can even lower your self-esteem

Socializing:

Socializing with a cheerful person in your neighborhood increases the likelihood that you'll be happy too. Surprisingly, this had even more of a mood-boosting impact than spending time with an upbeat sibling, according to a recent study.

We also can do a team event where we will celebrate team member's birthday or some celebration like sprint demo where we can do informal discussion.

Look at this photo, for 2 mins and close your eyes and feel the place for another 2 mins. Back to work.

Do you have any doubts about why we should not follow above all these steps as a leader? Please do a pilot and see the benefit of the team productivity.

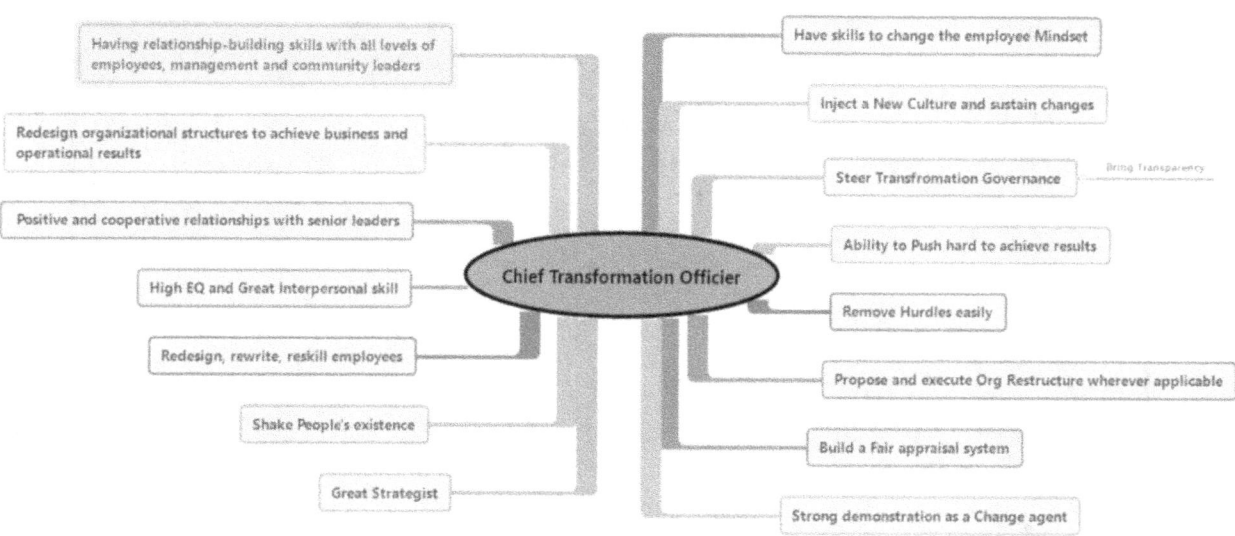

It is the responsibilities of the Chief Transformation Officer to create an ambient which is a breeding ground for the innovation and transformation.

The best way to cheer yourself is to try to cheer someone else up

—*Mark Twain*

What actions are you going to take from this lesson?

1. _____

2. _____

3. _____

Thinking Question:

Are you doing enough to make your team members happy by learning more about pleasure subject?

3.16 How to build an Excellent Team performance?

"Talent wins games, but teamwork and intelligence win championships."

—*Michael Jordan*

Why this topic?

Alone we cannot do much, what are the ways we can work together to deliver better?

Recently I visited a team, which is known to be a poor performing team. The Owner of the business asked me to check if I can recommend anything to improve the team performance.

I discovered some of the points which could be the reason for poor performance.

Do you agree that all these factors could potentially reduce the team performance?

An agile team has to resolve all these factors to become a high-performing team.

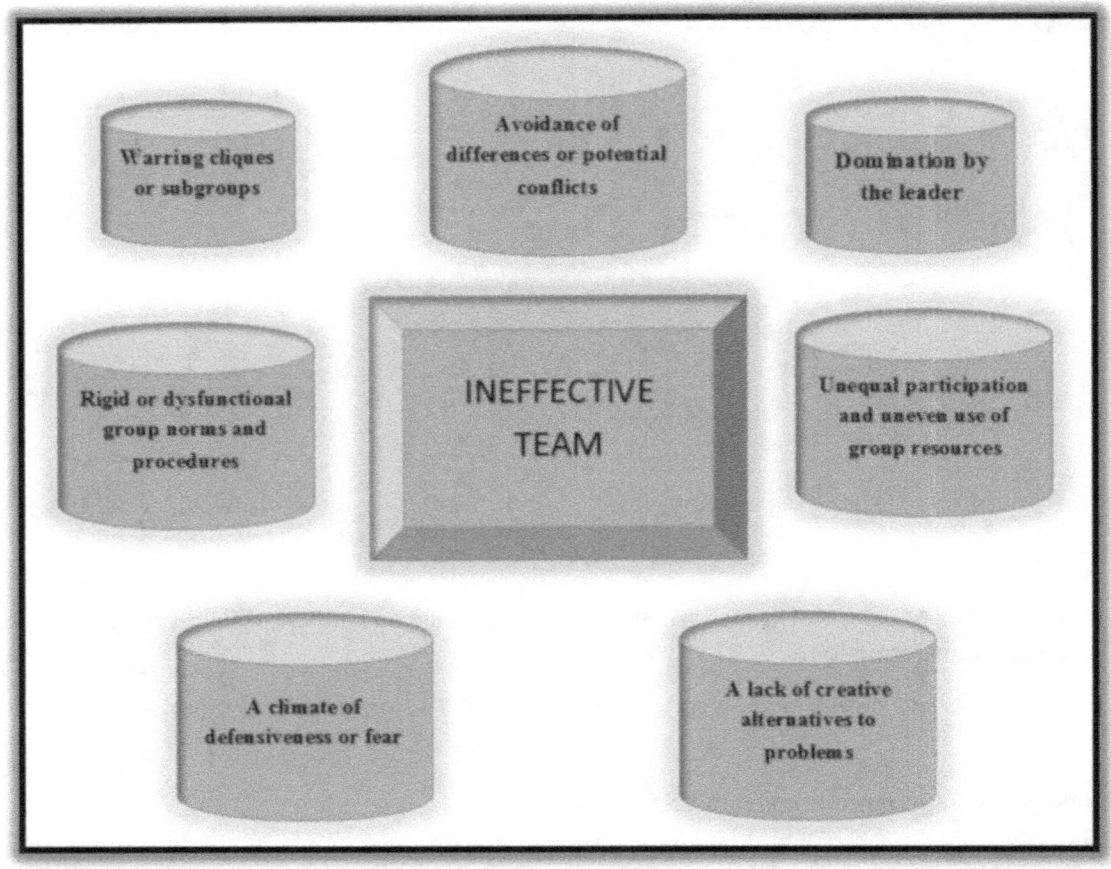

Anti Team pattern...

As a coach, we have to improve the situation by addressing all these weak links.

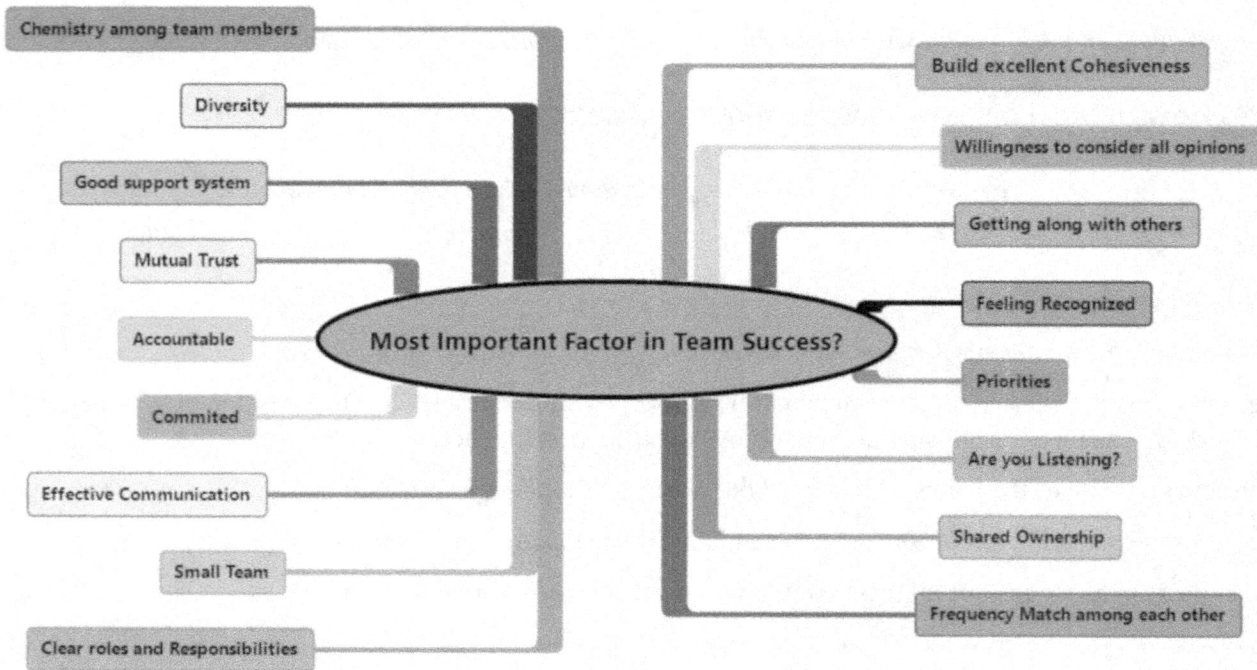

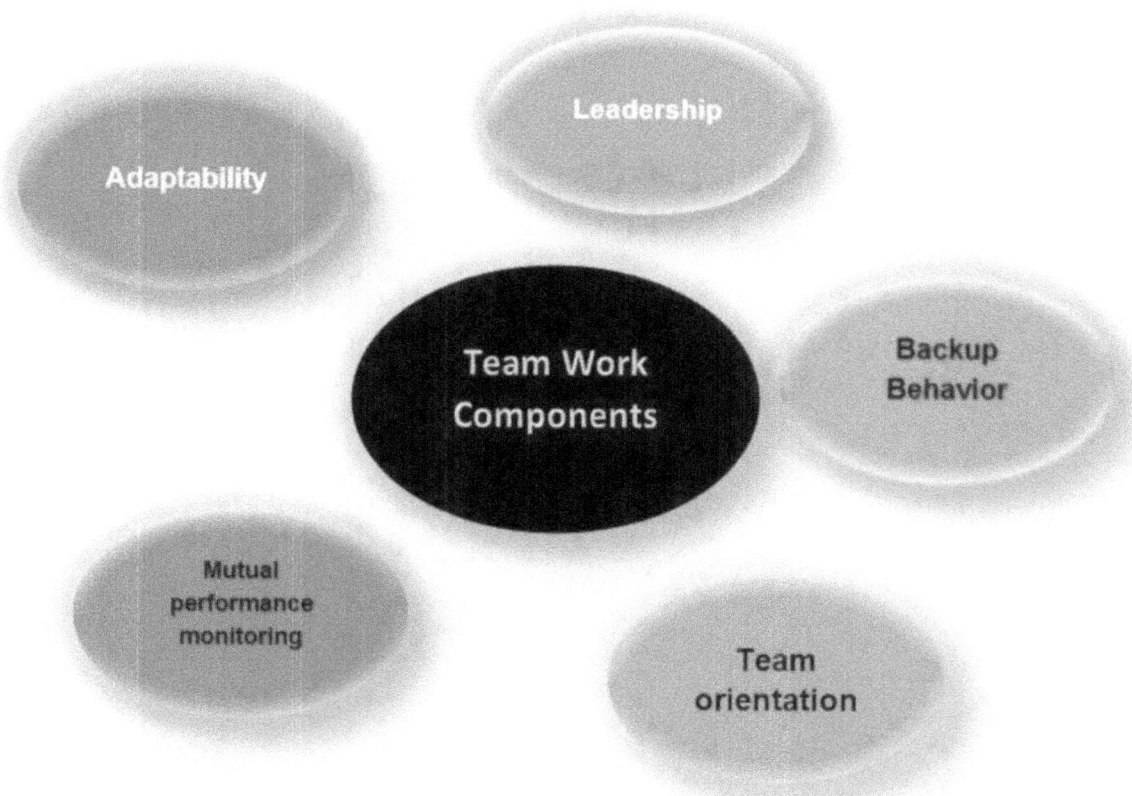

The Merit Principles Survey, which is administered to more than thirty-six thousand workers by the U.S. Merit Systems Protection Board ask questions to elicit information about these drivers:

1. **Pride in one's work or workplace**
2. **Satisfaction with the leadership**
3. **Opportunity to perform well at work**
4. **Satisfaction with the recognition received**
5. **Prospects for future personal and professional growth**
6. **A positive work environment with some focus on teamwork**

"If you can laugh together, you can work together"

—***Robert Orben***

What actions are you going to take from this lesson?

1. _____

2. _____

3. _____

Thinking Question:

Are you doing enough to increase your team member's performance by identifying all the elements which influence the team members?

3.17 How to select partners for collaboration?

Why this topic?

How to improve collaboration? Agile states we have to be collaborative but how to increase this skill?

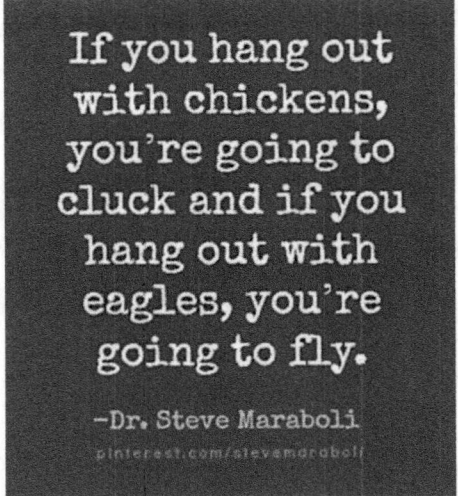

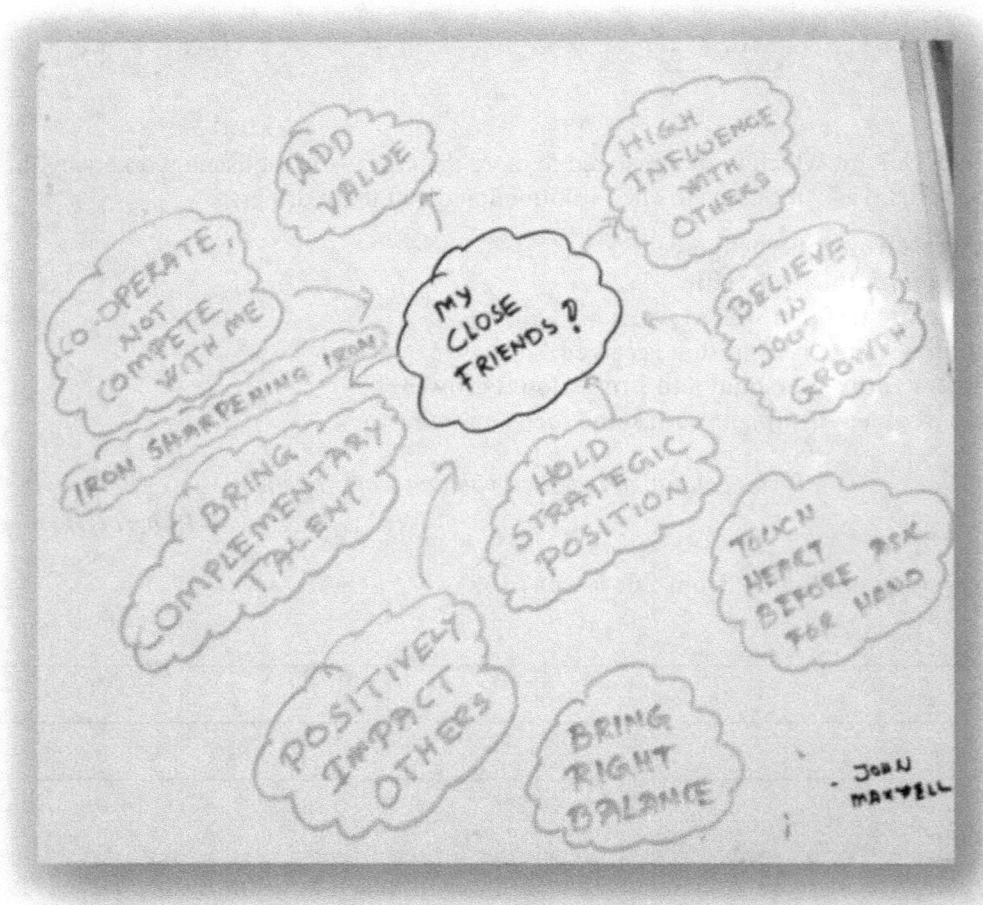

One way to drive fear out of a relationship is to realize that your partner's values are the same as yours, that what you care about is exactly what they care about. In my opinion, that drives fear out and makes for a great partnership, whether it's a corporate partnership or a marriage.

— Steve Jobs —

AZ QUOTES

As we know from the Agile Manifesto:

- **Business people and developers must work together daily throughout the project.**
- **The sponsors, developers, and users should be able to maintain a constant pace indefinitely.**

When I am thinking of starting my own setup, I always look for this point, and it comes to my mind, With Whom? Do I look into the current list of people with whom I have connected and find the suitability, why they would love to pair with me? Etc. points.

Let us build the partnership with the people to build better solutions.

What actions are you going to take from this lesson?

1. _____

2. _____

3. _____

Thinking Question:

Are you doing enough to build your partnership ability?

3.18 Extreme Collaboration? Is it needed

"None of us is as smart as all of us."

—*Ken Blanchard*

Why do we need to collaborate?

Most of the time, we were hearing that we have to work together as a collaborative team! Do we need to collaborate under all situations?

According to Thomas-Kilman, **Collaborating involves an attempt to work with the other person to find some solution which fully satisfies the concerns of both persons. It is a win-win** proposal.

Collaboration takes time, is it worth to invest so much time looking at the assignment? When both the parties are less interested, collaboration makes less sense.

When we have to quickly decide something. Collaboration is expensive.

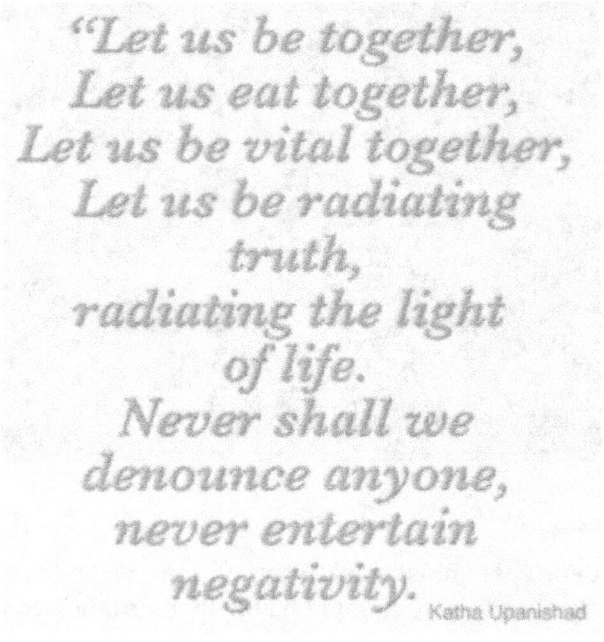

"Let us be together,
Let us eat together,
Let us be vital together,
Let us be radiating truth,
radiating the light of life.
Never shall we denounce anyone,
never entertain negativity.
Katha Upanishad

If time investment is not for the long term, it is not worth to do a collaboration.

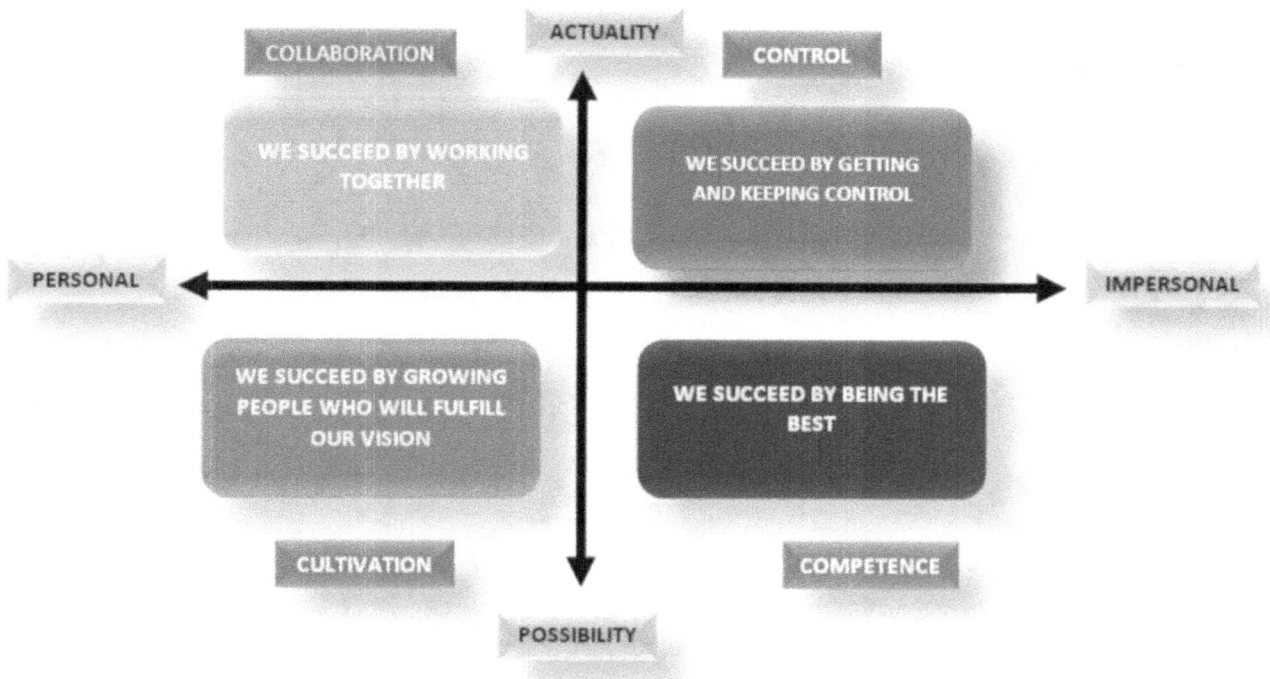

1. If I feel like, I am **not going to work for the long-term assignment with the party**, I may not go for Collaboration.
2. If I feel like, the current goal is **not so much important to me**, I may not be willing to go for a collaborative approach.
3. If I have to execute a certain assignment **quickly,** I may not go for a collaborative approach, as it is a time-consuming process.
4. If I find **some long-term benefit** by working with this person or assignment, then I will collaborate else not interested.
5. If I find that the team members I am working with, they are **knowledgeable** and **influential**, **ROI** will not be high, then I may be interested to collaborate.
6. If I realize I **cannot change the decision made by another person**, I will not be part of the game.
7. If I find the team members with whom I will be working **they are eating my pie**, I may not be willing to collaborate.
8. If I find the team whom I am going to work, I had a **previous bad experience** or some of my team members had an earlier bad experience I may not collaborate with them.
9. If I find the other party is **reliable**, and they **will not harm me** in any way, I can **trust** them, I will enjoy working with them, I can think of collaborating with the team.
10. If I find the subject is **not aligning with my passion**, I may not collaborate.
11. If I find **I am at risk** of doing too many things by collaborating with others, I may not progress much.

OR when we have many **MISSING** attributes, the collaboration will not happen.

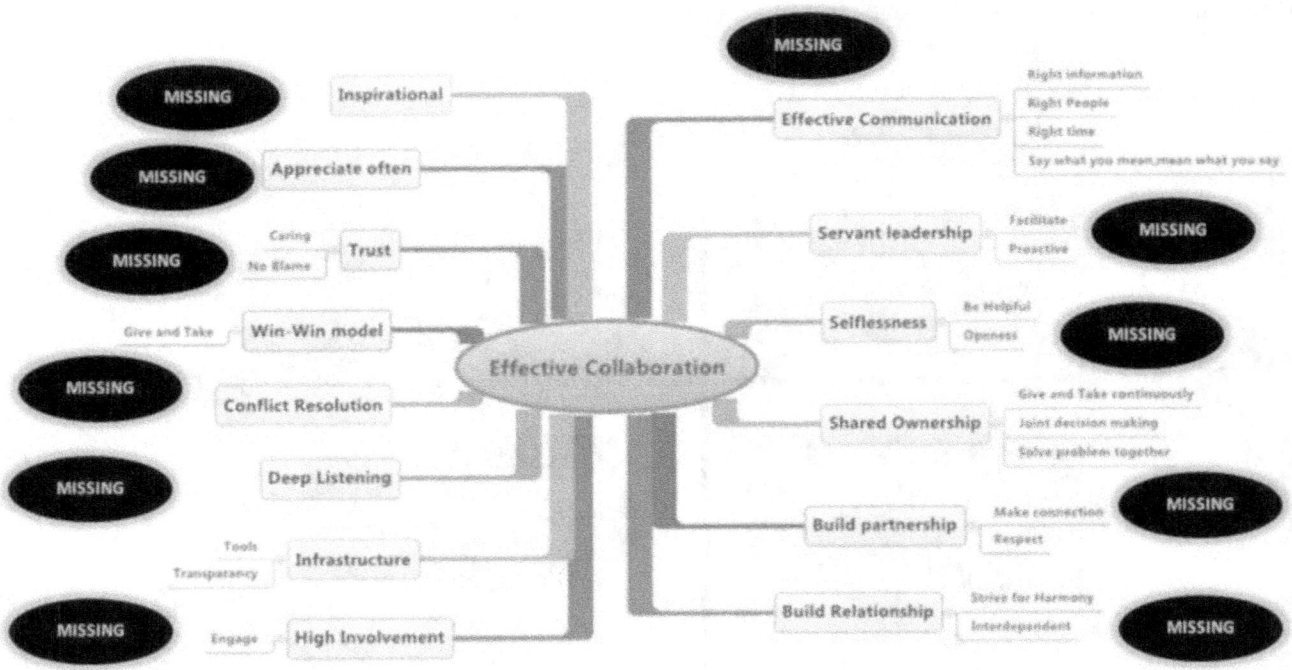

Do you all have the same feeling? Will you collaborate just like that? Too much collaboration is not always required. If I can run my show on my own, why do I need others?

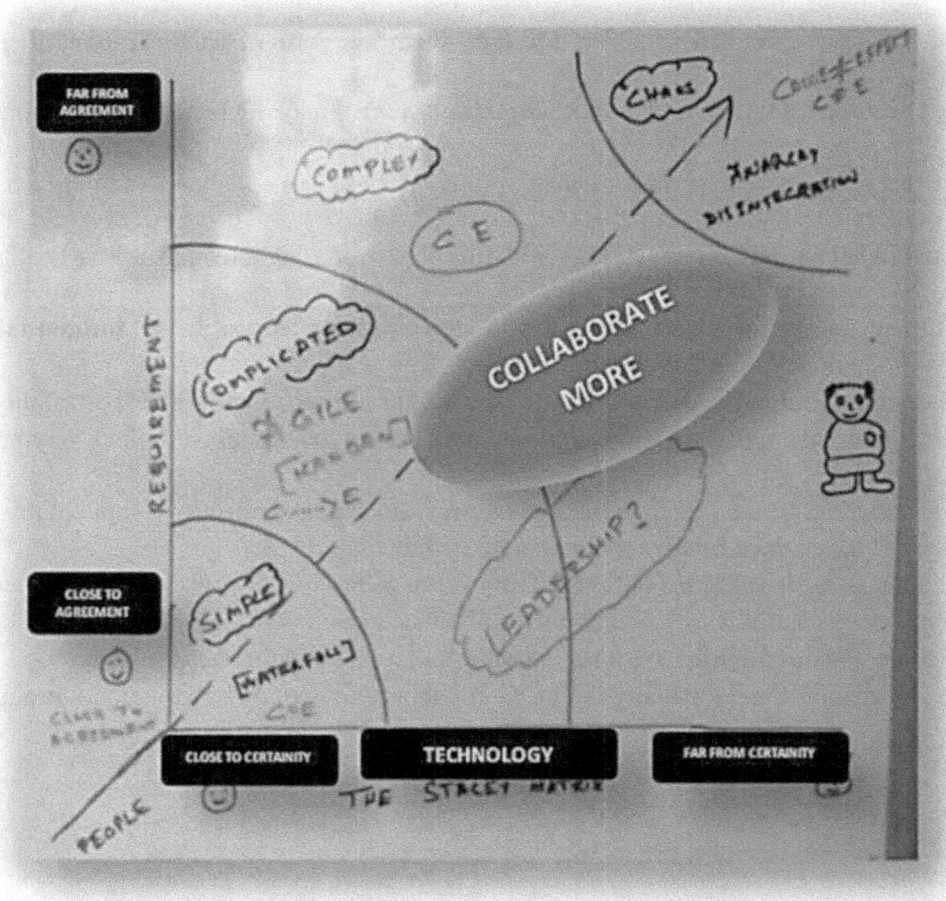

Maybe sometime when we have a common purpose, we may have to collaborate but not always.

What actions are you going to take from this lesson?

1. _____

2. _____

3. _____

Thinking Question:

Are you doing enough to understand when we should collaborate better and when we should reduce?

3.19 How to create a Sticky Presentation?

"There are three things to aim at in public speaking: first, to get into your subject, then to get your subject into yourself, and lastly, to get your subject into the heart of your audience."

—Alexander Gregg

Why this Topic:

As an agile team member, every moment team members are presenting each other. How can we build proficiency in the presentation?

John F. Kennedy—a powerful presenter in his own right—once remarked, **"The only reason to give a speech is to change the world."**

At Apple's 2010 Worldwide Developers Conference, CEO Steve Jobs presented the iPhone 4 to the public. AT&T had to stop taking orders almost immediately thereafter.

Our work should be that when presenting to marvelously convert an externally dull theme into an inwardly satisfying act.

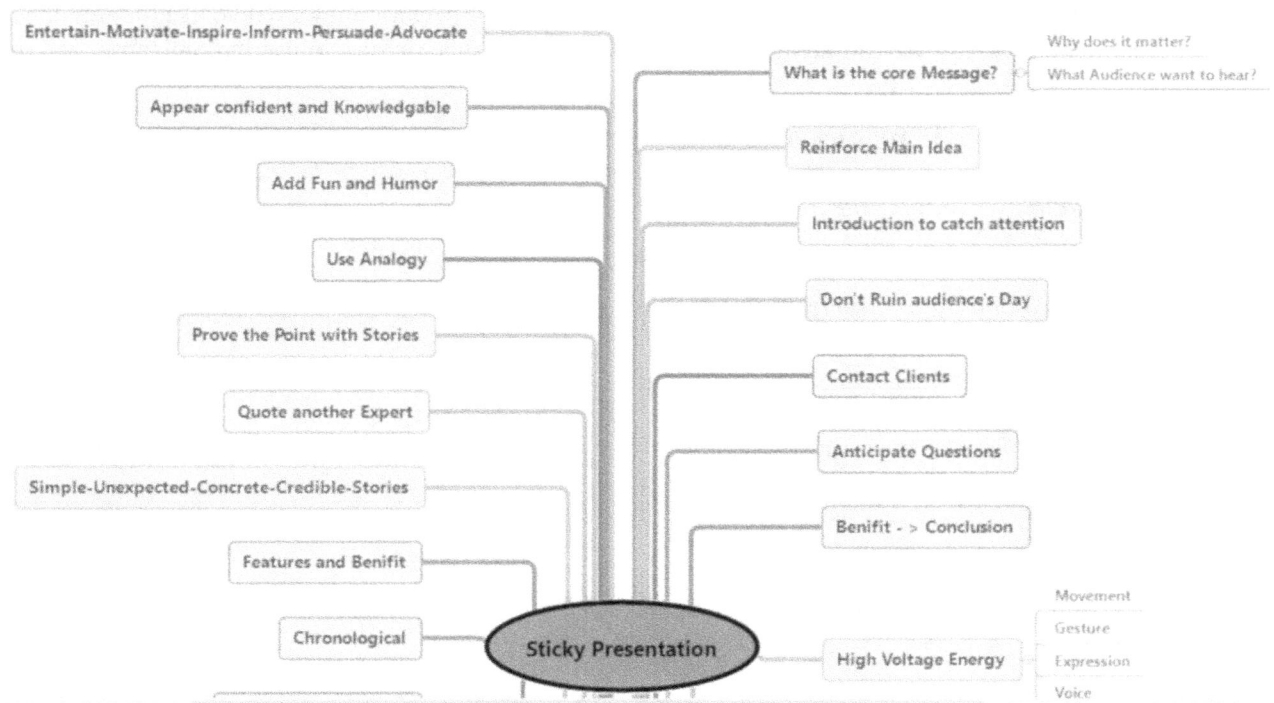

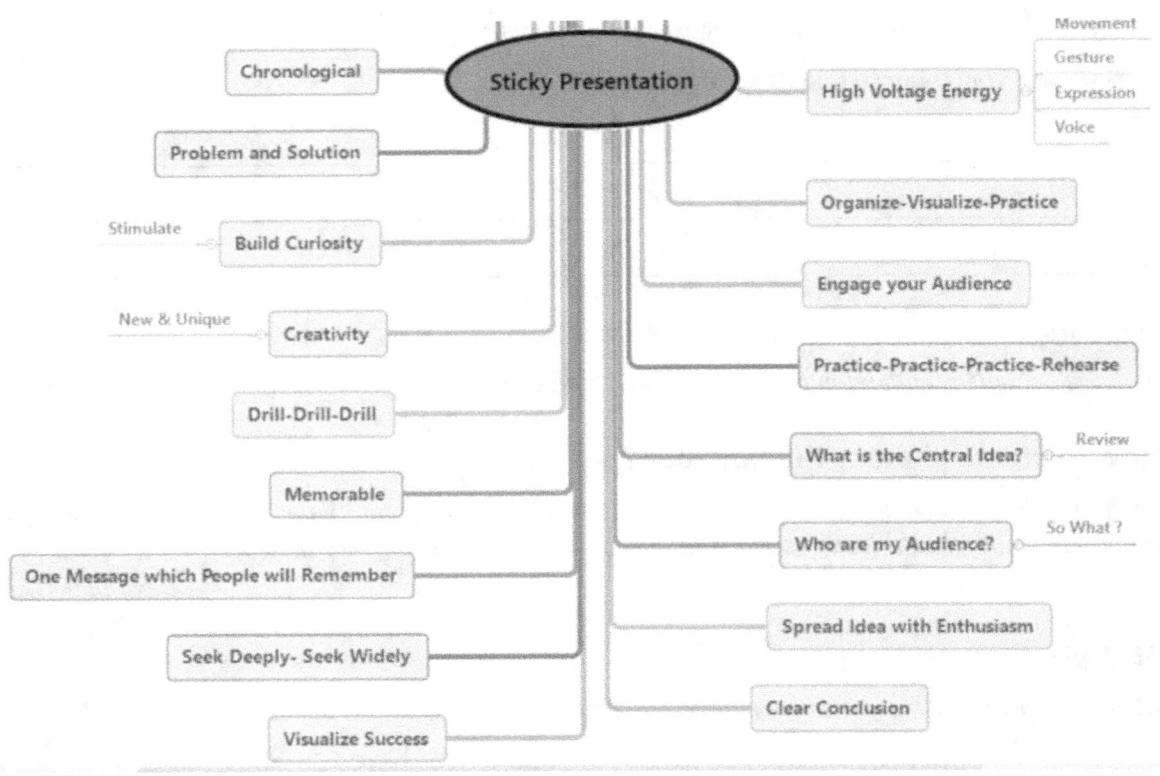

"Speakers who talk about what life has taught them never fail to keep the attention of their listeners."

Dale Carnegie

> *"It is not your customer's job to remember you. It is your obligation and responsibility to make sure they don't have the chance to forget you."*
>
> *—Patricia Fripp*

Stories are a powerful form of communication. They're engaging because they involve us emotionally, and they are memorable because we can mentally see the story. To be successful in our communication, we must use stories.

> *"Your purpose is to make your audience see what you saw, hear what you heard, feel what you felt. Relevant details, couched in concrete, colorful language, is the best way to recreate the incident as it happened and to picture it for the audience."*
>
> *—Dale Carnegie*

What actions are you going to take from this lesson?

1. _____

2. _____

3. _____

Thinking Question:

Are you doing enough to improve your presentation skills? What else can you make?

3.20 What's in it for me? Why should I contribute?

"If You Are Working On Something That You Really Care About, You Don't Have To Be Pushed. The Vision Pulls You."

– Steve Jobs

Why this Topic?

Every time I run an initiative, e.g. running the **Community of Practice (CoP)** *or any voluntary contribution, I notice it a challenge to get people to contribute. People will find many excuses not. How can we encourage people for maximum participation?*

Every one fundamentally asking this question WIFM? **What's in it for me** (WIFM)? Why should I?

I try to put into three BIG baskets

You will get

- **Learning, Exposure, and Experience**
- **Self-satisfaction**
- **Social Recognition, Personal Branding**

What are few tips which worked for me with the people I am working with to build such a community?

1) **Public goals**: We set public goals for all our decisions. In the process, team members are accountable publicly and so they all involved more to achieve their target
2) We display our outcomes through a **BIG Visual bang**! We scream, what we have achieved, and it satisfies all the involved party in the ecosystem
3) We set a **BIG purpose** in each of the events we drive. We **inspire** in a daily stand up what achievement each of the team members will obtain by doing this voluntary work.
4) Building a culture "**NO Fear from Failure**". We encourage failure, and we see much participation and many volunteers. Nobody to blame us.
5) Inspire team members as to what **impact** they are making through various voluntary services.
6) **Recognize in public**, and set a small target, do it more (Small, Consistent, rewards).
7) Build a team with a lot of **energetic** team members, who never run low on energy. They never give up on small hurdles
8) We as a team, help each other to make ourselves perfect with a lot of reviews, and training. Good **feedback** systems to improve.
9) We make a Physical board to demonstrate our work in progress items. Built-in **transparency**
10) We create **BUZZ about our happenings, upcoming items and alerts.** So that all the team members aware of our next steps. We build curiosity about our community to increase participation.
11) We create a **fun-filled ambient**, where the team members come to learn and have fun
12) We share, care and we build a family!

We believe if we inject a sense of achievement, responsibility, job satisfaction, purpose, involvement, empowerment, and ownership team members will run the show on their own.

Otherwise, we will have challenges to sustain voluntary community practices in the long run.

Give more public awards!

Community activities cannot be forced, Should not be forced!

"Knowing Is Not Enough; We Must Apply. Wishing Is Not Enough; We Must Do."

—Johann Wolfgang Von Goethe

What actions are you going to take from this lesson?

1. _____

2. _____

3. _____

Thinking Question:

Are you doing enough to improve community activities? What are the missing situations which require to improve?

3.21 I have completed my certifications, what should I do now?

> *"Unless you try to do something beyond what you have already mastered, you will never grow."*
>
> **—Ronald E. Osborn**

Why this topic?

I have been bombarded with the query regarding the certification and what next? Team members were seeking after completing one certification, what is the next certification? And what next? I shared the below points for myself and all the team members who want to know more about this area.

I am always getting these questions, from the team members, that team members have done all the certifications available in the market, then why we are not getting hike or promotion!

Most of the team members have the same mindset, and they want to do something in short and want to get the result immediately.

What does it take to become competent, or really good at something?

Let us look into this concept, which we can use in any knowledge base, be it agile certification or technology certification

I want to know and learn about Big Data and Cloud technology.

Lead me from the Unreal
to the Real
Lead me from the
Darkness to the Light
Lead me from the
Temporary to the Eternal

How can I apply below stages to enhance my knowledge of Big Data and Cloud Technology knowledge?

I have done the certification on Big Data and Cloud. What does that mean to my project?

Through certification, I might be in Conscious Incompetence.

- **Unconscious Incompetence.** Before you think of trying to learn something, you're not conscious of how incompetent you are at this skill; you didn't even think about it.
- **Conscious Incompetence.** When you begin to learn a new skill, you become quite aware of your incompetence.

- **Conscious Competence**. After some practice, you can become competent at a skill, but much of it is still very conscious—you have to think about what you're doing.
- **Unconscious Competence**. Ultimately, you can reach a point where you have learned the skill so well that it becomes unconscious. You just do it without having to consciously attend to it.

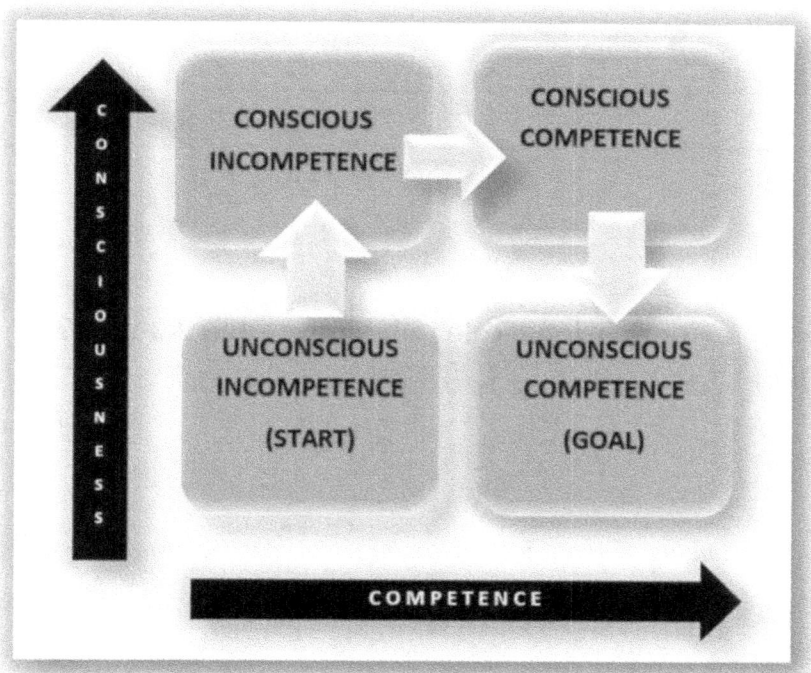

It is the same as when we start learning to drive a car. After several years of driving and several thousand miles of driving in a various jam-packed, mountains, the dangerous treks, we reach to a stage where we do not have to think how to drive while we are driving. It becomes an Unconscious competence for us.

"The only source of knowledge is the experience."

—*Einstein*

What actions are you going to take from this lesson?

1. _____

2. _____

3. _____

Thinking Question:

Are you doing enough to build up your unconscious competence?

3.22 How to enhance my professional role to become a blockbuster?

Find out what you like doing best, and get someone to pay you for doing it.

—*Katharine Whitehorn*

Why this topic?

Every time, our roles are changing, and our jobs are fading. How can we restore ourselves?

This is one of the techniques which helped me to significantly redefine my roles in the changing and emerging world.

Be it as a Technical Lead or as a Program Manager or as a Delivery Manager or as an agile coach, etc.

Peter Drucker's 5 Questions.

I Challenge myself to my core. Peter Drucker's five questions are about **Mission, People, Value, Expectations, and a Plan.**

To be successful in my professional endeavor, I must have thought, clear answers to these questions. Let us look into these.

To start with, PART 1: What is the **mission** of the team or the team members? Or Mine?

Who am I? What values do I consider the most important? What do I stand for? What do I want to achieve in life? How should I treat those closest in my life? How do I want to be treated? What is the purpose of my life?

We write down in detail why we are here for?

PART 2: who is our **customer**? How much do we know about them? What kinds of men and women do we want to interact with? Do they reflect our values and interests? Do they fuel our energy, our excitement for life?

PART 3: "What does the **customer value**? We must understand what is important to all of our friends, family, and colleagues. What are their goals and priorities? And what do they treasure in their relationship with me?

PART 4: What are the **expected outcomes**? Have the people around me clear about what the expectations were? If we have children, do they know what we expect? What about our spouse or partner? My boss? Employees or colleagues? Do I know what these people expect from me? Have I ever asked them what they need?

PART 5: What is MY **plan** now? Short, medium, and long-term actions that will get me to where I want to go.

Let us put it into the Business Canvas template

I use all these above questions when I am coaching or mentoring others.

I ask all these powerful questions to myself and encourage others to prepare themselves.

Do you see the value in this model? In the changing world where roles and responsibilities are changing rapidly, these questions are fundamental and not changing and keeping us relevant to our profession is not healthy. I have been using this model continuously and getting benefits in my career.

> *"I am not a product of my circumstances. I am a product of my decisions"*
>
> —*Stephen Covey*

What actions are you going to take from this lesson?

1. _____

2. _____

3. _____

Thinking Question:

Are you doing enough to equip yourself in this changing world to retrieve your roles and sustain yourselves in this job market?

3.23 Building a High-Performance Team by using the Pygmalion Effect

> *High achievement always takes place within the framework of high expectations"*
>
> —*CHARLES F. KETTERING*

Why this topic?

As part of building a world-class team, I was searching for some topics which can inspire team members to perform at their top

The core of this psychological phenomenon is the theory of a self-fulfilling insight: **If you believe something is true of yourself, eventually it will be.**

Greater expectations drive greater performance: Building a high-performance team.

Building a high-performance team actually already believes that having a high-performance team! We are all working for the world-class teams, world-class software solution! We are already with a high -performance team wherever we work, believing is bringing the reality.

Research has confirmed that people tend to act in ways that are consistent with what others expect of them. The source of low expectations in the workplace is often a boss who sees an employee as a pathetic performer and then treats the employee differently than high performers. The employee who thinks he or she is a weak performer in the eyes of the boss will often perform down to expectations.

Jeff Immelt, CEO and chairman of GE says, *"The ability to demand high performance without being heartless has been part of GE for a long time."*

When performance is measured against these high standards, productivity is likely to increase, and people tend to live up to the expectations of their superiors.

As an agile coach, we have to trust in this principle which is a proven concept to implement at the team level.

Ensure that all the connected parties believe and practice this concept. If not, let us correct them.

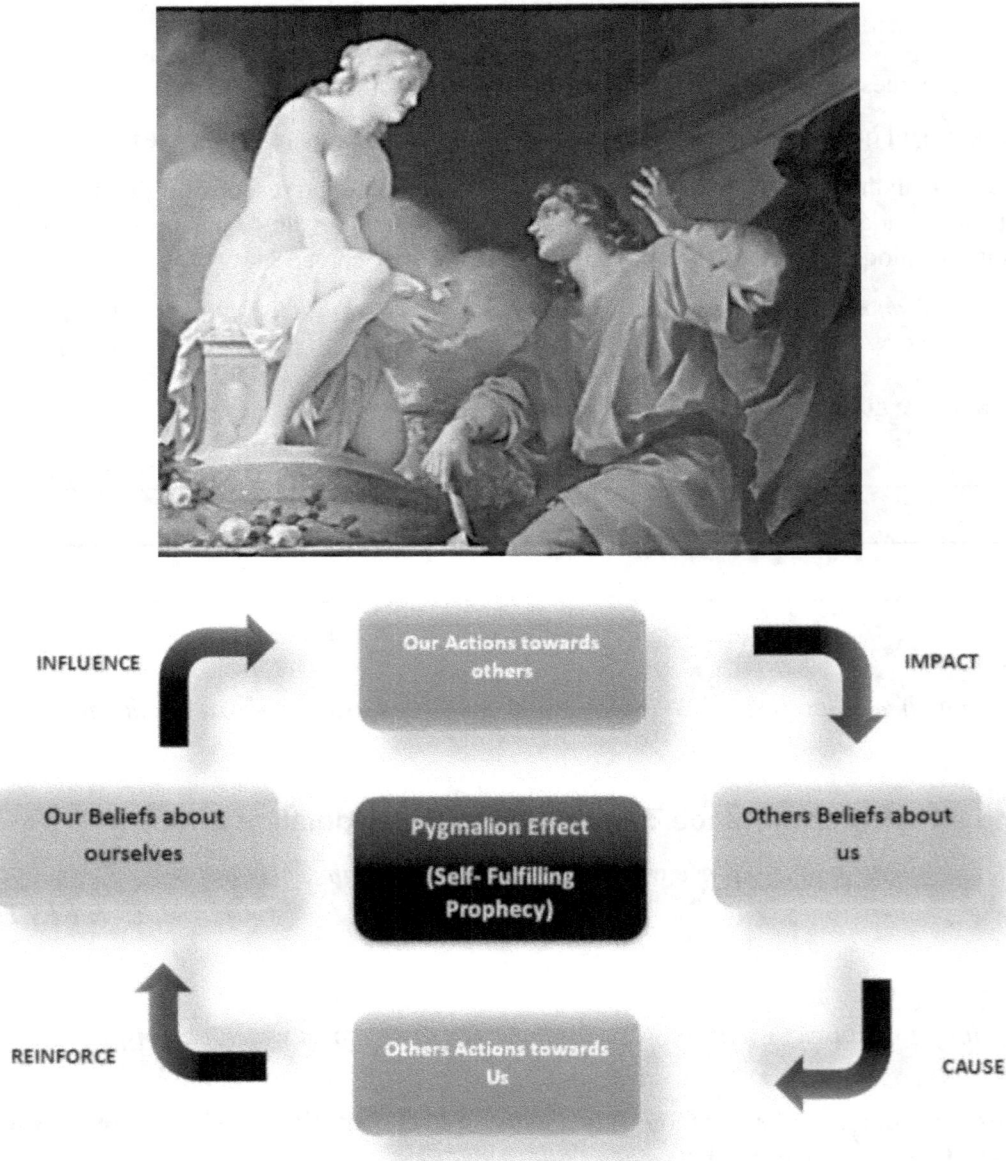

Pygmalion Effect

The first test of the Pygmalion Effect was performed by psychologist Robert Rosenthal and occurred in an elementary school classroom with first and second-grade students. At the beginning of the year, all the students took an assessment test, and Rosenthal led the teachers to believe that certain students were capable of greater academic achievement. Rosenthal chose these students at random, regardless of the actual results of the IQ tests.

At the end of the year, when the students were retested, the group of high achievers did indeed show improvement over their peers.

Why was this? Later tests concluded that teachers subconsciously gave greater opportunities, attention, and feedback to the special group. Their expectations for this group were higher, and their expectations created the reality.

Rosenthal summarized his findings-

What one person expects of another can come to serve as a self-fulfilling prophecy

The effect is named after Pygmalion, a Cypriot sculptor in a narrative by Ovid in Greek mythology, who fell in love with a female statue named Galatea that he had carved out of ivory.

People rise and fall to meet your level of expectations for them. If you express skepticism and doubt in others, they will return your lack of confidence with mediocrity. But if you believe in them and expect them to do well, they will go the extra mile trying to do their best.

—JOHN C. MAXWELL

Pygmalion Effect can help for both personal development and leadership. Exclusively, we can challenge ourselves with tough goals and jobs in an effort to rise to meet the contest. As a leader, when we believe great things from our team, we may see the enhanced performance in return.

Positive attention and caring improved individual performance. Given this finding, any coach or team member can use caring and outflowing concern at work to improve the performance of the organization or workgroup. Humans crave attention and want to be seen positively, which is why "saving face" is so important in many cultures.

As a coach how we are perceived is vital to our standing in the team and in the organization.

It feels good when management cares about you and it is motivating, as reflected in various studies.

Let us treat your team members positively, and reap real bottom line benefits.

Let us practice this at the team level to ensure that the team members believes the best and expect the best as they are developing world-class solutions.

I believe I am a part of the world-class organization and the team.

Perfection is not attainable, but if we chase perfection, we can catch excellence.

—Vince Lombardi

What actions are you going to take from this lesson?

1. _____

2. _____

3. _____

Thinking Question:

Are you doing enough to encourage your team whom you are coaching to establish a high-performance team?

3.24 Certified Feature Team

"Individual commitment to a group effort – that's what makes a team work, a company work, a society work, a civilization work."

—*Vince Lombardi*

Why this topic?

Most of the team claims that they are a feature based team! I have realized some way I need to check how we can confirm if the team is a true feature based team or not. Leader's want to know what is the maturity of each feature team and what can we do to improve the ability if it is less.

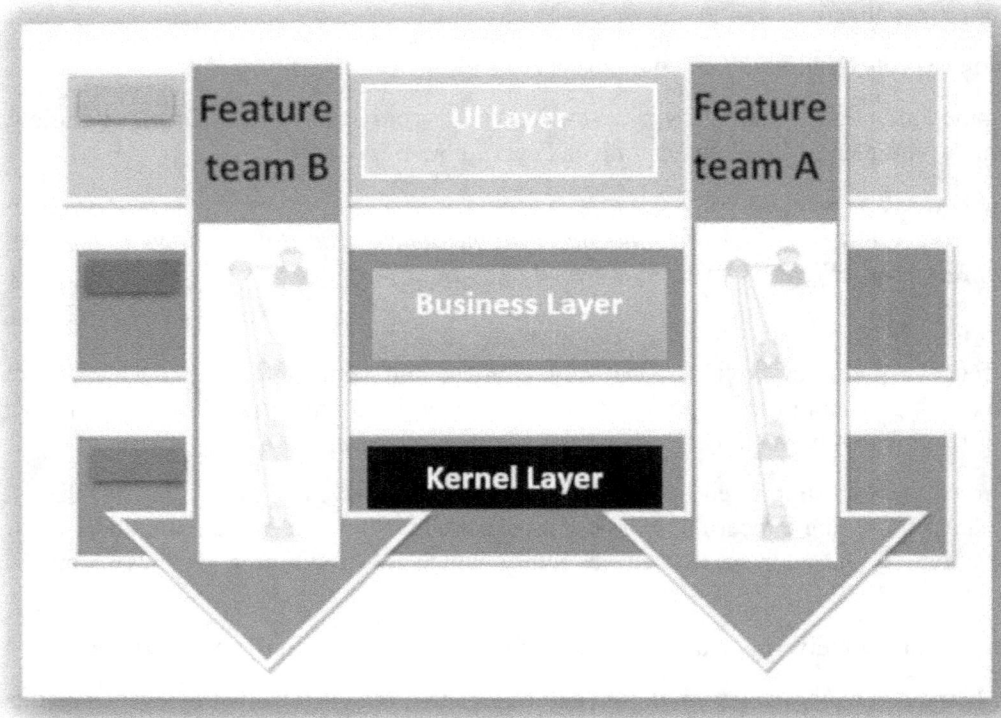

I have run through various questions and asked the teams to help me to get the data

1. Can we find if the team creation was based on the **business alignment** and if there is a continuous business value flow for the team? The rate in the 1-5 scale, 5 is max and 1 is the min level

2. Can we find evidence where the team has **minimized dependencies** between teams to increase the **flexibility**? The rate in the 1-5 scale, 5 is the max and 1 is the min level. Ask the team to show some use cases.

3. Can we find evidence where the team has team focuses on **multiple specializations "the whole team does the whole feature."**? There are no Solo specialists, the team invites roaming specialist. The rate in the 1-5 scale, 5 is the max, knowledge is spread across within the team and 1 is the min level, means hero culture is dominating

4. Can we find evidence where the team is mutually **accountable and have shared responsibility** for all the aspects of design, development, debugging, Quality Assurance, shipping, and so on? The rate in the 1-5 scale, 5 is the max and 1 is the min level

5. Can we find evidence where the team has the ability to **deliver end to end** user value and is able to build end to end functionality? Focus on the customer. The rate in the 1-5 scale, 5 is the max and 1 is the min level

6. Can we find evidence where the team has a **competency, to run the whole show**, they are able to demonstrate? The rate in the 1-5 scale, 5 is the max, the evidence says the team can implement all the functional and technical challenges and 1 is the min level, a team is struggling to deliver features

7. Can we find evidence where the team has a **high learning** to deliver end to end features? The rate in the 1-5 scale, 5 is max where we can find, team members are discovering the unknown and delivering the result and 1 is the min level where the team is struggling to deliver some feature

8. Is the team able to **manage change request faster** as the change planning is owned by one team and there is no dependency on the other teams? The rate in the 1-5 scale, 5 is the max and 1 is the min level

9. Can we find evidence where the team has the **working environment which is stable**, worked across architectural layers, and the team knows how to ensure stability? The rate in the 1-5 scale, 5 is max where issues from the dev environment, a production environment well controlled and 1 is the min level, means issues are messy

10. Can we find evidence where the team is **Self-managed**, and making their own decision? The rate in the 1-5 scale, 5 is the max and 1 is the min level

11. Can we find evidence where the team **avoids the effects of "Conway's Law"** which is "The software tends to mirror the structure of the organization that built it? If you have a big, slow organization, you tend to build big, slow software" the rate in the 1-5 scale, 5 is the max and 1 is the min level

12. Can we find evidence where the team is able to **reuse** wherever possible? The rate in the 1-5 scale, 5 is the max and 1 is the min level

13. Can we find evidence where the **team's time to market data** is improving and sustained at certain speeds? The rate in the 1-5 scale, 5 is the max and 1 is the min level

14. Same team members are **working for a long time** and a small team (8-10)? The rate in the 1-5 scale, 5 is the max where the change of inflow-outflow is 0 and last 12 months are together and 1 is 80-90% team members are new to the team.

15. Can we observe if the team is **free to share, care, improve, collaborate, and criticize, diverse points** of view? The rate in the 1-5 scale, 5 is the max(many Meetings are happening with sharing) and 1 is the min level

16. Is team able to deliver **vertically sliced features**? The rate in the 1-5 scale, 5 is the max and 1 is the min level

17. Are team members not **under-utilized**? If yes, the team takes care, how can we **maximize the utilization** through the right engagement (High-Value work)? The rate in the 1-5 scale, 5 is the max and 1 is the min level

18. Are team members **not shared among the various projects**? The rate in the 1-5 scale, 5 is the max and rate 1 when team members are spread in many projects, 5 means dedicated all the team members.

19. There are not many meetings called for, like "**Dependency Management Discussion**"? the rate in the 1-5 scale, 5 is the max(0 meetings) and 1 is the min level

20. There is no project manager **dedicated to coordination activities**? If yes, how much time spent on coordination? The rate in the 1-5 scale, 5 is the max(0 hrs. for co-ordination work) and 1 is the min level

21. If the team has a **community of practice (COP)** platform dedicated to sharing leanings and the meeting is happening frequently? The rate in the 1-5 scale, 5 is the max and 1 is the min level

22. If the team **co-located**? The Rate in the 1-5 scale, 5 is the max and rate 1 for scattered team members geographically, 5 for all team members are sitting together

23. **The customer is happy** as Customer is getting what he/she has been asking for, in the shortest duration of time with excellent quality? The Rate in the 1-5 scale, 5 is the max, Very happy customer and 1 is the min level.

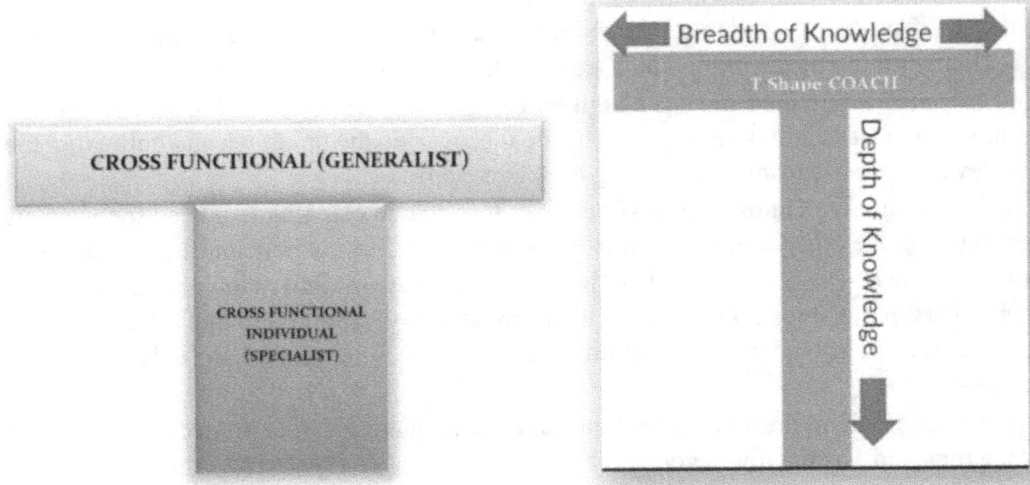

Let us measure what is the score for that feature based team, out of 110, how much they score and the improvement plan.

> *"A human being should be able to change a diaper, plan an invasion, butcher a hog, conn a ship, design a building, write a sonnet, balance accounts, build a wall, set a bone, comfort the dying, take orders, give orders, cooperate, act alone, solve equations, analyze a new problem, pitch manure, program a computer, cook a tasty meal, fight efficiently, die gallantly. Specialization is for insects."*
>
> **—Robert A. Heinlein, Time Enough for Love**

What actions are you going to take from this lesson?

1. _____

2. _____

3. _____

Thinking Question:

Are you doing enough to validate your feature team and help the team to take action for raising the tally?

3.25 How is Mother-in-Law spoiling the Agile Team?

> *"An employee's motivation is a direct result of the sum of interactions with his or her manager."*
>
> **—Bob Nelson**

Why this topic?

I am getting this complaint from many of my team members that Project Managers are intruding in their daily work. What can I do for those team members?

Mothers-in-law are spoiling the family life! Managers are spoiling the Agile Team!

"Monster-in-Laws:" A Leading Cause of Divorce. In a team context, it causes attrition

An article titled "Divorce Causes: 5 Ways to Destroy Your Marriage" in the Huffington Post states that in-laws can be a leading cause of divorce.

Author Francesca Escoto writes, "How spouses relate to the in-laws is a strong predictor of marriage longevity. A man who gets along with his wife's parents is wise — his chances of a strong marriage increases by about 20 percent. Women who get along with their in-laws actually have an increased probability of divorce, by about 20 percent."

What can we do about it? We need them, but they should not break the family.

In an Agile Team/Family, Mother-in-law is like a Manager! In the Agile world, they do not have many things to do, as they have retired from the active family life or delivery role. The Product Owner and Scrum Master manage this active life.

But Mother in law is interfering in every course of action like Managers.

What are those? Extracted from the happy family where the Mother in law is interfering!

HAVE YOU FOUND SUCH INSTANCES IN AGILE PROJECTS WHERE THE MANAGER IS HOVERING AROUND SCRUM TEAM?

Mothers-in-law are notorious for being controlling, judgmental, critical and overbearing (In the Project team, the Manager could be like this)

1. She is always right, without exception. Which means that she's never wrong. She'll never admit being wrong, and she will never apologize for anything. In her eyes, you (and possibly your spouse) are the only person to blame. (Similar things can be found with the Agile Team, where Manager will be doing exactly the same)

2. To establish her dominance, she will expect you to please her. That would include appearing at every family event, learning her way of cooking, cleaning and just about everything else under the sun (because her way is clearly better), If you fail to do any of that, you are indeed a rotten daughter-in-law, and she has a right to complain about you to anyone who'll listen. (Similar things can be found with the Agile Team, where Manager will be doing exactly like this and escalation goes to the senior leaders)

3. If you are still not bending to her will, she will move on to heavier artillery. She will start a smear campaign in her community, trying to turn everyone against you. If she succeeds, those people will start putting pressure on your husband to leave you, saying that they're just "worried about him" and they "want him to be happy."(Similar things can be found with the Agile Team, where the Manager will be doing exactly like this)

4. Try to mediate my son's marital disputes. Mothers-in-law don't get to have the inside scoop on the young marriage. Let them solve their problem. (In the Agile team, let the team members solve it, why managers in jumping into all these to become a hero.)

5. Rearrange daughter-in-law's house. Clearly, the coffee mugs should be stored in the cabinet over the coffeemaker. Any idiot can see that. But it's not Mothers-in-law kitchen, so Mothers-in-law don't get to decide where the coffee mugs go. (In the Agile team, the team decides everything with the help of the PO and the SM)

1. Fold daughter-in-law's laundry without her permission,
2. Buy daughter-in-law clothes only Mothers-in-law would wear,
3. Think daughter-in-law is perfect,
4. Enter daughter-in-law's bedroom without knocking,
5. Offer unsolicited advice,
6. Show up unannounced,
7. Criticize daughter-in-law's cooking.

(All these activities can be mapped to an agile team context where the Managers are getting into the team comfort zone and spoiling the self-organized culture)

Many of the items on the list are considered faux pas in any situation. They are a hundred times more egregious when put in the context of a mother-in-law (Manager)/daughter-in-law(SM/PO) relationship.

How to Manage her? Or the Managers:

What can the Scrum Masters do for the agile team?

a) **Respect her different viewpoints**. Even if you don't agree with what she has to say, listen to your mother-in-law. Don't immediately write off what she has to say. Hear her out (even if you feel it's ridiculous) and let her know you're listening. You don't have to agree to anything.

Respond to neutrally by saying, "Okay, I'll consider that" or, "Thanks for your input."

If she puts you in a difficult position, defer to your spouse. Say, "I don't want to answer right away. Let me talk to my spouse first."

b) **Use humor**. Deflecting criticism or other awkward interaction with humor can deflate conflicts and put everyone at ease again. Whether the situation seems tense or she's making things difficult, a little humor can go a long way.

c) **Work through your feelings** about your mother-in-law. Are you able to put yourself in her shoes occasionally and see just where some of her so-called interfering or judgmental behavior comes from? She values the person you're married to, so there must be something good inside her!

 - Keep in mind that whatever your feelings, your mother-in-law remains one of the most important people in your spouse's life. Be sure it's not your untamed jealousy causing problems.

- If your relationship with your mother is strained or difficult, consider if that is affecting your relationship with your mother-in-law. Remember that they are different people, and you can have a different relationship with each one.

d) **Create some ground rules**. If you live with your mother-in-law, establish some ground rules for living together. If you know there are things that might cause conflict, talk about them beforehand and make sure everyone understands the rules and why they are in place

e) **Make compromises**. You and your mother-in-law will inevitably disagree on certain things, especially when living together. Choose your battles and decide what things you can tolerate and what things you need to be firm about

f) **Create mutually agreed boundaries**. Both you and your mother-in-law may enjoy having your own space and ways of doing things. Ask your mother-in-law how you might make her comfortable in the home while enforcing your own needs and desires. As long as your boundaries don't conflict, try to respect her space and independence.

> *"A great manager is someone who says, 'You come to work with me, and I'll help you be as successful as possible; I'll help you grow. I'll help you make sure you're in the right role; I'll provide the relationship for you to understand and know yourself. And I want you to be more successful than me.'"*
>
> *—Curt Coffman*

What actions are you going to take from this lesson?

1. _____

2. _____

3. _____

Thinking Question:

Are you doing enough to help your team members who are the target of such a situation?

3.26 Key Takeaways

What we have discussed in this chapter is about the **Fire** elements of the **Pancha Bhoota Model**. If the team members are motivated and aligned with the organizational vision, Agility will assure achieved.

1) Business model YOU, important to set up one for yourself
2) People need the inspiration to contribute to CoP. How to engage the team members easily?
3) Creating awesome presentation steps
4) Develop extreme collaboration
5) Partnership and collaboration, developing the skill
6) Developing excellent team performance
7) Building happiness at the team level.
8) Developing better storytelling habits
9) Workshop facilitation tips
10) To be a Good Scrum Master steps
11) Awesome questioning skills
12) On successful partnership, steps
13) Applying a self-disclosure style for improving engagement
14) When excellent players fail, things to avoid
15) Tips for Motivating team members
16) Develop awesome Passion
17) Steps to Inspire adults to learn
18) Steps to work with difficult people
19) Entrepreneurial Mindset, spreading these ideas to the team members
20) Producing abundance ideas at work

In the next Chapter, we will take up the **mindset** which will strengthen the **Space element** in the **Pancha Bhoota Model**.

4 Enablement of Mindset Change

4.1 Introduction:

This chapter will highlight the mindset of the people and how a coach can encourage the team members to develop these skills. These skills are essential for inspiring people and energizing the team members to achieve a bigger goal. In the **Pancha Bhoota Model,** this is the **Space** element. It is the enormous where everything happens.

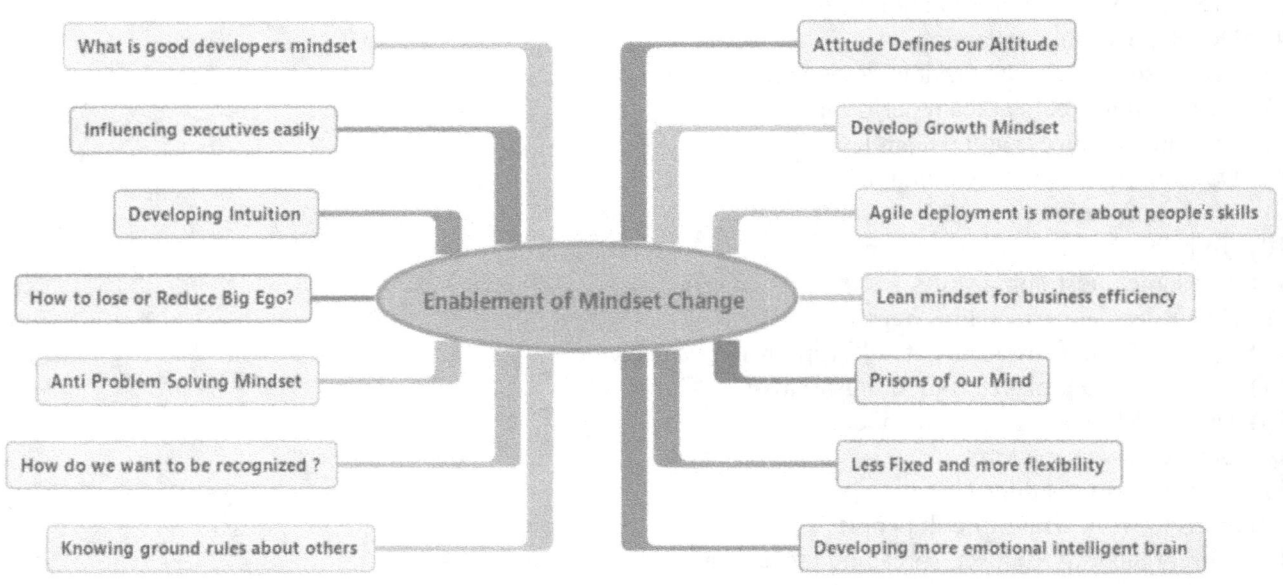

"Nothing gets transformed in your life until your mind is transformed"

—Ifeanyi Enoch Onuoha

4.2 Attitude defines our Altitude: How to improve?

People may hear your words, but they feel your attitude.

—John C. Maxwell

Why this topic?

I have always had this question what can I do with the individual who has a high attitude?

Attitude!! Attitude!! Attitude defines our Altitude not our Aptitude…which directly bonds with the employee's great Productivity. Spread this type of thoughts to our team members.

Somebody quotes: **"Ability is what we're capable of doing. Motivation determines what we do. Attitude determines how well we do it."**

Attitudes are beliefs that we have accepted as correct, and that leads us to think, feel, or perform positively or negatively toward a person, idea, or event. They represent an emotional readiness to behave in a particular manner.

Our values, beliefs, and preferences, we feel are important and serves as a foundation for our attitudes.

Attitude is often synonyms with self-esteem. People formulate a powerful first impression of our within the first 12-30 seconds. Judgement is based on the physical posture and appearance.

Each of us lives our life according to a unique set of core values.

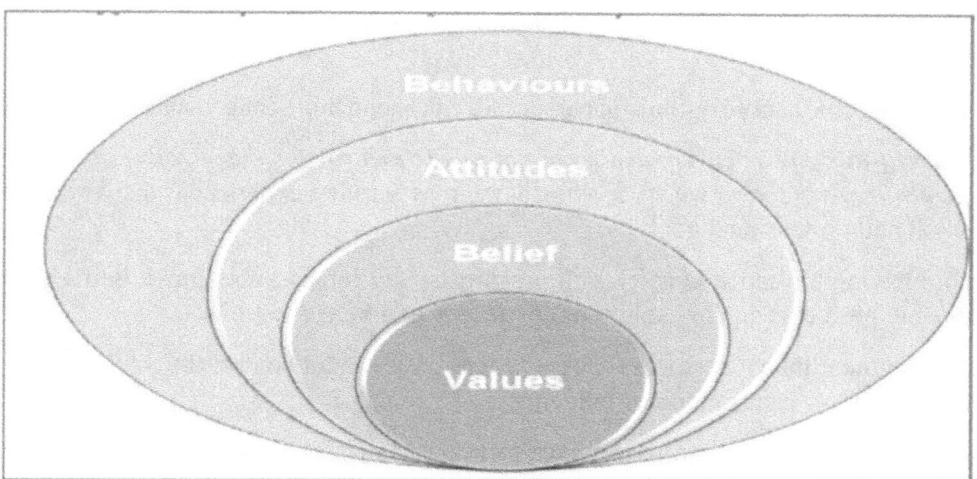

One of the most significant differences between high and low achievers is the **choice of attitude.**

People who go through life with a positive attitude are more likely to achieve their personal and professional goals. People who filter their daily experiences through a negative attitude find it difficult to achieve contentment or satisfaction in any aspect of their lives.

Jack Welch, the former chairman and CEO of General Electric, believes that an organization needs people with **"positive energy"** and needs to get rid of those people who inject the workforce with **"negative energy"**—even if they are high performers.

Many organizations have discovered the link between the workers' attitudes and profitability. This discovery has led to major changes in the hiring process.

Employers today are less likely to assume that the applicants' technical abilities are the best indicators of their future performance. They have discovered that the lack of technical skills is not the primary reason why most new hires fail to meet expectations.

It is their dearth of social skills that count. **Happy employees are productive employees.**

People who are self-motivated are inclined to set their own goals and monitor their progress toward those goals. *Agile team!! Self-Driven Team members.*

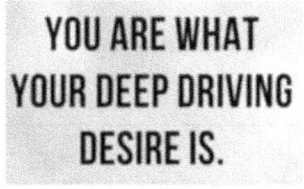

YOU ARE WHAT
YOUR DEEP DRIVING
DESIRE IS.

Brihadaranyaka Upanishad

Their attitude is

"I am responsible for this job." They do not need a supervisor hovering around them making sure they are on the task and accomplishing what they are supposed to be doing. Micromanagers will be forced to resign!

Many find ways to administer their rewards after they achieve their goals. Employers frequently keep and encourage those employees who take the initiative to make their own decisions, discover better ways of executing their works, read professional publications to acquire new things, and monitor the media for advances in technology.

Optimistic thoughts give rise to positive attitudes and effective interpersonal relationships. When we are an optimist, our coworkers, managers, and—perhaps most important—our customers feel our energy and vitality and tend to mirror your behavior.

If we feel the need to become a more optimistic person, we can spend more time visualizing yourself succeeding.

Let us monitor our self-talk and discover whether or not we are focusing on the negative aspects of the problems and disappointments in our life, or if we are looking at them as learning experiences that will eventually lead us toward our personal and professional goals.

Let us try to avoid having too much contact with pessimists, and refuse to be drawn into a group of negative thinkers who see only problems and not solutions. **Attitudes can be contagious.**

An attitude is nothing more than a personal thought process. We cannot control the thinking that takes place in someone else's mind, but we can sometimes influence it.

And sometimes we can't do that either, so we have to set certain rules of behavior. Some organizations have come to the conclusion that the behavior that offends or threatens others must stop.

When employees have positive attitudes, job performance and productivity are likely to improve.

We are constantly placed in new situations with people from different backgrounds and cultures. Each time we go to a new school, take a new job, get a promotion, or move to a different neighborhood, we may need to alter our attitudes to cope effectively with the changes when events, such as a layoff, are beyond our control. We can accept this fact and move on. **It is often said that life is 10 percent what happens to us and 90 percent how we react to it.**

Most companies realize that an employee's attitude and performance cannot be separated. When employees have negative attitudes about their work, their job performance and productivity suffer.

Excellent work + Poor Attitude = Poor Productivity

Excellent IQ+ Excellent Work + Poor Attitude = Poor Productivity

When employees work with the right mindset, the output increases.

"Excellence is not a skill. It is an attitude. "

How can we build such a mindset? Agile team ......as a part of the journey to build a world-class place to live in...

> *"Adopting the right attitude can convert a negative stress into a positive one."*
>
> —*Hans Selye*

What actions are you going to take from this lesson?

1. _____

2. _____

3. _____

Thinking Question:

Are you doing enough to help our team members to develop the right attitude?

Do we have allies, colleagues, and team members with such a mindset? What can we understand from them?

4.3 Do you have a Growth Mindset? How to improve?

"We need to realize that our path to transformation is through our mistakes. We're meant to make mistakes, recognize them, and move on to become unlimited."

—Yehuda Berg

Why this topic?

Most of the time in my coaching I have come across various challenges, and how do we analyze if I am having a growth mindset or a fixed mindset?

In today's world, we should be focused most of the time on a growth mindset based thinking.

Woody Allen once said, **"If you are not failing every now and again, it's a sign you're not doing anything innovative."**

How do we encourage leaders to apply the growth mindset in Emergent work? Look for the below characteristics in your personality.

Especially when we are living in a **Complex** world, and when things are **emergent**, we need to mostly apply a **Growth Mindset.**

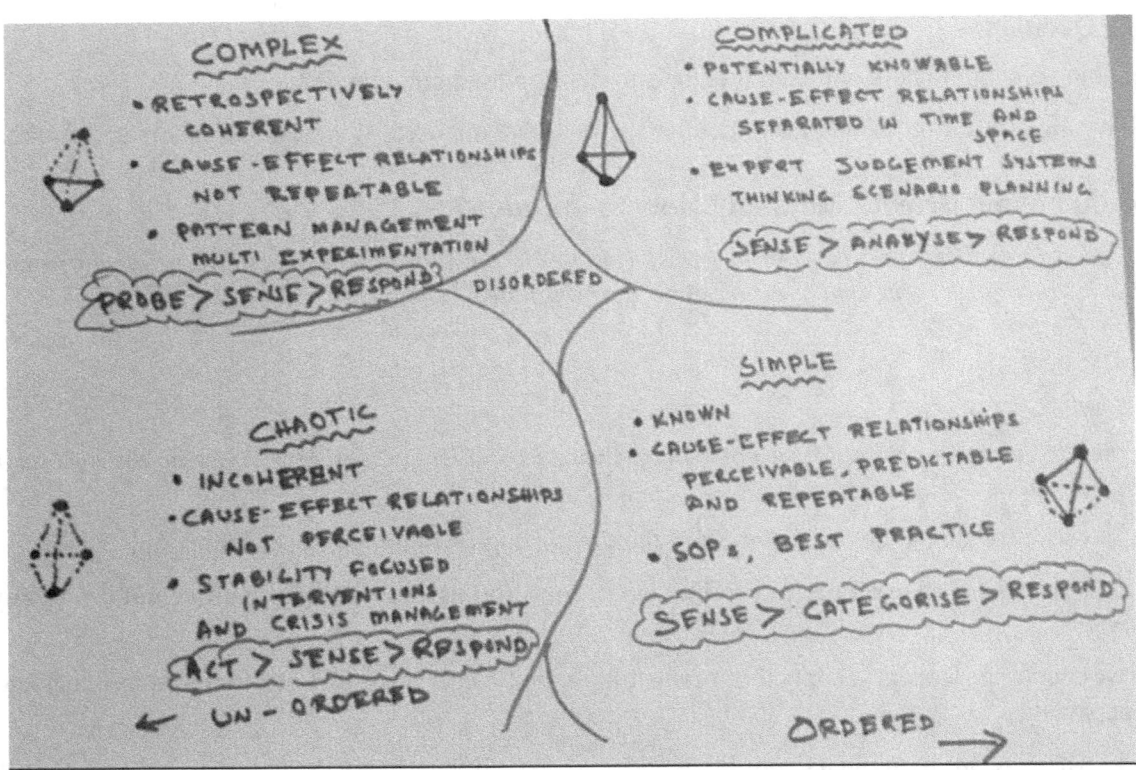

Michael Jordan: "I have missed over 9,000 shots in my career. I have lost almost 300 games. On 26 occasions, I have been entrusted to take the game's winning shot, and I have missed. I have failed over and over and over again in my life. And that is why I succeeded."

Saeongjima, pronounced "say-ong-jay-mah," is a Chinese–Korean saying that means "the horse of an elderly person living on the border." The phrase comes from a parable in which an old man encounters a series of lucky and unlucky events. But whatever happens, **the old man always shrugs off the congratulations or commiserations of his neighbors by saying, "Good or bad, who knows?"**

The story goes like this: One day, the old man's horse escapes and runs away across the border. It seems that it has gone forever, but soon enough it makes its way home again, accompanied by a splendid new horse. At the time this appeared to be a wonderful good fortune. **Months later,** the old man's son is badly hurt riding this new horse and ends up disabled, which at the time seems like terribly bad luck. However, the following year the son is spared from being drafted into a dreadful war because of this injury and goes on to live a long and peaceful life. **In our own lives,** events can have unforeseeable outcomes, so it's always worth remembering "saeongjima": **one "unlucky" or missed opportunity might turn into a new and better one later.**

"YOU BUILD ON FAILURE. YOU USE IT AS A STEPPING STONE"

—JOHNNY CASH, MUSICIAN

What actions are you going to take from this lesson?

1. _____

2. _____

3. _____

Thinking Question:

Are you doing enough to improve your mindset which can stimulate you to perform your tasks better in this complex world?

4.4 How to lose/Reduce Big Ego?

Ego is one of the biggest weapons that is used to take us down. It's self-destructive. It's a problem at all levels - even regular people can have big ego problems.

—Yehuda Berg

Why This Topic?

I have been working with a large organization where I am dealing with leaders who are with the same systems for 15-20 years! When we communicate with them that one common factor, that I have come across, all these team members are having huge confidence as they are living with the systems for a long time and they know the in-and-out of the systems and their customer expectations. How do we coach them? How do we coach them to check their ego for change initiatives?

Now there are slow changes are happening in these domains and the markets and which they are not noticing or not willing to listen, as they know it all!

We as a coach sometimes have to come across them! Influence them about business agility and a new leadership style! Most of them I have found have built huge **EGO**

Of course, they will pretend they are very humble and down to earth.

Most of the time I have failed by trying and experimenting!

How do we coach them to release the control style and be a servant leader!?

"Ego" is Greek for I. In the Greek New Testament or a Greek version of Plato or Aristotle any time someone says, "I…" they utter the word ego.

Ego According to Freud, this is the conscious, rational part of the personality. He saw the human psyche as being made up of three parts: the **Id**, which seeks instant gratification, the **Superego**, which makes moral judgments, and the **Ego**, which mediates between the first two. It does so use the 'reality principle,' which compels us to abide by current social norms. Freud said the **Id** was like a horse and the **Ego** like a man riding the horse and controlling its wilder instincts.

The ego deals with conscious thoughts and regulates both the id and the superego—our critical, judging voice.

157

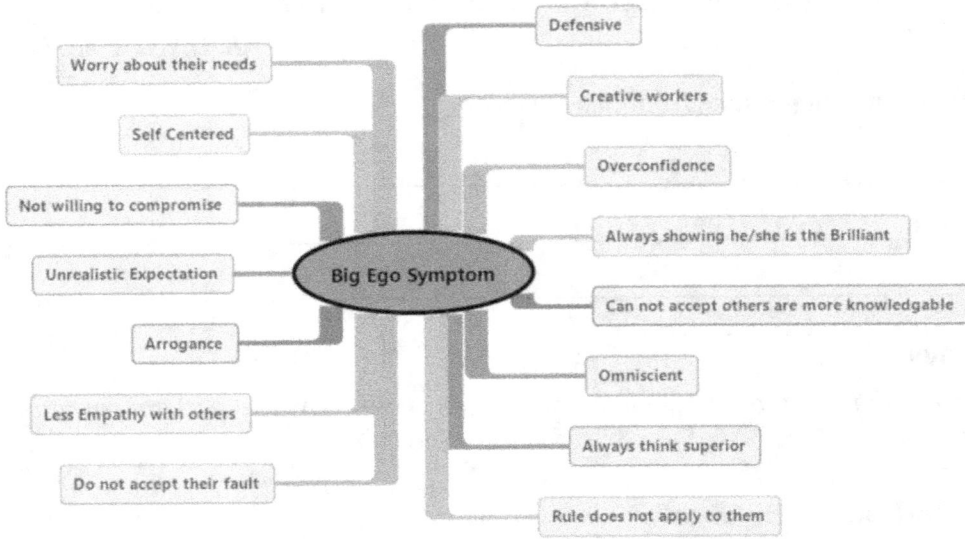

How to normalize big ego state through coaching? How to build an ecosystem where the team members would like to work with each other?

Let us start practicing the below characteristics for 15 days or help others to change and see the result or **apply this cream for 15 days!** It is only available in *Himalaya!!!*

It will surely improve the individuals and teams to improve the current situation and deal with the BIG ego guys!

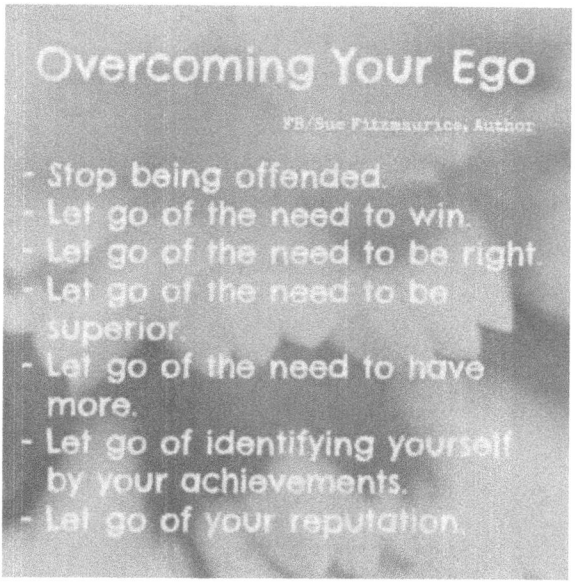

The ego is not master in its own house.

—Sigmund Freud

What actions are you going to take from this lesson?

1. _____

2. _____

3. _____

Thinking Question:

Are you doing enough to build your potential to encourage your colleagues who have to repair their ego?

4.5 How to escape from the confinement of our Mind?

"We are shaped by our thoughts; we become what we think. When the mind is pure, joy follows like a shadow that never leaves."

—Buddha

Why this topic?

How to coach some of the senior team members and demonstrate to them about the new way of working?

While implementing Scaling Agile, I came across many situations where I could find most of us are in the prisons of our mind. Some of the prisons are

- **Prison of Pride and Ego**
- **Prison of past achievements**
- **Prison of unknown**

These are deadly prisons because they are invisible prisons of the mind: we do not know that they are there and we do not know that they are trapping us inside.

Once we are successful in life, we are in the trap that we can do it again as we have done this so many times. We do not want to consult with anyone, as others are nothing in front of us! We are under the effect of the dark prison of success and repeat success.

But the world has changed, and our old styles may not be working in the current setup. We are trapped in our prison and we are not able to come out of the dark cell.

The process which has helped us to achieve the maximum success that may not work at all today, and if the wall of the prison is thick, we will not be able to accept or break those walls.

The old way of product development or the old leadership style has changed, but most of the seniors are living under the prison of the old styles as they are not able to come out from this prison cell.

You would like to repeat the good old memories and emotions, as it excites you and gives you a feel-good factor. Research has shown that emotion hinders observation. We are under the effect of the old prisons.

The prison of uncertainty is also a thick-walled prison, which most of us pass through. We all have this prison. This prevents us from experimenting, trying new things, and learning from falling over and getting up again.

Knowing that these prisons exist, at least to alerts us to their risks. If we know they are there, we have a chance of avoiding ending up in them. But to escape the prisons and to keep out of them, we need to establish positive routines for ourselves

If I say to my Leaders that you are in a prison, they will not accept that, they have to experience that and start breaking the prison wall

➢ Have you explained to your executives while coaching about the various prisons of the mind?

➢ What was your experience?

➢ How can they recognize those prisons?

Let us help each other and experiment to break these prisons.

"You must weed your mind as you would weed your garden."

—Astrid Alauda

'If you can change your mind, you can change your life."

—William James

What actions are you going to take from this lesson?

1. _____

2. _____

3. _____

Thinking Question:

Are you doing enough to help your senior team members to find out the new way of working and why they should look into the numerous new learning styles?

4.6 How to apply the Lean Mindset to Improve Business Efficiency

> *"The most dangerous kind of waste is the waste we do not recognize."*
>
> **—Shigeo Shingo**

Why this topic?

Learning from Lean and implementing the concepts in our various roles and responsibilities. How to perform better and the impressive?

My friend wants to start her own business. Looking for advice on where to start from, other than core competency, which she already has. I prescribe her to start with **Lean Thinking**.

One friend wants to start her coaching business and another one to start play home for small kids.

Lean Thinking?

Why Lean?

Several case studies— including Harman, Intuit, and GE Healthcare—show how the lean principles of **Focus on the Customers, Energize Workers, Learn First, and Deliver Fast** help companies develop breakthrough innovations before they get blindsided by someone else's disruptive innovations.

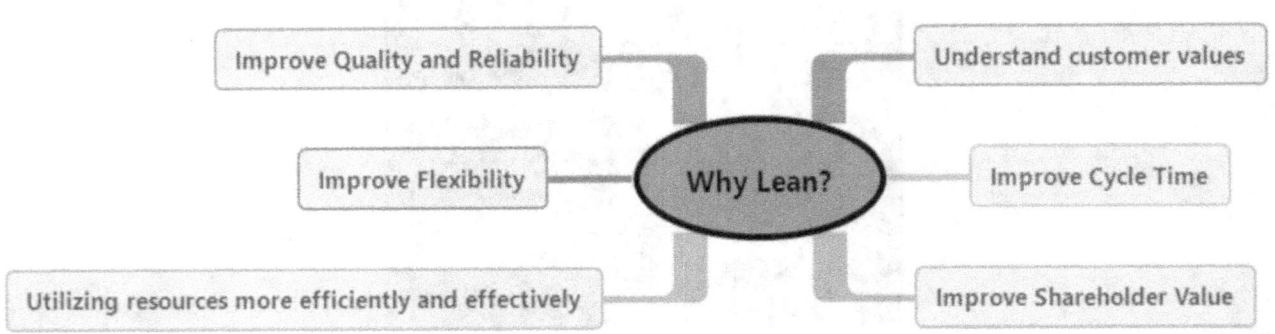

Lean is a customer-focused approach that concentrates on providing value by eliminating waste and increasing quality.

Lean is an approach that, when adopted, provides many benefits.

Adopt Lean Mindset?

Adopting a Lean mindset will be making the customer the center of attention by capturing a person or organization's specifications, or requirements, and satisfying those using value-added processes, operations, procedures, tools, and techniques deemed worthwhile by the customer.

> *A mindset is a set of assumptions, methods, or notations held by one or more people or groups of people that is so established that it creates a powerful incentive within these people or groups to continue to adopt or accept prior behaviors, choices, or tools*
>
> **—Wikipedia**

Need to change the mindset wherever applicable if it is not returning the expected result.

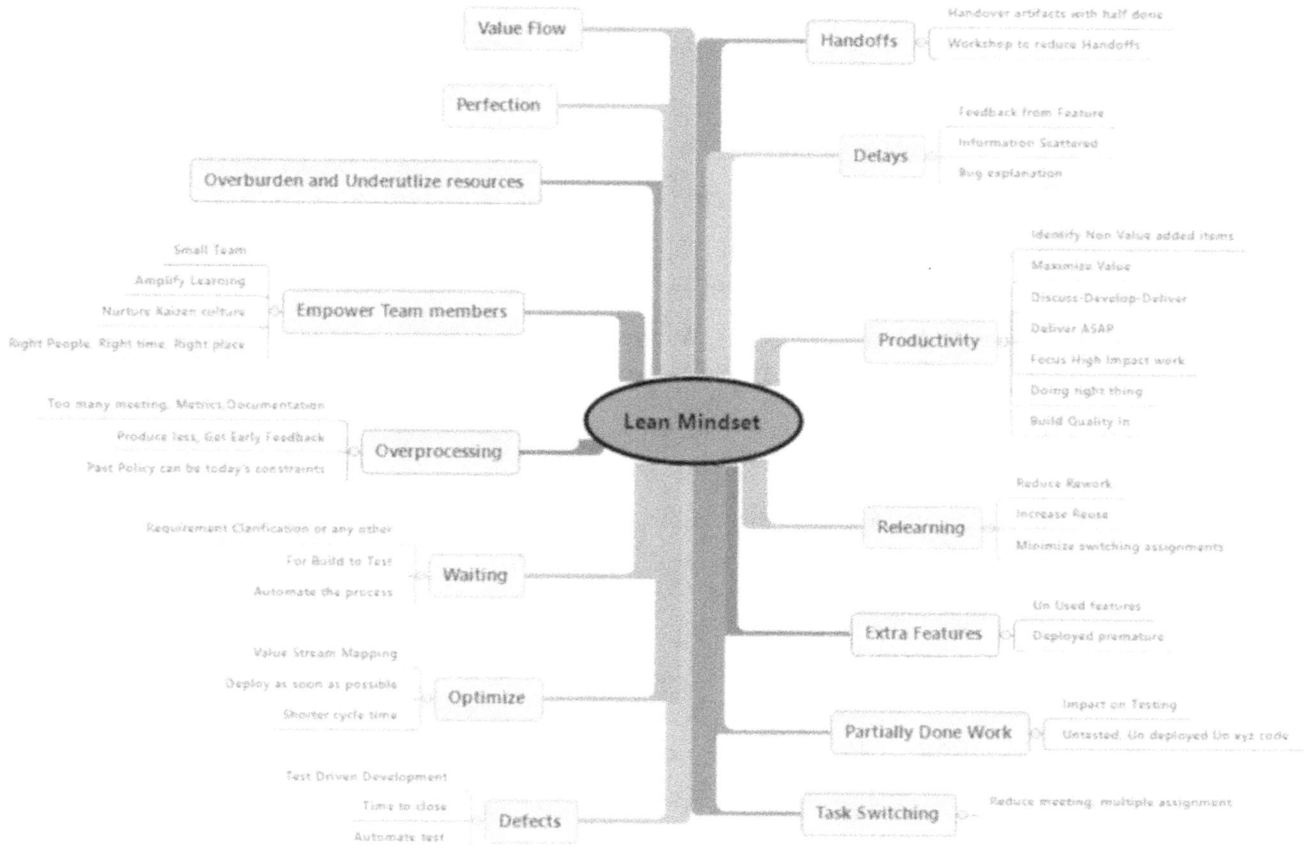

Value Flow — Handoffs — Handover artifacts with half done / Workshop to reduce Handoffs

Perfection

Overburden and Underutilize resources — Delays — Feedback from Feature / Information Scattered / Bug explanation

Small Team / Amplify Learning / Nurture Kaizen culture / Right People, Right time, Right place — Empower Team members

Productivity — Identify Non Value added items / Maximize Value / Discuss-Develop-Deliver / Deliver ASAP / Focus High Impact work / Doing right thing / Build Quality In

Too many meeting, Metrics, Documentation / Produce less, Get Early Feedback / Past Policy can be today's constraints — Overprocessing

Lean Mindset

Relearning — Reduce Rework / Increase Reuse / Minimize switching assignments

Requirement Clarification or any other / For Build to Test / Automate the process — Waiting

Extra Features — Un Used features / Deployed premature

Value Stream Mapping / Deploy as soon as possible / Shorter cycle time — Optimize

Partially Done Work — Impact on Testing / Untested, Un deployed Un xyz code

Test Driven Development / Time to close / Automate test — Defects

Task Switching — Reduce meeting, multiple assignment

"Lean is a mindset change", and when team members, takes a lean approach for each of the tasks they execute, efficiency improves.

See Big and beyond

Every member has to think from the organization, business point of view, customer and the stakeholder point of view.

When all the members are working from looking at the "big picture" point of view, we automatically achieve lean.

As Don Reinertson says in *Managing the Design Factory* (Reinertsen 1997):

"...we can improve effective capacity by cross-training our workers. Since critical bottlenecks are likely to occur in specialized areas, we should create backups for these workers. For example, test specialists can be supplemented by cross-training some of the engineering technicians to assist in this area during heavy periods. You might think that this is inefficient, because cross-trained people can never be as efficient as the specialist. This is true, but irrelevant. We do not cross-train to create an efficient resource, we cross-train to create a resource that can deal with bottlenecks. Remember, when the system is heavily loaded a small change of capacity can lead to a large change in cycle time."

Lean highlights accepting and gathering customer requirements as the elementary drivers of a process/ business.

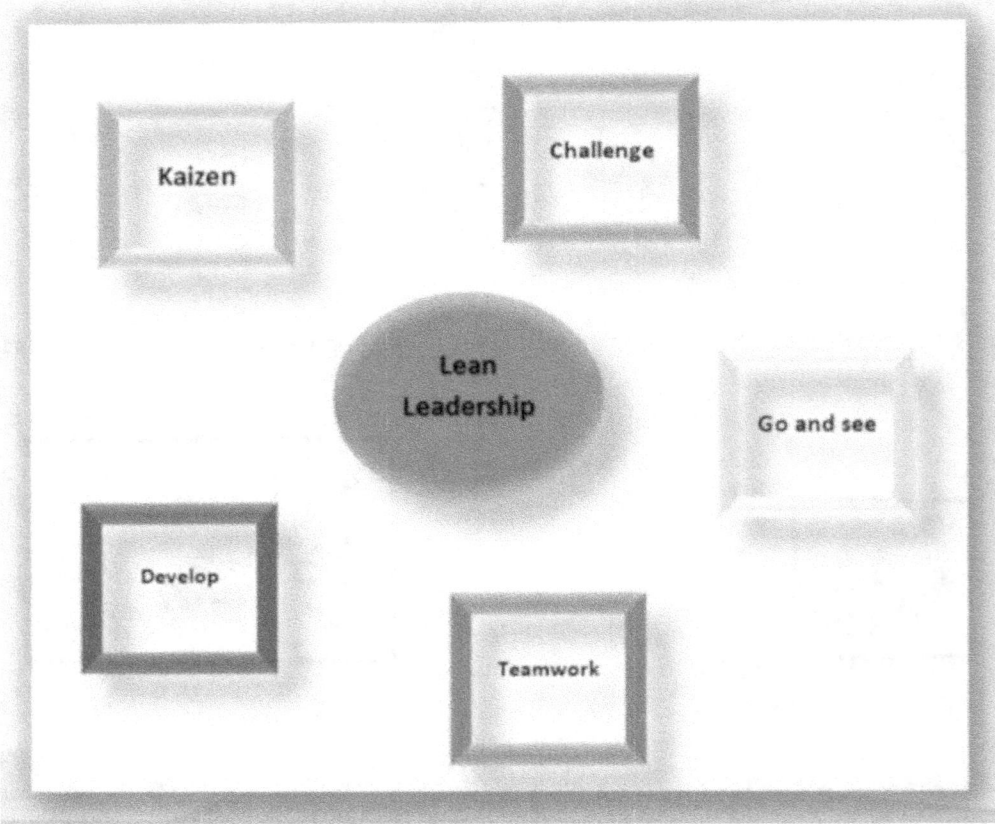

Start the journey with this concept and see the result.

Let us apply the same in our **Conference Business**

- **Customer Discovery:**

Do we have to create a list of participants, who they are? What do they do? Why do they want to participate in our conference? Can we satisfy most of their needs? What is the maximum service we should be provided so that they can keep coming to the conference? All these questions have to be brainstormed and answer appropriately. What type of topics, discussions, and events would they like to hear, talk and share?

- **Specify value:**

Discuss with as many participants as possible what they value about such a conference. Can we do something to maximize the value? What unique services are we providing regarding customer value generation?

- **Make value flow continuously:**

Identify the value flow and ensure the theme has been designed in such a way that there is a minimum waste in the flow and the maximum value is obtained. E.g., during tea breaks some conference various poster presentation stalls, where there are a variety of options to talk, share, learn and have fun.

- **Pursue Perfection:**

Have we done enough validation on the topics that the presenters will present? Have we done enough research that these are the topics the audience wants to hear? At the end of the day, can we get wow participants satisfaction through transparent feedback system?

- **Team:**

Do I have an empowered team to run the show? Can they coordinate efficiently to handle the whole event? Can I add some topics at the last moment based on the customer needs and deliver as fast as possible?

- **Transparency:**

Can I show the whole flow and the last moment change if any? Participants need to visualize the whole flow and based on the last moment change if any, everything should be visible on display board?

- **Kaizen:**

How can I build my expertise year-on-year in running such events where conferences become more popular? My learning is adding value to the next year's conference. The customer input for improvement has been taken care of, leanings are corrected and improved.

- **Innovation culture:**

Organization culture is innovative, fun and the best place to work. There is no fear of failure and the team members are free to experiment, learn and improve? Teams are taking calculated risks and sharing the learnings from each other. We need to apply more discovery-driven process to minimize the uncertainty.

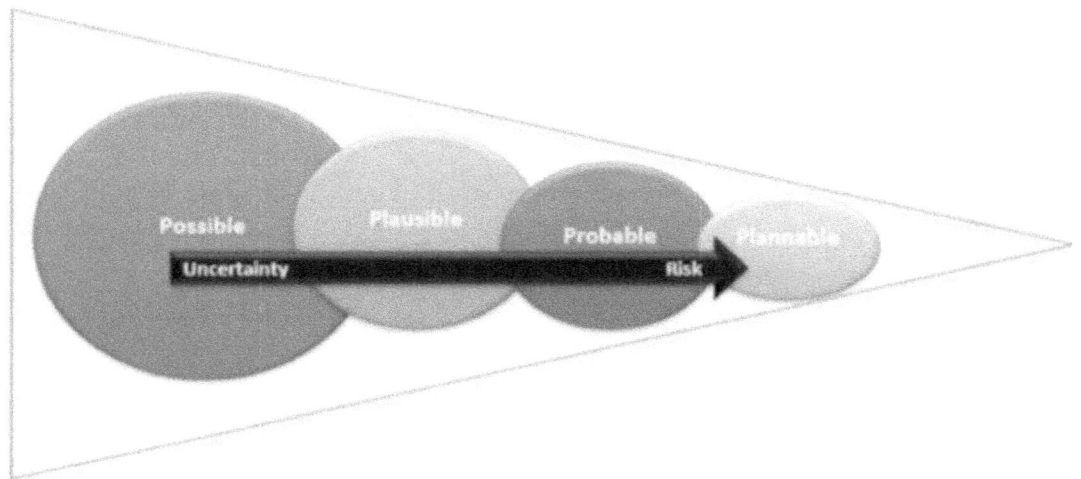

"Willful waste brings woeful want."

—*Thomas Fuller*

What actions are you going to take from this lesson?

1. _____

2. _____

3. _____

Thinking Question:

Are you doing enough to infuse the Lean thought into your regular work?

4.7 How to become Less Rigid and More Flexible in your mindset?

"Eliminate the mindset of CAN'T! Because you can do anything!"

—*Tony Horton*

Why this Topic?

Many team members, I have noticed, not willing to experiment, anything new, I was constantly studying how can I influence them to seek new things and learn from it?

Dr. Ilona Boniwell, one of the world leaders in the field of positive psychology, described how people tend to have either a '**fixed mindset**' or a '**growth mindset**'.

Her research discovered this often has to do with how we were taught at school or parented.

If, as a child, you were **praised** more often for getting things right, then you might have developed a more **fixed mindset**.

When things are going well, then all is good in your world; the trouble starts when you hit a setback.

You might find you have a tendency towards an all-or-nothing mentality in this situation – success or failure.

This is because you believe your abilities and talents are **fixed**, so if you fail the first time, you will often want to give up immediately and do **something** else.

If, however, you were praised for your efforts as a child, you will tend to have a growth mindset.

Failure isn't an immediate trigger to abandon ship, it's just an indication that you need to learn from the situation or try a new approach.

Flexibility is inbuilt as you enjoy the process of finding out how to make something work as much as the end result.

With a fixed mindset, over time we can start to back out on ourselves even as we approach a challenge; the voice of fear inside starts questioning,

'Are you sure you can do it?

What if you fail, how will you feel then?

What will everyone else think of you?'

As soon as things get tough, a person with a fixed mindset will often think to themselves, 'What's the point? I knew it.

Now I just feel stupid, so I'll get out while I can.' It's very difficult to take any criticism when your mind is in the fixed mode.

Constructive feedback sounds like, 'I'm really disappointed in you.

You're clearly not capable.'

Either that or you reject any criticism: 'It's not my fault, who do they think they are?'

You can train your brain to be less fixed and develop a growth mindset instead

- Know that you can't get everything right, but every day is an opportunity to learn something new and get better at something that matters to you.
- Practice using a growth mindset language:

'I'm not sure how to do this right now, but I'm willing to learn or ask for help.'

'If I don't get it right, I'm not a failure.'

Look at all the successful people who have overcome setbacks. **Failure is a chance for growth.'**

'If I don't try, I'll never learn anything.'

- Listen fully to constructive feedback or criticism and use it as it is meant, to help you grow.

'We must be willing to fail and to appreciate the truth that often life is not a problem to be solved, but a mystery to be lived.'

—*M. Scott Peck*

What actions are you going to take from this lesson?

1. _____

2. _____

3. _____

Thinking Question:

Are you doing enough to build a flexible mindset among the team members?

4.8 How to develop more EQ?

75 percent of careers are derailed for reasons related to emotional competencies, including an inability to handle interpersonal problems; unsatisfactory team leadership during times of difficulty or conflict; or the inability to adapt to a change or elicit trust.

—*Center for Creative Leadership*

Why this topic?

How to improve team collaboration and team bonding by improving the emotional aspects of people?

Planning to produce many such team members? Where to start and how to start?

A team member who excels in most of the emotional and social competencies below is going to significantly outperform a team member who is poor in most of the competencies below.

Only by **conscious practice,** we can develop, such as team members.

All these have to be practised in real-world situations. One needs to put in a lot of effort to develop mastery in these areas.

Emotional intelligence is something that's acquired through what is known as implicit learning, which happens in the areas of the brain other than the neocortex, where the thinking occurs.

Fortunately, this means that practicing behaviors in one setting, such as leading a group of volunteers on the weekend, will make it more likely that we exhibit the same behavior in other leadership contexts, such as at our workplace. The more often we practice a given behavior, the stronger the neural network associated with that behavior becomes and the easier it will be to behave that way in the future.

a) **Build Self-Awareness**: How well do you know yourself? How deeply do you understand your motivations? Get regular feedback at work and ask the trusted friends. Recognizing your emotions and the impact they have on your life.

"When you make people angry, they act in accordance with their baser instincts, often violently and irrationally. When you inspire people, they act in accordance with their higher instincts, sensibly and rationally. Also, anger is transient whereas inspiration has a lifelong effect"

—*Peace Pilgrim*

b) **Self-Management:**

- **Achievement Orientation**: Team members with a high achievement drive are self-motivated and tend to anticipate obstacles, take calculated risks, and take action rather than wait.
- **Adaptability**: Team members who are adaptable tend to juggle multiple demands well, handle rapid change easily, and adapt their ideas based on new information.
- **Emotional Self-Control**: Team members with high levels of emotional self-control don't become a victim of his or her emotions and is able to remain calm and collected under very demanding situations.
- **Positive Outlook**: Team members with a positive outlook tend to see opportunities rather than threats, have positive expectations about the future and about other people and see the positive side of difficult situations.

"In my 35 years in business, I have always trusted my emotions. I have always believed that by touching emotion you get the best people to work with you, the best clients to inspire you, the best partners and most devoted customers."

—*Kevin Roberts*

c) **Social Awareness**

- **Empathy**: This crucial skill is what allows Team members to listen well and understand the perspectives and emotional states of others
- **Organizational Awareness**: Team members with organizational awareness are able to understand office politics, the social networks, and the norms of an organization.

"We define emotional intelligence as the subset of social intelligence that involves the ability to monitor one's own and others' feelings and emotions, to discriminate among them and to use this information to guide one's thinking and actions"

—*Salovey and Mayer*

d) **Relationship Management**

The only way to change someone's mind is to connect with them from the heart.-Rasheed Ogunlaru

- **Inspirational Leadership**: Team members are able to inspire other team members by connecting their work to a larger purpose and being a living example of the team's values.
- **Influence**: The ability to influence the behaviors of others is the essence of leadership. Emotionally intelligent team members are able to build influence with others by understanding others and appealing to what's important to them.
- **Coach and Mentor**: Team members who coach and mentor offer feedback that improves others' performance, recognize strengths, and truly care about the development of other team members.
- **Conflict Management**: Team members who skillfully manage conflict are able to draw out and recognize the needs of all sides and help the parties involved find a shared solution.
- **Teamwork**: Team members who are most effective at fostering good teamwork are living examples of good team players. They seek to collaborate often and they value and invest in personal relationships.

When we start developing each of these areas, we are in the process of building a great team with an emotionally intelligent brain.

Let me share what we did.

As an Agile team, we need to adapt playfulness to our team members? We need to create a position called **Chief Fun Master** (CFM) at work.

We strongly believe that the best results come from motivated and engaged people, who knows how to collaborate with everybody involved. How do you create such a collaborative culture? Engaged culture? Motivated team members?

A game is an engagement engine—it attracts and engages players.

The game improves people collaboration. Improve **FUN@WORK**

Play brings joy. And it's vital for problem solving, creativity and relationships.

Playing at work fosters teamwork, allows employees to release tension, thus better concentrate on their work, and it also allows them to develop their creativity, adaptability and problem-solving skills. At the same time, it provides the body and mind with more energy and ultimately allows us to be happier.

Play can add joy to life, relieve stress, supercharge learning, and connect you to others and the world around you. Play can also make work more productive and pleasurable.

Sharing laughter and fun can foster empathy, compassion, trust, and intimacy with others.

George Bernard Shaw, "We don't stop playing because we grow old; we grow old because we stop playing."

Play teaches cooperation with others. The play is a powerful catalyst for positive socialization.

Play can heal emotional wounds. If an emotionally insecure individual plays with a secure partner, for example, it can help replace negative beliefs and behaviors with positive assumptions and actions.

Build projects around motivated individuals. Give them the environment and support they need, and trust them to get the job done.

Some of the game we played at a certain cadence with some team

a) Tell your employees to draw a caricature of their coworker. Surely a lot of us are not artists but they will at least try to scribble something and highlight those prominent features like maybe that ducktail mustache or hawk nose or weird hairstyle of a co-worker which would be fun to see!! Let the best resemblance be awarded. Also, you can have a guessing game where people try to guess the person in the caricature.

b) Employees can often find it fun to compete with each other and it is so easy for everyone to have a try at this. Do it with pro boards, a commentator, and scoreboards. You might probably want to add this as part of your annual sports event as well. And who knows, maybe the lucky guys can beat the skilled ones!

c) Indoor golf at workstation area!

d) Play Foosball as a team!@office

Bigger challenge you will face is to bring the crowd into the play mode. Most of the team members by design has become serious due to business pressure! The coach needs to put a lot of effort to bring life into those team members. We need lots of energy as most of the team members will not participate!

If you have more generation Z as a team members, you are lucky, as they are playful and fun-loving. Easy to influence them.

If you succeed in executing a few games, you will see the change you have brought about! It is a wonderful medicine!

Have you experienced such a need? Coach, Please facilitate the Game events.

> *Where are our Managers? Once the team has become self-driven they can own this role*
> **—Chief Fun Officer.**

> *No one cares how much you know until they know how much you care.*
> **—Theodore Roosevelt**

What actions are you going to take from this lesson?

1. _____

2. _____

3. _____

Thinking Question:

Are you doing some experiments with your team members to support them to improve their EQ?

4.9 Why do we need to know the "Ground Rules" of others?

> *"What lies in our power to do, lies in our power not to do?"*
> **—Aristotle**

Why this topic?

How do we connect with other easily? How do we influence others easily? This question invariably shows up in our coaching engagement, so what can we do about it?

Rules shape our behavior.

For example, we learn that "Big boys don't cry" and "You don't scratch Nose in public.

From our childhood, these rules have been imposed on us by our parents, Teachers, and Elders.

Many of these rules are also **transmitted** and **reinforced** by the organizations and institutions.

As we are growing old, these rules are part of our life.

Some of these rules were **building** our **character** and **personality**. It is working for us, guiding us.

Some of these rules we have been questioned and corrected on the way. Some of these rules we have redefined for ourselves. And all these rules are working for us.

By this time, we have learned how to act according to those rules. Generally, no one around us needs to remind us of the rules as our parents, teachers, and friends did when we were little.

THESE RULES HAVE BECOME OUR SECOND NATURE. WE ARE IN AUTOPILOT MODE!

We started sharing these rules with others as these rules are working for us.

We expect that others also should follow these same rules! We implicitly learn that the rules with which we were raised and that are true for us must also be true for others who share the same cultural heritage!

WE USE THE SAME "GROUND RULES"!!!!

When we come across some other people who have ***different*** ground rules, we become **upset**, and **negative** emotions build up, frustrated and annoyed. If they are culturally different from these ground rules are much more different!

Our emotional reactions often lead us to make judgments about others. We say someone is good when they align with our ground rules and we say someone is bad when they upset us with their ground rules and belief systems.

Ground rules play a critical role in connecting effectively with others which we make them align or enemy of ours. These rules of perceiving and interpreting form the basis of our own "filters" that we use in seeing the world. Stronger the rules, stronger is the filter!

These rules are inseparable and all part of our life, belief, and filters.

What do we do now?

- Align with other ground rules and understand their rules. Understand their filters and appreciate
- Your rules are not ultimate and it may need some changes based on the circumstances
- Believe that our way of perceiving and interpreting the world is not the only way of perceiving and interpreting.
- Recognize the existence of other possible interpretations
- Accept the possibility of me being wrong, being adaptive, and flexible
- MY WAY OR HIGHWAY will not always work in a globalized world. Wear their shoe and understand through their glasses.
- Understand the emotional changes and manage efficiently
- Crash course on others culture, go beyond defining boundaries.

THIS PROCESS IS A JOURNEY OF CONTINUOUS LEARNING

What actions are you going to take from this lesson?

1. _____
2. _____
3. _____

Thinking Question:

Are you doing enough to figure out the ground rules of others so that we can relate with them in the best way?

4.10 How Do You Want to Be Recognized?

"It is amazing what you can accomplish if you do not care who gets the credit."

—Harry Truman

Why this topic?

Every team that I coach, I have come across this question, people hunger to get recognition. But how should we recognize others? Money, appreciation, social focus, and what else?

Everyone wants to be recognized in some way.

Agile Development is often based on effective communication, collaboration, and coordination.

- **How can we increase engagement?**
- **How can we increase self-motivation?**
- **How can we increase sharing - caring culture?**
- **How can we encourage increased competence and growth?**

Agile practice discourages to build a Hero culture.

How do we build the team culture and encourage individuals to contribute their best and doesn't recognize!

Eric Berne, the originator of Transactional Analysis, identified what he called 'six hungers' that act as fundamental drivers that push us into action.

One hunger is **Recognition hunger**. When others recognize and acknowledge us, our sense of identity is reinforced as we know ourselves to exist as individuals and to have an accepted place in society.

For the agile team, we need to build a system where we continuously provide **feedback** and recognize each individual as an when we find there is something that can be **appreciated**.

Harvard Business School professor and international change expert John Kotter's work spotlighting the need to "**celebrate small wins**" in any change effort. Without such an acknowledgment teams often begin to lose direction, motivation, and enthusiasm.

What is the various way we can enable recognition?

Examples of **external rewards** include pay, bonuses, plaques, notes, and publicity in newspapers, commendations at a company party, certificates, gifts, trips, and dinners. Examples of **internal rewards** include satisfaction from accomplishing the team goal and a sense of well-being deriving from strong working relationships, creative challenges, increased responsibility, and learning opportunities.

What we can do to build such a culture. Eight points to focus on.

1. Look for the opportunities where you can appreciate others
2. Help individuals where he/she can perform better and You can appreciate
3. Share the goal with the members and share the expectation, Help them to set stretch goals
4. Create an appreciation platform. Make it shorter and frequent
5. Create many ways for appreciation, e.g., Writing best code, share best stories, Helping others in a crises situation, Best support team members, Creative team members, etc.
6. Celebrate the achievements
7. Make it Visual, on the board where all of the team members can see
8. Recognize best ideas, best solutions, Best knowledge shared, etc.

Recognize the skills, knowledge, behaviors, and demeanor that support agile performance to reinforce them at all levels of the organization.

A culture of recognition engages, energizes, and empowers employees.

Let us not recognize activities, but recognize outcomes.

> *"There is no limit to the amount of good you can do if you don't care who gets the credit."*
> **—Ronald Reagan**

What actions are you going to take from this lesson?

1. _____

2. _____

3. _____

Thinking Question:

Are you doing sufficient work to develop the appreciation skills so that you can help your team members?

4.11 Mindset Bias, Are you a victim of this?

> *"Quitting is never an option on the road to success. Find the way forward. If you have a positive mindset and are willing to persevere, there is little that is beyond your reach. The attitude of being ready to work even in the face of challenges and despite odds is what will make all the difference in your life."*
> **—Roopleen**

Why this topic?

I looked at the mirror and thought, do I have a problem-solving mindset? Let us talk about a few anti problem-solving mindset. What are those?

I could easily find those in my work with the team in various scenarios. Once I explained all these aspects to my team members, it helps the team to think differently.

Most of the time I find with all the intelligence and good problem-solving tools available with us we missed to apply the right mindset to solve the problem.

Prof. Jeff Malpas ("Problem-solving for Managers") says

"No problem is ever totally solved. Every problem has a solution, but every solution with it brings a new problem. Some well-known management techniques emphasize the idea of continuous improvement and successful problem-solving is seen as part of such a continuous improvement."

Are you aware of these factors?

A) "**BOUNDED RATIONALITY**" issue Coined by Herbert Simon.

Rationality of people is partial due to the information they have, the cognitive boundaries of their minds, and the finite amount of time they have to make a decision.

One of the key aspects is that **cognitive blinders stop people from seeing, seeking, using, or sharing relevant, accessible, and perceivable information during decision-making.**

This concept identifies that decision making takes place inside an environment of partial information and ambiguity. Herbert Simon highlighted that the best people are **only partly rational** and are in fact **emotional** and **irrational** in the remaining part of their actions.

As an Agile coach I might have helped a team in a certain way as I know the context, but in the inspection or audit by another agile coach for the same team, he or she may blame me saying I have not done them justice. We may be suffering from the Bounded Rationality effect!

B) **Satisficing effect**: I am a victim of this!

It is aimed at taking decisions that are **okay enough to tackle a situation**, but not the best possible decisions. If any solution takes too long, too much cost, I usually get into low hanging fruits, never think about the long-term solution.

C) **Groupthink**: Groupthink, a term coined by social psychologist Irving Janis (1972) occurs when **a group makes faulty decisions because group pressures lead to a deterioration of "mental efficiency, reality testing, and moral judgment."**

A group is especially vulnerable to groupthink when its members are similar in background, when the group is insulated from outside opinions, and when there are no clear rules for decision making.

D) **CONFIRMATION BIAS**: It is an affinity to hunt for or understand information in a way that confirms one's presumptions, leading to statistical errors. When people would like a certain **idea/concept to be true,** they **end up believing it to be true.**

They are motivated by wishful thinking. This error leads the individual to end, the gathering information when the evidence collected so far checks the views (prejudices) that one would like to be true.

We don't perceive circumstances objectively. We pick out those bits of data that make us feel good because they confirm our prejudices. Thus, we may become prisoners of our assumptions.

E) **FIXATION**: We fixate on one solution at the expense of alternatives. We do not look from another angle or from do not look for alternatives. Watch for those things that you are ignoring. Are these significant? Could they cause you problems later?

F) FEAR FROM FAILURE: From many attempts in the past you have discovered that people criticized you badly because of your solutions. Someone else has helped you to solve the problem, you will emotionally negative to solve any solution. You always think someone will blame you, you are scared. All these negative emotions will block your thinking pattern.

Feeling Stuck? Feeling Judged or worthless? Feeling powerless? It's also not good and needs to change this mindset.

G) Time spent on the problem?

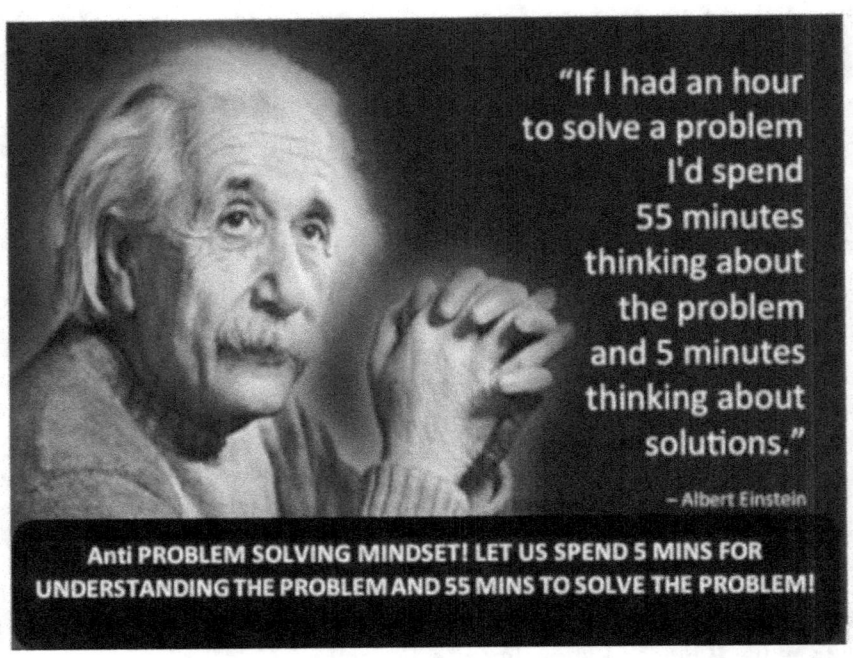

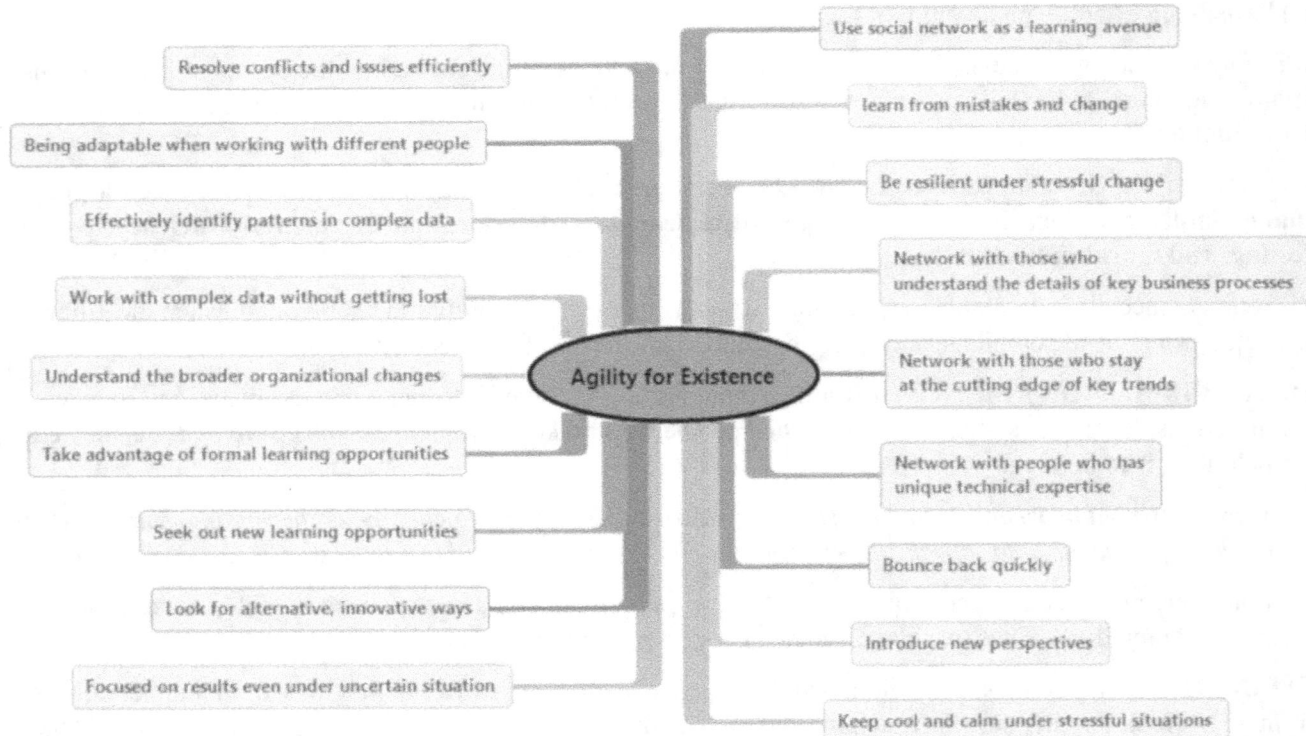

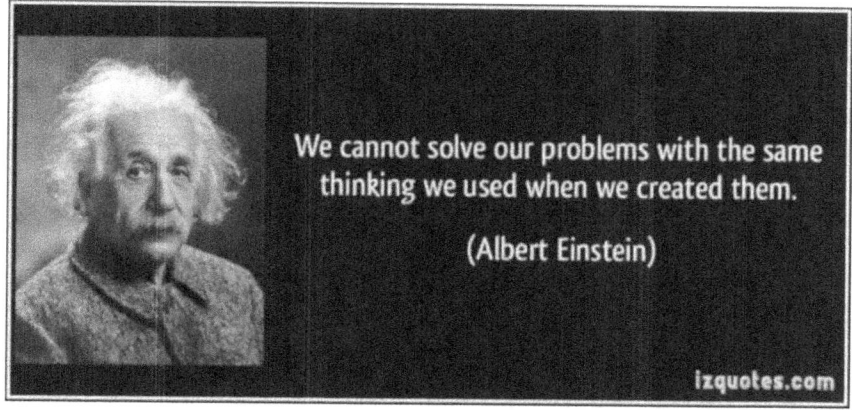

We need to look for the instances at our workplace and share with others about our learnings.

What actions are you going to take from this lesson?

1. _____

2. _____

3. _____

Thinking Question:

Are you doing adequate work to raise the problem-solving mindset?

4.12 Agile Deployment Requires more Soft Skills, More Leadership Skills, and More People Skills?

Why this topic?

This topic is to highlight why it is so important to focus on people development skills in an agile transformation? Software product development is by the people, and for the people. It is all about people skill.

Two of the four manifesto items and five of the 12 principles are **people oriented**!

This emphasizes that applying agile methods is more than simply having a different way of developing software.

The human element is just as important, as is delivering value to the customer rather than merely following a prescriptive development or a management process.

The team needs to discover *WHY* Agile, in the context where they are operating? Not just do agile because others are doing the same.

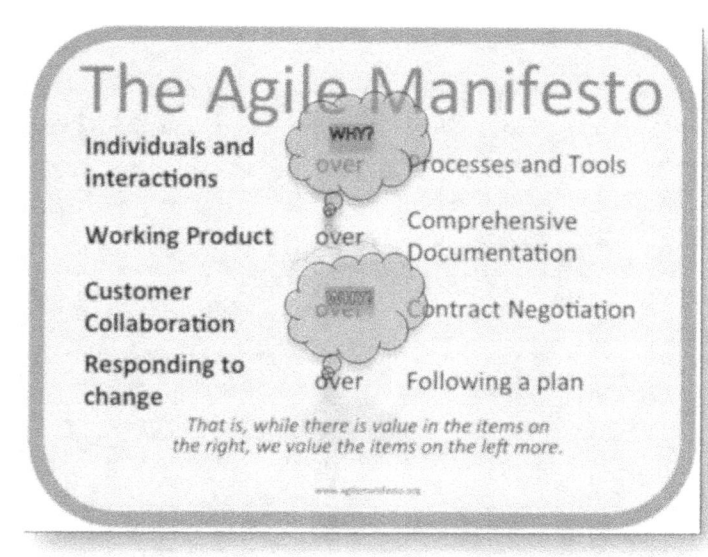

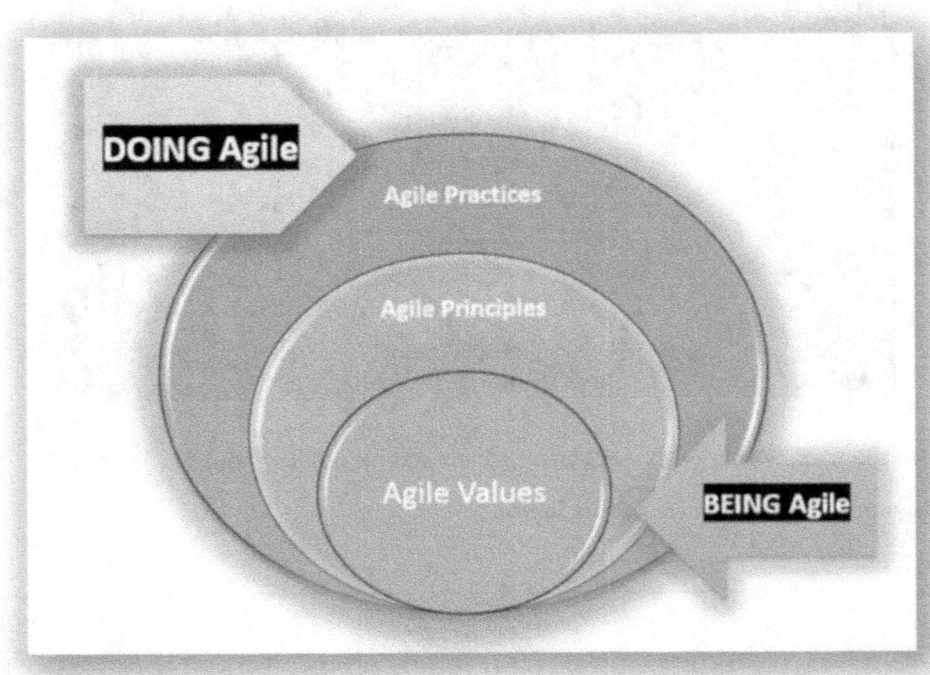

PEOPLE FOCUSED ASPECTS OF THE AGILE MANIFESTO		
Individuals and interactions over processes and tools		
Working software over comprehensive documentation		
Customer collaboration over contract negotiation		
Responding to change over following a plan		
PEOPLE FOCUSED ASPECTS OF THE AGILE PRINCIPLES		
1. Our highest priority is to satisfy the customer through early and continuous delivery of valuable software.		
2. Welcome changing requirements, even late in development. Agile processes harness change for the customer's competitive advantage.		
3. Deliver working software frequently, from a couple of weeks to a couple of months, with a preference to the shorter timescale.		
4. Business people and developers must work together daily throughout the project.		
5. Build projects around motivated individuals. Give them the environment and support they need, and trust them to get the job done.		
6. The most efficient and effective method of conveying information to and within a development team is face-to-face conversation.		
7. Working software is the primary measure of progress.		
8. Agile processes promote sustainable development. The sponsors, developers, and users should be able to maintain a constant pace indefinitely.		
9. Continuous attention to technical excellence and good design enhances agility.		
10. Simplicity--the art of maximizing the amount of work not done--is essential.		
11. The best architectures, requirements, and designs emerge from self-organizing teams.		
12. At regular intervals, the team reflects on how to become more effective, then tunes and adjusts its behavior accordingly.		

Agile transformation is all about culture and people. Work closely with your people and invest in them.

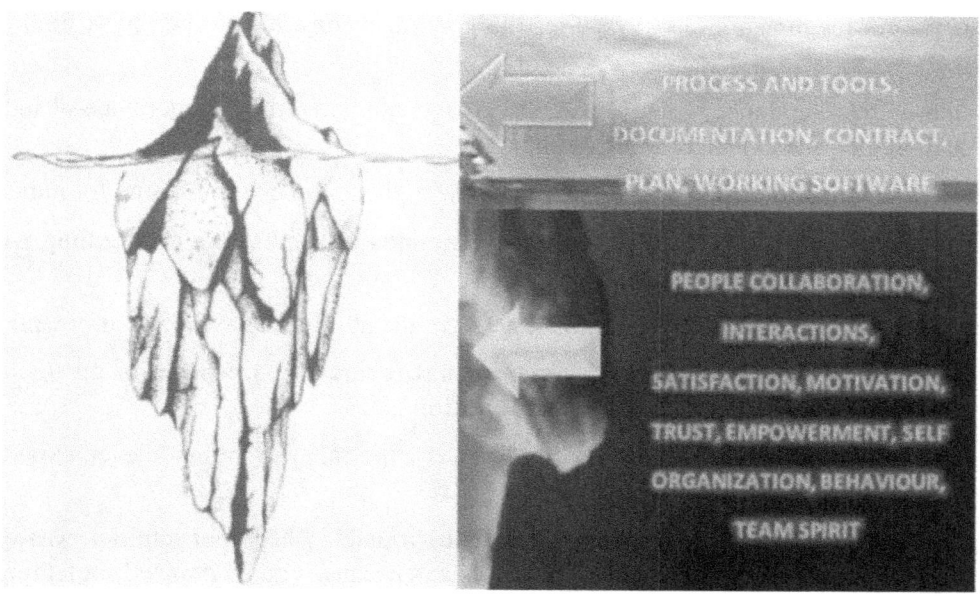

What actions are you going to take from this lesson?

1. _____

2. _____

3. _____

Thinking Question:

Are you doing enough to improve your people skill to help your team members whom you are coaching?

4.13 How do you develop Your Intuition?

> *"Intuition is seeing with the soul."*
>
> —**Dean Koontz**

Why this topic?

I have worked with many great leaders, I was always wondering, how they take some decisions instantly without much data. I was looking for the answer to these question...Learning from outstanding leaders...

We think of intuition as a **magical** phenomenon—but hunches are formed out of our experiences and knowledge.

How to develop these hunches?

> "Intuition is really
> a sudden immersion of the soul
> into the universal current of life,
> where the histories of
> all people are connected,
> and we are able to know everything,
> because it's all written there."
>
> Paulo Coelho ~ The Alchemist

So while relying on gut feelings doesn't always lead to good decisions, it's not nearly as flighty a tactic as it may sound.

Many great thinkers, from Immanuel Kant to Carl Jung have emphasized the importance of intuition and the great impact it had on their personal and professional lives.

They defined it as 'a priori' knowledge, and as being an essential and indispensable tool for humans.

According to Jung, **intuition is one of the four major functions of the human mind along with sensation, thinking, and feeling.**

By balancing all of these functions within ourselves, we have the ability to maximize our potential. He wrote:

"I regard intuition as a basic psychological function that mediates perception in an unconscious way. Intuition enables us to divine the possibilities of a situation......"

Daniel Kahneman's Thinking Fast and Slow is full of clever experiments that made even experts jump to the wrong conclusions.

Their sixth sense failed them. You can probably recall times yourself when your intuition was wrong —when you followed your gut and it turned out to be a mistake. That's because you recognized something familiar, but the rest of the situation was new. Your intuition only works when you encounter something very similar to what you've seen before. If the situation is new, your sixth sense isn't enough.

**"Have the courage
to follow your
heart and intuition.
They somehow
know what you
truly want to become."**

- Steve Jobs

For intuition—the sixth sense—that's very important.

You must study what can go wrong as well as what can go right.

For example, a music teacher might show you the most common mistakes in playing a certain piece. The teacher won't show you all the ways to do it wrong—that would take years, and most of them would not be useful for you. **But studying common pitfalls is a normal part of learning for deep expertise in any domain.**

"With practice, you start noticing the quiet voice within," explains David Stevens, professional intuitive and founder of Yoga of the Mind, a meditation and intuition training service. **"Some see flashes of pictures. Others have certain feelings. Some have pure knowingness."**

Mitchell and Stevens recommend these four techniques to help you tap into and trust your intuition.

1) **Meditate**
2) **Do a blind reading**
3) **Play red-light green-light**
4) **Learn more through readings and classes**

> *"Cease trying to work everything out with your minds. It will get you nowhere. Live by intuition and inspiration and let your whole life be Revelation."*
>
> *—Eileen Caddy*

Highly developed intuition is a "secret weapon," says Judith Orloff, MD, professor of psychiatry at UCLA and author of Dr. Judith Orloff's Guide to Intuitive Healing. *"It gives you all kinds of information you wouldn't normally have. This isn't the brain analyzing; this is nonlinear knowledge. It's the second kind of intelligence. You want to use both."*

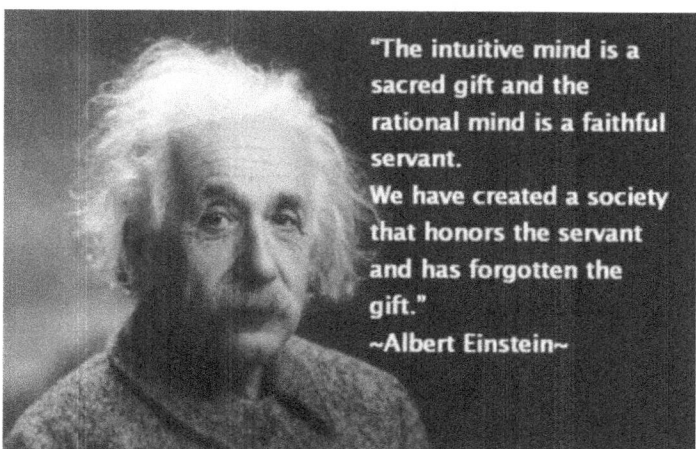

"The intuitive mind is a sacred gift and the rational mind is a faithful servant.
We have created a society that honors the servant and has forgotten the gift."
~Albert Einstein~

Even Einstein said, **"Logic will get you from A to B, imagination will take you everywhere."** And this takes you right to my first tip…

Intuition more often than not is a result of data analysis, pattern and trend spotting and rational and logical thinking – not a gut feeling - although this does come into it too.

> *Intuition is the supra-logic that cuts out all the routine processes of thought and leaps straight from the problem to the answer.*
>
> *– Robert Graves*

Intuition is an aptitude that simply requires a deeper consciousness of what is really going on around you and why. To activate simply start tuning in more by listening, observing and being more curious as to why people do the things they do and behave the way they do!

Again with Einstein: **"The intuitive mind is a sacred gift and the rational mind is a faithful servant. We have created a society that honors the servant and has forgotten the gift."**

Do meditation.

Pray. A 1995 study by William MacDonald of Ohio State University found that people who regularly pray are more likely to have telepathic experiences than people who don't pray. MacDonald explained these findings by saying, **"In one sense, the results aren't surprising. You can think of prayer as a type of mind-to-mind communication between a person and God**. So prayer and telepathy are related concepts.

Let us listen to our heart...

> *It is through science that we prove, but through intuition that we discover.*
>
> *—Henri Poincare*

What actions are you going to take from this lesson?

1. _____

2. _____

3. _____

Thinking Question:

Are you doing enough to enhance your knowledge to develop your intuition skill?

4.14 Why is it tough to influence executives easily?

"Executives owe it to the organization and their fellow workers not to tolerate nonperforming individuals in important jobs."

—*Peter Drucker*

Why this topic?

Influencing executives is one of the principal tasks which every coach will come across. What are the numerous choices we have to address this challenge?

Why is it tough to influence senior managers and executive members?

Have you tried to coach them on certain topics? What is your experience?

I was interacting with Product owners who are working with the system for the last 25 years. They exactly know how the things are working and how the system should behave.

> **Their beliefs are the result of years of experience and the objective analysis of the information they had available.**

For example, imagine that a person holds a belief that thick mustache people are more masculine than non-mustache people. Whenever this person encounters a person that is both non-mustache and Masculine, they place greater importance on this "evidence" that supports what they already believe. This individual might even seek "proof" that further backs up this belief while discounting examples that do not support the idea.

I was working with the Audit team members to inject agility, I get such instances. I was working with a Production support team where they use the ITIL process, I see instances of such a bias. They argue for hours and finally, they do not accept! Agile is not for them.

What do we call this phenomenon?

> **Confirmation bias is a type of cognitive bias that involves favoring information which confirms previously existing beliefs or biases.**

Confirmation bias is the tendency to accept evidence that confirms our beliefs and rejects evidence that contradicts them.

We Believe What We Want to Believe

In the 1960s, the cognitive psychologist Peter Cathcart Wason conducted a number of experiments known as Wason's rule discovery task. He demonstrated that people have a tendency to seek information that confirms their existing beliefs. Unfortunately, this type of bias can prevent us from looking at situations objectively. It can also influence the decisions we make and can lead to poor or faulty choices.

> **The confirmation bias helps explain why the traditional approach of trying to persuade people by giving them reasons to change isn't a good idea if the audience is at all skeptical, cynical, or hostile. Confirmation bias is a primary reason why the influence technique of logical persuading can be risky and ineffective.**

> **It is a subconscious process where the mind will automatically try to reject new information and instead seek evidence to support the current belief.**

Now if we are coaching executives who are having such biases, how can we find out a strategy to coach them?

Six points to look for

1. First, identify, if the person is the victim of confirmation bias
2. Seek information from a range of sources and consider a range of perspectives.
3. Encourage them to be open-minded. Nobody would like to be proved wrong. Without hurting their ego, try to share the data with them
4. Let them accept that they do not know all the things. Help them to control their emotions and ego. Practice humility when it comes to listening to others.
5. Ask powerful questions to understand their beliefs. A good question is "what do you believe about this topic?" A better question is "why do you believe this?" Asking questions that lead to deeper thoughts and conversations will help them to broaden their way of thinking.
6. Let us find enough points to prove that they are biased. Their belief system is not correct in the current context.

Michael Specter talks about "truth" and "facts in his TED talk from 2010:

"People wrap themselves in their beliefs, and they do it so tightly that you cannot set them free. Not even the truth will set them free. And listen, everyone is entitled to their opinion, they are even entitled to their opinion on progress [...], but you are not entitled to your own facts."

What actions are you going to take from this lesson?

1. _____

2. _____

3. _____

Thinking Question:

Are you doing enough to influence your executives? What else are you seeking to change due to these false beliefs?

4.15 What is a good developer mindset?

Why this topic?

I have been working with many developers in my coaching engagement. When I have encountered developers are not motivated, and they are not concerned to write good quality code, I try to find out why? What is the distinction between good developers with the poor developers?

What problem are we solving by **DOING** software Craftsmanship to BEING a better Software Craftsman?

Business always says that we are not getting benefit from the agile implementation! We have invested so much time, money, reoriented ourselves, but we do not find the ROI. Our developers are doing TDD, BDD and Test automation, but still, we have production issues? Our maintenance budget is still high?

Did they understand software Craftsmanship? I am not saying anything new, it is the same old statement, but every-time by taking some different steps, we are emphasizing the same old concepts.

Software development is a Social Process.
Software Development is a People focus.
Software Craftsmanship is an Art, Science, and an Engineering Process.

manifesto.softwarecraftsmanship.org/ says

Craftsmanship is about gaining mastery.
Continuous attention to technical excellence and good design

In our coaching engagement, we teach XP practices, and team members demonstrate the application of the XP practices in their work environment BUT once we assess after six months the team goes back to the original form.

Do we try to figure out why there is no motivation to build world-class awesome software?

How can we build Mastery in software craftsmanship? What have we done to achieve it? Listed below are few points.

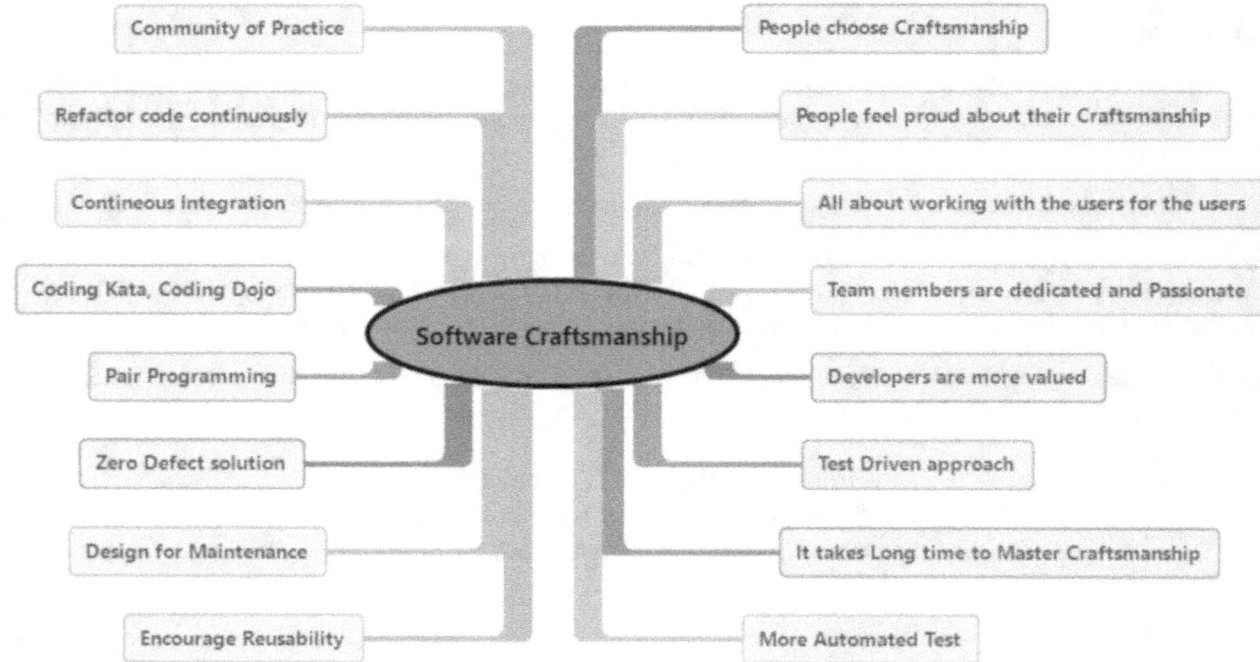

a) **What have we done**, Build a Community of Practice (CoP): Most of the developers demonstrate their capabilities in CoP, where they feel proud of their output. The learning organization which appreciates such initiatives that are the breeding ground of software craftsmanship engineers.

b) **What we have done**, Code contest or hackathon where a developer cracks the problem with an elegant solution is another way to identify and demonstrate the best capabilities. Encourage them to do more such instances. Organize such an event more often.

c) **What we have done**, in various project context the team members who are demonstrating the elegant level of contributions should be highlighted and recognized for their contribution. Developers are more valuable than Managers.

d) **What we have done**, Doing six months JAVA certification course and becoming a Java Architect! Need to be very careful about this certified candidate vs. real experience. Mastery is far from certification. We are cautious about recruiting the right candidates. Once we recruit an **A class** player, he/she will recruit another **A class** player.

e) **What we have done**, Good Craftsman developers are the very good collaborators. They easily engage with the end users and build exactly what is requested by the users. Develop people collaboration and communication skills to mastery in software craftsmanship.

f) **What we have done**: Most of the time too much delivery pressure compromises on the software craftsmanship. Developers never get quality time to craft their product there is always pressure on delivering something fast! On time delivery comes with a price. All team members have been coached to demonstrate the courage to demand for more time for developing solutions.

g) **What we have done**: There is always bad statistics that can be removed which drives poor output. People are behind the numbers, not the value. Avoid them, this drives poor performance, E.g. Number of paintings done in 1 day! Quantity vs quality

h) **What we have done**: Excellent craftsman is expensive, we have to identify and be ready to pay for it, and they will build the world-class software. Because they have put their best effort to increase their craftsmanship, skills, the client should be ready to reward for it. Let the customer decide if they want a diamond or glass. There is always a demand for diamond.

i) **What we have done**: Value-based measurement. Developer's outcomes need to be measured based on the value that the solutions has provided, not by some number e.g. Number of lines coded, the number of unit test cases written, the number of web services written, etc.

j) **What we have done**: Craftsmanship builds over a period with a lot of self-discipline and practices in place within the system. E.g., all the code should follow a standard coding guideline, developers do pair programming, code reviews are done, all the code is written with unit testing, there is BDD scenarios are written, and there is a daily build running with all the automated tests running. If anybody breaks the build they have to fix it in 4 hrs, coding kata sessions etc.

k) **What we have done**: Software Craftsman is full of Unconscious Competence, Good developers are humble and talk less, and work more. It is also the ecosystem which helps them to traverse these phases (Below Picture). They work as a team and build each other's expertise. They challenge each other and do pair programming for learning.

l) **What we have done**: IT IS A MINDSET AND AN ATTITUDE to become such a craftsman. Coach for the mindset change.

m) **What we have done**: The best way to achieve the mastery is to work with the best architects. If you are fortunate, you will get the master, you will be able to learn a lot. In my experience I have seen, many of the best masterpiece developers have worked with world-class architects over a period of time and learned a lot from them. Search for those masters.

n) **What we have done**: We encourage team members to write blogs, papers and contributes in seminars. We encourage people to write books and contribute back to the society.

o) **What we have done**: We have to build software factories wherever possible. All the team members worked under the applications are trained on the tools and infrastructure needed to build the delivery pipeline.

I am consciously looking for all these points while coaching and reusing some of my knowledge.

Manager and Leaders have to inspire developers to write the world-class software.

The Coach has to inspire team members to follow all the software development best practices.

Communities have to build where developers can demonstrate their capabilities.

Software craftsmanship is a mindset and an Attitude

We need to sustain this software craftsmanship movement by doing whatever is required to do, especially in the changing era where the digital is penetrating rapidly into our daily life.

My best developers are not only focusing on writing the best quality code but enhancing other required skills to enable each feature to be effectively consumed by the end users.

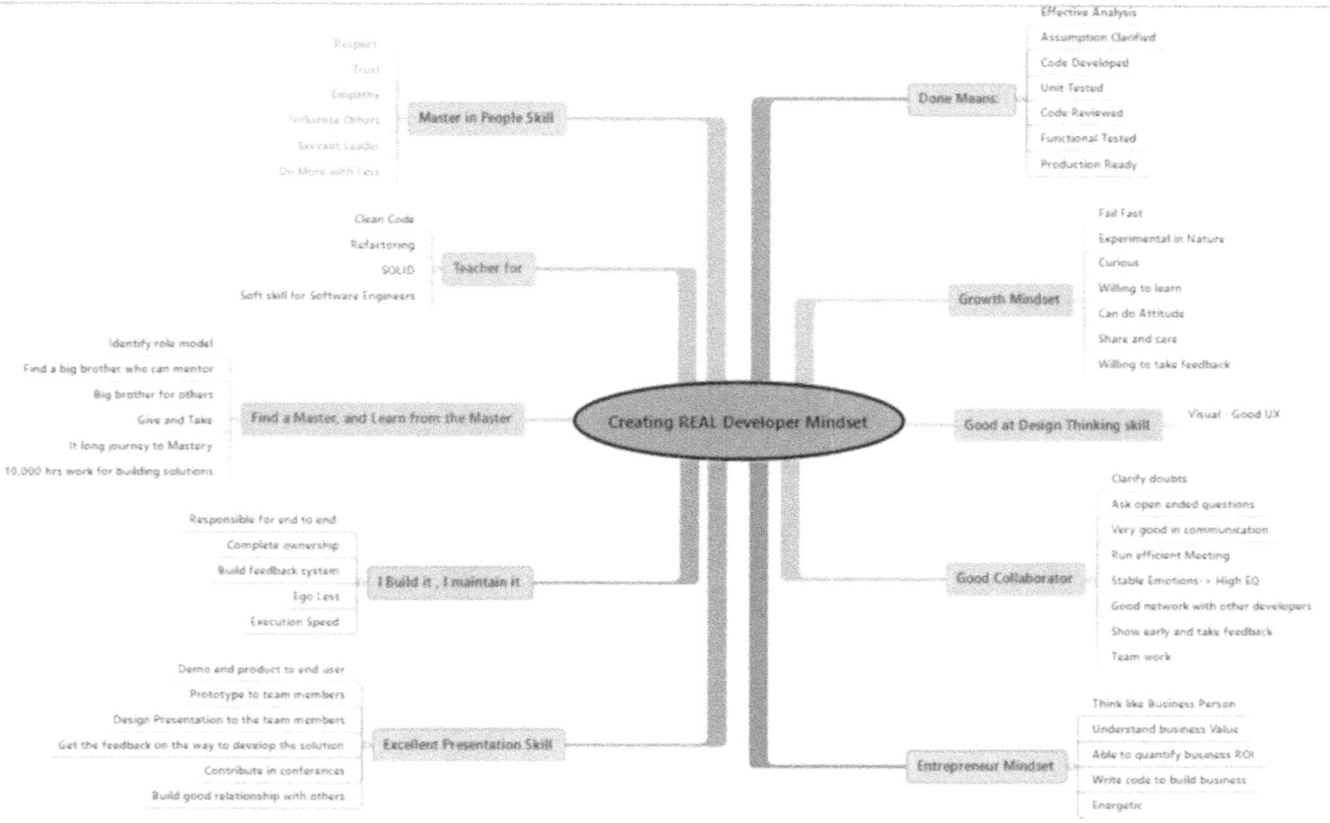

Master in People Skill
- Respect
- Trust
- Empathy
- Influence Others
- Servant Leader
- Do More with Less

Done Means
- Effective Analysis
- Assumption Clarified
- Code Developed
- Unit Tested
- Code Reviewed
- Functional Tested
- Production Ready

Teacher for
- Clean Code
- Refactoring
- SOLID
- Soft skill for Software Engineers

Growth Mindset
- Fail Fast
- Experimental in Nature
- Curious
- Willing to learn
- Can do Attitude
- Share and care
- Willing to take feedback

Find a Master, and Learn from the Master
- Identify role model
- Find a big brother who can mentor
- Big brother for others
- Give and Take
- It long journey to Mastery
- 10,000 hrs work for building solutions

Creating REAL Developer Mindset

Good at Design Thinking skill
- Visual - Good UX

I Build it, I maintain it
- Responsible for end to end
- Complete ownership
- Build feedback system
- Ego Less
- Execution Speed

Good Collaborator
- Clarify doubts
- Ask open ended questions
- Very good in communication
- Run efficient Meeting
- Stable Emotions -> High EQ
- Good network with other developers
- Show early and take feedback
- Team work

Excellent Presentation Skill
- Demo and product to end user
- Prototype to team members
- Design Presentation to the team members
- Get the feedback on the way to develop the solution
- Contribute in conferences
- Build good relationship with others

Entrepreneur Mindset
- Think like Business Person
- Understand business Value
- Able to quantify business ROI
- Write code to build business
- Energetic

185

What actions are you going to take from this lesson?

1. _____

2. _____

3. _____

Thinking Question:

As a coach what are the steps we can take to inject all these into developers mind?

4.16 Key Takeaways

This chapter features a few challenges which we need to strengthen to improve the **Space** elements of the **Pancha Bhoota model.**

Here are the key points to remember from this chapter

1. People skill is the key for any organizational Transformation
2. Importance to come out from the anti-problem solving mindset
3. Various way to Recognize the team members
4. Ground rules for the better engagement. Put the effort to learn it more.
5. Better emotional development of the brain and the benefits of it.
6. Benefits of improving flexibility
7. Many benefits of the lean mindset, if we apply it to our work thoughtfully.
8. Importance of providing positive strokes
9. Come out of the prisons of our mind and experiment with new stuff
10. Ego reduction mechanism
11. Develop a growth mindset, and how to reprogram our mind.
12. Attitude to altitude, and how they influence our growth

In the next chapter, we will look into Organization structure, cultural facets. In the **Panch Bhoota Model**, this will strengthen the **Earth** element.

5 Enablement of Organizational Transformation

5.1 Introduction:

This chapter features the issues with organizational transformation challenges and the countless factors which the coach desires to notice about the organization for easy, agile transformation. It is significant for a coach to learn more about the big picture. I have touched upon a few of the key aspects of organizational issues which benefits everyone to become aware of and work on these aspects. It requires a great amount of study on all these aspects. If we deep dive into each of these topics we will be able to equip ourselves in a better way of handling challenges emerging from these areas. In the **Pancha Bhoota model,** this is the **Earth** element.

This chapter covers the following topics depicted in the mind map:

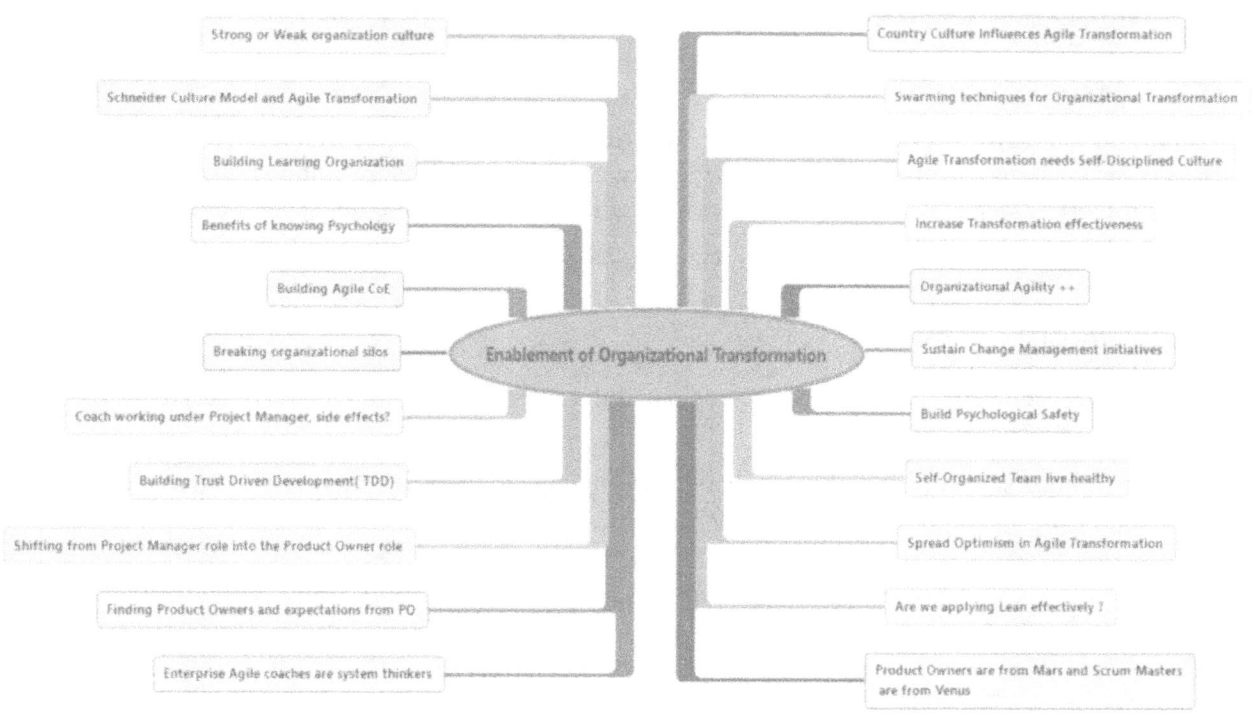

5.2 How Country Culture Influences Agile Transformation

> *"A nation's culture resides in the hearts and the soul of its people"*
> —*Mahatma Gandhi*

Why this topic?

Recently, one of my tours to a European country had induced me to think, how country culture can shape the agile transformation. As the Agile transformation is all about people and people are influenced by the culture

187

of the country where originated. If I am coaching a team from Brazil and coaching a team from Japan, there should be a distinct coaching approach.

As a Change Agent and agile coach, if I am not aware of about the country culture, an agile transformation will not be an easy one. Especially in the distributed team, if the majority of the team members are from the local country, its influences the team balance sometimes us vs them culture.

How can we prepare ourselves?

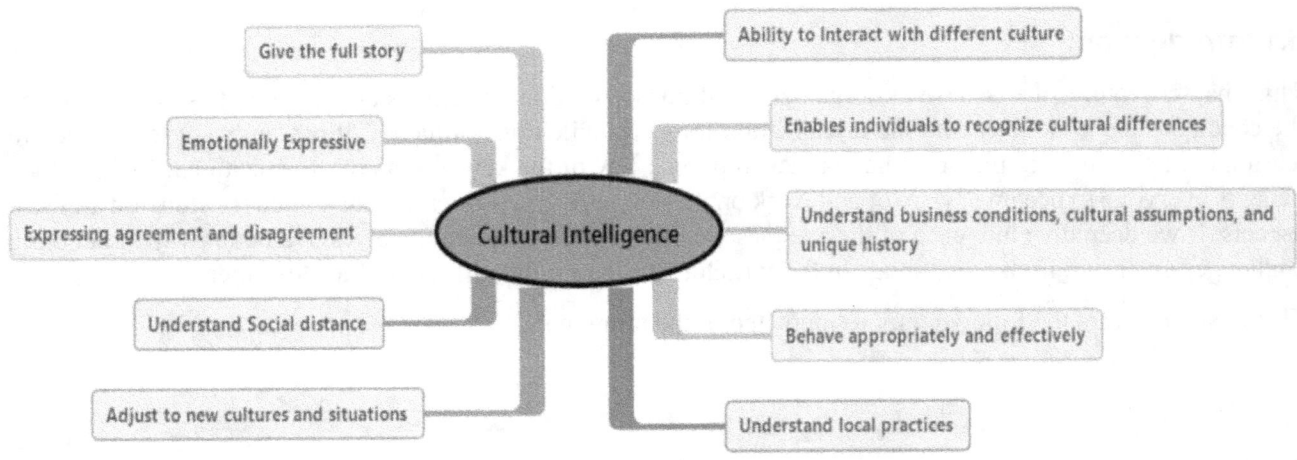

Wiki definition: **Culture** is a word for people›s **'way of life,'** meaning the way groups do things. Different groups of people may have different cultures. Different countries have different cultures. Culture can be viewed as the customs, arts and social interactions of a particular nation, people, or other social groups.

Cultures are what makes countries unique.

Each country has different cultural activities and cultural rituals. Culture contains physical goods, the stuff people use and produce.

Culture is also the **beliefs** and **values** of the people and the way they contemplate and comprehend the world and their individual lives.

The latest Versionone survey also highlights that understanding culture is the highest point to focus on

Challenges Experienced Adopting & Scaling Agile

From last year to this year we saw a decrease in respondents citing "organizational culture at odds with agile values" and "lack of business/customer/product owner availability" as challenges for adopting and scaling agile. Barriers that were cited more this year include "fragmented tooling", "inconsistent processes across teams" and "general resistance to change".

Challenge	%
Organizational culture at odds with agile values	53
General organization resistance to change	46
Inadequate management support and sponsorship	42
Lack of skills/experience with agile methods	41
Insufficient training and education	35
Inconsistent processes and practices across teams	34
Lack of business/customer/product owner availability	31
Pervasiveness of traditional development methods	30
Fragmented tooling and project-related data/measurements	24
Minimal collaboration and knowledge sharing	21
Regulatory compliance or government issue	14

*Respondents were able to make multiple selections.

VERSIONONE.COM   #StateOfAgile   12

I had prepared myself to discover more about culture to understand the cultural context better. It helped me indeed in a better way to get into the business.

1. How long I had to wait in the reception or in the building for someone to ask if they can help you.
2. How people value time?
3. How do people introduce themselves? How much time do they spend with you to share their initial thoughts, context?
4. How people wear dresses? How much time did people spend in the cafeteria? How are they talking during a formal and informal discussion? What does the lunch table look like? Many team members as a group or as many individuals eating alone?
5. How they interact and involve when they interact with people from a different place/country? Do they make you comfortable?
6. How do people treat each other? Is Respect demonstrated among co-workers?
7. Is there a sense of emotional and interpersonal openness inside the organization?
8. Do people demonstrate an understanding of the broader business or are they only given insight into their little part of the operation? Do they have the information they need from across the business areas?
9. Do you find an honest opinion? Do they talk from their heart?
10. Do you find a centralized decision-making style or empowered decentralized decision making style? In a meeting, what do you observe? Many people are talking, few people talking? Who talks more, the position of that person? Encourage to talk freely? Or dominated by a few?
11. Are people fearful–of bosses, competitors, expectations, failure, or something else?
12. How do the senior leaders behave? How differently do they treat each other vs. everyone else?
13. Do you find people are getting into small talk like before, during, and after meetings?
14. How much bad talk of others goes on when someone leaves the room or isn't present?
15. If you ask this question to the people, what answer do you get? "What words would you use to describe this organization? Give examples of each word"
16. If you ask this question to the people - What are the people more proud of their organization?
17. How does the organization support their professional development and career growth?
18. Is risk-taking encouraged, and what happens when people fail?
19. What is the purpose of the organization? Can people explain properly? Why do they think they are part of the important assignment? How do they create impact through their work?
20. What special attribute does the founder/leader possess that has influenced the character of the organization?
21. What makes this organization feel different or unique from our competitors?
22. What do people think that the organization focuses on and pays attention to?
23. What key values, if followed, would help this organization compete and thrive?
24. How are the office space and building layout designed? Who got which position?
25. What is posted on bulletin boards or displayed on the walls?
26. What is displayed on the desks or in other areas of the building? In the work groups? On lockers or closets?
27. How are common areas utilized?
28. What would you tell a friend about your organization if he or she was about to start working here?
29. Who is a hero around here? Why?
30. When anyone fails, how do people respond? What is the reward and recognition policy?
31. How is work-life balance?
32. Does the company host social outings or events for employees?
33. Is the company's strategic approach driven by processes or results?
34. Have the company's different departments ever collaborated with one another?
35. How has success has been celebrated?

Let us create a coaching culture in our organization where we coach each other.

It helps all of us to achieve a smooth, agile transformation.

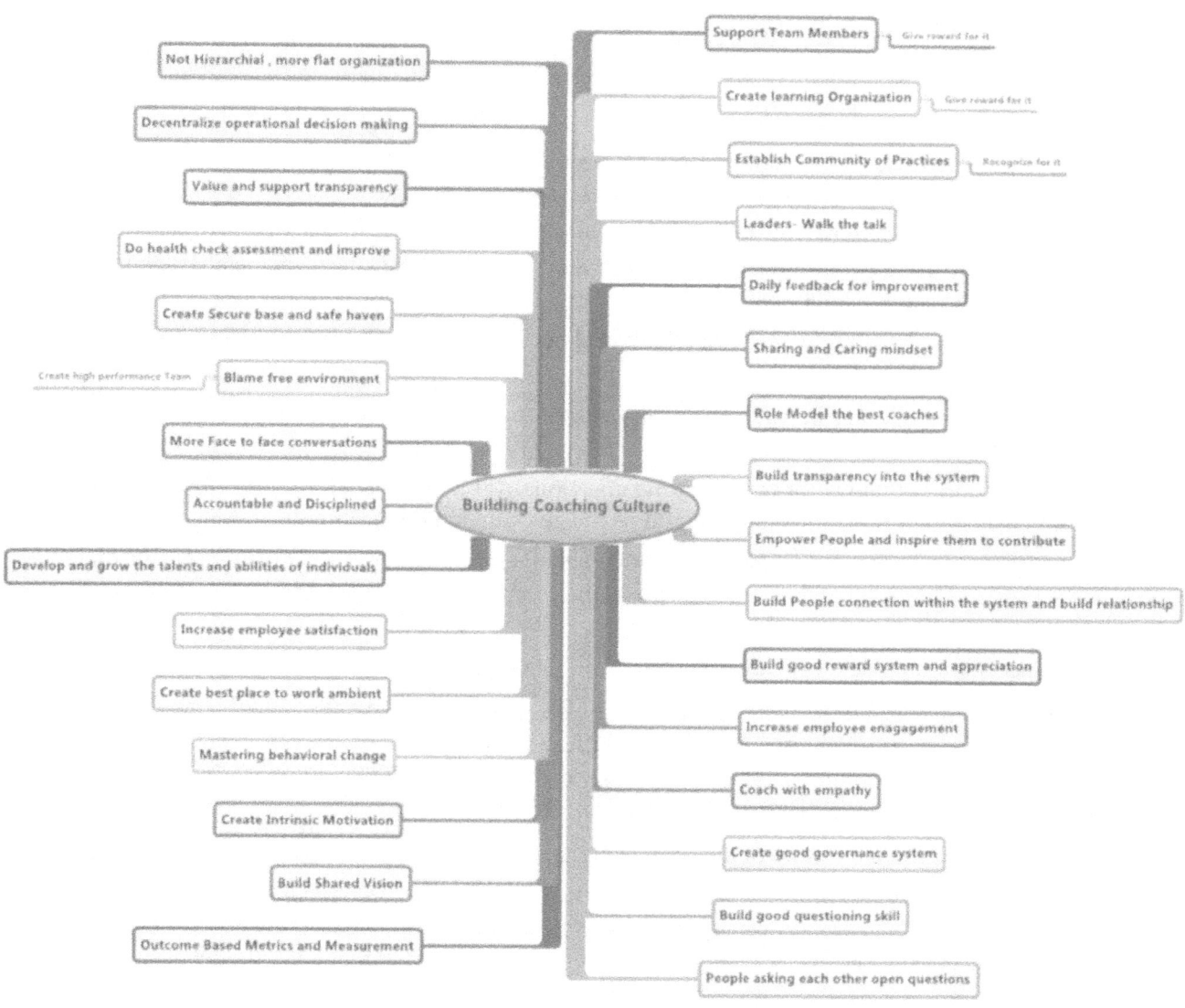

Look at this mind map, what action can you take to incorporate the changes in your current engagement? This mind map helped me to focus on all these aspects.

Culture is the arts elevated to a set of beliefs.

—*Thomas Wolfe*

What actions are you going to take from this lesson?

1. _____

2. _____

3. _____

Thinking Question:

Are you doing enough analysis to understand the culture where the organization is serving, the country it is operating and sharing the findings with the team members and work out?

5.3 How Schneider Cultural model helps successful agile adoption?

"Great leaders create great cultures regardless of the dominant culture in the organization."

—Bob Anderson,

Why this topic?

What is an agile culture? This question team members were seeking, leaders were demanding, with some approach, is there a way to explain the agile culture?

I have been extensively using below model for the last several years to explain the team members about the agile culture. I get very good acceptance from the team members.

Knowing the cultural facets of the organization is central before we start agile adoption. It helps the adoption process to be smoother.

Organizational culture is a set of values, norms, and standards that control how employees work to achieve an organization's mission and goals.

Bill Gates of Microsoft is famous for the set of organizational values that he created for his company, which include entrepreneurship, ownership, honesty, frankness, and open communication.

Culture shape employees' behavior. Company's culture becomes more and more distinct as when its members become more similar. The virtue of these shared values and common culture is that they increase integration and improve coordination among organizational members.

There are various cultural models which we can refer.

- The competing values framework (Based on Quinn and Rohrbaugh 1983),
- Harrison's culture model (Based on Harrison 1972, 1987),
- Deal and Kennedy's culture model (Based on Deal and Kennedy 2000a, b),
- Schneider's culture model (Based on Schneider)

 It is not easy to get the accurate picture of the organizational culture based on the survey and questionnaire. But we have to start somewhere…

Schneider Culture Model–an easy-to-use tool for assessing culture in any organization.

There are four aspects to look for

Collaboration Culture: How can we work together?
Control Culture: How can we control?
Competence Culture: Build a culture of world-class solutions, etc.
Cultivation Culture: is about learning and growing with a sense of purpose.

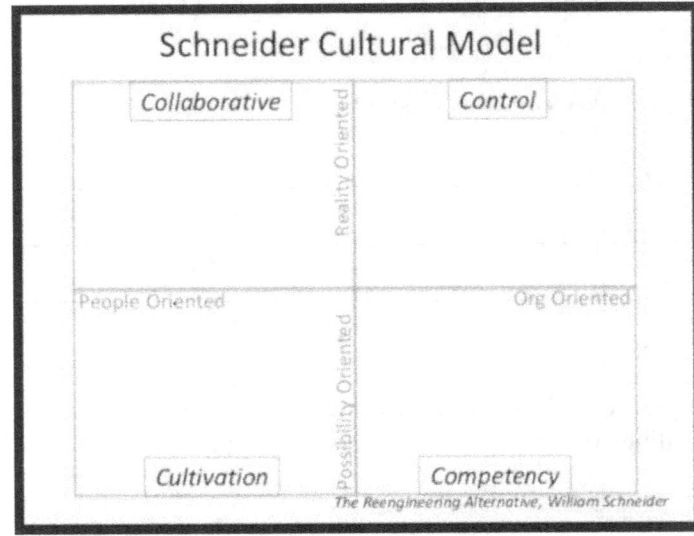

All these four cultural quadrants are good in their own context. Based on the context of that domain one cultural aspect may be prominent than others. More and more we are supporting each other's culture, there will be a smooth transaction else there will be more and more issues. E.g., it is not like Cultivation culture is better than Collaboration or Competency, all these are driven by the context in which the organization is operating.

The Schneider Culture Model Assessment is a simple tool to help Agile Coaches to judge an organization's current culture. If we use this assessment as a discussion tool, it can generate useful ideas that may help us during the transformation process. Each culture model defined has a descriptive quote and some words.

Cultures that are Reality Oriented (focus on what is happening now) and cultures that are Possibility Oriented (looking to the future for what is possible).

"The Collaboration culture springs from the household." It's "way to success is to put a collection of people together, to build these people into a team, to create their positive touching relationship with one another and to trust them with fully applying one another as resources."

This means that negative behavior and extreme self-interest do not go well with this culture. "Status and rank take a back seat."

"Control cultures prize objectivity. Emotions, subjectivity, and 'soft' concepts take everyone's eye off the ball and potentially get the organization in trouble. Empiricism and the systematic examination of externally generated facts are highly valued".

Important values in control cultures are order and predictability as well as maintaining stability. "Decision-making is highly detached and impersonal."

In describing the Competence culture, Schneider heavily refers to McClelland (1961). He argues "the competence culture is based in the achievement motive, discovered by McClelland in his research on individuals and societies and defined as man's need 'to compete against a standard of excellence'"

Schneider continues to explain that, "the need to achieve has to do with accomplishing more and doing better than others."

In a competence culture, being superior or the best is chief. This can mean having the best product, service, process or technology in the marketplace. "This culture gains its uniqueness by combining possibility with rationalism. What might be and the logic for getting there are what count".

Fundamental values are knowledge and information. Formalities and emotional considerations are not important compared to proven accomplishment.

"A competence culture values competition for its own sake even though it is not necessarily more competitive than other core cultures. There is a love for challenge; people like to be told that 'it can't be done'". This tool helps us to assess an organization or a team which particular quadrant they are dominating and the status of other quadrants.

If we look into the Agile Manifesto and then we connect these four quadrants, we can then check which area an organization should improve when adopting agile, based on the current state.

Individuals and interactions over processes and tools (Collaboration Culture)

Customer collaboration over contract negotiation (Collaboration Culture)

Working software over comprehensive documentation (Competency culture)

Responding to change over following a plan (Competency culture)

From Agile principles side

Business people and developers must work together daily throughout the project. (Collaboration Culture)

Continuous attention to technical excellence and good design enhances agility (Competency culture)

The best architectures, requirements, and designs emerge from self-organizing teams. (Collaboration and Competency culture)

At regular intervals, the team reflects on how to become more effective, then tunes and adjusts its behavior accordingly. (Collaboration culture) and so on.

So this gives information that if an organization is adopting an agile methodology which particular cultural aspect has to be more advanced. **Of course, this mapping shows an organization that is adopting agile practice has to be more collaborative, and it has to be people oriented and focused on the reality-oriented culture.**

We need to analyze the current cultural status and plan for the changes (Inspect and Adapt).

In the context of the Schneider culture model, a transformation would be a shift from one core culture to another. In agile terms, a transformation is a shift to an Agile Mindset – which entails a shift in culture.

There will be resistance, the reasons why people might resist a change in culture needs to be identified and plans formulated to overcome this resistance.

Participation, communication, and training are all seen as ways of overcoming resistance. The process of overcoming resistance involves a stage called unfreezing when the existing culture is questioned and is followed by a period of reformulation, where people consider what new beliefs they need to develop and share with each other. Finally, there is the re-freezing stage where the new culture is fixed in place.

The shift in leadership model is also expected: a move from a command and control to a collaborative model that builds trust and pushes ownership and decision making deeper into the organization, while retaining a good balance of process and policy.

What actions are you going to take from this lesson?

1. _____

2. _____

3. _____

Thinking Question:

Are you doing enough to help the organization to adopt an agile culture?

5.4 Are you part of a Strong or weak organizational culture?

Your position never gives you the right to command. It only imposes on you the duty of so living your life that others may receive your orders without being humiliated.

—*Dag Hammarskjöld*

Why this topic?

When we start our coaching engagement, we need to assess organizational culture, one of the prominent reasons for failure of the agile transformation is culture hence culture needs a lot of attention for an agile transformation.

Organizations can have either a strong or a weak culture.

Participants in a strong culture generally demonstrate a clear alignment with the organizational values and eagerly contribute to the common vision,

Participants in a weak culture must be more formally controlled usually through transactional or command-and-control management styles and driven to achieve objectives through process, bureaucracy, and authority.

Whether weak or strong, organizational culture can be evaluated through various methods and tools that have been used earlier.

Hofstede (1980) identified four dimensions of culture including:

Power distance–the degree of separation demonstrated between levels of power or authority within the organization

Uncertainty avoidance–the extent to which the culture accepts or resists risk (risk tolerance level)

Individualism versus collectivism–the extent to which people are able and expected to stand up or operate as part of a team

Masculinity versus femininity–the value placed within the organization on traditional gender roles such as competitiveness, assertiveness, ambition, and the accumulation of wealth

These four dimensions provide a framework for analyzing and classifying the organizational culture.

Another perspective on this is the four types of culture (Handy 1985)

Power culture–places the power among only a few within the organization with a central group or person driving the agenda and the purpose or the entity as a whole

Role culture–formally delegated authority structure generally operating within a greater hierarchy with power defined by the title of an individual

Task culture–teams formed and used to solve particular problems and generally lasting until a resolution is found or a task is completed

Person culture–where individuals believe that he or she is equal or superior to the organization itself and each member contributes what he or she feels is needed by the organization such as a professional partnership

Let us evaluate where we are performing in our current assignment and how best we can improve the situation.

What actions are you going to take from this lesson?

1. _____

2. _____

3. _____

Thinking Question:

Are you doing enough to help the organization understand various aspects of culture? And how these impacts organizational agility?

5.5 Sustaining change Management initiative in an Organization

"People don't resist change. They resist being changed!"

—Peter Senge

Why this Topic?

I got a question from one of my colleagues, she asked what do you do to sustain the change management initiative?

Why does change management effect not sustain for long?

Wherever there is a change, there will be resistance. It is tough to bring changes and sustain the same. We need to do a **force field analysis** and check in which area the force is more. <u>Driving forces need to be more than the resistance forces to do successfully do any change initiative.</u>

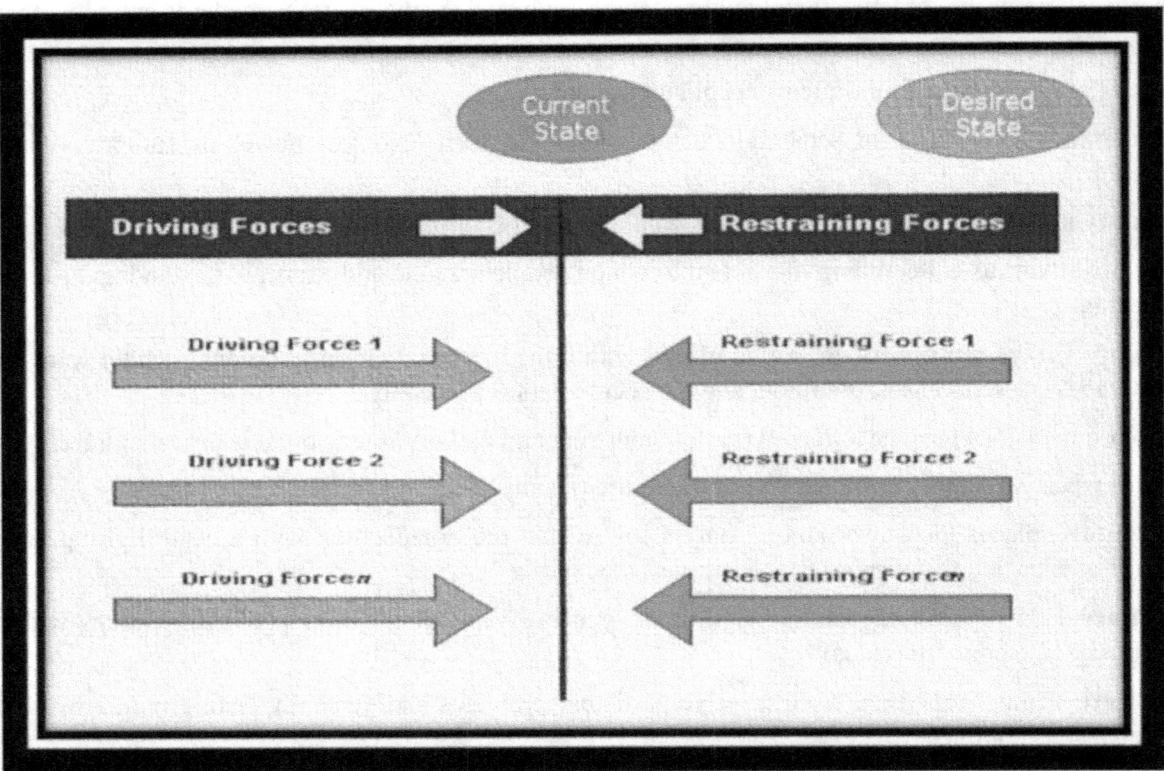

Any change will bring uncertainty. Most of the time employees think about the job security. Honestly, there is no job security in today's world.

As a leader, we look for various resistances for the changes. Some people like changes. Because due to change learning will be very high. Some team members hate changes. There will be neutral team members who will not say anything.

The Leader needs to communicate effectively about the changes. Impact analysis has to be done. **Various workshops have to be done** related to the changes and share the positive and negative impact on the new changes. **Team members have to be comfortable** and aware of what changes are coming. If there is ambiguity regarding the changes, there will be increased resistance.

William Bridges have written extensively on the topic of change in organizations for the past several decades. Bridges' work, *Managing Transitions*, is particularly helpful for the manager planning a technology change. His model views change as a series of events going from an ending, which is the way things used to be, to a beginning, which is the way things will be in the future when the project is complete. Between the two is the neutral zone. This is the stage in which few things are the way they were and it's not clear how they will be.

It is in the neutral zone, according to Bridges, where resistance can be found, because it is a stage that can be marked by confusion and uncertainty. In the neutral zone, there are no clear markers and no promises. The savvy leaders will be careful when dealing with people who may be in the neutral zone because they are seldom difficult on purpose. They are unsure and concerned and may not realize their resistance. Sensitivity to the neutral zone is important because the leaders can often help team members through this stage more quickly.

"The larger the scale of change, the greater the opportunity for success." If we try to do the work incrementally or if we try to shelter this work within a laboratory, particularly for too long a period, we will find that the organization as a whole will reject the new system.

When we face a large change—when we say we're going to make this change big time within the organization— we are forced to confront the larger issues of culture and management style that exist within the organization.

The probability of success is higher if these larger issues are taken on directly than if we try to introduce piecemeal change.

People are fearful of change when they don't know where they're going, but they can get excited about these changes once they have a sense of where the whole operation is heading. We have to be realists and recognize that some people will leave the organization because of these changes. Some will move on because they disagree with the company's new direction; others, because the management structure has been rewritten. But those who remain with the company can and do become excited when they experience how their work takes on new meaning within the altered processes.

We all want employees who care enough about their work that they are willing to want to understand and state their concerns. As new changes are presented, it should be expected that employees will have many questions. In fact, one of the best things a leader can do is communicate in many ways and many times what the changes entail. Some employees do better with written communication (email, blogs, websites, etc.), some with group meetings, and some with one-on-one casual conversations. All have their place in a plan for communicating changes.

Resistance to change in people can take many forms. Constant questioning about new concerns is a classic sign that resistance may be taking place. It can also take the shape of a form of confusion, in which the team member just can't understand how or why the project will be the way it is planned. Such a team member is probably not doing this on purpose. It's possible that this person is just not able to hear what is being communicated because of some discomfort with the message. This person may well be in the neutral zone and is just trying to find his or her way through it.

Other forms of resistance may include silence or easy acceptance. People may be silent for many reasons, but it is easy to assume that silence means acceptance.

How can we help the team to adapt to the change?

- **Training:**

Training is the best way to communicate and have employee awareness about the changes. People always want to be in their comfort zone. We have to encourage them about these changes which will shake their comfort areas. Some team members will not be able to understand the message clearly and they will resist all the possible ways regarding these changes. We have to communicate with them and answer all their genuine concerns. We have to repeat the training if required where all the team members clarify their queries if any.

- **Cowboy team members:**

There will be team members who are very good in the current system and if they are not part of the change initiative, they will create many issues with the change and try their level best to jeopardize the initiative.

Communicating the advantages of the new options may help, but when people are comfortable with the current situation, any change can be challenging and bring resistance into play.

In fact, it may be that our brains are wired for inertia. Christopher Koch reported in *CIO Magazine* on this phenomenon. He states that the:

"... Prefrontal cortex's capacity is finite—it can deal comfortably with only a handful of concepts before bumping up against limits. That bump generates a palpable sense of discomfort and produces fatigue and even anger. That's because the prefrontal cortex is tightly linked to the primitive emotional center of the brain, the amygdala, which controls our fight-or-flight response"

- **Job Security:**

Most of the team members are concerned about their existence what this new trend or changes are bringing. If we can help them by understanding how they should align themselves with the new changes, it will be easy to get the maximum of the people with the changes. Team members have to groom themselves with the latest trend, else they will not be able to survive for long in the organization.

 The way technology is changing the landscape, and if business or people are not aligning themselves with the latest trend soon most of the jobs/people will become obsolete. So for any type of change initiative people have to adapt though they will resist, they have to realize the benefit and rapid change.

Neuroscience research has uncovered information that explains a great deal about resistance.

According to David Rock and Jeffrey Schwartz,

Managers who know the fresh revolutions in cognitive science can lead and stimulate mindful change: an organizational transformation that takes into account the physiological nature of the brain, and ways in which it influences individuals to resist some forms of leadership and admit others.

Rock and Schwartz **stresses that change of any kind is a form of pain that causes serious reactions in the brain**. In fact, research using magnetic resonance imaging (MRI) indicates that **organizational change may be perceived by the brain as not being that different from being attacked by an animal in a forest.**

According to Rock and Schwartz, *"Trying to change any hard-wired habit requires a lot of effort, in the form of attention. This often leads to a feeling that many people find uncomfortable. So they do what they can to avoid change."*

How can we sustain the change initiative?

1. Have a focus group with experts, who can bring and effectively implement those changes smoothly
2. Let us have a review on the changes and improvements in the organization and communicate with all the people
3. Connect with the employees and understand their concern and implement wherever applicable and feasible
4. Series of communication at different levels and get the feedback
5. Encourage different ways to engage people to participate. Facilitate those events to connect with the people.
6. Let us talk openly, employee voice and concern in a common area so that there is no secret mission
7. Build win-win situation wherever possible
8. Take the help from all the team members wherever possible, slowly resistance will become cooperation

 We have to keep looking and calibrate the situation for sustaining the changes for long.

 "Everybody has accepted by now that change is unavoidable. But that still implies that change is like death and taxes; it should be postponed as long as possible, and no change would be vastly preferable. But in a period of upheaval, such as the one we are living in, change is the norm."

—*Peter F. Drucker*

What actions are you going to take from this lesson?

1. _____

2. _____

3. _____

Thinking Question:

Are you doing enough to understand the change aspects and the sustainability of these changes?

5.6 Swarming technique for Organizational Transformation

 "Culture does not change because we desire to change it. Culture changes when the organization is transformed; the culture reflects the realities of people working together every day."

—*Frances Hesselbein*

Why this topic?

Most of our discussions in the coaching circle, there is a talk on Structure vs. transformation, structure vs. culture, structure vs. leadership. The thought is to understand how all these concepts are co-related and as an agile coach why it is important to understand all these aspects?

One of the big barriers to organizational transformation is an organizational structure.

Wrong structure hinders the business agility.

What's wrong with the above structure? Except few a proud team members saying I am heading 200 people! I am heading this vertical! Etc.

Too Slow? Too rigid, too cumbersome to deliver the responsiveness we now need?

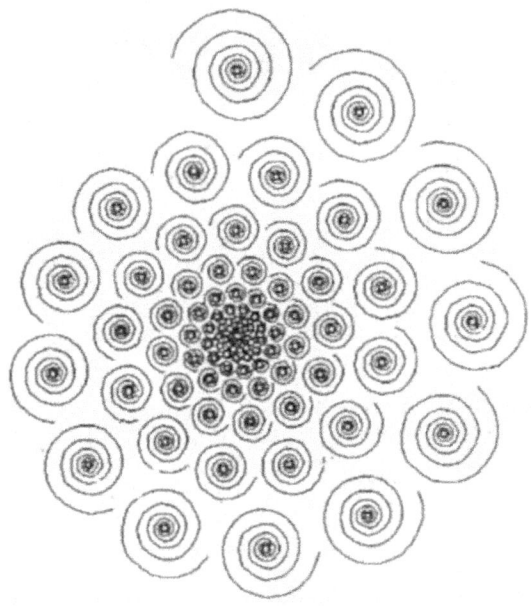

How about this revolutionary structure? The network of team members for different purposes.

Connected for a reason, no command and control. Interconnected families?

Why can't we build such a community?

The quick, coordinated behavior of large groups of individuals in these networks is called swarming.

In Swarming behavior, they are not just members of some clumsy hierarchy waiting around to be told what to do. Instead, they act fast on their initiative and their opponents must either flee or else be overwhelmed.

Swarms place more emphasis on decentralized coordination than on centralized control to get things done.

Wikipedia describes swarming as "an emergent behavior arising from simple rules that are followed by individuals and does not involve any central coordination".

Gartner predicted that by 2015, **40 percent or more of an organization's work will be 'non-routine' and people will swarm more often and work solo less.** This means that people work with others whom they know just barely if at all. Teams will also include people outside the control of the organization.

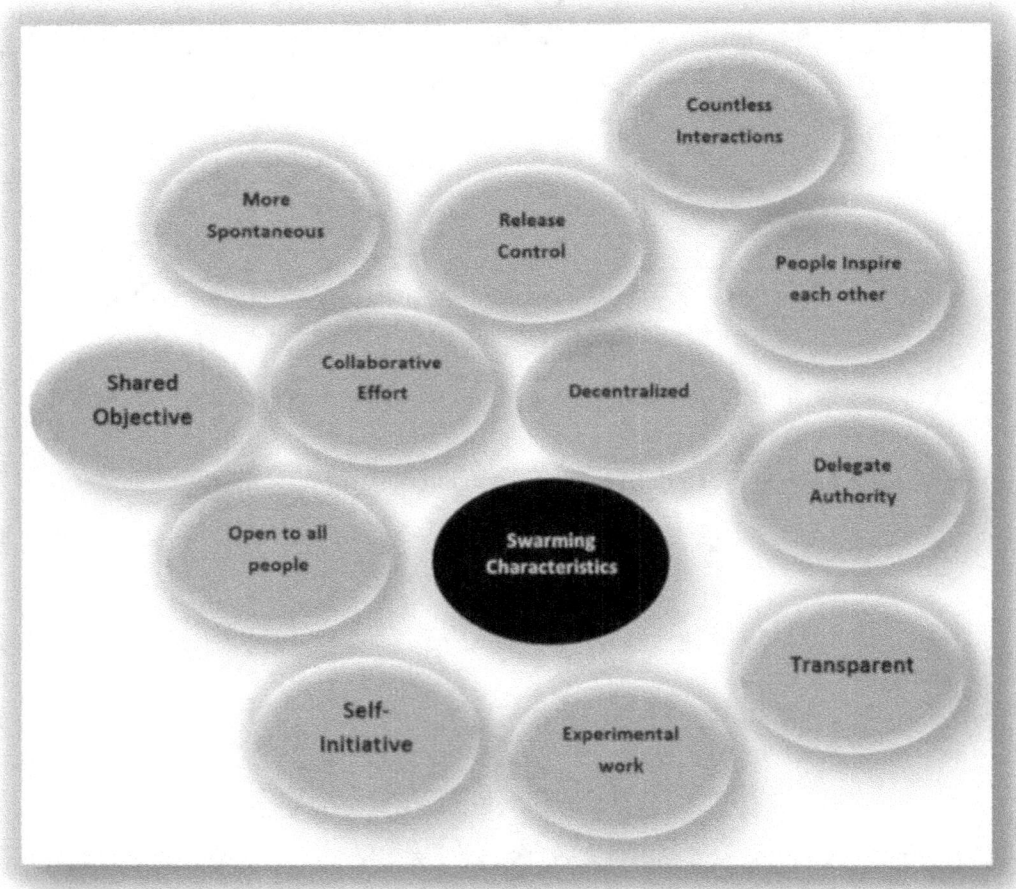

Swarming behavior emerges as people learn how their actions combine to create larger effects.

Those larger effects are the organizational responses that move their company toward achieving its performance targets even as the world continues to change.

This is swarming behavior in a company. It is fast, powerful, and continually responsive to change.

If we imagine our body, interconnected trillions of cells act as Swarming agents. They know how to connect and get the work done. Complete decentralized manner.

In an uncertain rapidly changing world, we have to change the way we are operating. Let us apply swarming at the organizational level and transform for the better business agility.

We have created many communities to establish a learning organization. Team members are sharing the learning for their own growth and to validate their knowledge.

The best organization model proposed by **Laloux** model for modern days, let us build such a culture.

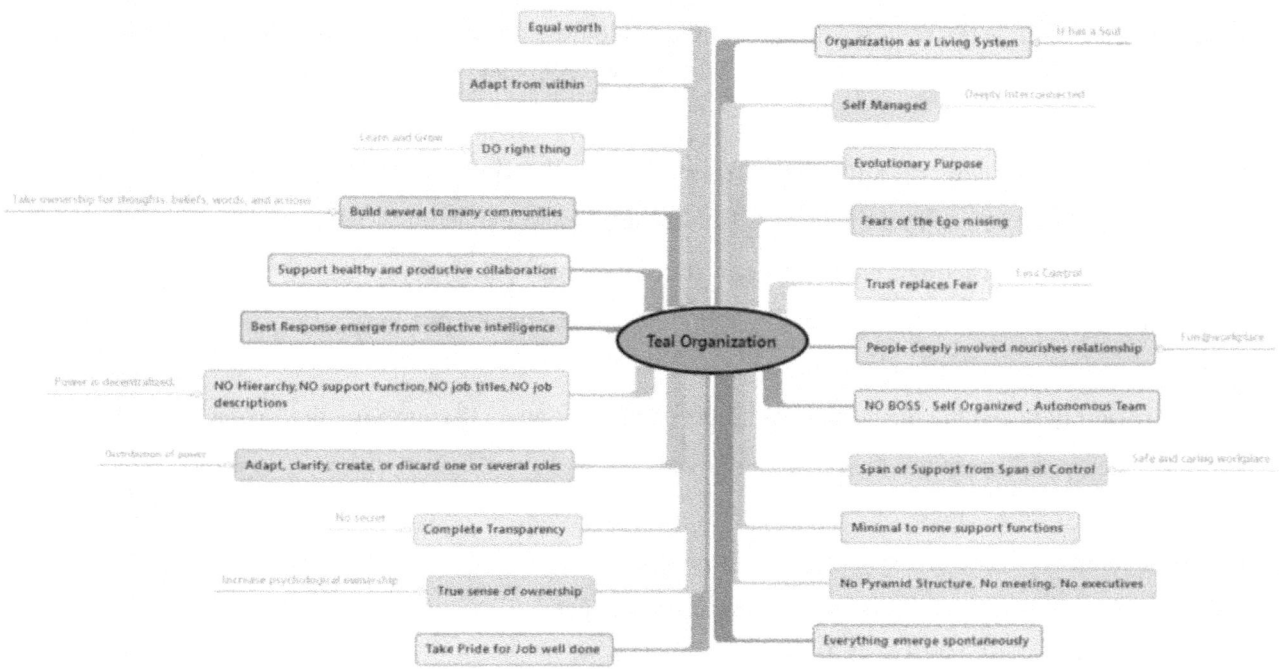

This mind map highlights the aspects of the teal organization. What can we do as a coach to create such an organization?

What actions are you going to take from this lesson?

1. _____

2. _____

3. _____

Thinking Question:

Are you doing enough to learn organization structure and its impact on organizational culture? Explain the same in your coaching sessions?

5.7 Agile Transformation needs a Self-Disciplined Culture

> *"Self-discipline is the magic power that makes you virtually unstoppable."*
>
> *—Anonymous*

Why this topic?

In my sustenance assessment, I observed this thought, how to sustain a transformation, and if there is a good connection with self-discipline vs. sustenance. How to explore this and explain the outcome to the team members?

Some questions to be answered

1. How do we sustain agility for transforming an agile project?

2. How do we sustain the team culture when we have significant attrition?

Self-discipline: It is the ability to control one's impulses, emotions, desires, and behavior.

Agile transformation is all about **Discipline and Self-disciplined** team members.

When we find discipline is missing, we do not get the value flow out from the team to the end users. Once the transformed team is not able to sustain the value delivery, agility disappears.

Lack of discipline?

All the 12 principles highlight regarding the self-discipline to be maintained or followed for a long time.

In our sustenance activities, we find the team is lacking self-discipline habits

1. Customer satisfaction **through early and continuous software delivery**

2. **Accommodate** changing requirements throughout the development process.

3. **Frequent delivery** of working software

4. **Collaboration** between the business stakeholders and developers **throughout the project**

5. **Support, trust, and motivate** the people involved

6. **Enable** face-to-face interactions

7. **Working software** is the primary measure of progress

8. Agile processes to **support a consistent development speed**

9. **Attention to technical detail and design** enhances agility

10. Simplicity-**Develop just enough** to get the job done right now.

11. **Self-organizing teams** encourage great architectures, requirements, and designs

12. **Regular reflections** on how to become more effective

Most of these activities come from self-discipline by understanding why we are doing all these initiatives.

How do we bring team members who follow such a self-discipline culture, build such a culture, and sustain the culture?

What are the team member's characteristics who are self-disciplined? Three eyes, four ears! How do we find them?

Without the right people on the bus, we will miss the target.

Building self-discipline culture is all about bringing the right people who are self-disciplined.

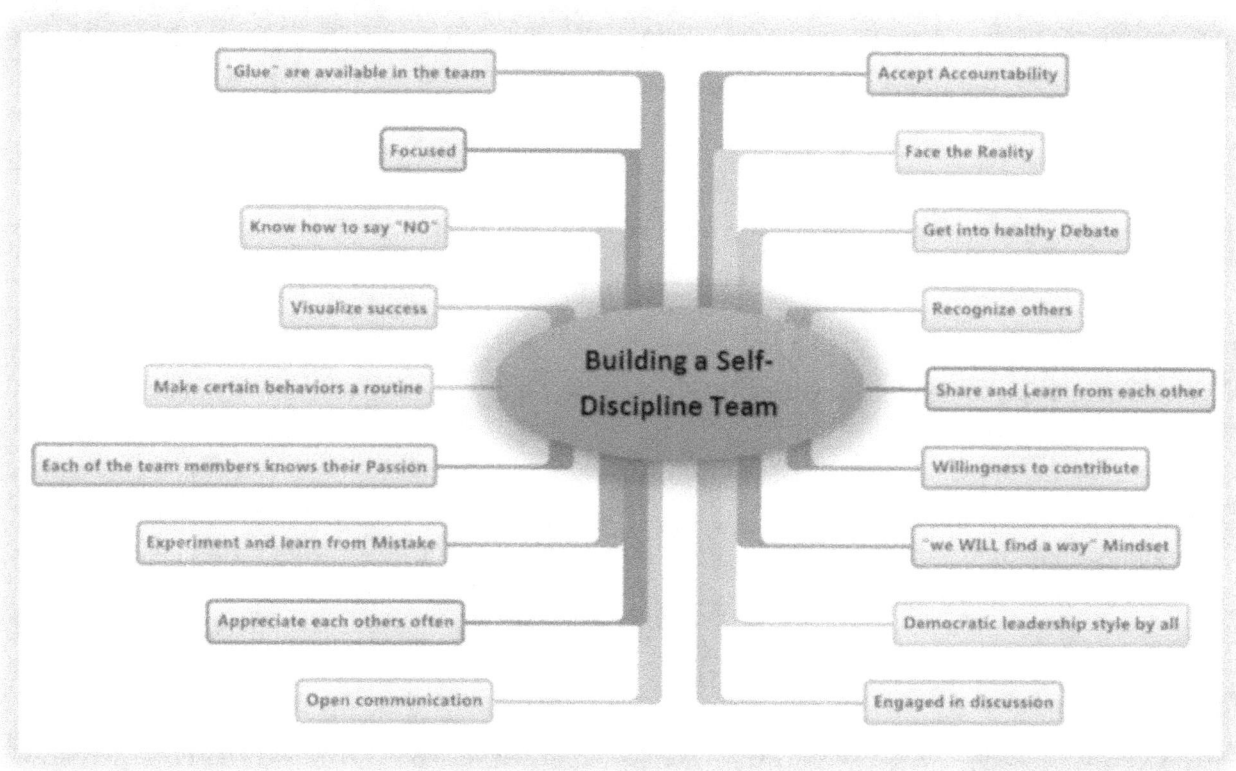

In Jim Collins's book, Good to Great, he argues that modern corporate culture is all about self-discipline.

He identifies three elements as central to creating this culture

- **Disciplined people**–have the right people on the team
- **Disciplined thought**–understand your company's strengths and weaknesses
- **Disciplined action**–take action based on this understanding

During our coaching, we look for all these elements,we recommend recruiters to follow this so that later we have fewer issues with the team members.

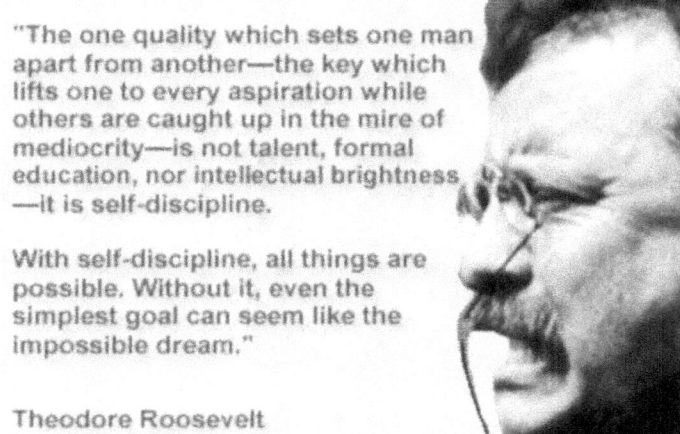

"The one quality which sets one man apart from another—the key which lifts one to every aspiration while others are caught up in the mire of mediocrity—is not talent, formal education, nor intellectual brightness —it is self-discipline.

With self-discipline, all things are possible. Without it, even the simplest goal can seem like the impossible dream."

Theodore Roosevelt

It needs immense dedication, practice, passion, and self-discipline to deliver performance in classical music conference which the audience appreciates. As a coach do we rehearse so much to scale ourselves up to such a higher level when we perform that the audience says "Awesome"? It needs discipline from ourselves.

"A great way to develop self-discipline is to make it a habit to do the things you should be doing when you feel the laziest. Every time you feel really lazy, do the opposite of what you feel like doing." - Anonymous

What actions are you going to take from this lesson?

1. _____

2. _____

3. _____

Thinking Question:

Are you doing enough to improve the discipline in a team where you are coaching? What else should you be doing to achieve the mastery?

5.8 Organizational Agility ++

"Agility is all about trusting in one's ability to respond to unpredictable events more than trusting in one's ability to plan ahead for them."

—"The Agile Manifesto."

Why this topic?

What are the factors which influence a super agile team? Why cannot we achieve super agility?

What is organizational Agility ++?

In the quickest timeline, how can an organization deliver solutions to the users and correct the received feedback in the quickest timeline?

Is the organization able to find its growth path?

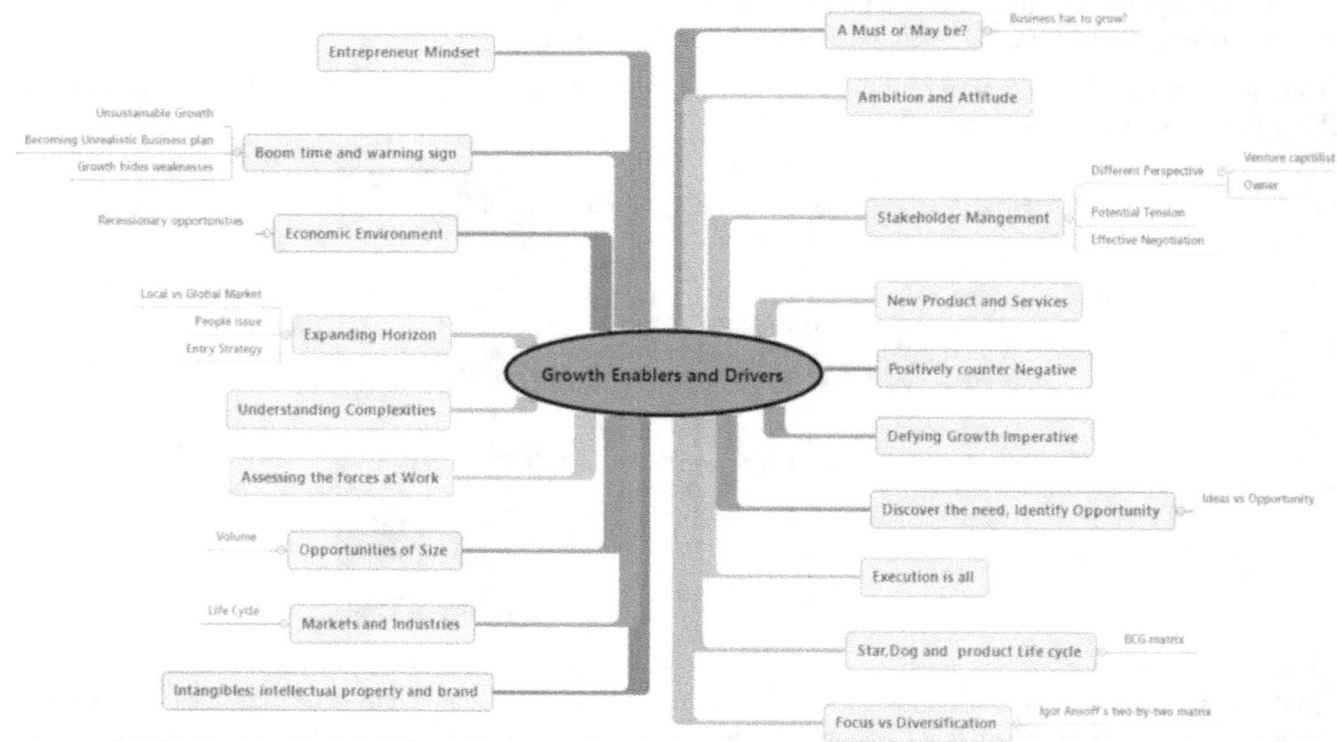

Ways to achieve Agility :

Cockburn's (2001) :1) *effective*, 2) *steerable*, 3) *rule-based*, 4) (about) *people*, and 5) *communication*

Anderson (2003):1) *speed*

Larman (2003): 1) *speed* 2) *flexibility* and 3) *responsiveness*

Schuh (2004): 1) *speed*, 2) *people*, 3) *empowerment*, 4) *change*, 5) *feedback*, and 6) *value*.

Lyytinen (2006): 1) *feedback*, 2) *adaptability*, and 3) *collaboration*.

Subramaniam (2005):1) *feedback*, 2) *adaptability*, and 3) *collaboration*.

Ambler (2007) : 1) *iterative*, 2) *incremental*, 3) *self-organizing*, 4) *less process-driven*, 5) *collaborative*, 6) *cost-conscious*, 7) (about) *speed*, and 8) *customer-driven*

IEEE (2007): 1) *iterative* and 2) *responsive*

Let us look into these below pictures and try to visualize the whole story.

When we are focused and we have goals to achieve, we can run as fast as we can towards the goal. No one can stop us. No friction, no baggage. We are standalone. Just run and deliver the solution.

Like a Pipeline which supplies the materials as fast as it can!

What if, we have many legacy issues to carry? What happens when we have much emotional baggage to carry? What if frictions are high? Pipeline gets clogged!

Slows down the execution speed.

Can we automate the dependent systems to get the benefits? Else we will be slow down the end to end process.

Can we integrate all the systems and make it as a single piece and automate the whole process? We need to break the silos of the dependent system to automate the whole piece.

Even as a team, we can achieve the speed when we have focused and we have no attached load with us.

Let us look into the implementation of such agility into the legacy enterprise.

What advantage **small startup company** has- Being able to start from scratch with their IT architectures—with no complex legacy systems to either reconfigure or maintain. And because those companies' main products of web applications are 100 percent customer facing, these companies have learned how to react quickly to the customer feedback and release new features and improvements on the fly.

They can achieve Agility ++ in the shortest timeline.

Most of the large legacy enterprises sitting on the applications developed long back, Once they try to implement Agility ++ they had all this baggage to carry as a load.

> *"Agile is more a "direction," than an "end," a philosophy and mindset at the board level."*
>
> *—Pearl Zhu,*

Their delivery pipeline **has clogged** with many legacy issues (People Issue, Infrastructure Issues, Architectural issues, process issue etc.).

The organization has to re-look at the setup and automate those steps, wherever applicable to get the benefits of agility++.

As an agile enterprise coach, we find such **clogged** pipes while bringing agility++, It takes time to clean such a pipe and we should have patience. These clogged pipes, block the business continuity flow.

What it takes to achieve Agility++

1. It takes time to completely **restructure** the current organizational setup (Remove silos, more and more mini-startups within the team)
2. It takes some time to complete **re-architecture** the solutions, wherever applicable
3. Need to Introduce new **focus roles** to achieve agility++ (Old roles become obsolete)
4. Invest and Drive for new **cultural** changes (Collaboration and Cultivation)
5. Invest in **tools and infrastructure (DevOps Tools)**.
6. **Re-skill** the team members on the required skill (**Intrapreneurship**)
7. **Standardize** the Continuous delivery process
8. Give a hard look at the leadership contribution, revamp if required

Build a smooth business continuity pipeline without any blockage to achieve Agility++

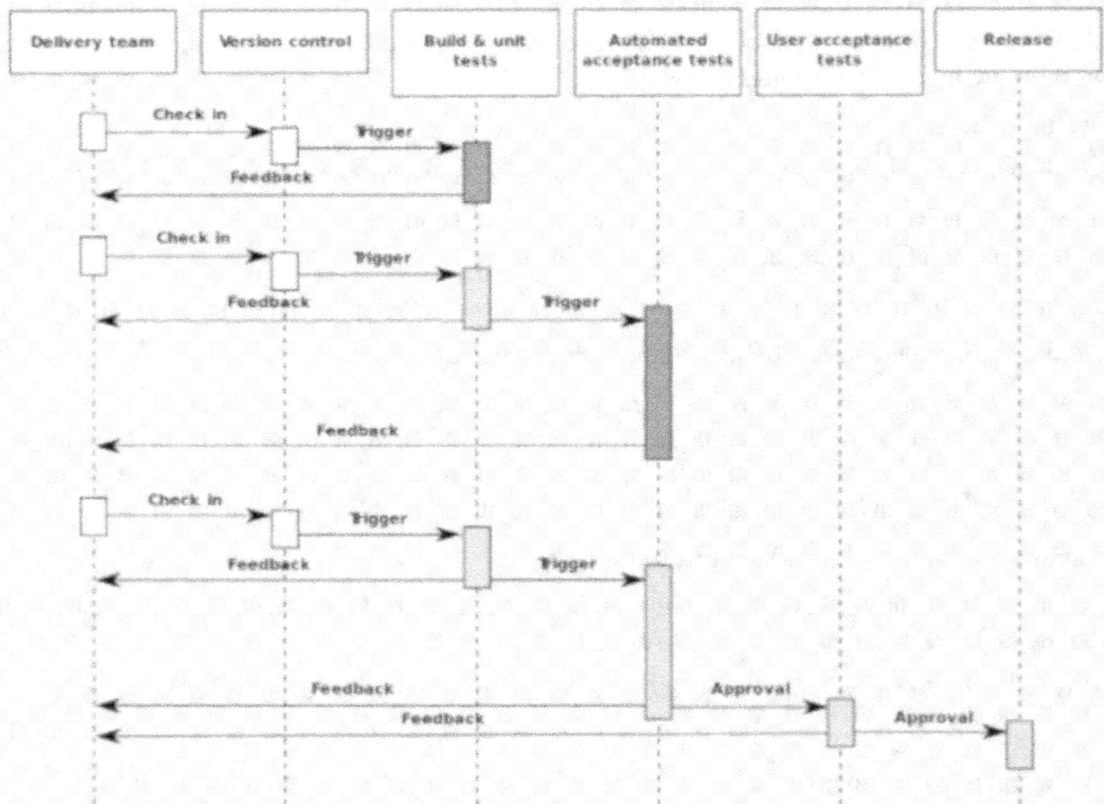

Source: Wikipedia

More and more digital transformation is penetrating across all the industry, all the organizations are forced to look into the Agility++ characteristics, else they will be left out of the business very soon.

Agility comes when the whole ecosystem reduces the feedback loop to a shorter timeline, e.g. gate 0 to gate 7 in 3-6 months the cycle.

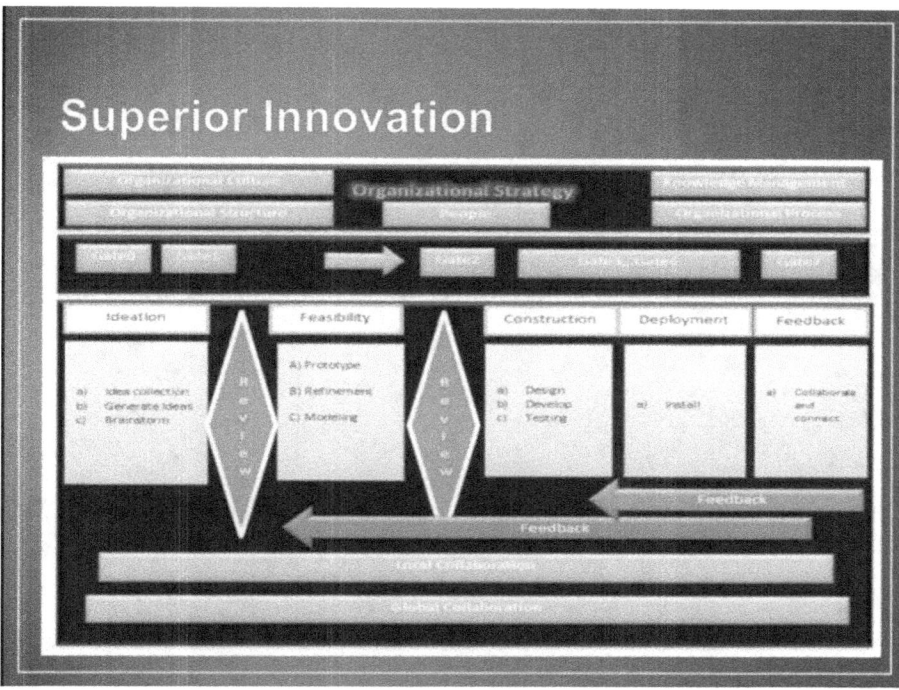

Team focus more on value based delivery

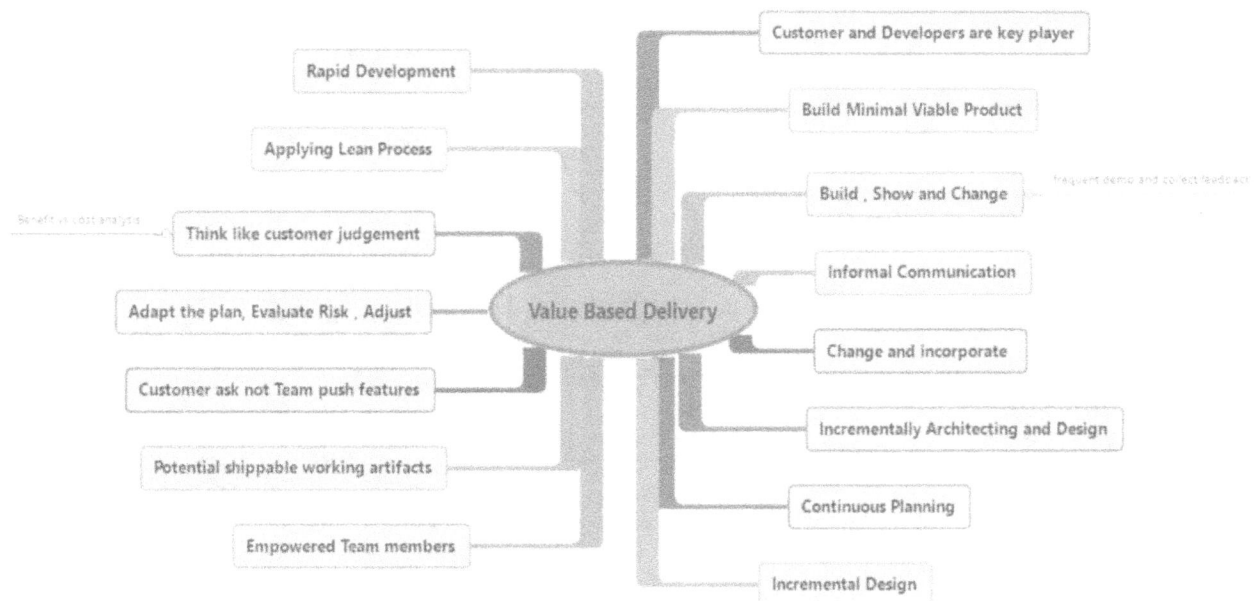

Survival kit for an agile coach. All these below image points has to be exercised.

Excellent interpersonal, negotiation and presentation skills

Able to forge relationships and influence effectively at Senior Management level

Drive improvement through examples and practical experience

Demonstrate a strong knack for identifying waste and helping teams devise streamlined solutions

Ask difficult questions, be focused, compassionate and uncompromising

Skillfully facilitates group dynamics and communications, regardless of the audience, and ensure that every voice is heard and heeded

Maintain and share relevant metrics with the leadership team

Act as an ambassador for teams, and facilitate trade-offs between business and technical needs

Ability to design and facilitate a group process, elicit contributions from group members, stimulate a focused group discussion, and achieve a desired outcome

Ability to encourage, motivate, and guide individuals or teams in learning and improving effectiveness

Challenges conventional thinking that interferes with change efforts

Effective in driving cultural change and leading transformation

Promotes and fosters a culture of collaboration, accountability, trust and transparency across teams

Introduce teams to the latest innovative systems thinking

Translates industry best practices into actionable recommendations

Acts as an enterprise thought leader

Coaches Release Train Engineers, Product Management, Epic Owners at the program level

Coaches/Facilitates business leads in lean thinking and development of Minimal Viable Products (MVP)

Create, launch, and facilitate Communities of Practice, and Agile Working Groups

Engage with clients / senior leaders — Define Agile transformation plan / Governance mechanisms

Enable Agile transformation — Act as champion and evangelist of Agile principles and values

Conduct periodic readiness / maturity assessments — Measure Agility

Represent Client in internal and external forum

Build Agile solutions and frameworks — For different technologies / domain

Coach the team to ensure Agile adoption

Conduct training workshops — Create and deliver methods, training, templates and tools / Create, build, and deliver customized Agile training

Promote delivery of business value

Influence changes that increases team performance at a sustainable pace

Work with Scrum Masters to increase the effectiveness

Address Team dysfunctions — Improve team's ability to achieve sustainable in

Work with organizational leadership and teams — To change and adjust or organizing teams within

Understand challenges with scaling agile teams across organizations

Capable of identifying and addressing dysfunctional patterns caused by external forces

Exhibits a deep-passion for continuous learning — Facilitate learning thro

Facilitate classes, workshops, and Agile sharing events — Create Enterpri

Adopt Continuous Delivery practices

Ability to garner respect from individuals/teams

Communicate with Team,larger practitioner community and Agile thought leaders internally and externally — Bring le

Understand challenges with scaling agile teams across organizations

Capable of identifying and addressing dysfunctional patterns caused by external forces

Define Agile transformation plan

Act as champion and evangelist of Agile principles and values

Governance mechanisms

Help team to deliver outstanding software as fast as possible

Measure Agility

For different technologies / domain

To change and adjust organizational design to promote self-organizing teams within an enterprise environment

Create and deliver methods, training, templates and tools

Create, build, and deliver customized Agile training

Create Enterprise wide initiatives: internal certification (SM, PO).

Improve team's ability to achieve sustainable increases in velocity and team efficiency

Facilitate learning through workshops, meetings, and team offsites

Coach the team to resolve internally

Bring industry knowledge from the Agile community

Eliminate Blockers, Risks, create opportunities

Develop and grow business trust

Deepen customer relationships

Not afraid to raise issues and drive change to remove impediments

Drive process implementation, standardization and simplification

"Learning agility means to learn, de-learn, and relearn all the time."

—Pearl Zhu,

What actions are you going to take from this lesson?

1. _____

2. _____

3. _____

Thinking Question:

Are you doing enough to enhance your knowledge to increase the organizational execution speed and share the same with the team with whom you are working?

5.9 How do we Increase the Effectiveness of Organizational Transformation?

"The only way you survive is you continuously transform into something else. It's this idea of continuous transformation that makes you an innovating company."

—Gini Rometty

Why this topic?

From Agile center this is an evergreen search, what can we do to improve the effectiveness of agile transformation? I have been working on this for the last several years and coming up with many proposals, some are successful, and some are not so good.

During coaching, we focus on the **Mindset** change.

What most of the time we observe once coaching is over, is that the team members go back to the original style? They fall back!

We discuss and debate and come up with different ways to address this problem.

Employees are altering their mind-sets only if they **understand the purpose** of the change and agree with it—at least sufficient to give it a try.

They ask, **what's in it for me?**

An organization has to be ready and ensure that they are encouraging employees to develop a new way of working. Employees are developing the skills that are required to do the tasks.

In 1957, the Stanford social psychologist Leon Festinger published his theory of cognitive dissonance the distressing mental state that arises when people find that their **beliefs** are inconsistent with their **actions**.

Festinger observed in his experimentation that a deep-seated need to eliminate cognitive dissonance by **altering either their activities or their views.**

If People believe in its complete purpose, they will be happy to alter their behavior to serve that purpose, they will suffer from cognitive dissonance if they don't.

Getting individuals to have an emotional response to a requisite new form of behavior isn't enough to encourage them to adopt it forever. It must also help them to satisfy their innate appetite to grow.

When they view the new behavior's meaning from this completely different perspective—not as the fulfillment of an external requirement, but rather as a way of satisfying a personal need— they are unlikely ever to give it up.

As a coach we need to create a story and tell why employees need to change and what benefit they will get as a result of the change.

Employees are falling back in the transformation process when they discover that **nobody is appreciating the new way of working or producing output**. System structure has to be ready with a **new way of operating with reward and recognition**. The whole ecosystem has to behave in the same way, a partial transformation is not sustainable.

If you are encouraging people to use alternative transportation to improve climate conditions, create a structure for it and celebrate it when they use it.

Company's goals for new behavior has to be **reinforced**, else employees are less likely to adopt it consistently.

Let us find the team who is demonstrating the best agile values and principles and recognize the team publicly.

Let us find the manager who is the best servant leader, let us find the best scrum master who has demonstrated excellent scrum discipline and output.

Let us find the best product owner where the team says he/she is a passionate product owner.

Let us find the best agile coaches who have transformed several teams and the team says they got the benefit, etc.

Once we take care of all these small aspects, the sustainability of the transformation will be generated.

Adaptability is not imitation. It means the power of resistance and assimilation.

—Mahatma Gandhi

What actions are you going to take from this lesson?

1. _____

2. _____

3. _____

Thinking Question:

Are you doing enough to enhance knowledge about the transformation? What else you need to do?

5.10 Challenges to Build Psychological Safety

"People often believed they were safer in the light, thinking monsters only came out at night. But safety – like light – is a façade."

—*C.J. Roberts, Captive in the Dark*

Why this topic?

One of the key requirements for the best performing team is to create psychological safety, why we cannot create? What are the bottlenecks?

Wikipedia definition: Psychological safety is a **shared belief** that the team is safe for interpersonal risk-taking. It can be defined as **"being able to show and employ one's self without fear of negative consequences of self-image, status or career"** (Kahn 1990, p. 708).

In psychologically safe teams, the team member's sense is accepted and respected. It is also the maximum areas studied, enabling situations in group dynamics and team learning research.

Psychological safety is the key to an agile culture. An Agile leader enables Psychological safety at the workplace.

Leaders who create psychological safety and hold their employees accountable for excellence are the highest performing.

Teams at Google include questions such as, **"How confident are you that you won't receive retaliation or criticism if you admit an error or make a mistake?"**

Highest-performing teams have one thing that is shared: psychological safety, the belief that you won't be punished when you create a fault

When as a coach you find below symptoms in the team, you need to increase the **Psychological safety** for that team. You need to coach them about psychological safety.

1. People get into blame style easily
2. Conflicts are getting into the fighting mode
3. Normal conversion getting into arguments and it gets escalated
4. Lobbyism and threat to the employees are as they are not part of the Lobby
5. Team members take feedbacks personally
6. Questions are marked as a silly question and marked as trivial
7. If we challenge one another, team members consider that pushing of their ideas
8. Team members are not willing to accept their mistake, they become defensive
9. Most of the team members are busy and are not open for discussion
10. People are not focused during the critical discussions
11. Team members always feel it is someone else problem, not mine.(Passing the ball)
12. Creative ideas are shot down by the experts
13. Accountability is missing most of the time, it has to be pushed from the top as team members are not willing to take it up
14. Team members are not free enough to share their some personal stories, too professional and no time for all these discussions
15. Measurement is only with numbers, efficiency, saving, ROI calculation. Happiness index is missing
16. Culture is, complete the job right at first attempt, so be cautious
17. The leader is very strict about the deadline, the pressure is very high, Delivery always today and now.

18. Team members know there is no place to go or share their stories.
19. Do it else leave the place
20. Leaders do not walk the talk
21. Cost is the center of all discussions. No money for the team outing, no money for travel, no money for the celebration, no money for recognition! Save the cost!
22. Rewards and recognition are rare, too much politics in the selection process
23. People are scared to become vulnerable
24. Team members sometimes reject others for being different
25. People do not share much about their personal story
26. Only a few team members are dominating the meeting most of the time
27. Retrospect actions related to impediments have not been closed for several months
28. Not much support from each other (individual contributor and hero culture)

As a coach, you need to coach the leaders and team members to bring back Psychological safety for the team.

What actions are you going to take from this lesson?

1. _____

2. _____

3. _____

Thinking Question:

Are you doing enough to understand psychological safety and help the team to maintain the same?

5.11 Self-Organized Team live Healthily, Being Agile is good for health

A self-organized team is possible when people carry shared purpose, principles, and values. They support and respect each other. And they want to succeed. The [Agile] team works together to respond to changes that happen together. They collectively do what needs to be done to build the software."

- Ken Schwaber

Why this topic?

The connection between health benefit and self-organization characteristics! At least for the sake of health we will ensure that we are self-organized, some interesting facts to connect between these topics.

Agile Manifesto says

*We are uncovering better ways of developing software by doing it and **helping others** do it. Through this work we have come to value:*

One of the Principles is:

The best architectures, requirements, and designs emerge from **self-organizing teams**.

The Self-Organized team helps each other on a daily basis.

High-performance team is HIGH IN **COMPASSION!**

When you are high in compassion and continue to do this practice for several years, you get many health benefits.

WHAT IS THIS COMPASSION?

Compassion is responding to the needs of others and protecting those who are suffering or in need.

Compassion is the expression of *love, kindness, and caring for those who need help.*

If you want others to be happy
practice compassion If you want
to be happy practice compassion
Dala Lama

Compassion helps us to gain a better perspective of our situation. No matter what our challenges may be, there is always someone out there who is worse off than us and could benefit from our kindness.

Some fascinating research suggests human beings have a built-in "**compassionate instinct**" that drives us to care and help others.

*The Act of being compassionate causes the release of brain chemicals that make us **feel happy and content**.*

These are stories I include in my coaching session with the team to inspire them to bring happiness to the team.

UCLA medical researcher **Steve Cole and Barbara Fredrickson** evaluated the levels of cellular inflammation in people who describe themselves as "very happy." Inflammation is at the root of cancer and other diseases and is generally high in people who live under a lot of stress. We might expect that **inflammation would be lower for people with higher levels of happiness**.

Cole and Fredrickson found that this was only the case for certain "very happy" people. They found that people who were happy because they lived a life of pleasure had high inflammation levels; on the other hand, people who were happy because they lived a life of purpose or meaning had **lower inflammation levels**. A life of meaning and purpose is one focused less on satisfying oneself and more on others. It is a life rich in compassion and altruism.

Using advanced brain-imaging techniques, researchers have shown that the brain's pleasure centers become more active when people *take money, a good dessert, or some other pleasurable thing*. And these same brain centers become equally active when people **witness money being given to charity**! Other studies have shown that children as young as two years old derive as much **pleasure from giving treats to others as they do from receiving treats**—and they are too young to be driven by the social conventions of politeness and fairness!

Research by Ed Diener and Martin Seligman, leading researchers in positive psychology, suggest that **connecting with others in a meaningful way helps us to enjoy better mental and physical health and speeds up recovery from disease.** Furthermore, research by Stephanie Brown, at Stony Brook University, and Sara Konrath, at the University of Michigan, has shown that it may even **lengthen our lifespan.**

The reason a compassionate lifestyle leads to **greater psychological well-being** may be that the act of giving appears to be as **pleasurable** as the act of receiving, if not more so.

Research also suggests that

*A **compassionate lifestyle may improve longevity,** which may be because it provides a buffer against stress.*

***Compassion may protect against stress** in that it is very **pleasurable**.*

Compassion may boost our well-being in that it can help broaden our perspective beyond ourselves.

Research shows that depression and anxiety are linked to a state of self-focus, a preoccupation with "me, myself, and I." When you do something for someone else, however, that state of self-focus shifts to a state of other-focus.

Just as importantly, the brain chemicals released through compassion can counteract the effects of other brain chemicals that promote stress. Thus, **compassion can serve as an antidote to stress, anger, catastrophic thinking, and other negative thoughts**.

In addition, many studies have shown that compassion can

- **Increase our resistance to stress**
- **Improve our marital relations, friendships, and workplace relationships**
- **Reduce our risk of heart disease**
- **Lessen our desire to get even with or harm those who have harmed you**
- **Lengthen our life**

One of the key ways **compassion** works is by increasing our **connections** to other people, deepening existing connections and helping to forge new ones, as when you reach out to help strangers. **Such "social connections" have been shown to reduce inflammation, anxiety, and depression, which, in all three cases, can add years to our life and life to our** years.

What actions are you going to take from this lesson?

1. _____

2. _____

3. _____

Thinking Question:

Are you doing enough to enhance your knowledge on self-organization and benefits?

5.12 Why do we need to spread optimism during an Agile Transformation?

"Don't be pushed around by the fears in your mind. Be led by the dreams in your heart."

—Roy T. Bennett

Why this topic?

The connection between optimism and developing a product in a complex world, how can we motivate team members? How can leaders inspire team members?

Agile demands more optimistic team members. Agile mindset is all about growth mindset.

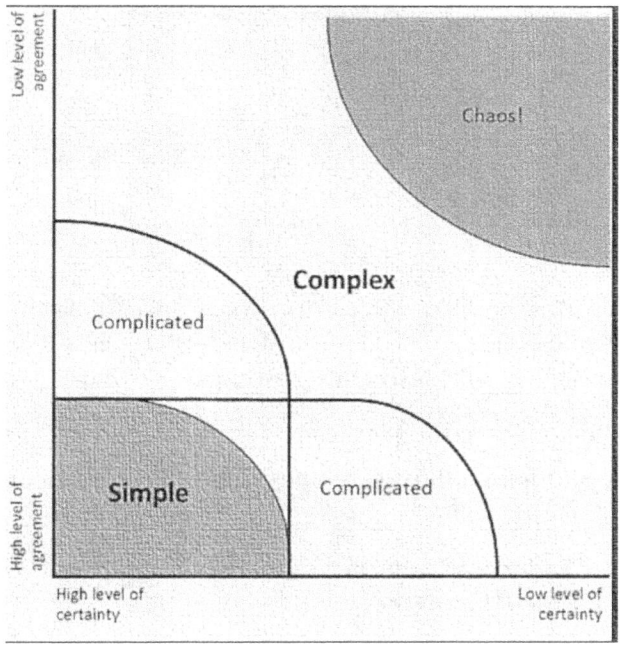

In a complex zone everything is **emergent**.

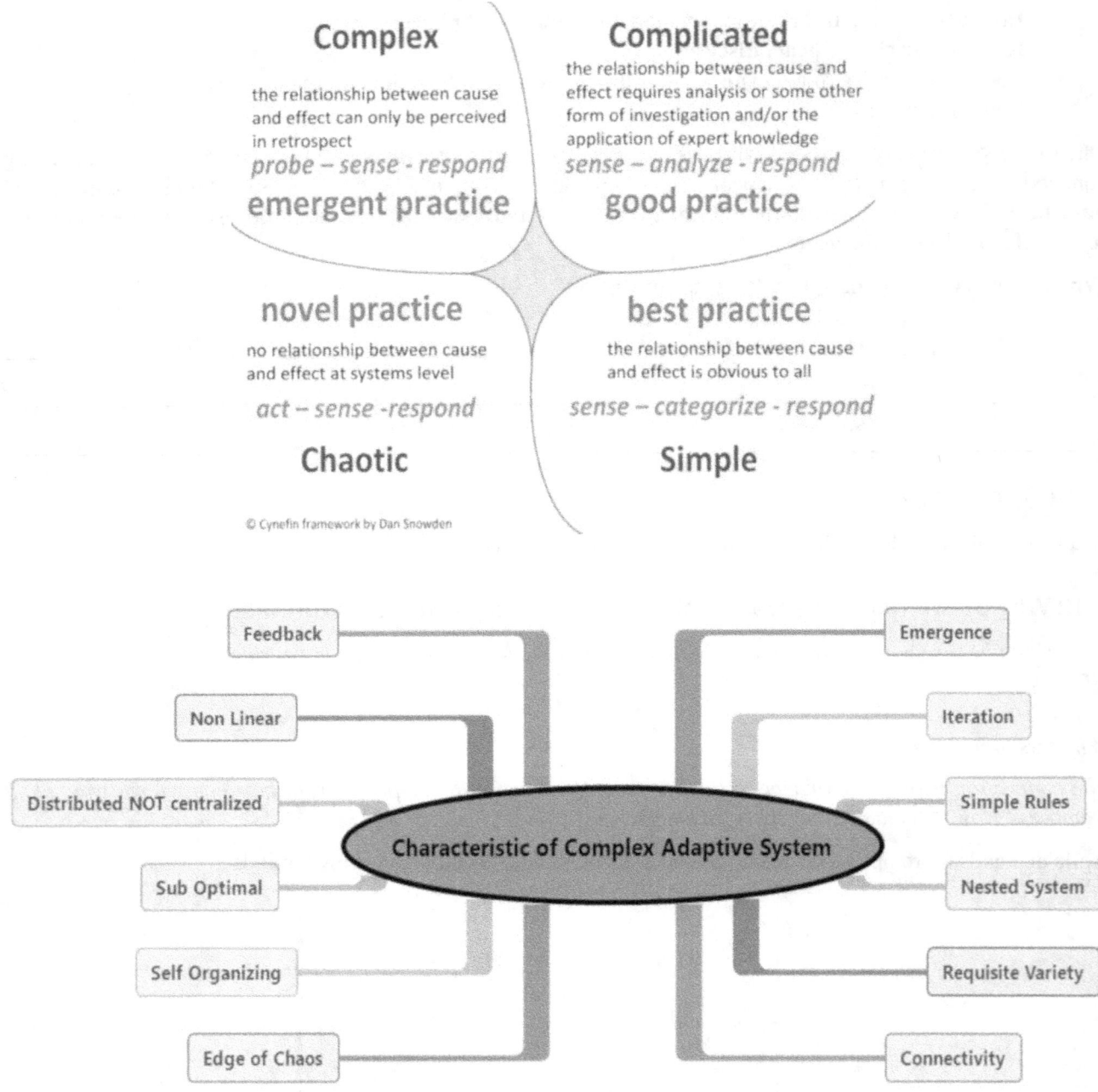

Agile is more suitable for complex scenarios, where **uncertainty and ambiguity are** very high and play with ambiguity is the part of the team culture. We need to do many experiments to find solutions. Team members should be **comfortable with ambiguity**. We need to hire team members who have a **natural optimistic attitude**.

What is that? Natural Optimism?

"... The optimist sees the rose and not its thorns; the pessimist stares at the thorns, oblivious to the rose," Kahlil Gibran.

Sir Winston Churchill states 'A pessimist sees the difficulty in every opportunity; an optimist sees the opportunity in every difficulty.' What do you see?

Researchers have zeroed in on a possible **genetic basis** for optimism, self-esteem, and mastery (the belief that you have control over your own life and destiny). It's rooted in the hormone **oxytocin**, also known as the **love or cuddle hormone**.

Earlier studies found evidence that particular variants, or alleles, of the **OXTR** gene, might be linked to stress-related traits and other psychological characteristics. OXTR codes for the receptor for **oxytocin**, a hormone that contributes to positive emotion and social bonding.

An increase in **oxytocin** tends to lead to more social behavior, especially under stress and especially in females, earlier research has indicated.

Research by British psychologists suggests that people **who carry the gene pay less attention to negative things going on around them and focus instead on the happier aspects of life.** By doing so, they end up being more sociable and are generally in better shape psychologically.

Genetic tests on the participants showed that a tendency to ignore negative images and dwell on the positive ones was strongly linked to a variation in a gene that controls serotonin, the brain's main feel-good chemical.

Why do I need these team members?

1. Optimism allows us to learn from failures, pick up the pieces and move on to something greater.
2. Optimism, opens us up to new ideas, new experiences and new possibilities.
3. Optimists had significantly better blood sugar and cholesterol levels, exercised more, and had healthier body mass indexes, and were less likely to smoke.
4. Focusing on the positive, instead of the negative, improves mental well-being, which can motivate individuals to take better care of their bodies, as well.
5. Optimism is contagious. Having an upbeat attitude can inspire everyone around us.
6. Optimism helps us see new opportunities, learn from different situations, and keep moving.
7. By nature, optimists don't sweat the small stuff.
8. Optimists Are Better at Bouncing Back

> *"It's only after you've stepped outside your comfort zone that you begin to change, grow, and transform."*
>
> —*Roy T. Bennett*

How do I detect those team members?

Look at these characteristics during your discussions with the team members, give them scenarios and ask them to tell what they will do under such scenarios?

1. Optimists bounce back from painful experiences faster than pessimists do.
2. "They turn to something else when it is clear [their current track] won't work."
3. "Optimists are more active about doing a range of things that are health-promoting,"
4. "There is some evidence that [optimists] are more forgiving," notes Carver. "Or perhaps [they] look on the good side of what they are being presented with."
5. "They're certainly less likely to dwell on the negative,"
6. "Given the same stress, they are less adversely reactive to it [than pessimists are],"
7. Lack of worry means optimists don't lie awake all night suffering from so-called "monkey brain" syndrome—they sleep a lot
8. "One's character to experience appreciation is positively related to optimism." Optimists' glass-half-full mentality leads them to count their blessings and appreciate what they have
9. Optimists are thankful for the least things in life
10. Whether it's helping at the local soup kitchen or being available to people you know, Wachob says, giving back is a habit optimistic people practice.
11. "No matter what you're going through, you need to be good to others and help when you can," he says. "The spirit of altruism can make you feel optimistic about your own life."

12. "People often think they're alone in their struggles, such as divorce, cancer, or financial problems," he says. "When they hear about people who've experienced the same thing and came out on the sunny side, it can give them hope, and hope is the foundation of optimism."

13. Optimistic people don't take the views of others too seriously when they don't agree.

How do I develop optimism if I am less in Optimism?

> *Optimist: Person who travels on nothing from nowhere to happiness.*
>
> **—Mark Twain**

1. Optimism is a learned habit, and it is positively contagious.
2. Consider your goals and dreams. Imagine that everything works out for the best.
3. Think of ways that you can create a pleasurable experience tomorrow
4. Spending as little as five minutes thinking and writing about a pleasant memory can improve your mood and optimism for the future
5. Find the opportunity in every difficulty.
6. Surround yourself with supportive friends who have the positive outlook.
7. Give love, receive love, and invest in love.
8. Prepare for the worst but hope for the best – the former makes you sensible and the latter makes you an optimist.
9. Feed your optimism with positive reminders
10. Acknowledge the things you can't control and don't become a victim. Stop thinking about what is happening to you and start thinking about what you can do to make it better.
11. Appreciate often and in smaller intervals

Optimism Bias:

The optimism bias is defined as the difference between a person's anticipation and the result that follows. If expectations are superior to reality, the bias is optimistic; if reality is better than expected, the bias is pessimistic.

Overly positive expectations can lead to terrible mistakes — makes us less likely to get health checkups, apply sunscreen or open a savings account, and more likely to bet the farm on a bad investment.

> *"Instead of worrying about what you cannot control, shift your energy to what you can create."*
>
> — Roy T. Bennett, the Light in the Heart

What actions are you going to take from this lesson?

1. _____

2. _____

3. _____

Thinking Question:

Are you doing enough to build optimistic knowledge for software product development in a complex world?

5.13 Lean into "Roles", Are you applying Lean effectively?

> *"Why not make the work easier and more interesting so that people do not have to sweat? The Toyota style is not to create results by working hard. It is a system that says there is no limit to people's creativity. People don't go to Toyota to 'work' they go there to 'think'"*
>
> **—Taiichi Ohno**

Why this topic?

How can I become more effective in my work? This is the question that came into my mind for several years. Applying lean concepts into our daily work. Can we get some more benefits of Lean Process?

The Effectiveness of our role and the value coming from one role are undergoing examination and someone always measuring the value.

How can we look at our current situation and see what can be done better?

You might be a Human Resource person or Developer or Manager, for any role this thought process can be applied to increase effectiveness.

Just imagining applying Lean concepts for any of these roles.

Basically, increase your value from your role.

I hear and I forget. I see and I remember. I do and I understand.-Confucius

I was talking to a Fish vendor and I could find instances of Lean in his role. I was talking to a Cab driver and I could trace the same Lean thinking. When I was talking to a recruiter, I could feel the same thoughts.

In general, I realized that we all can apply Lean practices to our role to increase the effectiveness and contribution of our role will improve. We become a Lean Leader.

Automation cannot take our job when we have Lean into our job. Because we optimize, improve our jobs by injecting creativity into the work.

"Lean is about constant ticking, not occasional kicking."
—Alex Miller, Professor of Management at the University of Tennessee

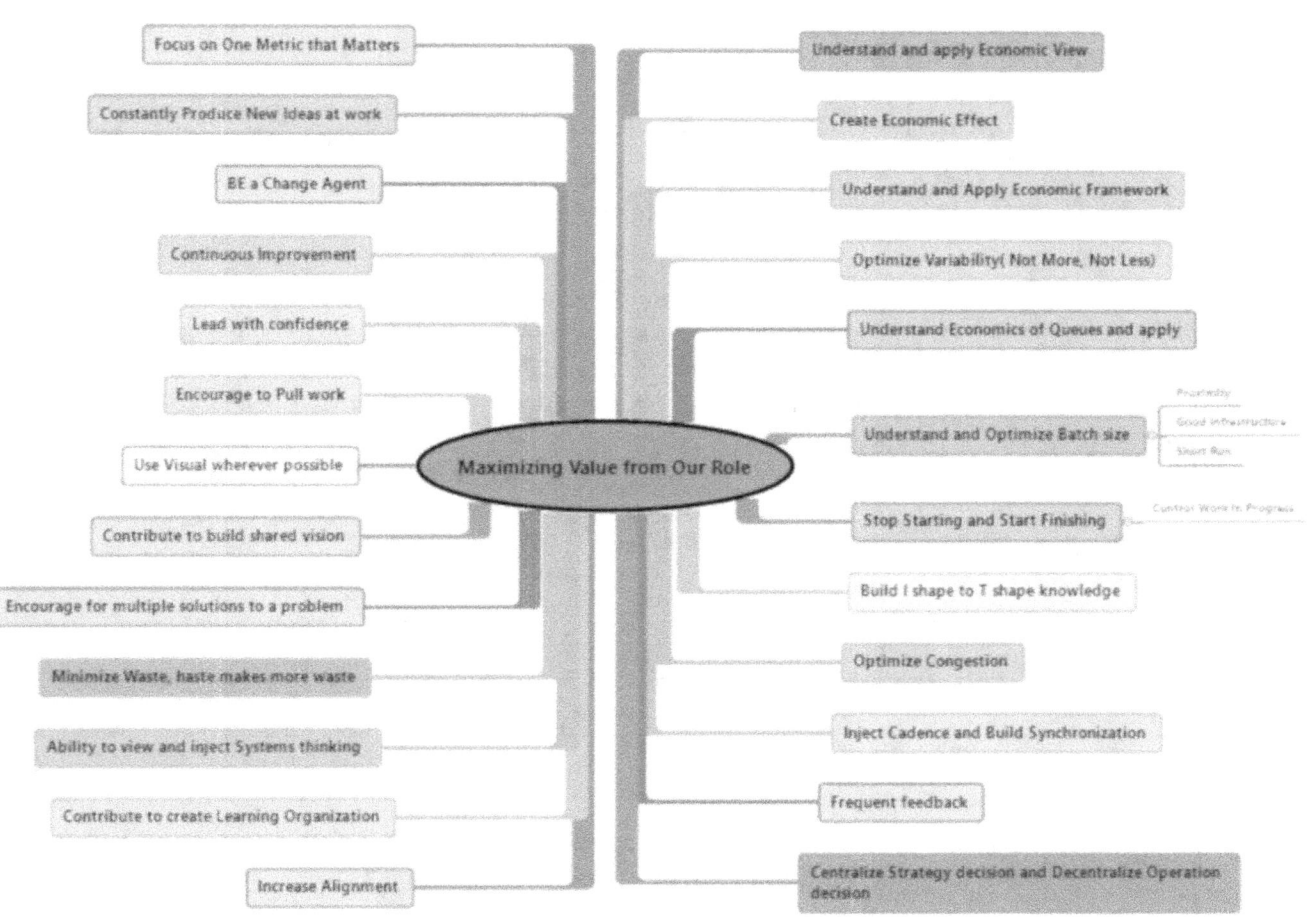

What can we do to maximize the effectiveness of our role? We have to re-look and redesign our contribution if required.

25 Rules to be followed:

1. UNDERSTAND AND APPLY ECONOMIC VIEW AT YOUR WORK
2. CREATE ECONOMIC EFFECT AT YOUR WORK
3. UNDERSTAND AND APPLY THE ECONOMIC FRAMEWORK
4. OPTIMIZE VARIABILITY
5. UNDERSTAND ECONOMICS OF QUEUES AND APPLY
6. UNDERSTAND AND OPTIMIZE BATCH SIZE
7. BUILD HABIT OF STOP STARTING AND START FINISHING
8. STRENGTHEN "I" SHAPE SKILL TO "T" SHAPE SKILLS
9. OPTIMIZE CONGESTION
10. INJECT CADENCE AND BUILD SYNCHRONIZATION
11. GIVE AND TAKE FREQUENT FEEDBACK
12. CENTRALIZE STRATEGIC DECISION AND DECENTRALIZE OPERATIONAL DECISION
13. INCREASE ALIGNMENT AT YOUR WORKPLACE
14. CONTRIBUTE TO CREATE LEARNING ORGANIZATION
15. ABILITY TO VIEW AND INJECT SYSTEMS THINKING
16. MINIMIZE WASTE, HASTE MAKES MORE WASTE
17. ENCOURAGE MULTIPLE SOLUTIONS FOR A PROBLEM
18. CONTRIBUTE TO BUILD SHARED VISION
19. USE VISUAL MANAGEMENT TECHNIQUES WHEREVER APPLICABLE
20. ENCOURAGE TO PULL WORK(DO NOT PUSH WORK)
21. LEAD WITH CONFIDENCE
22. BUILD KAIZEN CULTURE
23. BE A CHANGE AGENT
24. CONSTANTLY PRODUCE NEW IDEAS AT WORK
25. FOCUS ON ONE METRIC THAT MATTERS

These rules work for most of the team members, it will help us to perform better if we understand and apply judiciously in our work.

> *"Great companies will have a strong lean vision in place with the Senior Management Vision and are working daily at getting on with doing some important things consistently–day in, day out, week after week, month after month, year after year, as part of the middle management action plans. And finally, the results must be visible at the Shop floor level. That is what makes for effective lean leadership within companies."*
>
> *—TXM, Total Excellence Manufacturing*

What actions are you going to take from this lesson?

1. _____

2. _____

3. _____

Thinking Question:

Are you doing enough to enhance knowledge about the lean process and implement the same at your work?

5.14 Why Product Owners are from Mars and Scrum Masters are from Venus?

"Tell me what you pay attention to and I will tell you who you are."

—*José Ortega y Gasset*

Why this topic?

I am getting this question more often; can the same person play both the role of the PO and SM? Team Manager says my PO is good at communication and he/she is mature to handle the situations, why he/she cannot perform both of these roles?

Characteristics of Mars and Venus person:

Mars is to stand up, be noticed and get things done -- sitting on the sidelines belongs somewhere else in the heavens. Mars speaks to the power and confident expression of the individual. Whether it's at work or on the field of play, Mars encourages us to face challenges and to be our best -- or better. Aggression is part of the plan here, although Mars also values courage and honor. Assertion and a daring, fearless nature please this planet.

Venus rules our sentiments, what we value and the pleasure we take in life. Grace, charm, and beauty are all ruled by Venus. Through Venus, we learn about our tastes, pleasures, artistic inclinations, and what makes us happy. Venus rules attachments to others. The energy of Venus is harmonious, and this is why people with Venus prominent in their charts are often peacemakers.

In Venus, we find a need to be appreciated and to appreciate.

A Venus person is "a lover, not a fighter," preferring harmony and collaboration, rather than strife and competition, in all their relationships. They seem to know the right thing to say to defuse tense situations and have excellent manners.

Venus People gravitate to them because they are kind-hearted and have a way of talking to you that makes you feel like you are special. They will ask you about your family, your health, your opinions, and be interested in your answers. You feel like they "get" you.

Venus People value love, communication, beauty, and relationships. They spend a lot of time supporting, helping, and nurturing one another. Their sense of self is defined through their feelings and the quality of their relationships. They experience fulfillment through sharing and relating.

What should a PO and SM do?

Product Owner:

- Own the product on behalf of business owners
- Cares about the user needs and business goals
- Collaborate with the dev team and stakeholders
- Stakeholder vision while developing the product

Responsible for product success

- Able to see the big picture
- Accept or reject the work
- Responsible for ROI
- PO is a domain expert
- Demonstrated ability to understand, translate and communicate technical and complex ideas and situations to a wide variety of audiences including clients, coworkers, and management.

Scrum Master:

- Process check master
- Help the team to be self-organized

- Remove dysfunctional team work
- Able to remove team impediments
- With team ensures work demo is happening
- SM is a servant leader
- Great interpersonal skills and a proven ability to build strong relationships with team members fostering a repeatable development process
- Appreciate when the team does well (Reward and recognize team members)
- Facilitates meetings, discussions, decision making and conflict resolution to ensure work gets done
- Detail oriented, organized, and able to handle multiple tasks simultaneously

The roles are different and the expectation out of these roles is different.

Leadership team or organization has to build the machine to create such team members to get the expected level of output.

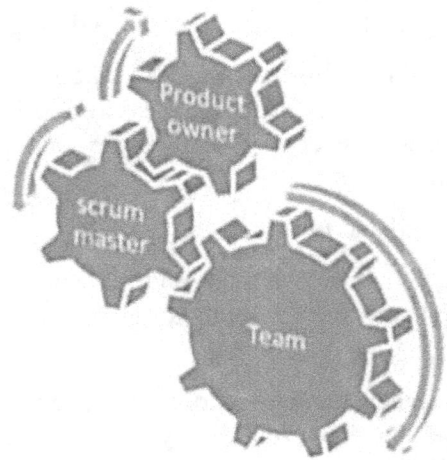

To get the expected output, it is not a good idea to play these roles by the same person.

> *"If you want to discover the true character of a person, you have only to observe what they are passionate about."*
>
> —*Shannon L. Alder*

What actions are you going to take from this lesson?

1. _____

2. _____

3. _____

Thinking Question:

Are you doing enough to strengthen the Product Owner and Scrum Master roles for your organizations?

5.15 How to Identify a Product Owner and what to expect from a Product Owner

> *At the end of the day, your job isn't to get the requirements right — your job is to change the world.*
>
> —*Jeff Patton*

Why this topic?

While doing business onboarding session, this is the very famous question asked by the business team members. We need to explain to them in a very simplistic way, before that we have to do our homework, how much do we know about them?

I was a part of a panel where I was helping the team to identify a suitable Product Owner for their product. My Team has asked me to help them find the best Product Owner (PO) for their product.

I was thinking if I should ask the below questions, I will get the best PO for the project need. Thought of asking the candidates to share with me a few stories related to the below areas.

1. **Business Model Canvas**: Please share with me, how you as a Product Owner have used Business Model Canvas at your work. What are the key challenges you have faced?
2. What are the key steps for **customer value creation**? Customer discovery steps?
3. Share your journey of creating a **customer profile**. And share with me the end results. Explain **Personas, Usability, and Empathy**, how you have used these concepts?
4. Tell me some benefits customers got from your products and services.
5. What are the various driving forces for you to decide **customer products and services**?
6. How have you applied **Minimum Viable solution**? Sketch it on a napkin. Take a couple of napkins and explain the thoughts.
7. What does your team's **shared vision** look like? Please write it down on a napkin.
8. Explain the User Story format. Explain **INVEST; DEEP**. Explain three Cs of user stories. Explain the **Storyboard technique**. Share a few Acceptance Testing strategies you have used.
9. Explain the characteristics of the **Product Backlog Iceberg**. Why is it called Iceberg?
10. Explain **Kano** and **MOSCOW** techniques.
11. Explain the rational to use of **Fibonacci** number during estimation.
12. Explain various **Slicing techniques**. Give us a couple of examples. What was your **Definition of Ready?**
13. Explain how you have used **Story Mapping** on your project. Explain **Minimum Marketable Feature (MMF)** and how you have used it in your project?
14. What are the various Non-Functional requirements you have considered? What is a **system quality card**? How have you used it? What are the various "**-ilities**"?
15. How do you calculate **Business Value**? How have you used **BVM (Business Value Modeling)** Techniques? What benefit did you get?
16. Explain to me how you have used **gherkin** language in your project?
17. Challenges in **Collaborative** exercise? Share with me a few key challenges. Explain a few key challenges to drive specification workshop.
18. Explain the **comprehensive Testing strategy** you have used for your product.
19. Explain to me a few scenarios where "before and after learning" about **feature development** was applied. Where have you corrected some key assumptions (Things you have learned about your proposed solution after validating the problem by interacting with customers)?
20. What key **challenges** have you faced during the **sprint review meeting**? Share with me some stories. How did you manage your **technical debts and spikes**?
21. Share with me some stories and actions where you have applied Inspect and Adapt approach. How have you applied the **Build-Measure-Learn** approach?
22. How have you applied **Design thinking approach** in your current product solution development context?
23. What are the **key metrics** you have measured? **One Metric that Matters most**?

I will be more interested to hear real-time use cases from the candidates. If He or She has built any solutions or products, he/she will be able to tell me some interesting insight into all the above points. In the Process, I am also planning to check the Attitude, Passion, and Curiosity to learn etc. soft skills and domain expertise.

The expectation from a Product Owner?

Organizations survive on great products and can be destroyed by bad products.

One of the critical roles is who builds the product. Behind every good product, there will be a good product owner or many good product owners. Product Owners are like bridges between customer needs and an organization needs.

In his seminal tech marketing book **"Crossing the Chasm,"** Geoffrey Moore recommended two separate titles that clearly distinguish the product manager from the product marketer:

"A product manager is responsible for ensuring that a product gets created, tested, and shipped on schedule and meets specifications. It is a highly internally focused job, bridging the marketing and development organizations and requiring a high degree of technical competence and project management experience.

A product marketing manager is responsible for bringing the product to the marketplace and to the distribution organization. It is a highly externally focused job."

In 1995, Ken Schwaber and Jeff Sutherland formalized the Scrum development methodology.

With it came yet another product management title: **product owner.**

"The product owner represents the stakeholders and is the voice of the customer. He or she is accountable for ensuring that the team delivers value to the business. Scrum teams should have one product owner."

Developing successful products requires that product managers understand what customers want. This is typically accomplished by defining and segmenting a marketplace by customer needs. By analyzing the segment through marketplace research, current product analysis, concept test, operational assessment, business and financial analysis and technical and risk assessment, we can ascertain the value that each places on a product. Stakeholders such as existing customers, prospects, sales managers, product marketers, and engineers can contribute valuable assessment information, such as requests for enhancement, defect reports, marketplace analysis, warranty data and call reports helping to define the needs of the target marketplace.

This information should be converted into metrics that will answer questions such as what type of customer is asking for this particular feature. And how large is thiss customer segment?

One of the best descriptions of what a product manager does was crafted by Martin Eriksson. Eriksson describes the product manager's role as it changes through the life cycle of a product. **First**, the job is not only to define the vision for the product but to understand the product's market and target customers and then to work with the product team to add a dose of creativity to make the product more alluring. It's then about evangelizing the product vision and inspiring those making the product with that passion.

As an Agile coach, I want to list down a few expectations for a Product Owner so that organizations can build world-class products

1. The organization expected the Product owner to own the product
2. The product owner should KNOW the customers
3. The product owner should KNOW the competitors
4. The product owner should KNOW all the stakeholders and connect, collaborate and communicate.
5. The product owner should KNOW sales and marketing team members
6. The product owner should KNOW operation team members (Installation, commissioning, Site engineers)
7. The product owner should KNOW the latest technological trend in the industry
8. Get information from all these team members to improve/build the product
9. Ability to do analysis (e.g., SWOT) from all the new ideas about product improvement or new features.
10. Build a case of investment in new ideas with strong business cases for each new requirement or initiatives

11. Build a prioritized product backlog with a product roadmap from 1 to 3 years and a 3 to 5 years horizon

12. Ability to build a case for the right product at the right time for the right market for the right people to use

13. Ability to understand organizational capability to build such features or how to build competency to build such features if there is a strong market demand.

14. Groom backlog frequently to adjust with the changing market needs

15. Share the vision and customer expectation with the team members and motivate them

16. Let the team visualize the solution through the customer representative i.e. product owner

17. Update and connect with the customer regarding what is upcoming and pulse checking with the end users

18. Build the roadmap, and build the capability to reach the destination.

19. The product owner should have good leadership skill, and good influencing skill to get the work done, and build strong relationships with many stakeholders

20. The Product owner is dedicated and focused

21. Build a trust culture where team members believe in the product owner and Product owner does not have to force to get the work done.

22. Evangelize the product, inspire others to use the product

23. Get the buy-in from top management; build a case for investment by understanding investors' concerns.

24. Connect with all the end users with various communication mechanisms.

25. Update sales and marketing team, end users, channel partners, etc. regarding what is upcoming and what benefit they will get. Set the expectation correct.

26. Participate in all discussions in product building discussion, help the team to build end-users expectation

27. Understand end user needs by spending time with them, and understand the cultural aspects, and empathize with them

28. Should have a passion for the product line, usages of technology to simplify product usage and make the customer's life easy

29. Smart and a good problem solver, come up with out of the box thinking to connect with the customer, understand their needs and take the various team's help to solve the problem, apply design thinking, etc. techniques

30. Connect with the problem and solution space and own the end result

31. Act like a sponge, be a good listener, check the assumption, believe in Kaizen culture

32. Not too much process oriented, preferably people oriented

33. Data-driven decision making, data tells what users are doing

34. Ability to do a gap analysis wants vs needs before investment, check the real pulse

35. Good storyteller and delight the customers

36. Eat the dog food first before giving it to the customers

37. No big bang failure, incremental learning with MVP, Product owner has to be vigilant about changes in the competitive market (New Technology, New positioning, new distribution mechanism) and come up with different ways build to the products to address the changing need.

In the end, the Product owner should help organizations and customers to build a world-class product which helps organizations to make a profit and the customers to solve their problems.

Product Owner should know design thinking concepts.

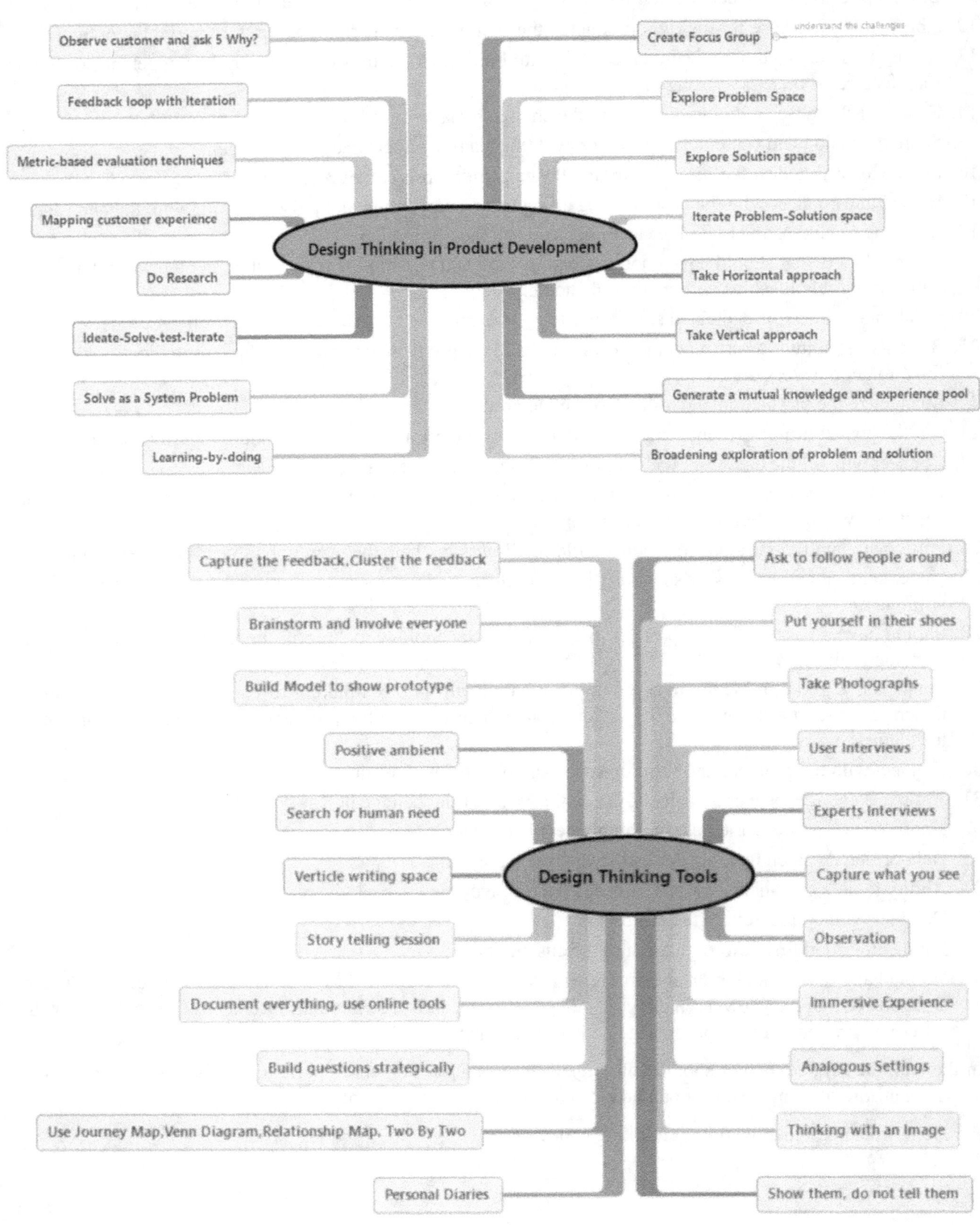

What actions are you going to take from this lesson?

1. _____

2. _____

3. _____

Thinking Question:

Are you doing enough to find a product owner who is eligible for our requirements?

5.16 Enterprise Agile Coaches are Systems Thinkers

Business and human endeavors are systems...we tend to focus on snapshots of isolated parts of the system. And wonder why our deepest problems never get solved.

—Peter Senge

Why this topic?

Enterprise agile and systems are interconnected, how can we connect both these concepts and explain, it to others with ease?

The speed and complexity of the global business environment call for a new appreciation of a system-focused view of the world, one that recognizes the interrelationships of people, processes, and decisions — and designs organizational actions accordingly.

Think about a system and interdependent cards. What will happen when one card loses its current position?

As an Enterprise Agile coach, he/she always has to think big for organizational transformation. Systems thinking helps to think efficiently. Think about scaling Agile at the organizational level, and the coach will start thinking about the whole, End to End value chain.

How to discover "Systems of Systems"?

Exhibit leadership skills when we are in such a system. Systems thinking isn't just for senior executives or engineers. Everyone who works within a system — including suppliers and line workers, designers, and marketers — should learn how the system works, develop their creativity, and apply that creativity to improve the system.

Systems are not easy to quantify, but we can map them.

Drawing system maps will help leaders understand their existence depends on being part of complex interdependent systems.

Systems Thinking?

Systems, like the human body, have parts and the parts affect the performance of the whole. All the parts are interdependent.

The liver interacts with and affects other internal organs—the brain, heart, kidneys, etc.

You can study the parts singly, but because of the interactions, it doesn't make much practical sense to stop there.

Understanding of the system cannot depend on analysis alone. The key to understanding is, therefore, synthesis.

The concept of systems thinking was popularized by Peter Senge in his book "The Fifth Discipline" where he describes system thinking as:

"A discipline for seeing wholes. It is a framework for seeing interrelationships rather than things, for seeing patterns of change rather than static snapshots."

The systems approach is to:

- **Identify a system**. After all, not all things are systems. Some systems are simple and predictable, while others are complex and dynamic. Most human social systems are the latter.
- **Explain the behavior or properties of the whole system**. This focus, on the whole, is the process of synthesis. The analysis looks into things while synthesis looks out of things.
- Explain the behavior or properties of the thing to be explained in terms of the role(s) or function(s) of the whole.

For enterprise transformation, use Systems Thinking, as the need to visualize the end to end value chain to maximize the value.

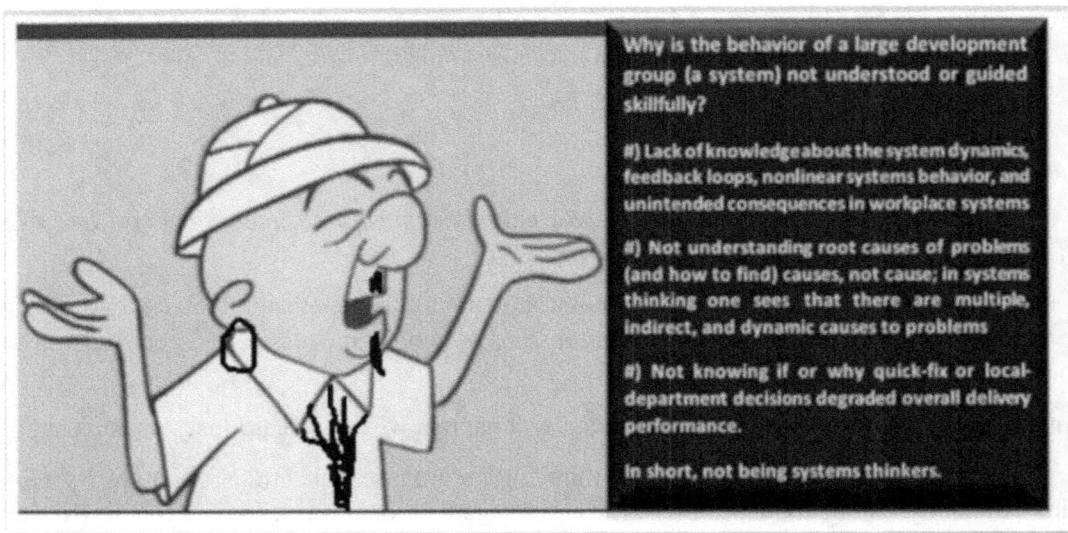

In The Search for Leadership: An Organizational Perspective, **William Tate**, includes the following which I have used during my scaling agile engagement

1. Concentrate on the whole and the interconnections between the parts.
2. Explain things in terms of the system's overall purpose.
3. Focus on the system's purpose ahead of its processes and procedures.
4. Look out for things (synthesis) more than look into things (analysis).
5. Put seeing, what is actually happening ahead of what needs to happen.
6. Check what is going on in the organization by personal examination.
7. Don't let short-term pressures get in the way of understanding the system.
8. Build and make use of feedback loops.
9. Understand complex dynamics through patterns and feedback loops rather than cause-effect links.
10. Facilitate and value emergence.
11. Be pulled by what the customer wants; to hear the customer's voice.
12. Understand the demand and respond to it (avoid provider-supplier dominance)
13. Make continuous improvement the goal.
14. Encourage self-adaptation.
15. Consider all the players and actors, of which the organization is one.
16. Be aware of natural oscillations.
17. Don't isolate strategy makers from the front line.
18. Stimulate and seek organizational learning.
19. Embrace the edge of chaos.
20. Make the most of uncertainty.
21. Recognize the system as a source of waste.

No product is an island. A product is more than the product. It is a cohesive, integrated set of experiences. Think through all the stages of a product or service - from initial intentions through final reflections, from the first usage to help, service, and maintenance. Make them all work together seamlessly. That's systems thinking.

—Donald A. Norman

What actions are you going to take from this lesson?

1. _____

2. _____

3. _____

Thinking Question:

Are you doing enough to learn system thinking, applying these concepts to the scale transformation and explain the same to my fellow coaches?

5.17 Why I want You to become a product owner from a Project Manager

The only way to do great work is to love what you do. If you haven't found it yet, keep looking. Don't settle.

—Steve Job

Why this topic?

In the Agile world, many of my colleagues were asking who is playing the delivery manager role, and what they should be doing in the agile world, where there is no role of project managers. Teams are self-organized and run by product owners and scrum masters. What could those Project managers do?

As I am a Project Manager, I do not find much growth in the new organizational setup which is adopting Agile Transformation.

Every organization is undergoing restructuring, and their setup is to become lean and efficient. All the roles are undergoing scrutiny, all the roles are redefined.

How do the best of the best project manager fit themselves into this new world?

The world market is changing rapidly, we are in a VUCA world, and every organization expects a greater value from each of the roles... risks are high when we are becoming a **LARGE FAT WHITE ELEPHANTS!!**

We cannot hide anywhere, and we are visible everywhere! **Every day people ask why you are on the payroll.**

We are building lean, small, and flat organizations, what role can you play to make us more efficient? How can my project manager friend reinvent himself/herself?

Let us look into the skill inventory, what we have built so far and what more we need to build for the project manager friends.

I want them to create their own position in the new organization.

In the Agile world, especially, scrum world, there is nothing much to do for a Project Manager, so this role is shrinking or going to be minimized.

All these agile coaches are transforming teams into a self-driven, self-organized, and self-motivated team where no project manager is required!

We have many team members who have spent a good amount of time in their career in a certain domain as a project manager.

I am proposing, **why do they not look for the Product Owner role?**

1. If they are not hands-on with technology.
2. If they are very good in a certain domain where they have spent a significant amount of their time.
3. If they are good at Technology, it is better to become a Solution Architect or a Technical Lead.

What needs to be done to become a Good Product Owner? Should I do some certifications to prove that?

When I am thinking about all the project managers, I feel I would let them aspire to become Product Owners and excel in this role. They can start looking into the below activities.

It is a journey, we need to master this journey by consciously practicing Product Owner skills.

Let us reuse most of the Project Management skills to shift into the Product Owner roles. Best of the Best Project Managers are good in all these skills, which can be reused in the Product Owner role

1. As a Great Project Manager, you were a good leader, Look into all those great leadership techniques (Mostly soft skills) which has worked for so many years. Polish all of those skills.
2. As a Great project manager, you were a great negotiator, use all these skills As a Great Project Manager, you were a good People person, and you need to extensively use this skill for customer collaboration.
3. As a Great Project Manager, you have very good communication skills, and you are a great motivator. You need all these skills as a Product Owner.
4. As a Great Project Manager, you were an expert in Budget and Cost Management, all these skills you can reuse as a Product Owner.
5. As a great Project Manager, you used to manage conflict effectively. You are going to use more of this skill with customers and team members.

What are you adding to the new Product Owner Role?

Your Product Management capability needs to multiply by 200X times in this new aspiring role and no certification can help you to achieve this

1. **Domain Expertise**: Think about a domain where you have developed mastery or have some depth. E.g., If I want to become product owner, in my career, I have spent a significant amount of time in the Industrial Automation domain, I could start developing mastery in the Industrial automation domain.

2. The product owner should be a **Domain expert**! It is good if you have done Doctorate into that domain! But we do not have so many people with a Doctorate, but some amount of mastery will help. The Product Owner should be able to understand the customer language and connect with them easily. E.g., If I am building software for a Nuclear Power Plant, and as a Product owner I need to know in depth about the power plant and the current technological advancement in these areas.

3. **Business Expertise**: The product owner is the face of the business for the development team. Product Owner on behalf of the business connects with the development team. Product Owner on a daily basis talks to the business and understands their pain points. Collect all those points which will help the PO to build the product Vision and the Product Backlog. Product owner studies the market and the trends, proposes a new feature for the customer, does the cost-benefit analysis, and influences all the stakeholders to create a new product roadmap.

4. **Influencing Ability:** One of the key capabilities is, ability to work with the business and executives to get the buy-in for investment. He/she has to prepare a business case, present the same to the business executives to influence them to believe his or her thought process. Same as the startup company, to get the fund from the venture capitalist, the founder has to give a sales pitch to tempo has to do the same for every six months or every year.

5. As a Product Owner, you are an individual contributor, you should be able to rely only on your own competency, capability, skill, and knowledge. There is no one who is working for you (that will be the mindset). You do not have an army of people working for you. A Specialist in Customer Management: Your mastery of customer discovery, customer building, Customer creation and customer validation has to be polished and shined. How do we achieve this? Practice, Practice, and practice! No exception.

6. You are an **entrepreneur**. You as a Product Owner is an entrepreneur for a product. You have a keen eye for opportunities, focuses on business value and Return on Investment and acts proactively on the possible risks and threats. Everything related to the growth (size, quality, market share) of his/her product is taken into account.

7. Product life cycle and Management: You are the owner of the product. You are aware of the market trends and take the right decision to build the right product for the right markets.

You are the master to fill this template with your excellent knowledge

In the end, the minimum requirement to become a Product Owner is

You have understood Agile Scrum way of developing the Product

What skill the Project Manager needs to unlearn? All these are anti-patterns in the agile world

1. Command and Control mindset
2. Everything cannot be planned upfront, full visibility will not be there.
3. Plan-driven mindset
4. Less experimental mindset
5. Outdated Project and Product Development knowledge
6. Uncomfortable with ambiguity
7. Too much Process focused

What actions are you going to take from this lesson?

1. _____

2. _____

3. _____

Thinking Question:

Are you doing enough to help your fellow project managers to reinvent themselves?

5.18 How to start Trust-Driven Development (TDD)?

> *"I'm not upset that you lied to me, I'm upset that from now on I can't believe you."*
>
> —*Friedrich Nietzsche*

Why this Topic?

To build a better team, trust is the key ingredient, but how to know more about how to build trust? This thought bothers me to deep dive into the world of trust.

Let us build a framework by taking the key messages from these below-related statements and apply it to our work environment. Trust building exercise for all.

- "The glue that holds all relationships together--including the relationship between the leader and the led--is trust, and trust is based on integrity." --**Brian Tracy**
- "Trust... the judgment one makes on the basis of one's past interactions with others that they will seek to act in ways that favor one's interests, rather than harm them, in circumstances that remain to be defined." - **E. Lorenz**
- "Trust is the reliance by one person, group, or firm upon .... duty on the part of another person, group, or firm to recognize and protect the rights and interests of all others engaged in a joint endeavor or economic exchange."
- Trust is "the expectation ... of ethically justifiable behavior – that is, morally correct decisions and actions based upon ethical principles of analysis." - **L.T. Hosmer,**
- "The leaders who work most effectively, it seems to me, never say 'I.' and that's not because they have trained themselves not to say 'I.' they don't think 'I.' they think 'we'; they think 'team.' They understand their job to be to make the team function. They accept responsibility and don't sidestep it, but 'we' get the credit. This is what creates trust, what enables you to get the task done." --**Peter Drucker**, author of Managing for the Future
- "Trust is built when someone is vulnerable and not taken advantage of." --**Bob Vanourek**, author of Triple Crown Leadership
- "The people when rightly and fully trusted will return the trust." --**Abraham Lincoln**
- "Trust each other again and again. When the trust level gets high enough, people transcend apparent limits, discovering new and awesome abilities of which they were previously unaware." --**David Armistead**
- "He who does not trust enough will not be trusted." --**Lao Tzu**
- "When the trust account is high, communication is easy, instant, and effective." --**Stephen R. Covey**
- "Trust is built with consistency." --**Lincoln Chafee**
- "Whoever is careless with the truth in small matters cannot be trusted with important matters." --**Albert Einstein**
- "I'm not upset that you lied to me, I'm upset that from now on I can't believe you." — **Friedrich Nietzsche**
- The Only way to make a man trustworthy is to trust him - **Henry Lewis Stimson**
- Do not trust all men, but trust men of worth; the former course is silly, the latter a mark of prudence.- **Democritus**
- Trust is like a vase, once it's broken, though you can fix it, the vase will never be the same again. **Walter Anderson**
- Respect people who trust you. It takes a lot for people to trust you, so treat their trust like precious porcelain. - **Brandon Cox**
- Trust is always earned, never given. - **R. Williams**
- In order to establish the trust, it is first important that you be trustworthy. This means you should be forthright with all your dealings. - **Paul Melendez**

- The best way to find out if you can trust somebody is to trust them.- **Ernest Hemingway**
- Building trust means thinking about trust in a positive way. -**Robert C. Solomon**
- Trust is a skill learned over time so that, like a well-trained athlete, one makes the right moves, usually without much reflection. **Robert C. Solomon**
- "Your words and deeds must match if you expect employees to trust in your leadership." – **KEVIN KRUSE**
- "Contrary to what most people believe, trust is not some soft, illusive quality that you either have or you don't; rather, trust is a pragmatic, tangible, actionable asset that you can create." – **STEPHEN M.R. COVEY**

You are the leader of the team and you wanted to build a trustworthy environment, by this time you know what you have to do...

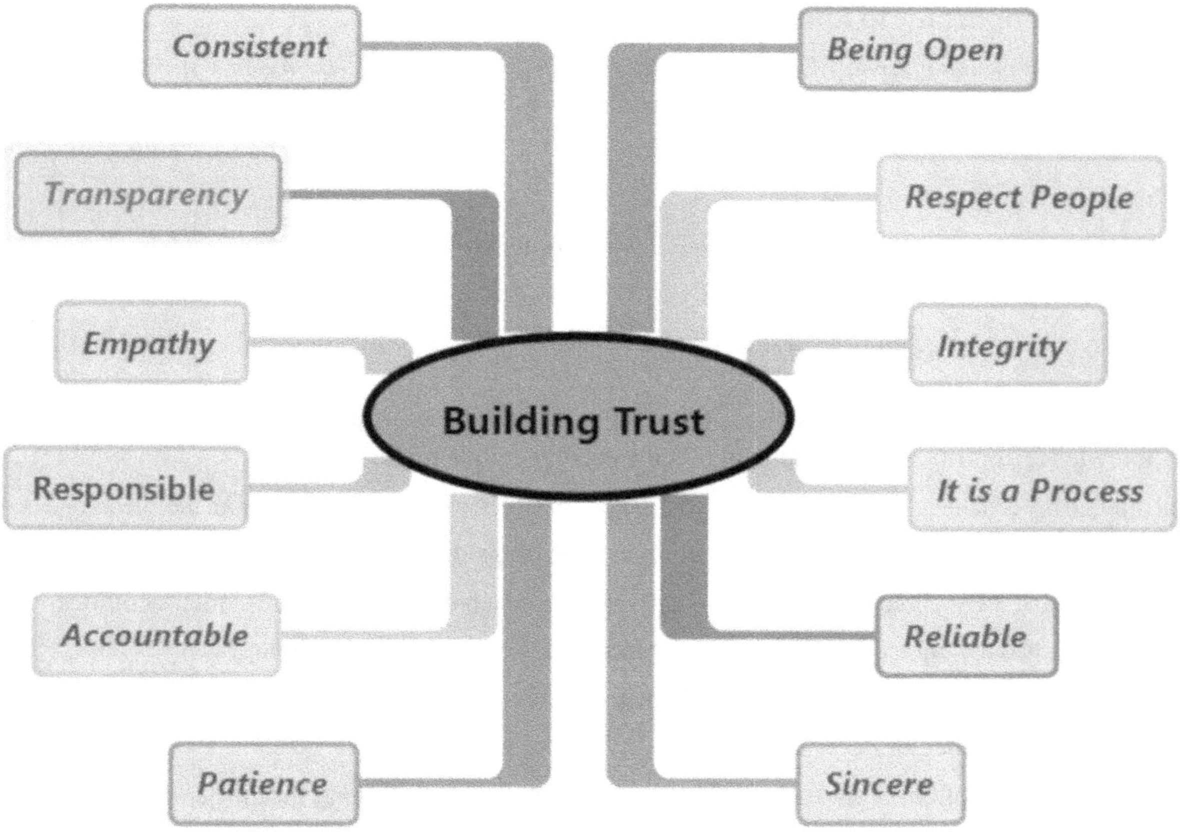

Consistent

Being Open

Transparency

Respect People

Empathy

Integrity

Building Trust

Responsible

It is a Process

Accountable

Reliable

Patience

Sincere

Most good relationships are built on mutual trust and respect.

—*Mona Sutphen*

What actions are you going to take from this lesson?

1. _____

2. _____

3. _____

Thinking Question:

Are you doing enough to build trust so that you can explain easily to your team members to improve trust effect?

5.19 Why it is important to know Psychology?

"There are some people you like immediately, some whom you think you might learn to like in the fullness of time, and some that you simply want to push away from you with a sharp stick."

—*Douglas Adams*

Why this Topic?

How to increase people skills? How can we coach others to improve people skills?

AGILE COACH AS A PSYCHOLOGIST OR BECOMING A PSYCHOLOGIST?

I believe, Psychology helps all of us, especially people are who are into building and running a business as an entrepreneur.

When I am playing various roles like Product Owner, Agile Coach, Servant Leaders, Technical Architect, etc. all this knowledge contributes exceptionally to the value generation process.

Several times in my coaching, training this knowledge helped me to get excellent feedback from the clients or customers.

They are happy because I have changed something in their life, at least thoughts, the way of thinking etc.

Let us look at what a Psychologist does, also we as an agile coach does some of the similar activities.

Textbooks often use the phrase "the science of behavior" as a definition of psychology.

Psychology is the study of people's behavior, performance, and mental operations.

What is coaching or sometimes counseling?

We are in the business of building software with the people, by the people, and for the people.

If we do not know the people, how to deal with the people, how to work with the people, the result will be disastrous.

Why not increase the knowledge about people, their behaviors, their belief, etc.? At the end of the day, we are building solutions for them.

Look at the Agile Manifesto and Principles, most of these are people focused

Coaching is meant to help "healthy" clients, but instead of helping them solve problems, coaching focuses on helping persons utilize their abilities more effectively than they have used it previously.

Advertising jargon would call this "achieving your full potential."

Counseling focuses on helping persons resolve problems or role issues related to work or school or family matters. In this setting, the counselor is a "problem solver" who through direct advice or non-directive guidance helps the client make rational decisions.

Psychologist collect Information through observations, interviews, surveys, and other methods. **Using interviews, questionnaires, and measurement tools, they can chart an individual's skills, personality features and personality style, emotional status and emotional style or problems they may be having in adjusting to life. So does by an agile coach.**

The Psychologist seeks to understand and explain the **thoughts, emotions, feelings, and behavior**. Depending on the topic of study, psychologists use techniques such as observation, assessment, and experimentation to develop theories about the beliefs and feelings that influence a person's actions. As a coach are we doing something similar with the team members?

Counseling psychologists advise people on how to deal with problems. They help patients understand problems, including issues at home, at the workplace, or in their community. Through counseling, they work with patients to identify their strengths or resources they can use to manage problems. As a coach are we doing something similar with the team members?

Social psychologists study how people's mindsets and behavior are shaped by social interactions. They examine both individual and group interactions and may investigate ways to improve negative interactions. As a coach are we doing something similar with the team members?

Psychologists can help people learn to cope with stressful situations, overcome addictions, manage their chronic illnesses and break past the barriers that keep them from reaching their goals. Are you doing the same as an agile coach in the work context?

Psychologist allows people to understand more about how the body and mind work together. This knowledge can help with decision-making and avoid stressful situations. It can help with time management, setting and achieving goals, and living effectively. Are you not doing? Mindfulness at work?

Psychologist makes it easier to live with others by understanding them more and working with their behavior. As a coach are we doing something similar with the team members?

Psychologists can work in an individual, group or organizational level and their ability to positively influence human behavior is called on by businesses.

Psychologist helps people and organizations adapt to change - advising on how to change attitudes and behaviors to improve customer service. Advising on the best type of management systems, identifying effective human resources strategies, and designing jobs to fit peoples' skills. As a coach are we doing something similar with the team members?

Psychologists are experts in human behavior. As a coach, you are also becoming the same?

Organizational Psychologists focus on the productivity of groups and individuals in the workplace. They work to improve the functioning of the organizations, and to promote the health of individuals within the organization. They also conduct research on "human factors" or the interaction between people and machines. As a coach are we doing something similar with the team members?

By knowing all these concepts, I have applied some of these on a need basis to help others.

What actions are you going to take from this lesson?

1. _____

2. _____

3. _____

Thinking Question:

Are you doing enough to build psychological knowledge and help the team members to improve this skill?

5.20 Challenges to building an Agile Center of Excellence (CoE)?

"Marketing is too important to be left to the marketing department."

—David Packard

Why this Topic?

Working with CoE is not easy, why CoE exists and how they can contribute to the organizational transformation journey is crucial. How can we develop it better?

Why CoE? The purpose:

CoE can have a wide range of purposes.

1. Providing research, solutions in the context
2. Supporting the organization for growth,
3. Offering guidance to all the team members,
4. Providing training and oversight of the employees,
5. Governing the organization through appropriate resource allocation.
6. Reduces the costs of running the business by eliminating inefficient practices and by cutting the time required for implementation of new technologies and skills.
7. Defining a common set of best practices and work standards
8. Assessing (or helping others to assess) the maturity profile of the plans against these best practices and work standards
9. Providing direct (i.e., in-person) and/or indirect (e.g., instructional content, tools & templates, etc.) guidance and support to assist plans in implementing these best practices work standards
10. Drive top-down, centralized initiatives for change management

CoE creation and sustenance got into challenges when below pictures related activities are not able to be fulfilled by the CoE due to situations like

1. **Insufficient Competency**
2. **Internal power conflicts**
3. **Availability of the budget has cut**
4. **Complaints from other business units**
5. **Not able to provide customized solutions for the need at the right time**

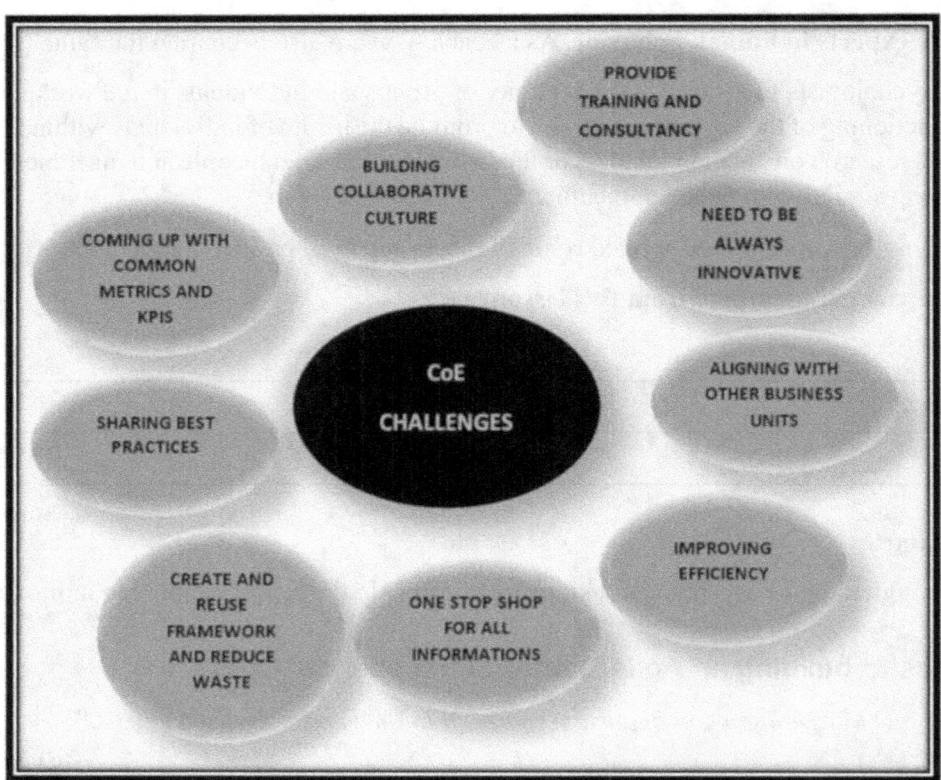

When we should we dismantle CoE?

1. CoEs are not always viewed as adding value, but are considered bureaucratic auditors that police an organization under the guise of promoting 'best practices.'
2. CoE needs different degrees of expertise, managing different processes, with different outcomes, and with different success metrics. As CoEs try to be "all things to all people," the business is left wondering what is the overall value the CoE is providing. "If you try to please everyone, no one will be happy."
3. A one-size-fits-all mindset
4. Global drive and initiative, imposing the same in the local setup without understanding local needs
5. In the absence of competent team members, CoE will not be able to meet the expectation.
6. Centralized decision making, if driven by politics and bureaucracy will impact the organizational growth
7. Delays in providing services to the waiting team due to various reasons.
8. Become a power center and a hierarchical, bureaucratic organization

What should we do for the Agile CoE?

Silos decentralized, the Agile CoE is more beneficial when every business unit is unique, and their challenges are unique to the context, e.g., agile coaches working for Power Automation business Units, or Agile coaches working for Industrial Automation business units or Aerospace Business Units.

I have worked under such circumstances in my previous organizations where we have worked in both CoE, Centralized, and Decentralized.

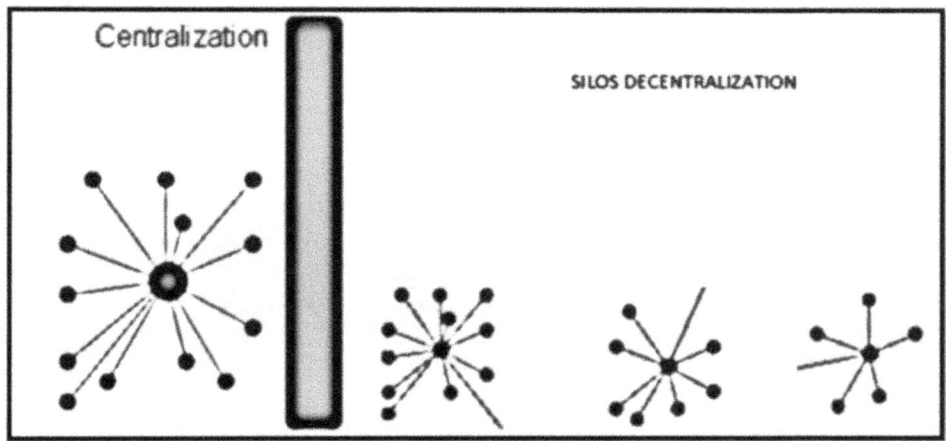

In the decentralized model, the team does not have much power to bring cultural transformation at a bigger level. As the support system is not strong, bringing standardization will invite criticism.

Business drivers for all these units are different, the dynamics are different, One size fit all, does not work. If we try to deploy a Centralize approach, the outcome is not appropriate.

We may go for a Centralized CoE approach when an organization wants to bring change management as a top-down approach in a quicker timeframe with a dedicated effort and focus.

What actions are you going to take from this lesson?

1. _____

2. _____

3. _____

Thinking Question:

Are you doing enough to build an agile center of excellence?

5.21 How to Break Organizational Silos?

"Until every team member views the company as an interdependent enterprise, you will never have an owner company."

—*Daren Martin*

Why this topic?

An organization which has grown over a period of many years, builds several departments and those departments create silos. How can we break these silos to increase the execution speed?

Breaking silos for Business through scaling Agile?

Business and IT (Information Technology) collaborate for large enterprises. What thoughts come to our mind? Layers? Large? Slow? Multi-locations?

Sometimes we have observed that Business is blaming IT and that they are not getting the benefit from IT. Business is too busy, and they do not have time to participate in the solution building process. IT claims that they are already Agile. IT is blaming that business is not appreciating their deliverable. At the end of the day, the end users are the victim.

The end user is not getting a faster solution so they look for other vendors who are quick in providing the solution in a rapidly changing world.

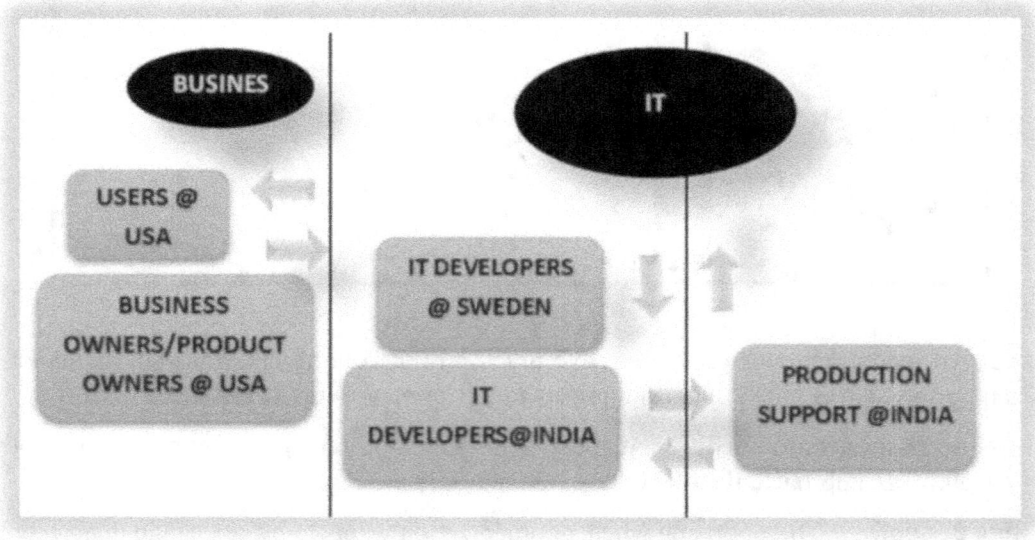

What can we do about it?

Shared ownership? How to build that?

Let us look into the current Value stream Map and discover what we can do about it.

The purpose of these maps is to create a 'wake-up call,' to get employees to question the current practice, to identify what needs to change and also to indicate which tools and techniques are likely to be required.

Maps help to define the value streams of the firm and the activities that support the primary principle of **'understanding customer value.'**

The primary principle of 'understanding customer value'

a) Let us identify our key value streams within our business. It should be a sequence of activities intended to produce a consistent set of deliverables to produce customer value and the customer is willing to pay for those deliverables.

b) How to identify Value stream (flow-level kaizen)? - Identify the product line with the various process steps or various services. With the clear picture of how the entire process is currently operating.

c) Once we identify the value steps, we need to discover how we can maximize execution speed by discarding non-value added steps. Understand the Real Constraints.

d) Some questions we may have to look (to identify the waste in the system)

1. Highest Product/Service volume in units
2. Products/Services with the highest errors or defect rates
3. Product/Service with the highest customer related issues
4. Taking more time to deliver solutions
5. Delay, waiting time, downtime etc.
6. Underutilize resources

e) How can we optimize the release by addressing all these challenges currently organization is facing? Create a Value Backlog. Value Backlog will have Theme, Epic, Dependencies and timeline

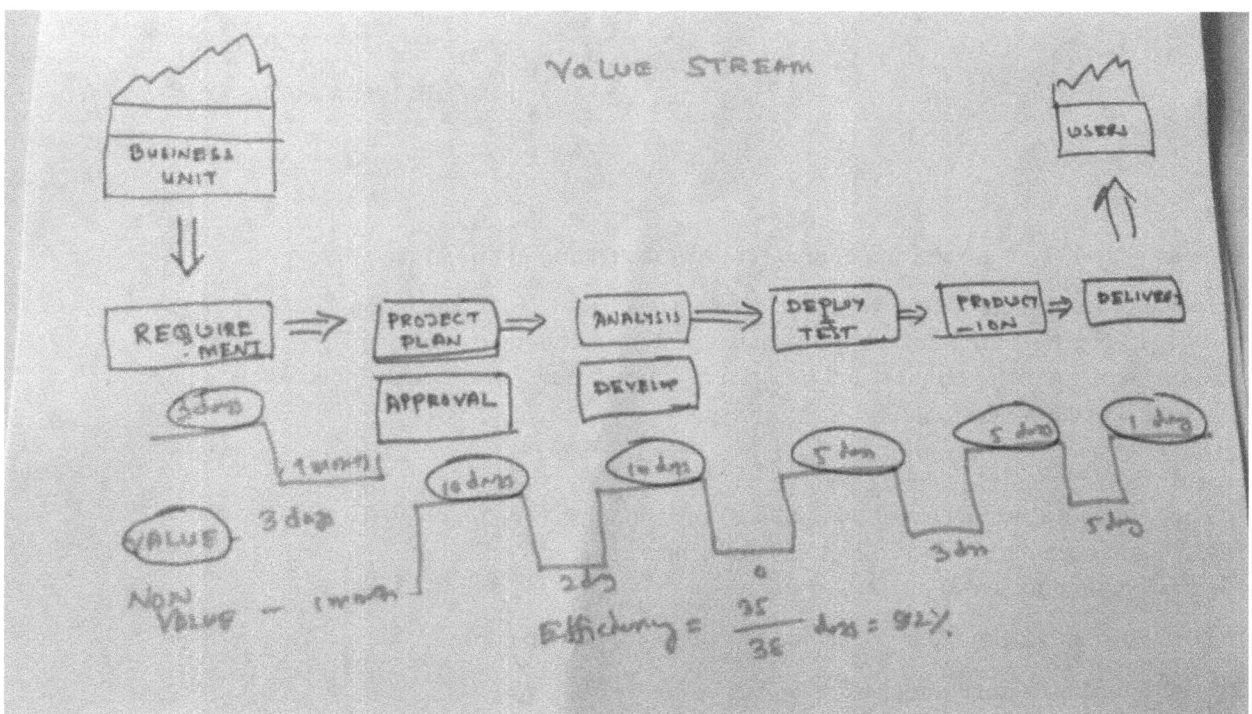

Value Stream Mapping makes it visible that the biggest problems aren't individual people, but the system in which they work. Everyone focuses on how to improve the system.

f) New Team structure. New release process. New Governance. The most important process that must be designed is **how the senior managers can lead change by becoming 'change champions.'** The position of power of the senior manager means that they can **'unblock'** problems and **promote change throughout the business**

We may stop treating Business, IT and support as a separate entity. They are all one and working for a common goal. Who will bell the Cat? All of us has to bell the Cat.

The purpose of a value stream map is to develop a common understanding and identify activities that **don't add value to the end product**. By eliminating these activities, you will gain a faster throughput, a higher level of quality and reduced inventory.

To achieve this, we may remove some organizational layers, and make it lean. We may remove local optimization and politics by giving the end to end ownership. You build, you own and you maintain, and you face to the consequences.

The Proposed solution could be, we break the silos and optimize the flow

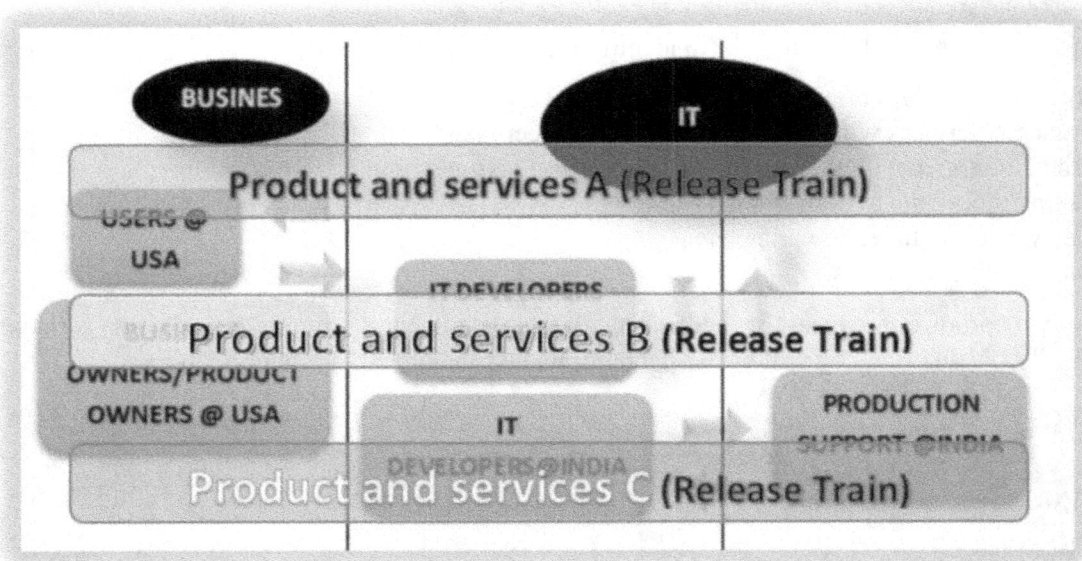

Some changes what we are recommending for the organization in this structure are

1. Deeply interconnected self-driven and self-managed team and organization
2. Fewer layers (flat structure), Self-Organized, and the autonomous team
3. The span of control is reduced and the span of support is increased. Distributed power
4. Sharing and caring ecosystem.
5. The true sense of ownership
6. Decentralized decision making
7. Support healthy product collaboration. Fear of failure has been eliminated.
8. Best solutions emerge from collective intelligence.
9. Many Communities to support the system

We will achieve faster time to market with great customer satisfaction.

Let us look into one more use case:

How do we involve all of these team members in one release cycle?

Their goals used to be different? Dev Team, Release Team, and Prod team...

Dev team owns only the Development environment and developers build and deploy code in a test lab and the development team tests the application at the most basic level.

In the System Integration Testing environment, the application is tested to ensure that it works with the existing applications and systems.

In the User Acceptance Testing environment, the application is tested to ensure that it provides the required features for the end users. In the Production environment, the application is made available to users. Feedback is captured by monitoring the application's availability and functionality.

All these activities were completely owned by different teams, goals were different, silos were built to last so many years, competencies were different, and the career paths were different.

Silos occur due to job specialization as well as differences in time zones, cities, and countries.

Distributed teams using different solutions and processes often discover that these differences double or triple their efforts and make them unable to deliver on time.

Bringing them into one vision, a roadmap is not so easy and that too when we set a timeline by saying that by this time all these team members have to work like one family! Wow

Who will create that family environment? The Organization decided that let us hire a coach and they are supposed to break these silos and build a path. There are many monsters waiting to eat them alive. Last 20+ years, they have been doing monotonous jobs and someone comes and take away the routine work!

To satisfy the customer or end users, we have to pass through all these stage gates and increase the speed of delivery.

Every gate there is a gatekeeper whose goals and expectations have to be the same. The more critical and large the application is, the time and the checklists will be big and stringent. The more legacy is the technology, so much manual effort will be.

The larger the team, the conflict will be high. Every team member is worried, as the automation pressure is increasing, manual efforts are reducing, and manpower requirement is coming down. Release time has to come down.

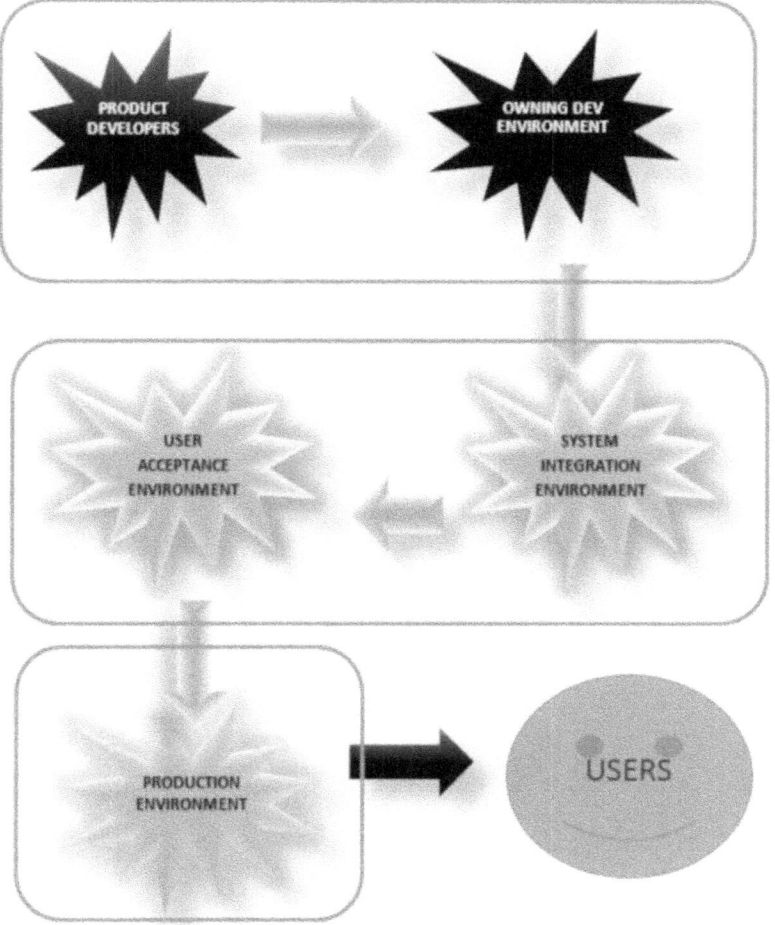

How do we improve the shorter feedback loop? When we have so many cycles and the end users are? We have many silos to break.

How do we break all these silos? How do we reduce the timeline?

It will always be overloaded with a partial Continuous Delivery implementation.

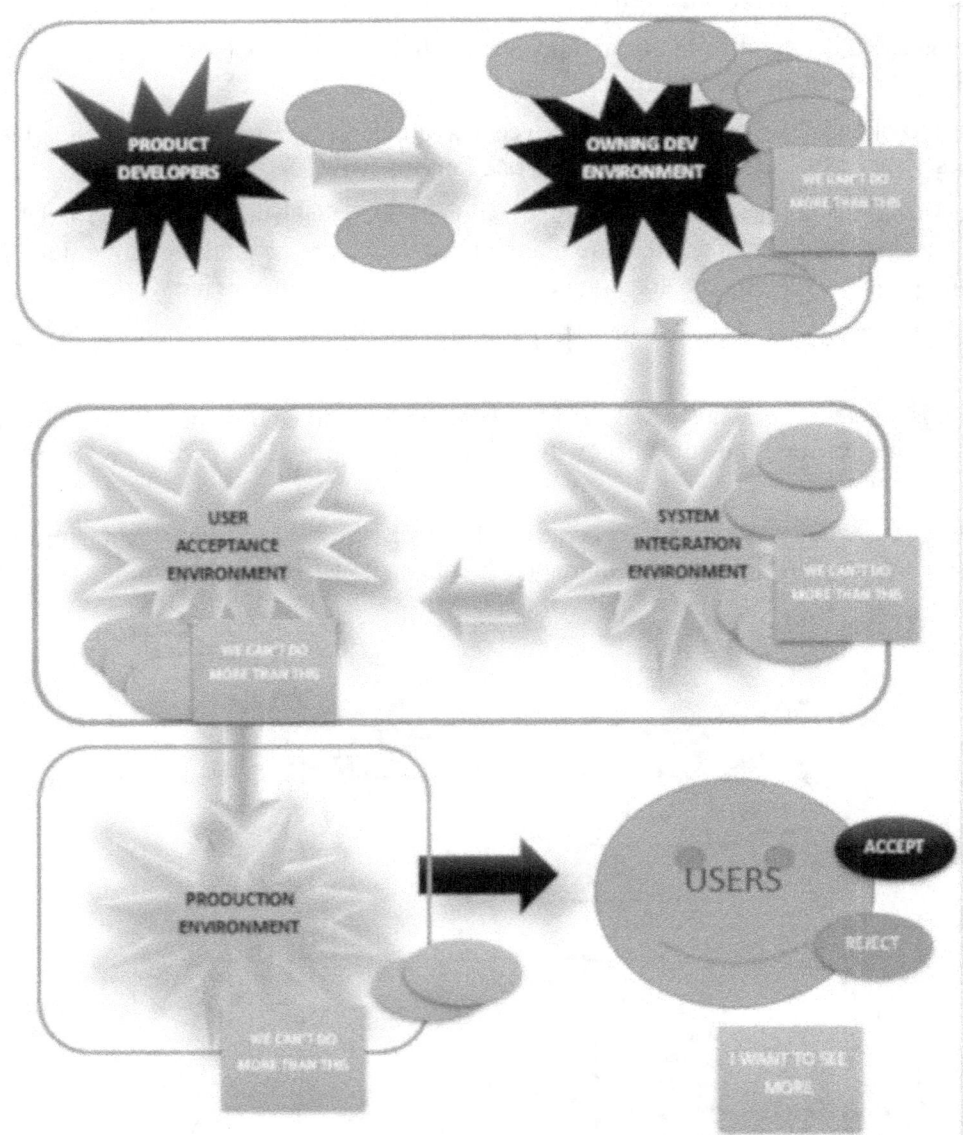

How do we collaborate with such a large team?

The amount of time that the customers are willing to wait for a desired new service keeps shrinking.

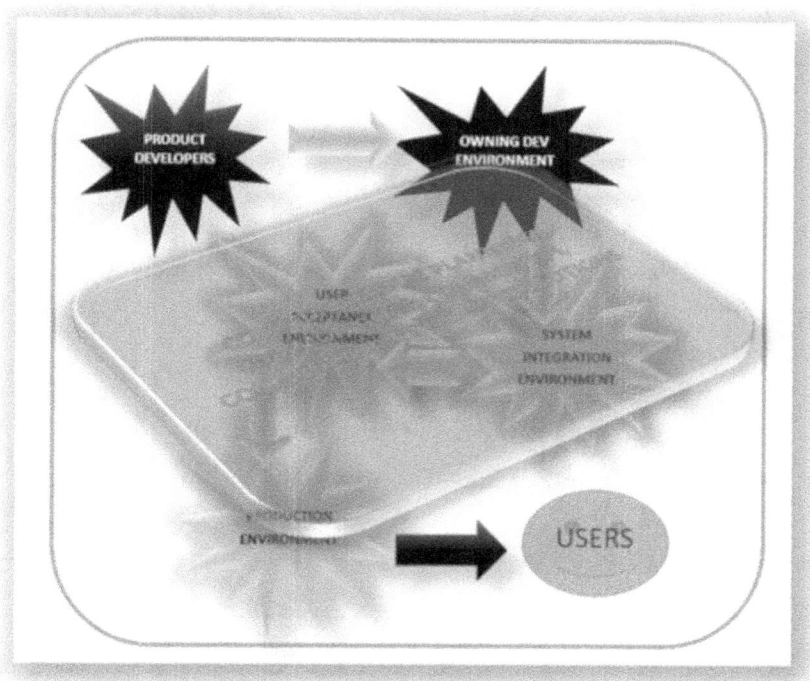

How can we streamline a common department goal for all these departments? How can we motivate all these different teams when we are working on a large, mission-critical application?

1. How can we create a **common goal** for all these team members?
2. They will get **rewarded and recognition** based on the delivery speed?
3. Cost of failure is **owned** by all these team members
4. How to have **common events** to increase cultural transformation?
5. How can we ensure **people's career** and their growth by achieving execution speed?
6. How to design cloud-based, virtual, physical, local environment helps the team members?
7. How can we involve changes for individuals, interactions, processes, and solutions?
8. We should prepare our teams for the shift, expect resistance, and remain aware of what works and what doesn't work for our organization
9. We have educated all these department team members to help each other. They should know each other's pain points and help each other. Every one's KPI should have some common elements

Let us reward for collaboration among the development, operations, and release engineering teams

Let us **encourage collaborative release planning and execution**.

Encourage a Culture of Openness and Honesty

Coordinate across all groups and individuals with interest in the release, by creating a single source of truth, updated in real time, which helps eliminate surprises for stakeholders.

The collaboration will help to achieve the below result.

> ✓ Reduce time-to-market for new features.
> ✓ Increase overall availability of the product.
> ✓ Reduce the time it takes to deploy a software release.
> ✓ Increase the percentage of defects detected in testing before production release.
> ✓ Make more efficient use of hardware infrastructure.
> ✓ Provide performance and user feedback to the product manager in a more timely manner.

What actions are you going to take from this lesson?

1. _____

2. _____

3. _____

Thinking Question:

Are you doing enough to build your knowledge to help the organizations to break their silos?

5.22 Agile Coach working under a Project Manager?

"Get the right people. Then no matter what all else you might do wrong after that, the people will save you. That's what management is all about."

—Tom DeMarco

Why this topic?

In an organization, agile transformation, sometimes transformation is a program run by a few project managers. When the coach works under such Project managers what will be the side effect regarding the agile transformation?

What will be the situation regarding the Agile Transformation when the agile coaches are working under a project manager?

The BIG project manager will take your appraisal! You will be speaking PM language!

Agile coaches wearing glasses of Project Managers

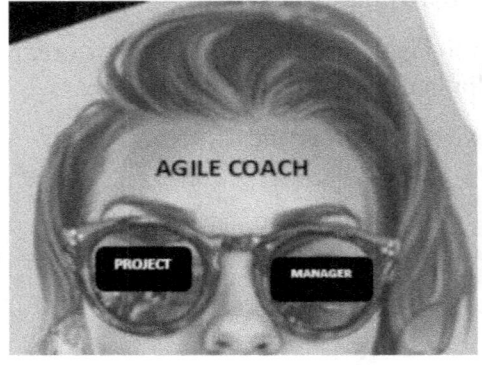

She is my friend Sheela, who is working as a consultant under a Sr. Project Manager for a couple of Agile Transformation projects in a reputed Healthcare company. She has to engage herself with the projects to get to continuous business (Billing) and PM will decide the contract date. Every three months she has to renew her contract.

What will happen when the Project Manager takes in charge of the Agile Transformation?

1. Every transformation will become a Project!!
2. Every Transformation will have a start date and end date! Every transformation will have a critical path!
3. Every transformation will have a fixed budget. He/she (PM) will ask the monthly budget consumed and to forecast data. Cost management is a big agenda for the discussion.
4. Every Transformation will have metrics and measurement!!
5. He/She (PM) will ask to maintain the monthly Risk backlog for transformation Projects!
6. He/She (PM) will call for governance meeting, review the status and will note action items, and capture the details in Excel.
7. If agile coaches miss the transformation deadline, the PM will force it to finish it on time, or else there will be an escalation.
8. If there is any budget change or timeline change, Coach needs to call for the change control board for approval.
9. Every project will have monitoring and be reporting at the monthly level.
10. Project Manager may get into the micro-level of discussions with the agile coaches! And influence coaches the way a coach is working. (Command and Control)
11. Resource planning; PM will ask for it, every now and then. What is coaching capacity utilization? Can she take some more transformation projects? If not, Justify
12. The PM will come up with many complex excel based templates to fill, track and will ask an Agile coach will fill all these data. Some coach will spend hours to fill this data (Data Analytics through excel file and produce complex graphs).
13. PM wants everything to be PLAN driven, they are uncomfortable with uncertainty or ambiguity.

Is it bad the Project Manager is driving agile coaches? Not at all, it has its own pros and cons.

Slowly the coach will behave as a project manager, instead of becoming servant leaders, they will become a command-and-control person in order to get the target result.

Though the project manager will empower the agile coach, the PM is influenced by the PM practices which will have side effects on the agile transformation.

What have we done?

We made an agreement in terms of what we measure and what we value. We introduce a visual management board and educate them to track the transformation project in an agile way. It took several months to change the way of working. We are not fully successful, as the influential project managers will argue to death for their existence. Until the day when one top guy will say, I do not need these projects managers.

What actions are you going to take from this lesson?

1. _____

2. _____

3. _____

Thinking Question:

Are you doing enough to build your knowledge to help agile coaches to run the transformation program in an agile way?

5.23 How to Build a Learning Organization?

An organization's ability to learn, and translate that learning into action rapidly, is the ultimate competitive advantage.

—Jack Welch

Why this topic?

As a part of deploying Spotify engineering culture, we need to deploy Chapters and Guild. This is a part of creating a learning organization. How to act?

Agile, heavily emphasizes **continuous improvement and learning.**

The learning often takes place within an agile team, and there is no vehicle for capturing the lessons learned across project teams and then feeding those lessons learned back into the process so that other teams could share.

Business Dictionary.com defines a learning organization as follows: **Organization that acquires knowledge and innovates fast enough to survive and thrives in a rapidly changing environment**.

Learning organizations:

1. Create a culture that encourages and supports continuous employee learning, critical thinking, and risk-taking with new ideas
2. Allow mistakes and value employee contributions
3. Learn from experience and experiment and
4. Disseminate the new knowledge throughout the organization for incorporation into the day-to-day activities

The culture of a learning organization creates an environment where that information is used for ongoing, continuous improvement.

Peter Senge said in building a learning organization there is no ultimate destination or end state, and it is a lifelong journey.

The most critical objective to accomplish from an organizational culture perspective is the creation of a Learning Organizational environment.

"Building a Learning Organization," David A. Garvin in 1998 said,

Learning organizations are skilled in **five** main activities:

1. **Systematic problem solving**
2. **Experimentation with new approaches**
3. **Learning from their own experience and past history**
4. **Learning from the experiences and best practices of others**
5. **And transferring the knowledge quickly and efficiently throughout the organization**

Each is accompanied by a distinctive mindset, a toolkit and a pattern of behavior.

Many companies practice these activities to some degree. But few are consistently successful because they rely on happenstance and isolated examples.

By creating systems and processes that support these activities and integrating them into the fabric of daily operations, companies can manage their learning more effectively.

Quote from Peter Senge on learning, **when a group of people collectively recognize that nobody has the answer, it transforms the quality of that organization in a remarkable way**. And so we teach executives to live with uncertainty because no matter how smart or successful you are, a fundamental uncertainty will always be present in your life.

That fact creates a philosophic commonality between people in an organization, which is usually accompanied by enthusiasm for experimentation.

If you are never going to get the answer, all you can do is the experiment. When something goes wrong, it's no longer necessary to blame someone for screwing up—mistakes are simply part of the experiment.

Barry Sheehy, Hyler Bracey, and Rick Frazier **Winning the Race for Value** said **the big difference between learning and non-learning organizations is not measured in their capacity for error but in their capacity to respond to the error**.

Persistence in error is a sure sign of an organization which, in today's politically correct parlance is "learning-challenged" . . .

But don't be fooled. Dumb organizations are not necessarily staffed by dumb people.

In fact, there may be many very smart people in a dumb organization. They are trapped there by a brain-dead organizational apparatus and are often very frustrated.

The learning disability usually lies at the organizational level, not with the individual.

Scaling agile will not be successful without building a learning organization where the whole organization is experimenting and learning continuously from its mistake-fail fast and learn fast.

If we deploy Spotify Model in the system, we are encouraged to build a learning organization.

Chapters are another way that Spotify promotes team collaboration and innovation. This is a great way to promote innovation and the 'cross-pollination' of ideas across teams.

A guild is a community of members with shared interests. These are a group of people across the organization who want to share knowledge, tools code and practices.

As a coach let us contribute towards building learning Organizations.

What actions are you going to take from this lesson?

1. _____

2. _____

3. _____

Thinking Question:

Are you doing enough to build a learning organization?

5.24 Key Takeaways

This chapter will strengthen the **Earth** element of the **Pancha Bhoota model** to enhance the organizational agility.

Here are the key points to remember from this chapter:

1. Lean and aids of applying Lean in our roles
2. Optimism and the effect on agile transformation
3. Self-organization and the health benefits from it
4. Building psychological safety
5. Transformation effectiveness steps
6. Building organization agility and the elements to look into.
7. Self-disciplined team and the impact on an agile team
8. Swarming techniques and impact on Organization transformation
9. Sustaining change management
10. The connection of country culture and the agile transformation. Things to look into.

11. Different planets and different roles but a common goal
12. Building a center of excellence and the various challenges to be addressed to make it a success
13. More we know about the country culture it helps the team to connect better with each other.
14. Getting a good product owner is a key, and we need to apply various techniques to identify a reasonable product owner.
15. Building Trust among team members steps
16. A learning organization is crucial in today's rapid change era, discussed various challenges to build such an organization
17. Systems thinking and how it is significant?

In the next chapter, we will examine a few case studies linked to the organization agile transformation.

6 Case Studies

Agile Transformation Case Study-1

Company **"Power Auto"** was under enormous pressure from its legacy power products. The products are already cash cow products and dominating the European market. They are expanding fast into the USA. With the current legacy product portfolio, this company cannot expand in the USA market. The product maintenance cost is becoming excessively high. Existing customer bases are very high, but with the outdated technology the product was built on, product features are no more extendable. Demanding customers were asking for more and more features. The company has a development center in Germany with 35 team members and testing center is in India with 20 team members. The product was 20+ years old with many legacy outdated technologies and a few of the original team members are still working with the product. With the new generation getting into the workforce and the introduction of the mobile technologies, the organization has to improve with the products.

Top management has determined to develop a similar type of product with cutting-edge latest technologies within 2-3 years. The growing market demands a rapid product lifecycle with the latest features and the shortest feedback time.

The company has team members who have been working with the company for the last 20 years.

Very few team members have expertise in the latest technologies. 50% budget goes to maintain the existing products (Bug/issues/enhancement request from the current customer base). New Development investment is always challenging.

The company has agreed to adopt the agile transformation for the product to address these demands.

Challenges

1. How can we migrate faster to the latest technology for expanding the market?
2. What should be the strategy the company can take to address such a situation?
3. How can technology migration and up-gradation happen?
4. How to address the existing customer base?
5. How to motivate the team members to learn new technologies and apply at work?
6. The Competitor has already launched a similar solution with the cutting edge technology. How to beat the competition?

As an Agile coach, how can you help the team members? What will be the important action steps that you will take initially? What is your engagement model and strategy?

Agile Transformation Case study - 2

Company **"Real Data"** was already dominant in the real-time database market. Their real-time database product was already ruling the market and the product mostly used in the Industrial Automation segment. The management agreed to expand the real-time database into other the IoT technologies. The company head office is in **Norway**. There were ten developers in Norway, and 10 test team members in India. Sales and Marketing office is in the US. The product is seven years old into the market and a highly robust product. Highly configurable with excellent extensible product features, and it can be configured and adapted to any database segment/Market. The company decided to enter the Wind turbine market, Shipbuilding market, etc. There are similar types of products within the same company as other units. Both the units are fighting with each other for its existence. The other unit is in **Italy**. Both the product testing centers are in India with the release management capabilities completely driven from India. The current release cycle is too long. There are regional politics and built-in bureaucracy.

The company has agreed to adopt an organizational agile transformation to focus on these challenges.

Challenges

1. How can we expand the product portfolio into the other IoT Markets?
2. How can we break the internal rivalry for existence?
3. How can we increase agility and enhance feature ready for IoT?
4. What should be the marketing strategy?
5. How can we reduce the hierarchies and make it a flat organization?
6. Today the current release cycle for both the unit products is around 1.5 years

As an Agile coach, how can you help the team members? What will be the important action steps that you will take initially? What is your engagement model and strategy?

Agile Transformation Case Study - 3

Company **"Soft bank"** was under pressure owing to the fintech world. Their existing products are doing well, but due to virtual money, wallet and mobile banking, the banks are rapidly losing the customers. The bank is also under threat from new small entrants. The company is within the top three in Bangladesh and it is supported by the Bangladesh government, dominating from last 50 years. There are many private banks competing with **Soft bank** and they are already becoming famous in a short time due to simple mobile based solutions. Also, there are many startup companies which are coming up with similar banking, and mobile products and threatening the **Soft bank's** existence. Recently **Soft bank** acquired a few startup companies in Bangladesh to get into the digital world. The company has 300 team members in **Bangladesh** and 50 team members in India.

The company has decided to adopt organizational agile transformation to address these solutions.

Challenges:

1. How can a company sustain in a volatile market?
2. How can we quicken the delivery process?
3. How can we help the bank which is running on a legacy system? To move into the digital world?
4. How can we help a company to wed startup and legacy culture (Indian and Bangladeshi culture)?
5. How can we improve innovation in the ecosystem?
6. How can we change the leadership mindset?
7. How can we bring business agility into the organization?
8. How can we handle PMP driven project managers who want the whole show to be run in a waterfall manner?
9. How can we reduce the cycle time?

As an Agile coach, how can you help the team members? What will be the important action steps you will take initially? What is your engagement model and plan?

Agile Transformation case studies -4:

The Company **"Super Health"** has many products in the healthcare market which are regulated by the government and compliance agency. The company brand is truly loyal to the people. The present product delivery cycle is three years. Due to regulatory issues, there are many entries and exit criteria have to be maintained for the certified agency to give clearance for the products to sell. The company is under significant threat from many low-cost products which are spread in the market. The company headquarters is in **Sweden** and the offshore development center is in USA and India.

The company has many legacy products and large teams to maintain these monolithic products. The company has many layers in the organization and 20 years of its existence. Within the company there are many silos, the teams are operating as a separate company. There are many kingdoms dominated by different kings within the organization. The quality of the product is very stable. Solutions are remarkably robust. The company has 500 people worldwide.100 in Sweden, 150 in the US and 250 are in India. Affordability of the product is becoming a question mark. Product acceptance are slowly turning into a question mark (Easy to use criteria). The primary market is in Europe and the US.

The company has decided to adopt organizational agile transformation to address these solutions.

Challenges:

1. How can we speed up the delivery process by maintaining compliance?
2. How can we break the silos and make it a lean organization?
3. How can value stream help organizational restructuring?
4. How can we address distributed team conflicts?
5. How can we address headstrong product owners?
6. How can we influence the team members to deliver large solutions which cut across many departments?
7. How can we convince senior executives that the new change will work?
8. How can we reduce hierarchy, reduce the lobby effect and convince the compliance agency?
9. How can we look into the monolithic architecture and simplify the same?
10. People prefer to retire from here, but they have become obsolete and redundant. What do we do? They have friends who are in influential positions within the organization.

Kanban Transformation case study -5

Efficient Executive Health Checkup: Done by Kanban Way!

Kanban is two Japanese words put together: Kan, meaning visual, and ban, meaning card. Put together, it becomes something like "visual card" or "signaling card."

The Visual record refers to the card used to control the flow of production through a factory.

Kanban is a pull system and Kanban is Less Prescriptive.

Kanban (sometimes lowercase k, sometimes capital K)—Sometimes refers to a **"visual process management system that tells what to produce, when to produce it, and how much to produce"**

Kanban executes the Lean thinking in practice (Becker and Szczerbicka, 1998; Chai, 2008). It is one of the key operational management tools in Lean manufacturing (Liker, 2004, 176). It drives project teams to visualize the workflow, limit work in progress (WIP) at each workflow stage, and measure the cycle time (i.e., the average time to complete one task) (Kniberg, 2009).

The origins of Kanban can be traced back to Taiichi Ohno and the Toyota Production System. In its more modern form, **David Anderson** has identified five core principles that support successful implementation of Kanban.

They are:

- Visualize your work so that you can see the work and in the context of other work.
- Limit the work in progress (WIP) using a pull system so that there isn't an overflow of work at any step along the way and the pace is understood.
- Manage the flow of work, and applying measures so that the team knows how much work to commit.
- Make the process policies explicit so that improvements can be made to acknowledge the baselines.
- Improve collaboratively so that there is an opportunity to improve the working process and the workflow.

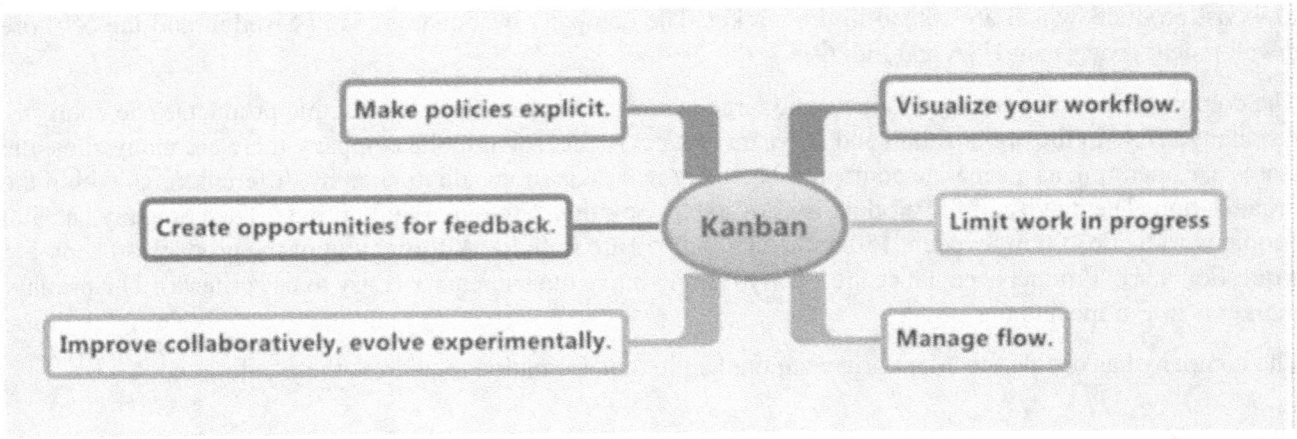

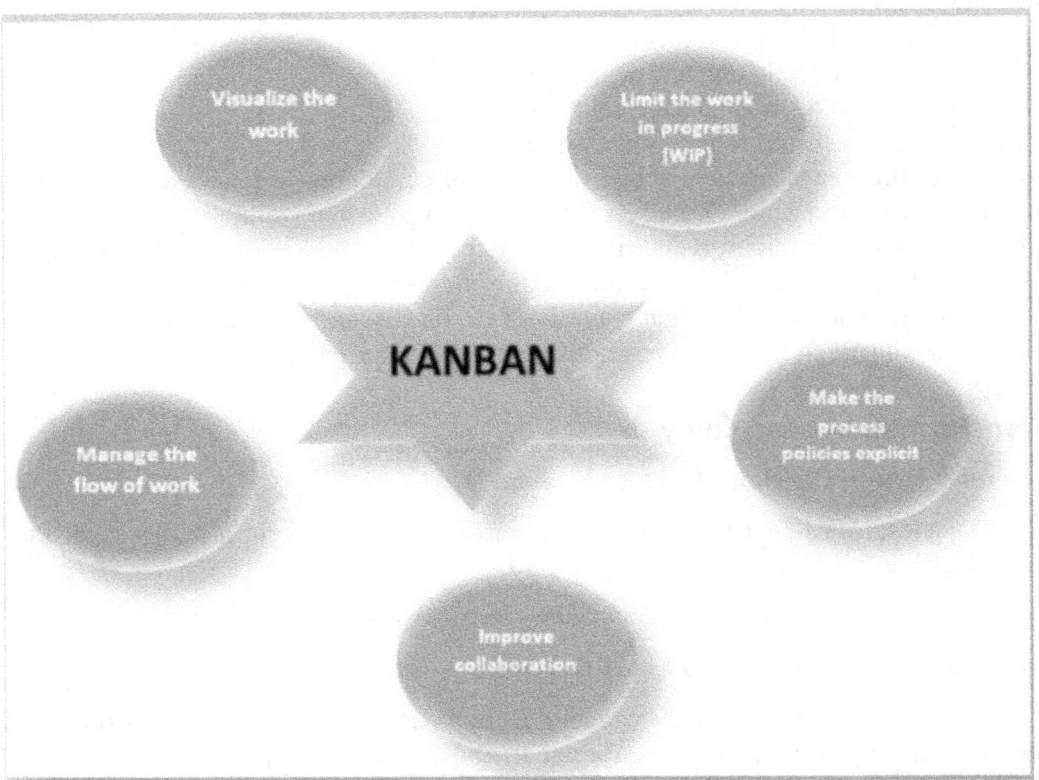

Last week I had completed my pending executive medical health checkup at one of the renowned Hospitals in Bangalore where I have observed how efficiently the Kanban practices have been followed and which has simplified my life. I have provided the highest customer satisfaction rating because of the service I have received. Of course, my health report was also good!

Practice 1–Visualizing your work

The first practice in Kanban is to visualize what you are doing. This includes both the steps in the process and what work you currently have in each step.

In my medical checkup curriculum at the hospital, they have provided me, a list of tests that will be done, the sequence has been provided, and the time, the room and places have been provided. They have a similar tracking on the system where they can find the movements and happen. One person is in charge of the flow management. She was guiding us all the time.

The complete information has been handed over in the morning when I had arrived at the location.

A complete sequence of the activities and the flow has been provided. Before a food test, after a food test, where to take the food and all the information has been in a single piece of A4 size paper. Including car parking!

The complete information in the checklist sheet has been handed over to us and each item has been ticked when it is done, and next items have been triggered automatically in the system. The next items people are also aware of the sequences of execution and they were ready.

Practice 2–Limiting work in progress

The second practice is about limiting work in progress, also called WIP. By setting limits, you are not allowed to bring more work than you are able to handle. If the persons working in the earlier process step works faster than the ones in the next step, then the work stays in the column until there is available capacity in the next step and they are ready to bring it in. Because of rule 2, the earlier steps are not allowed to bring more things in than what its limit allows. This is to prevent you from building queues of half-done work inside the system.

In Kanban, chaos is limited by directly limiting the amount of work in progress

(WIP)— Literally, the number of note cards allowed at each step. **Simple, yet effective**.

The booking system for the health checkup does not allow one to take more than 20 patients in a day. I had to do the booking for my test one month ago to get the slot.

Early in the morning twenty of us who will undergo the tests were assembled for the test and which took four hours for the complete set of tests, including the doctor's consultation.

Practice 3–Managing flow

The third practice is about improving the flow of a process so the time-to-market, also called lead-time is decreased.

The lead-time is from when we start working on the item until we have deployed it. It would also make sense to measure the time from when the item was requested until it was deployed.

Since the third practice tells us to optimize the lead-time, here is where we start changing organizations and the way they work. This is not simply because a selected process tells us to, but because we believe the change will decrease the lead-time. Our belief is that the organization is more willing to change when they know why.

Last year, the whole day it took for me to complete these executive medical health checkups because of too many patients were allowed, the report was not completed on time, and the doctors were not available etc. But this time it was flawless.

Every time they approached us and checked how things were flowing and they tracked the situation. There was good teamwork among hospital staffs.

Practice 4 – Making process policies explicit

The fourth practice is about being clear about the process and the policies and principles behind it. This is to make sure everybody involved knows and follows the process and can suggest improvements to it. The reason is that it is very hard to discuss and improve a process unless you know the current process.

Since morning, several times we have been educated about the flow and the sequences and the team members from the hospital were guiding us regarding the execution and the next steps.

So, we were relaxing and following the process flow as things were moving on its own.

Practice 5 – implementing feedback loops

What the customers, and the end users think, and will decide how well the product contributes to your company's revenue and wellbeing. Here is where practice number 5 comes into the picture, the need for getting feedback

from people outside of your system. There is also a need for feedback loops within a system to make sure you deliver the expected functionality with the right quality.

We had to give feedback and improvement suggestion at various transactions about the way things are going on and the results we are getting.

I have observed the below lean principle. The right process will produce the right result: I have observed all these steps in the entire flow chain.

- **Create continuous process flow to bring problems to the surface**
- **Use the "pull" system to avoid overproduction**
- **Level out the workload (heijunka) – work like the tortoise, not the hare**
- **Build a culture of stopping to fix problems to ensure quality right from the start**
- **Standardized tasks are the foundation for continuous improvement and employee empowerment**
- **Use visual control so that no problems are hidden**
- **Use only reliable, and thoroughly tested technology that serves your people and the processes**

Overall, I was quite happy as it took less time to complete all these process steps, and it did not take my whole day like the last time! I felt it was only because of the systematic way of applying Kanban practices. Hospital staff will be looking at all these points frequently

- **Where are we now?**
- **When will it be done?**
- **Who is working on what?**
- **What should I be doing now?**

Cycle time and lead time was good, which means they were measuring how fast the work is moving through the process and where it slows down.

By measuring lead time, they can see the actual improvement in time-to-deliver/market and predictability. They can also see the due-date performance—whether a certain item is on target against what you think it should be. With the lead time captured, they can also analyze where the work item has spent its time and start tracking lead-time efficiency to see whether the work item is mostly waiting, blocked, being reworked, or actually being worked on. Cycle time refers to the time a work item takes to go through a part of the process

Lean case study-6

Lean-ification: Lean-ified everything at the restaurant (Lean Restaurant)

We have started a Lean initiative for my friend at his restaurant business. We looked into the Lean philosophy and realized that Lean processes can maximize our customer satisfaction and optimize the process.

Lean thinking emphasizes **value-adding services** which in turn helps us to achieve **high customer satisfaction and profitability.**

We have started with the famous quote from Taiichi,

> *"All we are doing is looking at the timeline, from the where the customer gives us an order as to where we collect the cash. And we are reducing the time line by reducing the non-value added wastes".*
>
> *– Taiichi Ohno*

We have started this initiative as a batch of waves. The first wave focused on the below steps

Specify Value: As we know, the value is defined by the customer in terms of specific products and services. We have taken feedback from the customer what they want as an improvement. Observe the customer and their expectations and brainstorm with the team members for improvements. We came up with certain points which defined the value for all of us and started implementing those points.

Identify the Value stream: Map out all end-to-end linked actions, processes, and functions necessary for transforming the inputs to outputs to identify and eliminate waste. We have tracked the flow of operation and figured out different wastes in the end to end delivery cycle.

The different wastes we have identified after several observations and discussions. We have used the VSM (Value stream mapping) tool to capture the flow chain. We have several versions of it over a period with the improvements.

Make Value Flow Continuously: Having eliminated waste, make the remaining value-creating steps "flow": The order booking should seamlessly continue. Customer satisfaction rates should be high. Let us design the service from (understand the Current, as-is State as a precondition for the design of the Future, to-be State). That was the key focus area.

Let Customers Pull Value: Customer's "pull" cascades all the way back to the lowest level of the supplier, enabling just-in-time production: At a Restaurant, We do not prepare upfront all the menu fully. All the general materials have to be ready so that we can prepare the menu just in time. We observe the order pattern and predict which items are selling more and those items are kept mostly ready, and other items partially made ready and we prepare them when we get the order.

Pursue Perfection: Pursue continuous process improvement, striving for perfection. Several areas we have got improvement ideas from the customers. A couple of ideas have come from our friends as well. Though some ideas implementation cost was high, like creating a parking place, creating more space inside the room, etc. We had several introspective sessions each month to improve the current situation. Every activity, all the teams performing we look for "makes it a world-class solution."

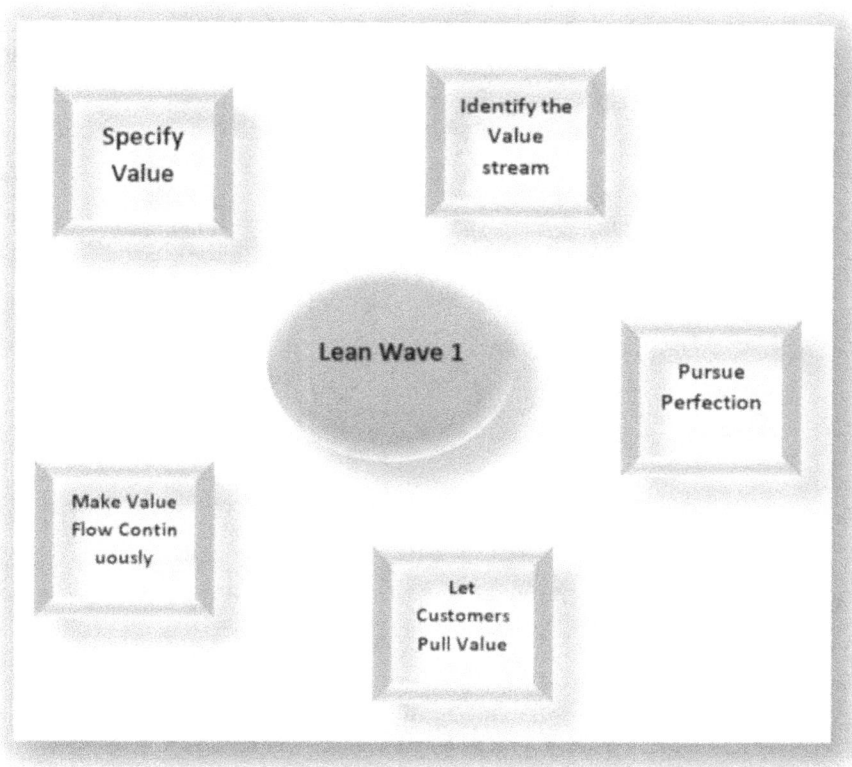

After executing the above steps for a couple of months, we observe that our feedback rating has improved and the customer visit also had improved. Now we have one baseline process which we can scale.

As the **next step** of the improvement, we thought about what other ways lean could help. We are looking at Lean which is about the focus on **Customers, Energizing Workers, Learning First, and Delivering Fast.**

Are all these steps enough for the business? The purpose of business is to maximize long-term shareholder value. Are we doing enough? What else can be done?

We decided to look at our below factors as kind of a second wave.

Let us analyze fast because of the first wave we did not have to spend much time understanding the below steps.

Customer: who are they? What is their profile? Do we have the right customer? Do we have the right items to satisfy the customer? Do we have the right stuff to evoke passion? Let us prepare a story about them.

Capability: Do we have the ability to deliver on the organizational and individual promises? Infrastructure, tools, process, and skilled employee's, etc. Do we have enough? What can be done to improve? Let us capture the missing weak factors and improve.

Control: Do we have a mechanism to measure and improve the processes, services, and products? We created a few KPIs to start with and which we closely track.

Coordination: Do we have an efficient way of understanding the working model with the suppliers and customers along the entire value chain? We have improved the relationship with the supplier within a couple of months and become good vendor list. A Couple of them, we eliminated.

Context and culture: Recognize the environment within which the restaurant is operating, including the competitive forces(another nearby restaurant), the culture of the restaurant(North Indian Restaurant), industry dynamics, and the economic environment(e.g., at festival season order booking is high etc.).

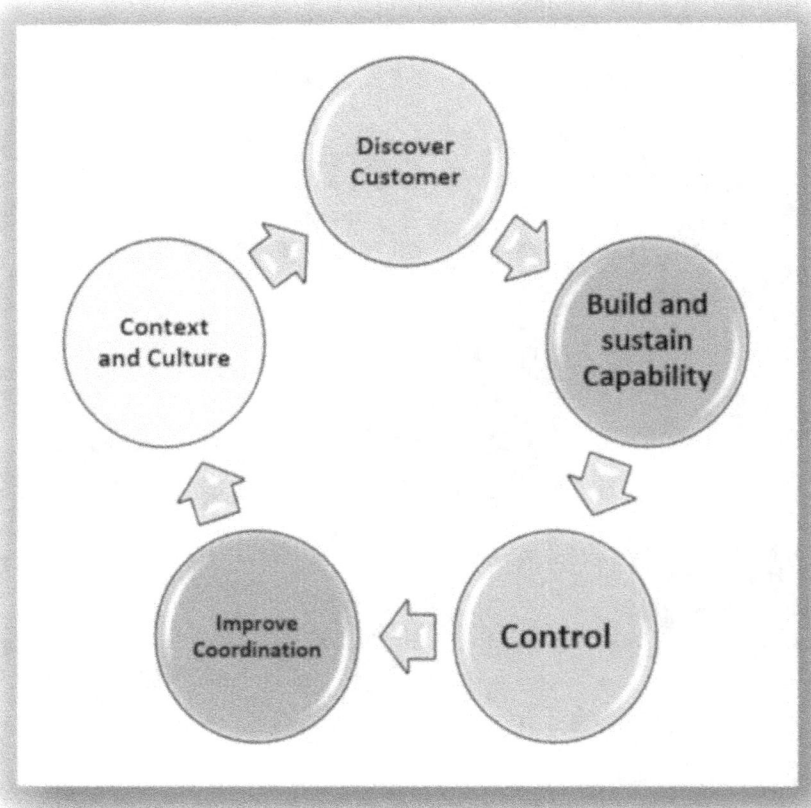

We drove these five factors for a couple of months and checked the improvement ideas. Learning in this process was very high. We are becoming smarter in this process and the same thoughts are applied in different restaurants of the chain. There is no negativity due to this initiative, and only positive returns. Employee satisfaction is also improved.

During the Third waves in the fourth quarter, we looked from different angles for deploying lean into the same chain of restaurants for additional improvement. Though the system was almost ready but slight improvement were expected in this initiative.

We looked into the below initiatives.

Eliminate waste: - we are focused on these aspects and we observed what else we can do about this waste reduction.

Amplify learning: - what can be done for our cook and waiters and cleaners, accounts, and security guards. We ensure they learn and we all learn.

Decide as late as possible: - do not jump into any small decision, let us discuss every purchase, investment etc.

Deliver as fast as possible: - We were capturing the time taken from order booking to delivery to the table and which steps we can automate and which steps we can optimize further.

Empower the team: - all the team members are trained well so that they can decide and later we analyzed the decision if it was the right decision at that moment and we help them to learn better. We appreciate our team members frequently. We build a culture of trust, in whatever possible way it is possible. Let us decentralize the decision-making process.

See the whole: Focusing only on some areas cannot make the process flow. We have to check end to end. We have used visual control systems to make problems visible. The entire flow is displayed where we are taking maximum time.

The challenges are many, and sustaining all these initiatives with the changing population who are part of this system in the restaurant was very high. We observed our entire process like a Zoologist and improved by doing plan-do-check-act. We go to the happening place and see the thing happening and improve (GEMBA walk).

The Lean initiative helped us to run the business efficiently by knowing what we are supposed to do. We have also used A3 thinking where we are able to see the problems (which is an art) in the first place, and in their apparent absence, to make problems visible, on the general assumption that there are always problems to solve.

Understand the problem correctly and the solutions can be readily identified. The second critical aspect, of course, is actually doing something about the root causes, they are the potential wastes. We remove those wastes from the system.

Improvement is a journey and continues to improve and share the best practices in the next venture.

Case Study on Agile Teams-7

I have two teams to work with and my job is to spread agility or coach agile process. At the end of the day, success or failure to deploy agile process are going to me and my team's responsibility. Both the teams are unique in the way the team has been structured, the business these teams are working for and the customer, the market they are serving, all are different. But the core software development is always the same.

The team has to deliver usable software which the customer is expecting.

It has been communicated to the customer that the team will be following the agile process and there are some changes in the delivery process. The customer was getting involved and assessing the delivered software for early feedback.

"Project_Satisfiedcustomer_A" is the team which is located in India. Total seven team members are based in India. They are physically collocated. The Product Owner and the Architect are based in Europe. The product is planned to be released in two-years, and it is to be delivered in 2.5 years. The complete product development solutions to be used by a Business unit, say a "Power Plant."

Product development was followed by "Stage Gate Review" process for decision making. Gate-2 to Gate-5 took a two-year timeline which is from concept development to market release. It was a huge successful project from the sales point of view. The team has undergone a complete team building cycle, forming, storming, norming and performing the process, the complete journey. Gate-2 to Gate-5 was an agile software development process.

"Project_NotsoSatisfiedcustomer_B" is a different type of a project. The team is based in manifold locations in Europe. The testing activities are done in India. There are seven test team members working with various development teams in Europe. It was a research-based project catering to manifold business units. There were Level 4 cases (Maintenance cases), which need to be supported by the developers from the various locations in Europe.

There were new technological developments which are experimental in nature. It was a complete distributed agile development where a lot of communication, and collaboration was required. There were many challenges to deploy agile and reduce the cycle time. Product release varies from 1.5 years to 2 years. The project team yet to establish a high customer satisfaction and the value generation (Work in progress).

Both the projects are technologically very complex where the domain expertise (Industrial Automation) plays a critical role.

How can a team ensure success by following certain practices? The end result and customer inputs are the only evidence that the team is performing and producing excellent output.

The roles designated by an agile process to play a significant contribution to success and failure of the project. The leadership skills from each role can play a significant value addition for the project.

All these roles have to contribute continuously, especially the Product Owner and the scrum master.

There are no excuse if these roles are not producing any value. The Product Owner and Scrum master have a major role to play in the entire delivery cycle. The line management organization has to motivate, ease and energize the team members. Once the energy level goes down it is the line management, the leadership team has to kindle the fire and boost the team's energy.

Agile philosophy believes all team members will be highly motivated, passionate, self-organized, but most of the time team does not have the required expected level of skilled team members.

Customer satisfaction: Have we achieved the highest customer satisfaction for both the project teams? The team was taking input from the customers in every sprint demo meeting and there is a separate feedback form filled by the customer every six months.

The team got inputs from the different channels to improve and satisfy the customer need. In the end, we got a happy customer rating.

Predictability: One of the main factors which the team identified initially need improvement is the date when the software will be released, i.e. it improves the predictability of the software release. Teams have started doing better estimation after several sprints and improved predictability. After a few iterations, it was easy for the product owner to commit to the release date.

Face-to-face interactions, the communication which plays a critical role, was missing in the "**Project_NotsoSatisfiedcustomer_B**" as there was a budget cut (Travel restriction). The team was not able to meet with each other in a distributed agile project which can cause certain soft skill issues. The collocated team was able to resolve all these types of issues rapidly through video conferencing, was an effective discussion but nothing like face to face.

Availability, and knowledge of the product manager were excellent for both the teams and it was showing excellent results. Sometimes the "**Project_NotsoSatisfiedcustomer_B**" team members did not have the information immediately, but it was available after some time (response time).

Developer's competency: For both the projects, the team members were competent and excellent and had the necessary level to execute the project. "**Project_Satisfiedcustomer_A**" had many young developers where they had the urge and hunger to learn rapidly by executing various approaches. It was a journey to build a mature, and competent "A" class team.

Collaboration with the whole team was not up to the mark for some time for both the projects and it needed elaborate discussions. It had later improved with a lot of workouts. These factors played a significant role in the success and the failure of the project. Cultural fitness also played a role in smoothly handles the issues, and good leadership practices removed all the bottleneck and increased collaboration effectiveness.

Organization Culture means that the agile values and principles are accepted as being part of the way the organization works.

Knowledge sharing: Was not happening properly to the expected level for "**Project_NotsoSatisfiedcustomer_B**." Not much-used wiki, blog, sharing was mostly forced. It has been observed for the project "**Project_Satisfiedcustomer_A**" sharing has improved significant domain knowledge, and understanding about the customer needs.

There were lots of push required to get the work done: Initially, a few team members were self-driven but not all the team members. The culture slowly transformed, but it took some time. Today, most of the team members are self-organized, they need minimal follow-up and they are self-driven. Both the teams are doing excellent test-driven development, Test Driven Development was being followed at the expected levels. There need some noteworthy improvements needed for the Acceptance Test Driven Development for the team "**Project_NotsoSatisfiedcustomer_B**."

Indicators of failure: Team members were closely watching the signals for failure and correcting the project situation. They were looking for various smells and discussing at retrospect meetings. As an agile coach, I have always looked for an opportunity to find the points which need to be aligned to meet the agility requirements.

"**Project_Satisfiedcustomer_A**" has fetched more revenue and more orders as the customer was able to use the product and decide quickly.

So What I am sharing?

Am I comparing one project with another project?

No, I am not doing Apple to Apple evaluation. What I would like to share is my learnings from both of these team which make them unique and successful. There are a few factors which I realized significantly influences to successfully deployed agile or bring agility into the team. As a result of these steps, the organization could able to bring agility into the system.

Below are the few factors which exhibited fabulous output when we have followed it across all the areas. All these factors are important and the agile coach has to ensure these have been followed religiously. No excuses in the below process to get excellent output. The team can look for these indicators and ensure that all these factors are running smoothly.

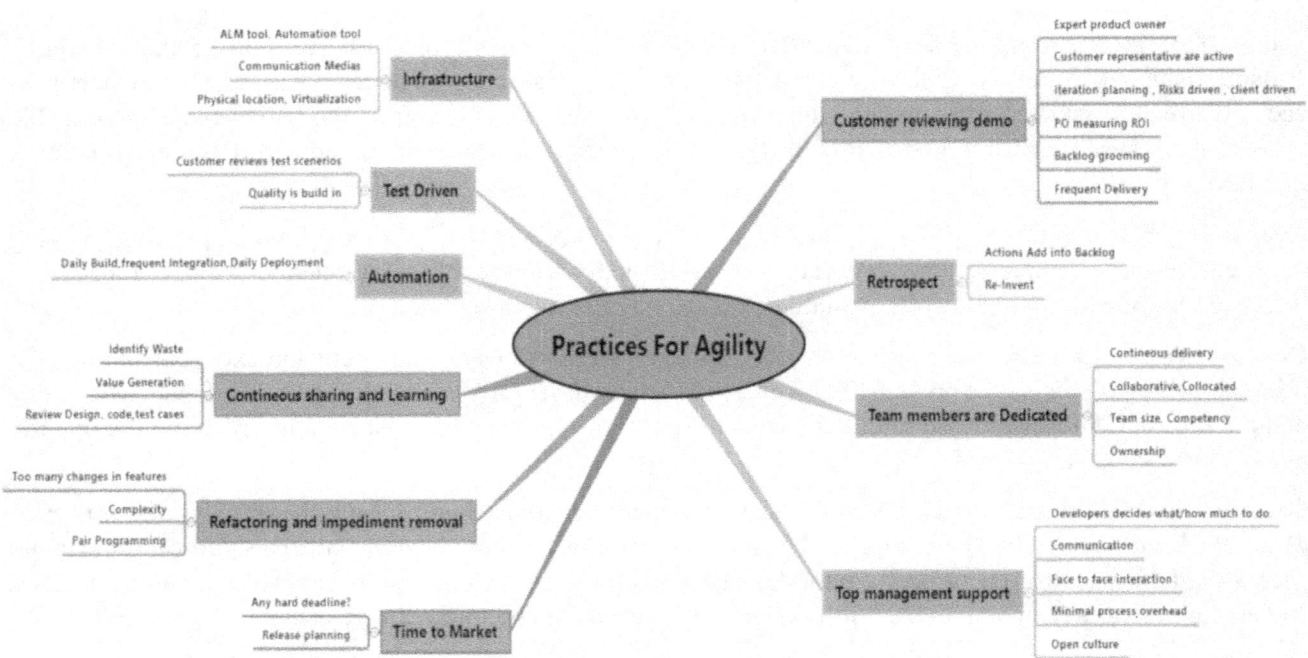

Few good points to mention:

Customer Involvement:

What we have observed is that "**Project_Satisfiedcustomer_A**" team was consistently engaged with the customer and satisfying the need of the end user. The team was correcting the steps wherever required to meet the end result. The customer was correcting their expectation on a continuous basis and the team was improving their capabilities.

Both the party was understanding each other better and the ambiance led to healthy teamwork. The "You" and "Us" has become "We." In the absence of these kinds of engagement, the waste is high, rework is high and the cycle time is high. The Product owner or customer representative can measure the ROI and feedback for all the improvement.

The Product Owner measures the doneness and grooms the backlog accordingly. "**Project_Satisfiedcustomer_B**" was not able to do this kind of an exercise. It was not the full-fledged and it was not consistent. Sometimes the team was doing a demo. There was not much continuous input for improvement has been identified. The customer can come back with changes when the product development is at an early stage and the changes are much easier and less expensive to implement.

Moreover, the customer can raise a concern if some features which are not needed and we should not develop the same so that we can avoid non-value added items.

Retrospect:

The Scrum masters and product owners were playing a great role to make continuous improvement. "**Project_ Satisfiedcustomer_A**" team was getting most of the input from self and external demonstration about the work. Backlog grooming was a major activity which refines based on the input. The Team retrospect provides refactoring input, and improvement input, which goes into a sprint backlog. Competency development inputs come from retrospect and demo meeting.

The customer was appreciating the sprint on sprint improvements. It was necessary for the product owner to calculate value when the team is doing KAIZEN.

The team is identifying all types of risks and sharing the same with all the stakeholders well ahead. Every time the team is reinventing themselves in new ways. There was lots of learning in every sprint. Organizational maturity was growing systematically. Whenever there was a sustainable velocity dip, the team brainstorms and identifies the impediment to improving the velocity in the next iteration. Just to ensure that the team knows how fast or slow they are moving and the team is on the right track (Self-assessment). "**Project_Satisfiedcustomer_B**" was struggling to do this exercise as other priority work were taking upmost of their time. Most of the team felt that this is not lean, so this is a waste.

Team Members are dedicated:

One of the aspects we have observed team members should focus on one project. If the expertise, and the resources are shared then the team members are disturbed in many assignments and multi-tasking can takeup a lot of time in switching which is a waste. It creates a problem for agility. Any amount of planning will not be helpful. There will be issues. Consistent resources are needed. Team members have to be 100% for one assignment for a sprint. Sharing resources causes lots of long-term issues. The organization needs to find a way to address this issues may be SCRUMBAN could help but the need has to explore. If there is an architect who is being shared with various assignments, he or she will not be able to do justice to most of the assignment (Switching time).

On the surface level everything looks good but most of the time we have always viewed the tip of the iceberg and later we blame the agile process or the team members. I could see the excellent team bonding, energy, and teamwork in "**Project_Satisfiedcustomer_A**." Team members have become like family members. Once a month, all the team members were going for outings funded by them. Most of the team members were on an average with seven years of experience.

Top Management Support:

In the "**Project_Satisfiedcustomer_A**" and **B**, we have an open culture where a team can experiment and make mistakes. Team members decide which items will take how much time, and they decide more or less about the backlog items.

Time to Market:

"**Project_Satisfiedcustomer_B**" team was something like the research type of the project, which is working on a next-generation technology solution. Whenever the product is ready, a team is supposed to release it. As there are lots of experiments, and prototype involve and the first time something of this nature has to be developed, even end customers also not sure how it looks like, this type of project is having a lot of challenges "**Project_ Satisfiedcustomer_A**" was a two years delivery targeted project at high-level planning.

In the end, the customer was pretty much aware of what is the expected from the deliverable at a very high level. The customer was able to use the features more or less at every sprint. So in every iteration there is a refinement and something which adds value to the customer.

Test Driven Development and Automation:

"**Project_Satisfiedcustomer_A**" team could be able to achieve the complete automation, unit testing attached with the daily build which deployed automatically which has integrated unit test result showing the coverage and demonstrated build success or failure, also capture the automated regressing test result report. The team has a dedicated developer who worked for a few sprints to automate the test cases. Developers were acting as a toolsmith to speed up the automation process. "Project_NotsoSatisfiedcustomer_B" team was also following the same approach more or less, but many improvements are on the way and needed.

"Project_Satisfiedcustomer_A" has broken the barrier between a developer and a tester. There is some improvement required for "Project_NotsoSatisfiedcustomer_B" team. When all these types of checking are happening on a daily basis, team members are well aware where the potential issues are triggered from. The same code is ready after each iteration as potential deliverable which goes for acceptance test at the customer location at the real target system.

These are few observations from both these teams. There are many more, but a few highlighted.

Measuring Organizational Agility Index:

Organizational Agility index in these **Pancha Bhoota Model** where Coaching, Mindset, leadership, High-performance team, Organization structure, and culture are measured.

Choose one number, 5 being the highest and one being the lowest against all these questions.

Area	Items	Scale
Leadership	1. Have leaders and team members demonstrated comforts with ambiguity and uncertainty? 2. Have leaders allowed the team members to experiment and learn from failure? 3. Do leaders trust the team members and empower team members? 4. Are leaders inspiring the team members, and using minimal command and control style? 5. A lot of new ideas are coming from the team members?	1: Not Applicable 2. Started 3. Doing daily 4. Part of the culture 5. Have mastered
Organization Structure	6. Is the Organization able to respond very fast once there is a need? Scan and change wherever applicable? 7. Is the Organizational team structure is stable and long-lived? 8. Is the organizational structure not pyramid shaped but it is more a network style, and a team is more swarm in the structure (Stable but dynamic)? 9. Is there customer involvement and good customer collaboration? 10. Is the culture is always changing, more coaching culture? 11. Have many platforms created for learning and sharing?	1: Not Applicable 2. Started 3. Doing daily 4. Part of the culture 5. Have mastered
Team	12. Are team members flexible to mobilize when needed? 13. Are team members more collaborative and more partnership-oriented? 14. Do team members have many governance platforms to measure, share and get feedback? 15. Do teams have the good processes defined, less rigid, but flexible to modify on a need basis? 16. Are sprint retrospect actions are closed at all the levels? 17. Self-organized, self-driven and self-motivated? 18. Competent full stack team members?	1: Not Applicable 2. Started 3. Doing daily 4. Part of the culture 5. Have mastered

Mindset	19. Is the organization is an organism, not a machine? 20. Is the decision being taken quickly at all the levels, and nothing is stuck due to the silos? Decentralized Decision making? 21. Is customer satisfaction and team member satisfaction are high? 22. Do we have most of the team members with a bounce-back mentality? 23. Are Team members thinking like a businessperson? 24. Trust each other, share and care, learn from each other?	1: Not Applicable 2. Started 3. Doing daily 4. Part of the culture 5. Have mastered
Coaching	25. Are Leaders acting like a coach and mentor? 26. Is there an Agile CoE to spread agile transformation? 27. Bring Change management initiative and ensure sustainability? 28. Is there a coach on technical craftsmanship and tools deployment? Transparency through tools? 29. Are there value-driven development, metrics, and measurement? 30. Maintain an informal management style with the focus on coaching and inspiring people	1: Not Applicable 2. Started 3. Doing daily 4. Part of the culture 5. Have mastered

E.g. Agility index for a team A is if all the questions answered are 5, total 100/100 = 1 if some teams are not doing good, 20/100 = 0.2

In the health test, all the five elements what we have discussed in the previous chapters are very strong.

Final Thoughts

We have considered that an Organization is an organism. The Organization is a like a living thing. In the complex system when the organism functions, it emerges with the distinct characteristic. For survival, the organization has to adapt and evolve.

Once we strengthen and purify the five elements of the organization by concentrating on the **Pancha Bhoota Model**, the Organization will be healthy. And it will have the ability to survive in the dynamic marketplace. All these five elements **Earth, water, fire, air and space**, the same five elements exist in our bodies and the same with the organization. The percentage of each element differs in every individual. These different proportions cause an interruption in our body. All these elements in the organization should be in precise balance to build a healthy organization.

All these chapters highlight various challenges an Agilist will come across and how to overcome them. These are all very context specific and someone has to do the experiment and deploy.

Let us concentrate on all these five elements **Leadership, Mindset, Coaching, high-performance team and organization Transformation** and work to strengthen these.

All these challenges and possible solution has helped me to perform my work better in my workplace. I am sure, these concepts will help anybody. These are universal concepts and universal challenges. Let us experiment at your context and share your learnings and observations to the world.

Let us build an impressive organization!

References

1. Agile Alliance. "Principles behind the Agile Manifesto," www.agilemanifesto.org/principles.html, 2001.
2. AGILE BUSINESS, A Leader's Guide to Harnessing Complexity, By Bob Gower & Rally Software, Published by, Rally Software Development Corp
3. Agile Excellence™ for Product Managers, A Guide to Creating Winning Products with Agile Development Teams, By Greg Cohen, published by Super Star Press
4. Making Sense of Agile Project Management: Balancing Control and Agility Charles G. Cobb, PMP, Published by JOHN WILEY & SONS, INC.
5. Agile and Lean Program Management, Scaling Collaboration Across the Organization, Johanna Rothman
6. The Agile Consultant Guiding Clients to Enterprise Agility, by Rick Freedman, Published by Apress
7. THE SCRUM FIELD GUIDE, Agile Advice for Your First Year and Beyond, by Mitch Lacey, Published Addison Wesley
8. Becoming Agile, IN AN IMPERFECT WORLD, GREG SMITH, AHMED SIDKY, published by Manning Publications Co
9. Beyond Requirements, Analysis with an Agile Mindset, Kent J. McDonald, By Addison Wesley
10. Agile! The Good, the Hype and the Ugly, Bertrand Meyer, by Springer International Publishing Switzerland 2014
11. The Agile Mindset, Making Agile processes work, by Gil Broza, Published by 3P Vantage Media
12. Agile FOR DUMMIES, IBM LIMITED EDITION, by Scott W. Ambler and Matthew Holitza, John Wiley & Sons, Inc.
13. Agile Metrics in Action, How to measure and improve team performance, by CHRISTOPHER W. H. DAVIS, by Manning Publications
14. Agile Development & Business Goals, Bill Holtsnider, Tom Wheeler, George Stragand, Joseph Gee, by Morgan Kaufmann Publishers
15. Becoming Agile... IN AN IMPERFECT WORLD, GREG SMITH, AHMED SIDKY, by Manning Publications
16. Beyond Requirements, Analysis with an Agile Mindset, by Kent J. McDonald, Publish by Addison – Wesley
17. The Art of Agile Development, by James Shore and Shane Warden, Published by O'Reilly
18. Enterprise-Scale Agile Software Development, by James Schiel, Published by CRC Press
19. Agile Project Management with Kanban, by ERIC BRECHNER, WITH A CONTRIBUTION FROM JAMES WALETZKY, PUBLISHED BY Microsoft Press
20. Scrum in Action: Agile Software Project Management and Development by Andrew Pham and Phuong-Van Pham, published by Course Technology
21. Being Agile, by Mario Moreira, Published by Apress
22. AGILE METHODS IN LARGE-SCALE SOFTWARE DEVELOPMENT ORGANIZATIONS, by Maarit Laanti
23. The Agile Manager, Leadership in an Agile Environment, Angel Medinilla, Published by Springer
24. Lean-Agile Acceptance Test-Driven Development, Better Software Through, Collaboration, by Ken Pugh, Published by Addison-Wesley
25. THE AGILE CULTURE, LEADING THROUGH TRUST, AND OWNERSHIP, by Pollyanna Pixton, Paul Gibson, Niel Nickolaisen, Published by Addison-Wesley
26. Agile Productivity Unleashed, by JAMIE LYNN COOKE, IT Governance Publishing
27. The Agile Organization, by Linda Holbeche, published by Kogan Page Limited
28. Coaching Agile Teams, by Lyssa Adkins, Published by Addison-Wesley
29. Agile Software Development, by Alan S. Koch, published by Artech House
30. The Principles of Product Development Flow, Second Generation Lean Product Development by Donald G. Reinertsen, CELERITAS PUBLISHING
31. The Lean Machine, How Harley-Davidson Drove Top-Line Growth and Profitability with Revolutionary Lean Product Development by Dantar P. Oosterwal, Publish by AMACOM
32. The Lean Anthology, A Practical Primer in continual Improvement, By Rebecca Goldberg and Elliott N. Weiss, Published by CRC Press
33. Lean Enterprise, by Jez Humble, Joanne Molesky, and Barry O'Reilly, Published by O'Reilly
34. The Lean Mindset, by Mary Poppendieck and Tom Poppendieck, published by Addison-Wesley
35. The Lean Leader, A personal Journey of transformation, Robert B. Camp, Published by CRC Press
36. The lean entrepreneur: how visionaries create products, innovate with new ventures, and disrupt markets by Brant Cooper, Patrick Vlaskovits, Published by Wiley
37. Leadership Theory, Cultivating Critical Perspectives, John P. Dugan, Published by Jossey-Bass
38. The agility shift: creating agile and effective leaders, teams, and organizations by Pamela Meyer
39. Follow the leader: discover the one thing great leaders have that great followers want by Emmanuel Gobillot, Published by Kogan Page Limited

40. Mindset: the new psychology of success by Carol S. Dweck, Published by Random House
41. Mindset Mastery, David de las Morenas, Published by Beast Industries,
42. Effective Teamwork, Practical Lessons from Organizational Research, Michael A. West, published by Blackwell Publishers
43. Team Geek, A Software Developer's Guide to Working Well with Others, Brian W. Fitzpatrick, Ben Collins-Sussman, Published by O'Reilly Media
44. Debugging Teams, by Brian W. Fitzpatrick and Ben Collins-Sussman, Published by O'Reilly Media
45. Reinventing Organizations, A Guide to Creating Organizations, Inspired by the Next Stage of Human Consciousness, by Frederic Laloux, Published by NELSON PARKER
46. Leading a learning organization: the science of working with others by Casey Reason, by Solution Tree Press
47. Power Questions, Build Relationships, win new business and Influence others, by Andrew Sobel and Jerold Pans, Published by John Wiley & Sons
48. The Coaching Solution, by Renée Robertson, Secant Publishing
49. Presentation Zen: Simple Ideas on Presentation Design and Delivery, by Garr Reynolds, Published by New Riders
50. Design thinking for strategic innovation, By Idris Mootee, Published by John Wiley & Sons, Inc.
51. Building a DevOps Culture, by Mandi Walls, Published by Oreilly
52. The Story Teller's Secret, By Carmine Gallo, Published by St. Martins Press
53. FLAWLESS CONSULTING, A GUIDE TO GETTING YOUR EXPERTISE USED, PETER BLOCK, Published by Pfeiffer
54. BRINGING OUT THE BEST IN EVERYONE YOU COACH, By GINGER LAPID-BOGDA, Ph.D. - Author of Bringing Out the Best in Yourself at Work, Published by McGraw-Hill
55. Agile Coaching, By Rachel Davies and Liz Sedley, Published by Pragmatic The Bookshelf
56. THE SOFT EDGE where great companies find lasting success, BY Rich Karlgaard, Published by Jossey-Bass
57. Team Building, Proven Strategies for Improving Team Performance, by W. Gibb Dyer Jr., Jeffrey H. Dyer, William G. Dyer, Published by Jossey-Bass
58. Building a High-Performance Team, Proven techniques for effective team working, Soft Skills, by SARAH COOK, IT Governance Publishing
59. AGILE AND BUSINESS ANALYSIS, Practical guidance for IT professionals, by Lynda Girvan and Debra Paul, published by BCS Learning & Development Ltd
60. Radical Transformational Leadership: Strategic Action for Change Agents, by Monica Sharma, Published by North Atlantic Books
61. Organization Development - A Process of Learning and Changing, Third Edition by W. Warner Burke and Debra A. Noumair by Pearson Education, Inc.
62. DESIGN FOR HOW PEOPLE LEARN, SECOND EDITION, by Julie Dirksen, published by New Riders
63. Lean UX, Second Edition, Designing Great Products with Agile Teams, Jeff Gothelf and Josh Seiden, Published by O'Reilly Media, Inc.
64. Systems Thinking, Coping with 21st Century Problems, John Boardman and Brian Sauser by CRC Press
65. Scaling Lean & Agile Development: Successful Large, Multisite & Offshore Products with Large-Scale Scrum, Larman & Vodde, Publish by Addison-Wesley.
66. Behavioral coaching, How to build sustainable personal and organizational strength, by Suzanne Skiffington and Perry Zeus, Published by Tata Mcgraw- Hill Edition
67. SPECIFICATION BY EXAMPLE, how successful teams deliver the right software, By Gojko Adzic, Published by Manning Publications Co
68. Leadership Research Findings, Practice, and Skills, by ANDREW J. DuBRIN, Rochester Institute of Technology, Published by South-Western Cengage Learning
69. Positive Psychology in Practice, Promoting Human Flourishing in Work, Health, Education, and Everyday Life, Stephen Joseph, Published by John Wiley & Sons
70. LEAN BUT AGILE, Rethink Workforce Planning and Gain a True Competitive Edge, by William J. Rothwell, James Graber, Neil McCormick, Publish by American Management Association
71. Design Thinking for Entrepreneurs and Small Businesses, Putting the Power of Design to Work Beverly Rudkin Ingle, Publish by Apress
72. How to be a presentation God ,Published by John Wiley & Sons, by Scott Schwertly
73. Team Geek , A Software Developer's Guide to Working Well with Others, by Brian W. Fitzpatrick, Ben Collins-Sussman, Publish by O'reilly
74. Presentation Zen, Simple Ideas on Presentation Design and Delivery, by Garr Reynolds, published by New Riders
75. THE FIFTH DISCIPLINE, THE ART AND PRACTICE OF THE LEARNING ORGANIZATION by P e t e r M. Senge, PUBLISHED BY DOUBLEDAY
76. Building a High-Performance Team, Proven techniques for effective team working Soft Skills, by SARAH COOK, IT Governance Publishing

About the Author

Chandan Lal Patary, lives in Bangalore, Karnataka, India, with his wife and two kids. He had commenced his career as an apprentice engineer in an Electrical Machine renovating company. He had started his software career as a Software Trainer, subsequently played various alternative roles like Test engineer, Developer, Technical Lead, Project Manager, Program Manager, Global Program Manager, Engineering Manager and as an Agile coach for last several years.

He has been conducting research on Organizational Development and Transformation for a decade. He is a practitioner and captures his analysis and shares his views through his writing.

His focus areas are **Organizational Transformation and Business Agility, Innovation, Strategy, Execution excellence and correlation with People Leadership** and the impact of all these into Organizational growth.

He is performing as an **Enterprise Agile Coach.**

He has **two decades** of deep experience in developing software products across various domains and has executed many large Projects.

He has served in product development for domains like **Banking software, Healthcare, Aerospace, Building automation, Power automation and Industrial Automaton** under real-time mission-critical product development to large-scale application development.

He has worked with the startup and large companies like **GE Medical system, Honeywell, ABB and Societe Generale**.

He has worked with the team members of the **USA, Germany, Sweden, China, Australia, Finland, Switzerland, France, and Poland**, which has shaped his knowledge, personality, and skills.

He is a certified PMP from 2008 and Green Belt certified holder since 2005. He is an agile practitioner, a Certified Scrum Master since 2011 and SAFe Agilist since 2017.

He has accomplished a **Bachelor of Engineering** from National Institute of Technology (National Institute of Technology–Agartala, Tripura, India) in Electrical Engineering-1998.

He has finished one year **Executive General Management program** from Indian Institute of Management-Bangalore (IIM-B), Karnataka, India in 2007.

He has composed seven different free e-books available for download at Slideshare. He has written **300+** blogs in LinkedIn. He has presented **10+** seminars as a speaker in numerous conferences. He has uploaded **30+** presentation at Slide share on diverse topics. He has written **20+** technical papers in various national and foreign journals. He has earned many rewards in all the enterprises he has served for. He has received **PM World Journal, 2017 Editor's Choice Awards** for the paper "Increasing Business Agility through Organizational Restructuring and Transformation".

His free e-books

1. *"COACHING SUTRA BOOK FOR AGILE COACHES"*
2. *"MINDMAPS TO CHANGE MINDSET"*,
3. *"STORIES YOU LIKED MOST"*,
4. *"LEADERSHIP SKILLS FOR SCALING AGILE"*,
5. *"HAPPINESS AT WORK"*,
6. *"DELIVERY EXCELLENCE IN SOFTWARE PRODUCT DEVELOPMENT"*,
7. *"THE COMPLETE REFERENCE BOOK FOR MOTIVATING SELF AND OTHERS"*

All these e-books available for free download from Slideshare.

All the 19+ years he has worked in software product development projects and companies have taught him how to build better software while working with world-class team members.

His real software product development experience started when he worked with the company, Datex Ohmeda (now known as GE Datex Ohmeda). He had spent seven months in Finland working with world-class software architects. He had worked for 3+ years with this product to build a system for monitoring the patient's vital sign under critical condition. He has acquired awesome learning experience on Software architecture and real-time system development.

His next splendid experience accumulated from the Honeywell Aerospace system, where he had served as a software developer with Honeywell world-class aviation software team. He had delivered products for cockpit systems to many companies including Airbus and Boeing. He had worked seven months in Seattle, Redmond, at Honeywell office. He had worked with many aerospace system engineers and great software architects for this mission-critical product development. He has flown with Honeywell plane for flight testing at the Seattle Honeywell facility. It was a Great experience for him! He had worked for 3+ years for this product.

His next world class exposure was in the ABB Power automation division with the Sweden-based team. He also visited Sweden, Vasteras office and worked with the team members who had built this system many years back. An outstanding team, they had an excellent robust product built over a period. This product development experience provided him with extensive knowledge of Distributed Agile software product development in a mission-critical situation. He had worked 3+ years for this product.

He has many tales about these product developments. These 3 products where he involved in hands-on development changed his life.

Other than these projects, he had many engagements as Manager which had a different exposure about building a better team for software product development. He has worked with Honeywell HVAC system, worked with ABB Industrial Automation control system products and Societe Generale (SG) banking system products.

He made a coach by accident! During his assignment as a global program manager for one of the Industrial Automation project, Head of Global Product Management from Finland, shared with his manager that Chandan should be their agile coach! This was in January 2012 when his journey as an agile coach begins. He was born to be an agile coach. And he is enjoying the role.

www.ingramcontent.com/pod-product-compliance
Lightning Source LLC
Chambersburg PA
CBHW081132020726
47504CB00010B/2054